Praise for Sarah Steele's evocativ

'A fantastic read. I was grippe
Wonderful storyte......
Jill Mansell

'Fascinating, moving, romantic and utterly gripping.
I couldn't stop reading'
Katie Fforde

'Readers will adore walking through occupied Paris
in the footsteps of the brave. A fabulous story'
Mandy Robotham

'A tense, heart-in-mouth story about courage in
occupied Paris, and secrets'
Gill Paul

'I felt so passionately involved in Flo's journey.
A GORGEOUS read'
Prima, **Book of the Month**

'An engaging novel, strong on character and place,
that kept me wanting to know more'
Daily Mail

'A lovely read, with the descriptions of the 60s jet-set
particularly evocative'
Heat

'A gorgeous, tender debut'
Kate Riordan

'I loved reading the entwined stories. This book is
warm and true, and it pays tribute to the heart and
backbone of women who support each other'
Stephanie Butland

Sarah Steele trained as a classical pianist and violinist before joining the world of publishing as an editorial assistant at Hodder and Stoughton. She was for many years a freelance editor, and now lives in the vibrant Gloucestershire town of Stroud.

Keep up with Sarah on X
@sarah_l_steele

and on Facebook and Instagram
@sarahsteeleauthor

Or visit her website at
www.sarahsteeleauthor.co.uk

By Sarah Steele

The Missing Pieces of Nancy Moon

The Schoolteacher of Saint-Michel

The Lost Song of Paris

The Traitor's Wife

The Last Letters from Villa Clara

The
LAST LETTERS
from
VILLA CLARA

Sarah Steele

REVIEW

First published in 2024 by Headline Review
An imprint of Headline Publishing Group Limited

1

Cataloguing in Publication Data is available from the British Library.

ISBN 978 1 0354 1299 0

Typeset by EM&EN
Printed and bound in Great Britain by Clays Ltd, Elcograf S.p.A.

Headline's policy is to use papers that are natural, renewable and recyclable
products and made from wood grown in well-managed forests and other
controlled sources. The logging and manufacturing processes are expected
to conform to the environmental regulations of the country of origin.

Headline Publishing Group Limited
An Hachette UK Company
Carmelite House
50 Victoria Embankment
London EC4Y 0DZ

The authorized representative in the EEA is Hachette Ireland,
8 Castlecourt Centre, Castleknock Road, Castleknock, Dublin 15, D15 YF6A, Ireland

www.headline.co.uk
www.hachette.co.uk

To Kate, Molly and Gus,

my own remarkable artists

Prologue

London, March 1964

As the taxi crawled towards the Royal Courts of Justice, Leonora Birch savoured the last moments of calm before she was devoured by the press pack and spat out as tomorrow's newspaper headline. She turned to her companion, wondering whether they would be making the return journey together later that day. If he were nervous too, Bruce Cato hid it well, the expression behind his untrimmed beard as relaxed as the shabby cream linen suit that had seen better days.

She examined the palm of his bear-like hand, ingrained with decades of paint, tracing the love line that had known they would find one another again. 'What do you think will happen?' she said.

He shrugged. 'The judge refused my bribe, so he'll probably throw us both in prison.'

She cuffed his arm. 'How can you joke about it?'

'My darling Leonora, I joke about everything. As you well know.'

'But this isn't one of your games, Bruce. This is real.' As the traffic slowed, she spotted a newspaper vendor hawking the morning edition. 'Judgement due in the Battle of Bond Street', screamed its headline above a photograph of Leonora looking all of her sixty-one years as she was accosted on her doorstep the previous evening.

Why hadn't she just put a stop to this? Apologised and coughed up the costs, then got out of London to begin her new life with Bruce in Italy? Instead, she had upheld her claims about Sir Edwin Viner, the man who had nearly destroyed her twenty-five years earlier, and now commanded a ferocious legal attack from his prestigious Mayfair art gallery.

The taxi growled onwards until she could make out the cathedral-like façade of the courts, the crowds below waiting for their quarry as photographers perched on stepladders for the best shot.

'Let's get the driver to drop us around the back,' Bruce said.

'Why should I creep in? It's Edwin who should be hiding,' she said as faces pressed against the cab window, a shout going around as she was recognised.

Bruce snorted. 'Fat chance. Look who's pulled up in front of us.'

A chauffeur opened the door of the sleek grey Bentley, and a roar of support went up for Sir Edwin Viner and his wife, dressed in a cream suit with matching feathered hat, every inch the debutante model Edwin had plucked from the conveyor belt. How dare a frumpy Pimlico landlady challenge such people?

The cabbie pointed to his meter. 'That'll be five shillings. Call it eight, including the valet job my paintwork's going to need now this lot have had their sticky paws all over it.' He must have sensed her distress, however, and as she held the money out to him, he shook his head. 'Second thoughts, you've got a tough enough day ahead. Have this one on me.'

Tears pricking her eyes at this small act of kindness, she turned to Bruce. 'This is it, then. Are you ready?'

'Ready to get it over with so we can finally carry on with our lives,' he said, then frowned, stroking her hand. 'You're really sure you want to see this through?'

'As sure as I ever have been about anything.' She took a deep breath, steadying herself as Bruce leapt out to open her door, hellish chaos breaking noisily into the privacy of the cab.

'Good luck, Leonora Birch,' the cabbie shouted as she stepped out on to the pavement. 'Don't you let him get away with it.'

The sound of the baying crowd was deafening against the machine-gun click of camera shutters as a galaxy of popping flashbulbs blinded her, reporters pressed so close that she could smell the pints they had drunk the night before, the washing powder their wives used. She glanced once more at Bruce and smiled. 'Let's get him.'

1

Tuscany, June 1989

Phoebe stepped off the aircraft steps and on to the sticky black tarmac, cheeks burning and nostrils stinging as the distant terminal shimmered through the heat haze. Beyond lay rolling hills dense with ripening vines and ancient villages, their bell towers ringing out the daily rhythm of this timeless, sleepy region, cradle of the Renaissance and her second home.

Tuscany.

As she walked away from the roar of the cooling engines, she felt London slip from her, shed as a skin from another life. She pulled off her blazer, longing to swap her neat jeans for one of the summer dresses packed in her luggage. Even through the acrid cloud of aviation fuel, she could already smell the tinder-dry grass surrounding her uncle Bruce's hilltop villa with its medieval watchtower, the mellow oil produced in the Villa Clara olive groves.

It still saddened her that she had only been permitted to get to know Bruce properly when, at the age of eleven, she was deemed old enough to be despatched alone to Italy for school holidays – every school holiday, she noted. Life in the former Hampstead family home had been fraught with the ever-present danger of fierce rows between her parents in the chaotic

Edwardian villa until her father's death three years ago and her mother's subsequent relocation to Cornwall. Of course Phoebe missed them both, but in truth Bruce Cato had been her primary parent for most of her life, and she the daughter he never had.

She hurried through to the arrivals hall, scanning the crowd for her old friend Stefano, whom she spotted lounging against a pillar in chinos and a linen shirt, floppy dark hair pushed back from his eyes and looking as though he had come from the pool rather than his desk at the law office in Florence. For once Bruce wouldn't be collecting her from the airport, but she could hardly contain her delight at seeing the housekeeper's son there in his stead, and ran across to greet him.

'Hey, Topolino!' he said, tussling her into a playful hug.

She sighed. '*Vero?*' Even though she pretended to be irritated at the nickname he had given her when they were children, its familiarity was a kind of homecoming.

'You were such a little mouse when you first arrived at Villa Clara,' he went on, slipping into Italian, as they always did when they were alone. 'How was I to know you would be so bossy?' And it was true: once Phoebe had settled into life at Villa Clara, picking up Italian as quickly as she picked up a suntan, she had forced Stefano to play anything from wildlife explorer to medieval knights. 'Nice hair, by the way. I like it shorter.'

'Really?' Phoebe said, suddenly embarrassed. The previous week, she had paid a fortune she didn't have, in order for her long blonde hair to be lopped into a stylish bob, encouraged by her friend and colleague Tilly, on whose sofa she had been sleeping for the last week. After the recent dramas in Phoebe's romantic life, she had needed a change, and she certainly felt better for it.

'Reminds me of when you made me cut it off when we were twelve. Boy, I got a hiding from Mamma for that. So, no boyfriend with you this time?' Stefano asked lightly, taking her suitcase and heading towards the car park.

'No boyfriend ever,' she replied. 'Seems you and everyone else was right about James.'

'I'm glad,' he said, pausing to push his long, dark fringe from his eyes. 'I mean glad he's gone. He wasn't good enough for you.'

'And is Jocelyn good enough for you?' Phoebe would never be best of friends with Stefano's latest girlfriend, a shiny London lawyer he had met at a conference, but she could at least show an interest.

He shrugged. 'Maybe.'

'Maybe for now?' Stefano's inability to make relationships last was legendary.

'I don't know. But I'm sorry that *pidocchio* hurt you.'

'I think you're being unfair on the common louse.' Phoebe pulled out her sunglasses. 'Now, can we please go to Villa Clara? I'm in dire need of a glass of Bruce's hideous house white and Angelina's excellent lasagne.'

'Mamma's recipe is legendary, for sure,' he said, leading her towards a silver Lancia parked nearby and opening the passenger door. 'I can't stay for lunch, but maybe after dinner I can take you into the village? There's a fiesta all weekend. We can dance your worries away.'

If only it were that easy. She waited whilst he climbed in beside her, then turned to him. 'Stefano?'

'*Si?*'

'Is everything OK at Villa Clara? Bruce wrote that he'd been undergoing a few medical tests.' 'Nothing to worry about' had been Bruce's throwaway comment, but the fact that he'd even mentioned his health led Phoebe to believe there was everything to worry about.

Stefano's green eyes clouded over briefly. 'I don't know for sure.'

'I sense a but?'

He hesitated. 'He asked me to update his will.'

'Really?'

Stefano pressed his tanned hand over hers. 'Probably just doing his housekeeping – he is in his eighties, after all. I wish more of my clients would. Try not to worry.'

'Easier said than done. On all fronts.'

'I'm sorry. You said things weren't great at the museum when we spoke last week?'

'They're really not,' she said. The idea for the Cato Museum of Artifice had been born five years earlier at Villa Clara, one evening when too much wine had inspired Phoebe and Bruce to imagine a museum of their own. Bruce had been serious, it seemed, signing the lease three months later on a quirky four-storey London townhouse to showcase some of his finely crafted reproductions of Old Masters and a few curiosities he had collected over the years. And yet now Phoebe was coming to realise that the numbers would never add up. The building had recently been sold to an American management consultancy, along with those on either side, and with the rent about to double unless she accepted their offer to buy her out of the lease, the museum's future seemed uncertain.

'Need to talk it through?'

'Only if you can tell me there's a crock of gold sitting somewhere in Bruce's estate.' She watched as he shrugged uncomfortably. 'Right. Then let's forget it until I've had a chance to talk to Bruce, if that's OK?'

'Of course. So, shall we go?'

She nodded. '*Andiamo.*'

He crunched the car into gear and headed out to the trunk road that would take them south to the tiny village of Monte-leone and the old villa at the end of a rutted track.

Bruce Cato was in animated discussion with Stefano's father Marco about where to plant some new lavender bushes when Phoebe appeared beneath the vine-covered pergola. Stefano's parents had arrived at Villa Clara not long before Phoebe herself began to visit in the early seventies, and while Angelina ran a tight ship looking after the house, Marco cared for the terraced garden that was Bruce's pride and joy.

An Italianate formal space that defied the blistering heat and provided shady reading corners amongst the gravel paths and low hedges of scented herbs, the garden was where Phoebe had spent long childhood hours whilst Bruce tried to pass on his mastery of watercolour techniques, finally admitting that his ability to create art, if not his love of it, had bypassed her entirely. Beyond the wide bed of dahlias that Bruce insisted on tending himself each summer, until they burst into a blaze of autumnal colours, stood the solid mass of the ancient watch-tower, which for six hundred years had warned of intruders, and now housed his art studio.

Angelina had laid two places at the table, where a large

green garden salad sat in a wooden bowl beside ruby-red tomatoes and creamy buffalo mozzarella, a cold roast chicken and a condensation-frosted carafe of almost colourless white wine.

'Sit, sit,' Bruce said to Phoebe, lowering himself into his seat with the help of a walking stick. Although the once-black hair and beard were now snowy white, his tanned, freckled arms were strong and dark eyes still roguish. 'Tell me your news,' he said.

She started with the easy stuff: a few pieces she was considering for the museum, in the unlikely event that she could find the funding; how she was moving back into the Notting Hill flat soon, now James had moved out; how her mother had managed to fall out with half the village over a postcard-sized scrap of land.

'Your mother could fall out with herself,' Bruce said, ripping off a chunk of rosemary-flecked focaccia. There was no love lost between Bruce and Phoebe's parents, which saddened her. Bruce had played a small part in some court case in the sixties, in which his word stood against that of Sir Edwin Viner, acquaintance of her parents and pillar of the London art world. Phoebe's parents had picked their side, and in the way that only siblings can, the brothers had nursed an ice-cold grudge for over a quarter of a century, leaving Phoebe stranded in the middle. 'Why do you think I've always stayed out of the way here?' he added.

'Because you wouldn't live anywhere else?'

'Exactly. The world comes to me, and I don't have to endure any more wet English summers.'

Phoebe looked at him, noticing the slight catch in his breath. 'But you'll be back in London to visit the museum? I need your help with that empty room we've not curated yet,' she said, trying to sound positive about their joint project, even though the truth was far from positive.

He shook his head. 'My travelling days are over.'

He was tired, she could see, his lightly imparted news perhaps more serious than he was letting on so far. 'Because of the tests you mentioned in your letter?'

'Maybe. But you don't need me at the museum. Trust yourself, Phoebe. Besides, I'm done with London.' Phoebe watched as a twinge of sadness crossed his face. 'Too many memories.'

'What sort of memories?' Phoebe asked gently, pouncing on a rare moment of candidness.

'We thought we could change the world back then,' he said, staring out across the gardens.

'When?'

'The sixties. Was there any other time? We tried to turn the Establishment on its head with our miniskirts and pop music, our marches and protests, but nothing has changed. Strikes everywhere you look, and nothing gets through Parliament without a bunch of landed gentry in long red dresses saying so.'

'Still the revolutionary?' Phoebe asked, smiling.

He sat back, wincing slightly. 'Only in spirit. If you want to make a dent in the Establishment, you need a very sharp stick and a very thick skin.'

This was a Bruce she had not seen before: deflated, tired, a smaller version of himself, and Phoebe knew she really did have to worry about him. 'Like when you challenged Edwin Viner?' she asked, hoping to re-energise her uncle by poking at the hornets' nest she had never quite been able to reach. There was an injunction in place, she knew, but surely it didn't extend to his closest relative?

'Viner?' he spluttered, topping up his wine. 'Even if I were allowed to, I'm not wasting our time together talking about that crook. I want to focus on things that bring me joy rather than peptic ulcers. And speaking of peptic ulcers, tell me what happened with Shameless.'

Phoebe rolled her eyes at the nickname Tilly and Bruce had given James during a recent visit to Villa Clara. She'd protested at the time, but she had to admit, he'd lived up to his name. Phoebe had met James at her first job as an apprentice curator at the Fitzwilliam Museum in Cambridge. James had done various internships at auction houses where his parents knew the board, but there was always a reason it hadn't worked out: he wanted to experience the art market from the bottom up; he wanted to be an artist himself; he wanted to go travelling. Or the truth: that he was killing time until he got his inheritance. 'It didn't work out,' she said, wincing at the understatement. 'Same old story,' she explained to Bruce. 'Girl falls in love with boy, boy moves in with girl, who discovers he is sleeping around . . .'

'I'm sorry. Want me to set my London gangster friends on him?'

'You don't have any gangster friends,' she laughed.

He narrowed his eyes. 'Are you sure?'

'With you, I'm never sure about anything.' And it was true: for all his joking, Phoebe would not be surprised to discover Bruce had known the Kray twins.

'Get yourself a chap who's not afraid to earn his own living next time. Or better still, find yourself an Italian who knows how to treat a woman.' He smiled. 'You might not even need to look that far.'

Bruce had long hinted that she and Stefano should be together, but she brushed his comment aside. 'I think I might take a break, to be honest,' she said instead. 'It was exhausting keeping up with James and his awful friends. They actually pitied me because I work for a living. Good riddance.'

Bruce laughed. 'I met a few of those back in the day. Called themselves hedonists in the twenties, bohemians in the thirties, and now they're just plain old spoiled brats. Well, at least you have the museum. So tell me, did you manage to chase up that fake Fabergé egg? I heard that instead of a portrait of the Tsarina hidden inside, there's a rather terrifying Russian clown with a striking resemblance to Rasputin. I was thinking it could go in the Bloomsbury Room.'

She hesitated. This was her moment to explain about the books that didn't add up, the falling footfall and rising rent, the American management consultants; to tell him she'd had enough. 'Maybe,' she said instead.

He looked deflated. 'Well, you decide where it goes. Your museum, after all.'

'Bruce . . .'

He frowned. 'I don't like the sound of that tone. Are you about to spoil this lovely lunch?'

'I don't want to, but I need to talk to you. The museum is struggling,' she said, deciding to simply come out with it. 'Really struggling.'

'I can help with that. Who do you think will get this money-gobbling place and my enormous debts when I go?'

'I don't know. Who?' There were parts of her uncle's life she knew nothing of, other than a brief, disastrous marriage in the fifties to a woman with a temper equal if not superior to his own. She looked at him now, still raffishly handsome but with no obvious love interest, other than the professed infatuation with Angelina, whom Marco offered to exchange for the Alfa Spider. Where did he disappear off to on his long, solitary drives every day or so? What, or who, was running through his mind when he sat alone with a cigar on the terrace late at night after everyone had gone to bed?

'You will get the villa, you silly woman,' he said. 'And if I could give it to you now, I would. All I want is for you to be happy. But you're clearly not. You walked in here like a wet Sunday afternoon in February.'

'I'm sorry.' She looked up at him. 'I've had an offer for the lease on Bedford Court.'

'An offer?'

'The Americans who bought the building want to re-develop it.'

'But we can't let them. We must fight.'

'Not we. Me. I'm the one at the coal face every day. I'm the one supplementing the coffers with—' She stopped suddenly – he didn't need to know she had begun dipping into her savings to pay Tilly. 'I just know I've done as much as I can.'

He sighed. 'And the collection?'

'I'd have to sell it.'

'Even the not-Vermeer?' He suddenly slammed his glass down on the table. 'No, that is yours, Phoebe. I painted it for you, not the museum. You are never to let that work go. Promise me.'

'Of course. I promise.'

'And Tilly? I hate to think of her talent going to waste. She's been a huge asset to the museum.'

'She would find something else – as you say, she's brilliant.' And it was true: Tilly was not only Phoebe's best friend in London, but a fearsomely capable second-in-command at the museum. 'It might not come to that. Miracles do happen.' Phoebe leaned across and took his hand. 'I didn't mean to upset you.'

'And I didn't mean to snap. I haven't . . . well, I haven't been myself of late. Speaking of which . . .' He felt in the pocket of his shirt and pulled out a small bottle of tablets, knocking back two with the rest of his wine. Even beneath his deep suntan, she could see his colouring was a little sallow.

'Bruce, please tell me what's wrong.'

He stood, pushing his chair aside. 'Come. It's a beautiful afternoon. Let's take a walk. I want to show you the vines – there should be a bumper crop this year. Then let's have a drink in the studio, where Angelina can't badger us and we can talk frankly.'

2

Phoebe followed him inside the squat tower that sat across from the gardens, unable to shift the sense that Bruce wanted to show her everything one last time. She glanced around at the stacks of paintings, scruffy chests of drawers containing pigments and brushes, the desk with his neatly stacked blue notebooks. 'I've always loved it in here,' she said.

'As have I,' Bruce replied, gesturing for her to sit beside him on a dusty velvet sofa.

As she sat, she spotted the ladder and trapdoor that led to the next floor. 'What *is* up there?' she asked now. 'You've never let me see.'

'On the first floor?' He shook his head. 'Mainly rubbish. Old canvases, that sort of thing. And,' he added, 'rats. Why do you think I've always stopped you going up there?'

'I was never frightened of rats.'

'You think your mother would have let you come here again if you caught bubonic plague on my watch? Or died from rat poison?'

'If only rats go up there, what's that for?' she said, pointing to a dusty bell hanging from a chain next to the hatch.

'So I can call Angelina for my evening gin,' he said a little sharply, then sighed. 'Since today seems to be about honesty, you're right, there's something I need to talk to you about.'

She wanted to tell him to stop, that she didn't want to hear it, but instead she nodded. 'Go on.'

'Phoebe, I am unwell. Very unwell, as it turns out.'

'Please, don't . . .'

'But I must. I can't pretend.' He smiled. 'I'm very proud of you, you know?'

'I'm proud of you too.'

'Despite what they say about me?'

'No one says anything about you.'

'Then it really is over. The cancer may as well take me.'

'Cancer?' She felt tears prick at her eyes. It was worse than she had feared. 'Why didn't you tell me sooner? I'd have come out here and helped.'

He waved a hand dismissively. 'Exactly why I didn't. You know I hate a fuss. Besides, it's untreatable. I broke my lungs, and now I'm paying the price. I don't regret a single cigar, however,' he said, taking one now from a drawer and lighting it, his eyes closed as he released a stream of bittersweet smoke.

'Dare I ask how long?'

'Six months, maybe more, but I'm not interested in outliving my useful life. Once I can't paint, I'm done.'

'Surely there are things that can help?'

He shook his head. 'I'm eighty-six. I'm not interested in chemotherapy.'

'Bruce, I don't know what to say.'

'There's nothing *to* say. I've had a good life, with only one regret.'

Phoebe looked at him. 'What?'

He narrowed his eyes. 'I'd be breaking the law if I talked about it.'

'Even to me?' she asked, wondering whether he might finally explain what had happened in a London court over two decades ago, which he refused to divulge in case even one word got back to her parents' London circle.

'Restricted information, even now. Get yourself a court transcript in twenty years' time.'

She smiled. 'You are incorrigible.'

'You can put that on my gravestone: "An incorrigible old fart who smoked too many cigars."' His gaze drifted suddenly. 'Did I ever tell you about the time I met Churchill? A weekend house party, back in the twenties. Full of artists. He was trying to tout his shabby watercolours. One of the Sitwells was there. Can't remember which. And a rather extraordinary woman who'd married old Roland Penrose, great friends with Picasso. Now what was her name?'

Phoebe sat up straight. 'You met Lee Miller? The war photographer? Sometimes I feel I don't know you at all.'

'I am just a man who has loved and been loved. I've been lucky.' He glanced towards his desk, his eye alighting briefly on a black and white photograph of a woman. Phoebe had noticed it many times over the years, yet never really looked at it.

'Who did you love?' she asked, but a fit of coughing overtook him before he could answer.

'Get me a brandy, would you?' he said eventually.

Phoebe shook her head. 'I'm glad I'm not your doctor.'

'My doctor also wishes she weren't.' He reached for the tortoiseshell glasses he kept in his shirt pocket, so spattered with paint that they could barely be of any use. 'Come, let's play the old game, shall we?'

'A treasure hunt?' Phoebe said, recalling the elaborate trails he would leave around Villa Clara and its grounds, using works of art to punctuate the clues. She and Stefano had lost entire days deciphering cryptic messages, checking behind paintings and statues, in order to find Easter eggs, Roman coins, even a kitten once.

'Not quite. I've got a new acquisition to show you. Want to test your eye?'

She had spent hours in the studio over the years, poring over art books while Bruce trained her never to trust the evidence of her eyes, to question the provenance of a piece, until she was almost good enough to pick a Bruce Cato reproduction out of a line-up – only ever almost, for he was unquestionably a master. 'If I get it right, do I keep it?' she asked.

He laughed. 'You might as well, my dear. You might as well.'

Phoebe gradually came to realise that her visit was as much about helping Bruce put his affairs in order as it was about spending time together. It was a difficult time, and she was grateful to Stefano for taking her into Siena for dinner one evening when Bruce had gone for one of his regular drives. It was good to talk to someone who understood what it was to love and to lose Bruce Cato. Stefano let her laugh and cry, often joining in himself. There had been a difficult conversation as Stefano prepared the ground for what might have to happen if Bruce needed palliative care. The Villa Clara finances were not in great shape, but they decided to cross that bridge when they came to it. These few days felt too precious to be loaded with more worry.

The next day Phoebe helped Bruce crate up a Leonardo da

Vinci replica he had made for the Cinecittà studios in Rome, the perfect excuse, he said, for a trip to the post office in Siena in the old red Alfa Spider. During that perilously fast drive along the tiny lanes, Bruce had looked across at Phoebe, protected from the dust and wind by large sunglasses and a scarf tied Grace Kelly-style over her hair. He had suddenly slowed down, pulling on to the verge at the edge of the road.

'What is it?' she'd asked.

'You just reminded me of someone, sitting there like that.'

And that had been it: a tiny glimpse into the secret world of Bruce Cato, before his foot hit the accelerator and off they shot again.

The week passed too quickly, and Phoebe hated the thought that she was helping her uncle clear the decks. 'Think of it as a spring clean,' he told her cheerfully as they went through the house, sorting old paperbacks and throwing away ancient correspondence.

'Bin or bonfire?' she said, sitting on the study floor one afternoon and holding up a manila envelope full of newspaper clippings, airmail letters, postcards and other correspondence.

'You needn't think that's going in your black bin bag, young lady,' he said, snatching it from her.

'I'm beginning to think nothing is.' She shook her head. 'If I do give up the museum, I could have a full-time job here, just sorting you out.'

'Promise me you'll give it another six months, and I'll let you throw everything away next time you're here.' He was joking, but she knew that next time she was here, at best he would be a little less himself. At worst . . . maybe he was right. Keeping busy was the only way.

They'd arranged she would return in six weeks, but already that felt like a lifetime away as she said her goodbyes in the early morning sunshine on the gravel driveway, Stefano waiting nearby at the wheel of his Lancia. The tickle of Bruce's beard on her forehead as she hugged him was the same as ever, the whisper of linseed oil and white spirit, but within her arms he felt smaller, and his breathing was laboured as Phoebe closed her eyes, memorising the hum of crickets warming up for the new day, the whickering of horses in a nearby field and the rhythmic swish of Angelina's broom. And then it was time to go.

'Look after her,' Bruce called out to Stefano as the car pulled away.

'What did he mean?' she asked Stefano, his eyes firmly fixed on the road ahead.

'He wants me to drive you safely, I suppose.' The forced lightness of his tone kidded neither of them, however, and it was a difficult, silent journey before he dropped her at the airport.

3

Phoebe was still half-asleep as she emerged from the Underground a few days later, a bicycle courier yelling as he swerved to avoid her. Her reactions were dulled after a night on Tilly's sofa and rather more Hungarian cab sav than she was used to – the last one, thankfully, since James had finally moved his stuff out of the Notting Hill flat and she could at last go home.

She checked herself – Tilly was not only the best employee she could ever have hoped for, but her lifesaver, of late. The closest thing she had to family in London, now Dad had passed away and Mum moved to the deep South-West, Tilly had been at Phoebe's side ever since they'd met as Art History students at the Courtauld Institute years earlier, through their various relationship break-ups, trips to Phoebe's uncle's estate in Italy, and the formative years of the museum that now just about paid both their wages. So no, she wouldn't miss the late nights and daily hangovers, but she would always be grateful for Tilly's generosity. If the museum ever made enough of a profit, she would promote Tilly to joint director, but those days were a long way off.

Having sent Tilly on an early morning scavenge for materials for the school trip booked in that afternoon, Phoebe made her commute alone through the Georgian streets and verdant squares that made up Bloomsbury, the elegant, bookish corner of London that lay behind the British Museum and had once found notoriety as the home of Virginia Woolf and her racy set. She passed countless blue plaques that marked the history of the area until she reached Bedford Court, a tiny, cobbled enclave of blue-brick buildings.

She paused, using the sleeve of her trench coat to polish the brass plate on the door of number 11: The Cato Museum of Artifice, where each room was dedicated to an artist or period. With the help of Tilly, Phoebe had trawled auctions and flea markets to create a series of beguiling domestic vignettes. It was a labour of love, and she couldn't be more proud of what they had created with Bruce.

Phoebe scooped up the post from the black and white tiled floor: bills, junk mail, a letter from the Arts Council probably confirming another rejection for funding. She would deal with these later, and instead focus on opening up the museum for the day.

She let herself into the drawing room inspired by the homes of the Bloomsbury Group who had lived close by in the early twentieth century, pulling back the heavy velvet curtains to cast light on Edwardian red-velvet sofas and a spindle-legged Arts and Crafts desk. On the sideboard sat Bruce's framed photograph of a young girl staring wistfully at a troupe of fairies. The Cottingley Fairies had caused uproar in 1917, until years later the girl in the photograph admitted it was a hoax. Further rooms included a Georgian salon upstairs, where visitors could work out which of the portraits on the walls were genuinely eighteenth century, and which were by Bruce Cato – it always amazed her how people missed the wristwatch he had added, or a vapour trail in the sky. If that weren't enough, in a sixties-style bedsit-cum-studio, anyone could have a go at creating their own Andy Warhol print to take home.

This carefully curated museum was a joy, and yet if visitor numbers continued to decline, she would be accepting the Americans' escape route. A route that was increasingly tempting, now Stefano had described the financial difficulties at Villa Clara. Besides, if – when – Bruce's health deteriorated, she wanted to be free to look after him.

Hearing Tilly arrive, she went to switch on the kettle in the office, pulling a packet of chocolate Hobnobs from a cupboard in anticipation of her temporary landlady's low blood sugar.

'Hi, babe,' Tilly said, slinging her denim jacket on the rack, and shaking out her shock of dyed satsuma-orange hair. She tipped a carrier bag out on to the desk. 'Here you go. Crayons, paper, glue, glitter . . .'

'Glitter?' Phoebe asked, aghast.

Tilly looked deflated. 'OK, so maybe not the glitter.' She brightened suddenly. 'Hey, you'll never guess. I got talking to some bloke on the bus.' She tipped her head coquettishly. 'We're going for a drink tonight.'

'I don't know how you do it.'

'Nothing to stop you, now you've dumped Shameless. You'll have them queuing up, with that new wardrobe.'

Phoebe looked down at her new tailored black dress, worn with a long, knotted necklace. It had been an eye-wateringly expensive Saturday spent on the King's Road with Tilly the previous weekend, tempered by a few charity-shop bargains,

24

but her friend had been right: she needed a revamp. 'I don't want anyone else. Not yet.'

Tilly narrowed her eyes. 'Not even Stefano? You obviously like each other.'

'Stefano's my oldest friend. Of course we do. Besides, he's got a girlfriend. Not that it makes any difference.' Phoebe looked at her watch, unsettled by an unwelcome blush. 'We'd better get on,' she said briskly. 'Twenty minutes before the hordes start banging the door down.' Or more likely the bailiff. 'I'll open up the studio.'

Even after five years, she still experienced a thrill whenever she stepped into the large, north-facing room at the back of the house, laid out by Bruce as a seventeenth-century Dutch artist's studio. A traditional ivory-coloured lime wash covered the walls, contrasting with a striking black and white chequer-board floor skirted with antique Dutch blue and white tiles. A heavy velvet curtain had been pulled halfway across the fake-leaded window beside a simple wooden desk and blue-upholstered chair. On top of the ornate patterned rug spread on the table lay a writing quill and paper, and a shallow pewter dish was pooled with the wax of a burned-out candle, a large monochrome map hanging on the wall behind.

Across the room, an artist's workbench had been set with antique glass jars of linseed oil and pigments, their labels written by hand – lapis lazuli, yellow ochre, vermilion, green earth – alongside a selection of worn paintbrushes, handmade affairs of squirrel hair bound with string. A deep stone bowl of walnuts waited to yield their precious oil to the master, perfect for creating light skin tones.

Nearby stood a paint-spattered antique easel, with a wooden palette and painting stick the artist might have used to steady his hand. The easel was covered out of opening hours, to protect the paint that should have taken decades to dry, rather than the several hours in Bruce's Tuscan bread oven, and Phoebe smiled as she pulled away the cloth. There, set behind a sheet of glass in an ornate frame, and no larger than an A3 sheet of paper, was one of the most skilful copies Bruce had ever executed.

To say the painting was a copy was to misinform, however. If the original of this work ever existed, it would be shielded by a high-security system in the Louvre or the Met, discussed by experts and insured for a king's ransom. But this was a figment of Bruce's imagination, the result of years of study, so that the composition, the execution, the pigments used, made it appear that an undiscovered Dutch treasure had found its way here. Such a painting had been mentioned in a seventeenth-century Amsterdam sale, but whether the original had looked anything like this was anyone's guess.

The painting depicted the tableau set up in the room, with the addition of a young woman in a striking blue gown, hand poised over the pages of a letter. Her yellow ermine-trimmed jacket thrown on the back of the chair echoed the blonde tendrils of hair escaping dainty plaits and tiny red ribbons arranged on her head. The slight flush on her cheeks and hint of moisture on the bottom lip she gently bit suggested she was excited, disturbed, the burned-out candle and screwed-up former drafts a sign she had been there for hours, trying to find the right words.

So convincing was this work, that art experts occasionally contacted the museum, but when Phoebe explained it was from the hand of Bruce Cato, they melted away.

It broke her heart to think of how he had been treated over the years, of how her parents' friendship with Edwin Viner had essentially cast Bruce from the family fold. Phoebe knew very little of what had happened, other than that there had been a court case, in which Bruce and Viner clashed. Reporting on the trial had been restricted, so that newspapers at the time, and subsequently, were barred from printing any details, and as far as Phoebe knew, the trial transcripts that she had secretly tried to track down whilst a student were still not in the public domain. Bruce, under a lifelong injunction preventing him from speaking about the case, had long since decided he had better things to think about than an ancient spat with 'that pompous arse'.

Phoebe had come across Viner at various dinner parties at the Hampstead home when she was a child, and found him to be exactly that, as from behind the door she heard him drawl the silver-spoon aristocratic vowels she would come to know from his occasional lectures at the Courtauld Institute. If it were an integrity contest between Bruce and Viner, Phoebe knew whose side she would be on. Shame her own parents had been too starry-eyed to agree.

She looked at the painting once more. It almost didn't matter that it was of no material worth, based merely on rumours of a missing piece: as a work of art, it was perfection. Even if Phoebe lost the museum, if she gave everything up, she would still have this thing of beauty, this thing made for her with love, which she had promised her uncle she would keep at all costs.

Her very own bespoke Vermeer.

A few weeks later, Phoebe was sitting at her desk poring through a pile of funding rejection letters. It was 20 July, four weeks since she had left Villa Clara, and she was trying to work out how easy it would be to get back there soon. Bruce's goodbye had troubled her, and she longed to walk out on her responsibilities in London and jump on a plane to Tuscany. Could she and Tilly share running the place, she wondered, short or long term, if she spent half her time at the Villa, looking after Bruce? It wasn't ideal, but her life was split into two, and compromises had to be made.

As it happened, such decisions were made pointless when she received a telephone call from a tearful Angelina later that afternoon.

'*Mia cara*,' she sobbed from the echoey hallway of Villa Clara.

Phoebe was instantly on alert. Bruce had taken a turn for the worse, perhaps? The doctor had perhaps misjudged how long he had before he became incapacitated. 'What is it, Angelina?'

'Oh Phoebe, may the Blessed Virgin preserve us.'

'Angelina, please . . .' Phoebe pressed, in no mood for Angelina's dramatics. 'Just tell me what has happened.'

'Mr Bruce, he took the car out this morning to San Gimignano,' the housekeeper gabbled on in Italian. 'As he does at the same time every morning. Day in, day out . . .'

'Yes, I know.'

'But when I came to serve lunch – a saltimbocca I had been preparing for two days, you know how it is his favourite . . .' There was a pause as the housekeeper blew her nose noisily. 'He hadn't come back. Four hours, he'd been out. He never stays out for four hours.'

'So where was he?'

'I didn't know. I was frightened for him. He'd seemed so sad at breakfast, so quiet. It worried me, and then when he didn't come back I called the carabinieri.'

'You called the police?' Phoebe asked, shocked. 'What did they say?'

'They went to look for him.'

'And did they find him? Where is he? Where's Bruce?'

An almighty wail blasted through the receiver, and Phoebe was forced to wait for Angelina to compose herself, time in which she imagined every scenario except the one she was finally told.

'They found his car. He had veered off the road and crashed through a copse. The car hit a tree full on.'

She hardly dared asked the question that hovered between them, the sound of the street outside muffled beyond the deafening beat of her racing heart. 'Is he all right, Angelina?' she eventually whispered, already sure of the answer, but relishing the last few seconds in which she could pretend that the world remained unchanged.

'All right?' Angelina sobbed. 'Oh, my dear Phoebe . . . He died instantly. Mr Bruce is dead.'

4

It was the sort of sky Bruce would have described as Turner with a chance of Constable, the landscape he loved so dearly putting on its most ravishing display as Stefano drove Phoebe back to Villa Clara a week before the funeral.

'Thanks for picking me up,' Phoebe said. 'I know you must have loads to do. You look shattered.' He did indeed look exhausted, his green eyes set within dark circles.

'Death certainly keeps the lawyers busy,' Stefano replied, accelerating as he overtook a three-wheeled Ape farm truck, two bewildered-looking goats staring out from its flatbed.

'You know, I keep thinking about what he said as we were leaving for the airport.'

Stefano glanced briefly at her before turning his attention back to the road. 'What did he say?'

'He said, "Look after her." Maybe he knew I wouldn't see him again.' Phoebe had been plagued by a suspicion that Bruce's fatal drive was a deliberate swansong: out in a blaze of glory on a sun-kissed stretch of road.

Stefano sighed. 'And he was right.' He slowed down, turning into the long, cypress-lined drive. 'Here we are. You ready?'

She had thought she was, but as they stopped in front of the house, the absence of the red sports car suddenly floored her.

'It's OK,' he said, holding her until she was able to put back on the brave face that had served her well in London.

'Sorry,' she said. 'It feels even worse than I thought it would.'

'I do understand.'

Of course he did: Stefano missed Bruce as much as she did. 'I really appreciate how much you've done,' she said, 'with the legalities and everything. It must have been a nightmare.'

He sighed. 'I've barely started. Listen, I know you won't want to think about this yet, but we should try to find some time to talk about the will. And about what you want to do with the villa. There's something else I was hoping you could help clear up, too.'

As executor of the will, and a partner at the law firm Bruce had used for years, Stefano had already explained that according to Italian hereditary laws, everything would go to Phoebe, but things with Bruce were never straightforward, even in death. 'Sure,' she said. 'What kind of thing?'

'Just a payment that's been going out regularly. But we can talk about it later.' He squeezed her hand. 'Come on, Topolino,' he smiled. 'You can do this.'

The front door, adorned with a funereal wreath of lilies and laurels, promptly opened, and Phoebe was swallowed up in Angelina's black-jersey soft embrace as Stefano quietly took her bags away.

'How have you been?' she asked Angelina.

The older woman shrugged. 'I would be better if every bugger within ten miles stopped dropping by with runny stews and cakes you could build a house with. They think Angelina can't cook any more, just because Signor Bruce has gone?' she complained.

Phoebe saw the worry etched on her face and knew that at some point she would have to address the issue of what would happen to Stefano's parents, who lived in an apartment attached to the villa. If she sold Villa Clara, they would be homeless; if she kept Villa Clara, she would be jobless. A rough estimate from Stefano over the phone a few days earlier had suggested that Bruce's few stocks and shares would pay the old retainers' salaries for twelve months, but Villa Clara was a ticking clock with a leaky roof and medieval plumbing. 'Flog it,' had been her mother's suggestion as she wrote to explain she was far too busy to make the funeral, but it was much too early to make any decisions.

They went inside, where all the mirrors had been covered with black cloths, the air sweet with the scent of lilies. 'Let's work out what has to be done, once I've unpacked,' Phoebe said, trying to be businesslike.

Angelina smiled. 'Everything has been done. Bruce knew exactly what he wanted.'

'I can believe it.' Bar the date of his funeral, it seemed Bruce had planned everything: the guest list, the catering, the string quartet who would play a Mendelssohn slow movement in the church, the wine waiting in the cellar. A jazz band had been engaged for the evening, when Bruce demanded his guests dance on the terrace and celebrate his life. He'd even had invitations printed, on which Angelina had filled in the space for the date, posting them in pre-addressed envelopes.

The silent farmhouse gradually came to life, with Angelina restocking the outdoor dining table every few hours to accommodate the string of visitors. Phoebe found herself greeting old family friends and members of Bruce's Italian circle whom she had never met: the owner of a prestigious Rome gallery, art professors and members of his *scopa* club, the fiendish Italian card game guaranteed to fuel angry arguments, especially after a glass or two of Bruce's grappa. It was wonderful to hear him spoken of so fondly, and with such respect: one Florentine dealer told her there was no one in the world who could restore a painting so sensitively and accurately as Bruce Cato.

As if to celebrate the life of the man who had created them, the gardens put on a dazzling display of colour, from the lavender beds and peppery geraniums to Bruce's beloved dahlias, which glowed in every shade of orange from rose gold to deep blood red.

To keep up with the flow of guests, Phoebe was initiated into the secret art of Angelina's Tuscan kitchen, collecting tomatoes from the garden as the two women recalled the childhood capers that had kept the young Phoebe and Stefano only a hair's breadth from the back of Angelina's hand.

And yet Phoebe still couldn't face going to the studio, which Angelina had kept closed since the accident. Seeing it as Bruce had left it would drain her of the strength she needed for the next few days.

Before she knew it, the day of the funeral was upon them, and beneath a beating sun Phoebe and Angelina led the mourners behind the coffin borne by Stefano and Marco and some of Bruce's friends from the village, into the medieval church. She took her seat at the front, fed tissues by Angelina whilst Stefano sat at her other side, the calm façade of the black-suited lawyer belying the shake in his hand as he clutched hers.

She glanced briefly at the congregation behind her, local farmers in dusty black suits sitting alongside tailoring straight off Rome's Via Condotti. An elderly lady with dyed black hair and livid red lips was apparently the former housekeeper at Villa Clara, Angelina told her sniffily, sitting with her son. Amongst the feathers and net adorning an array of millinery, one woman in particular caught Phoebe's attention, large sunglasses obscuring her eyes and her dark hair tucked Jackie Kennedy-style within a black scarf tied at her throat. Was she a friend of Bruce? Business associate?

Bruce's coffin stood beneath a wreath of Villa Clara dahlias as friends and neighbours shared memories of the man who had made his life here. Phoebe was stunned to hear of Bruce's bravery during the war, when he hid resistance fighters at Villa Clara and couriered messages for the Allies, hidden within painting frames.

Phoebe thought back to a telephone call she had received before she left for the funeral, from an obituary writer digging for titbits about the court case with Edwin Viner. She had given the woman short shrift, but the resurrected accusations of Bruce being a fraud rankled, and Phoebe wished there were a way of putting these tired stories to bed.

As the service drew to its conclusion, she glanced around once more, just in time to see the dark-haired woman at the back of the church remove her sunglasses. Phoebe realised with a jolt that she was looking at Margot Stockton, art critic and dealer, part of the British art establishment that Bruce had loathed – an establishment apparently moved to tears by his passing.

5

The last guests were still dancing on the terrace to the dying strains of a love song, and although Phoebe's energy was drained by a long day of speaking Italian and painting on a brave face, there was one more conversation to be had. As she watched Margot Stockton head across to the old watchtower, she knew her moment had come.

A standard lamp had been switched on in the corner of the studio beside Bruce's battered velvet armchair. Close by, his desk was piled high with *catalogues raisonnés* and reference books, alongside his meticulously kept blue notebooks charting every piece that had passed through his hands. A half-full glass beaker of red wine sat alongside them, as though he might return at any moment, and nearby Phoebe spotted Margot Stockton browsing the bursting shelves of a bookcase.

'Ah,' she said. 'You must be Phoebe. I've been hoping to catch you alone. You don't mind me looking around?' Margot Stockton was even more intimidating up close, her heirloom pearl earrings mirrored by the choker around her neck. Nothing, from the patent pumps and tailored black shift dress to the perfectly coiffed dark hair, said 'approachable'.

'Of course not.'

'I always wanted to visit Villa Clara. I knew Bruce from a long time ago, and had heard so much about it.'

'You were close?'

'Acquaintances, really. I hadn't seen him for over twenty years.'

'Thank you for coming, in that case.'

'I wanted to pay my respects.' She smiled. 'He also gave me little choice.'

Phoebe frowned. 'How so?'

'Bruce included a note with the invitation, asking that I talk to you about someone.'

'Who?'

'We had a shared friend.' Margot wandered towards the desk and picked up a framed black and white photograph. 'Here,' she said.

Phoebe took it from her, looking at the slight smile on the woman's strong, handsome face. It was a photograph she had seen many times, but whenever asked, Bruce had just said she was an old friend from his student days. 'Who is she?'

'Leonora Birch. She studied art at Chelsea School of Art with Bruce, back in the twenties.'

'She was an artist too?'

'For a short while. She had a sick father to care for, or it would have been she on the Rome Scholarship, instead of your uncle.'

'She was that good?'

'I only ever saw some of her sketches, a couple of paintings, but yes. What I wouldn't give to represent her at my gallery, if she's still working . . .' Margot frowned. 'You haven't got a drink of anything here, have you?'

Phoebe smiled. 'In Bruce's studio? I think that's a given.' She began rummaging inside the desk, eventually producing a dusty brandy bottle and two glasses. She handed a small measure to Margot, who sat in Bruce's armchair, her feet tucked debutante-style to one side. 'So why did Bruce suddenly want me to know about Leonora Birch?'

Margot frowned. 'You really don't know anything about her?'

'Only what you just told me. Is she still alive, even?'

'I hope so. I was very fond of her. We all were.'

'All?'

'Oh yes. You see, Leonora Birch had a talent for bringing people together, creating a family of sorts, I suppose you could say. One I was lucky enough to be part of.'

'An artistic family?' Phoebe asked, wondering how Bruce might fit into this narrative.

'Not exactly. More of a sort of ark, really.'

'And how did you end up being part of this . . . well, family?'

Margot smiled. 'That's easy. It was 1963 and the day I thought my life was over.'

6

London, 9 March 1963

Margot wished everyone would stop fluttering around her. She longed to shrug off the girl from the Ronald Paterson atelier, constantly checking that the ivory shantung silk of her wedding gown fell in perfectly even folds from its boat-necked bodice. She wanted to elbow away the hairdresser smoothing for the hundredth time Margot's glossy, backcombed bob, curled at the top of her long, bare neck.

She felt as though she were being prepared for a photo shoot, not marriage to Hugo, but perhaps that was exactly what was happening. Ever since the engagement notice went into *The Times*, the Right Honourable Margot Stockton-Jones had been courted by society magazines, her mother secretly cutting a deal with the *Tatler*, whose photographer had now joined the circus on the top floor of Belgravia's Davenport Hotel.

'Darling, don't frown,' Arabella Stockton-Jones, Countess of Abingford, tutted as she pressed a tissue to her crimson lipstick, an exact match to her bracelet-sleeved shantung-silk coat dress. 'You'll get lines, and that will never do.'

Nothing had ever 'done' for Arabella, as far as Margot had experienced in the brief windows of mother–daughter interaction between terms at Roedean and Swiss finishing school. One's daughter studying Art History at Oxford was certainly not done: 'University?' her mother had said. 'Books make a girl so dreary.' Popping pills from her pet Harley Street doctor and criticising her two remaining children were apparently 'done', however. No wonder Margot's brother Cosmo was a functioning drunk and her father kept a mistress in Paris.

Thank goodness for Hugo, she supposed, and the new life they would soon make together, running the estate in Cumbria between his work as a London barrister.

Cumbria.

Margot closed her eyes as the hairdresser carefully attached furlongs of tulle net to the diamond-studded tiara virtually stapled to her scalp. She tried to imagine herself on the other side of this spectacle, dressed in tweed, mud and dog hair. Yes, sharing the Chelsea flat with Diana was trying – Cumbria, though? No one would ever visit. And of course she was fond of Hugo, but the way he sighed every time he took a sip of tea or telephoned his mother to help him decide what tie to wear, the mother who would be living in the dower house . . .

'Margot.'

She opened her eyes to find Arabella assessing her like a prize filly. 'Yes?'

'Diana has your bouquet,' she said tightly. It was generally perceived that Diana Viner, with her 'fast' ways, passed muster for the big day only because their mothers had been at school together and her father Sir Edwin was a well-respected Mayfair art dealer. 'Now where are those ghastly children?' she said, moving away to choreograph the offspring borrowed from distant relatives and influential friends.

'Here you go,' Diana said, holding out the heavy posy of peach-blush roses. 'You know, Escargot,' she whispered, using the teenage nickname Diana found hilarious, and Margot less so, 'you don't have to do this if you don't want to. In fact, I've put a fiver on one of you not turning up.'

Margot was shocked. 'You bet on my wedding?'

'Well, that and the three-thirty at Cheltenham.' Diana shrugged. 'Plus, I'm pretty sure you don't really want to be some provincial wifey serving sherry to dull women.' She shuddered. 'Ugh.'

'Of course I want to,' Margot bristled. 'Well, apart from the sherry. Besides, half of London is waiting in the Brompton Oratory.'

'You'd get married for other people? Lord, I wouldn't even give the time to other people.' Diana caught sight of her reflection in the overmantel mirror and brushed her sharp black fringe from the heavily made-up eyes still red from the bottle of whisky they had drunk together the night before. Or, rather, Diana had.

'Isn't that what all weddings are about? Other people?'

'Nonsense. When I marry, it will be in Gretna Green with someone utterly unsuitable and no one else there.' She lowered her voice. 'Besides, you don't even love each other. This is madness. Don't come running back to your aunt Diana in tears when it all goes wrong.'

She had expected Diana to tell her not to be silly the previous evening as she sobbed that she and Hugo had not done 'it', and that in fact he hadn't ever kissed her properly. Diana hadn't even teased her when Margot said Hugo's best friend was coming on honeymoon with them. When Diana's naturally catty streak was silenced, there was usually cause for concern.

'Margot!' Arabella called from across the room.

'Off you go, little lamb,' Diana whispered, a little meanly for Margot's liking.

That just about sums it up, she thought. A lamb to the slaughter.

She suddenly recalled a moment sitting in the back of a cab with Hugo, on the way to some dinner or other. He had leaned forward to tie his shoelace, and as she watched his pale fingers, long and soft like a woman's, she had tried to imagine what it would feel like if – when – they touched her.

'Mother, I need some air,' she said suddenly, waiting for Arabella to be distracted before seizing her chance and slipping out on to the landing.

She hadn't really planned it, but she headed towards the carpeted staircase. Down she went, flight after flight, in a flurry of silk shoes and petticoats, until she was looking down on the mirrored foyer and the teeming pool of top hats and feathers preparing to decant to the Brompton Road, where her husband-to-be and his weirdly long fingers awaited her.

'Darling!' Across the sea of guests, her father stood in tails and pinstripes, his glow of pride fading to concern as she stood in front of him. 'Margot, what is it?'

'I'm sorry, Daddy,' she said, then turned away, forcing a path through the crowd.

Her brother Cosmo broke away from chatting up the wife of some MP or other and caught her arm. 'Marge, what are you doing?'

'Let go of me. I have to . . .' Have to what? she asked herself.

'Bloody hell, sis. Are you bolting?' Cosmo laughed.

'Cos, please. Get out of my way.'

He stood back, his arms wide as he smiled at her. 'Poor old Hugo. At least one of you has balls. Run free, old girl. Don't look back,' he called out as she pushed through the glass doors, pausing briefly to hook the slingbacks of her satin shoes across her finger before she broke into a run.

She didn't stop running even as she tossed the most expensive roses in London into the gutter.

She didn't stop running even as she ripped the veil from her tiara, letting it catch on a set of iron railings and wave her a long, fluid goodbye.

She didn't stop running even as she tore through Eaton Square and the smart white stucco of Belgravia morphed into terraces that made up the shabbier district of Pimlico.

She only stopped when she had no breath left in her and was forced to plonk herself down on the nearest doorstep.

The front door behind her opened suddenly and Margot stood, gathering the acres of silk in her arms.

'Well, what have we got here?' said a tall woman in men's brogues and a neatly pressed housecoat that belied her educated accent, her greying hair knotted in a low bun at her neck.

Margot noticed a sign propped in the front window: 'Mrs Birch's Boarding House for Young Ladies.' She looked up at the woman. 'I don't suppose you've got a room free, have you?'

7

'And don't bother coming back this time, my girl.'

Dolly Carter grabbed her daughter by the arm and pushed her through the open door, so that within minutes of the row exploding, Joan found herself on the street for the whole of Bethnal Green to see, in the short-skirted dress she'd been wearing when she crept into the house at six a.m. Joan had got halfway up the stairs before Dolly caught her.

'Your father would be disgusted . . .' Joan had heard it before, but Dad was in no position to be disgusted at anything whilst sitting in his cell at Wormwood Scrubs with all the other wife-beaters and petty crooks. Unfortunately, she had told her mother so, earning herself an extra slap.

Usually these altercations ended in a two-day house arrest until Dolly smiled grudgingly at Joan's mimicry of the neighbours, the butcher, the postie. Blonde, blue-eyed Joan could charm the pants off anyone, even if Dolly Carter's sensible drawers provided a unique challenge.

This time, however, not only had Joan come in with the milk, but she'd been seen the night before with Alf in his fancy car, and wearing a new fur-collared coat she'd certainly not paid for with her job at the dry-cleaner's on Bethnal Green Road. Or rather the job she'd had until three days ago, when she turned up late again.

As the coalman leaned out of the cab of his truck, she countered his 'In trouble again, Joanie?' with a 'Get lost, Stan.' Joan looked around to see that most of the doorsteps at this end of Percy Street were now occupied by women in hairnets and pinnies, cigarettes hanging from their lips as they stared at the dirty stop-out. 'You lot can get lost, an' all,' she shouted.

'Look out, love,' Mrs Jones called out from over the road, laughing as she pointed upwards.

Joan moved just in time to avoid the suitcase Dolly threw from the upstairs window. As it exploded on the street below, a shower of shoes followed close behind before the sash window was slammed shut. She scrabbled around, scraping together nightdresses and stockings, sweaters and short skirts and stuffing them back inside. 'See you kept the bloody coat, Mum,' she muttered as she forced the clasps shut and heaved the case on to its side.

Joan smoothed her hair and straightened her shoulders, trying to pretend the suitcase didn't weigh a ton as she tottered down the street. Mum would change her mind – she always did. But maybe Joan didn't want to come back. Maybe she'd just go ahead and prove them all wrong. Alf had promised he'd look after her – well, now was his chance.

Joan took a corner table at Wilson's Eel and Pie Emporium on Bethnal Green Road. It was nearly closing time, but Daphne wouldn't boot her out. She'd once even given Joan a job clearing tables, until they both realised Joan's skills lay in chatting to customers rather than serving them. She took a compact mirror out of her handbag and looked at herself. Last night's mascara had bled black lava down her cheeks, and her nose was shiny with crying. The worst day of her life had started so well, with Alf dropping her round the corner from home in his new white sports car, but things had gone downhill ever since.

Joan was not sure exactly where Alf lived, as he always picked her up, but everyone knew him and his mum, and so she had eventually dragged the suitcase to a little street stranded between two vast moonscapes of bomb damage. As she hammered on the door of number 29, it turned out that not only did Alf live there, but also the flame-haired fiancée just arrived from Dublin.

And now here Joan was, at five p.m. in Wilson's with a cold cup of tea and nowhere to go.

'You done, love?'

Joan looked up and nodded. 'Thanks, Daph.'

'Going on your holidays?' Daphne glanced down at the suitcase.

'Moving house.'

'Where's that, then?'

Joan shrugged. 'I'll tell you when I find out.'

Daphne came around to the other side of the Formica-topped table, limping a little from what Joan had been told was an old war wound. There were stories that Daphne had been a spy in the war, but no one really believed it. 'So, you left home?' she said, pulling a packet of cigarettes from her apron pocket.

'Mum chucked me out, and this bloke I've been seeing, well, turns out . . .' She stopped, reluctant to say the words.

'Turns out Alf's getting married?' Daphne said.

'You heard?'

'Half the East End has heard. Oh, you poor love.'

45

Joan felt fat tears drip down her cheeks once more. 'I don't know what to do, Daph.'

'I've got a settee in the flat upstairs?'

'Thanks, but I don't want to stay around here. Everyone knows.' She looked across at Daphne, with her bottle-blonde hair and mask of make-up. She was the kind of woman Joan wanted to be, the sort of woman you never messed with, but instead she was the classic naïve idiot.

Daphne tapped her cigarette in the ashtray then pulled a notebook and pencil out of her pocket. She scribbled something down and ripped the sheet of paper out, passing it across to Joan. 'Here,' she said. 'Mrs Birch will sort you out. Nice lady. Used to do bed and board for some of the girls I was in the typing pool with during the war. Round the corner from West-minster, so it was handy.'

Typing pool? That was a new one. She read the note then looked up. 'Pimlico?' she said. 'But I've never been to Pimlico.'

Daphne smiled. 'High time you went there, then, my girl.'

8

Little of London was visible through the tiny top-floor window. It was like being in a cave fifty feet above the ground, Margot realised, the anaglypta walls the sludgy olive-green of the Blythmere swimming pool if it was left uncovered all winter. She ran her fingers over the wavy-ploughed brown counterpane, taking in the painted floorboards, the boarded-up fireplace and ropy-looking electric heater.

The room had two beds, a small chest of drawers over which one was presumably to argue with one's room-mate, a mahogany wardrobe and a table with a jug and bowl. It being a twin room, Mrs Birch had said that at some point Miss Stockton – Margot having dropped the double barrel – might have to bunk up. Until then, she could have it at half the rate of two sharing.

Her new landlady had the air of an educated lady, her walls decorated with fine art and bookcases stuffed with erudite volumes, her taste more bohemian than boarding-house. Margot was curious to get to know this stiff-backed, smartly dressed woman who had explained the rules of the house briskly.

The bathroom was on the first floor, Leonora Birch had told her. Five minutes maximum at rush hour. Sunday lunch was included, as Mrs Birch believed in her household getting to know one another, and a Baby Belling oven was provided in each room, washing-up to be done in the downstairs kitchen.

Lodgers needed their own change for the communal telephone in the hallway. Rent was £3 a week, and if you couldn't pay, you did chores until you could. Unlike other landladies, Mrs Birch didn't believe in curfews: of her other two tenants, Miss Stevenson was a civil servant who kept funny hours, and Linda, as well as being a secretary, had a waitressing job in the evening to help save for her wedding. Mrs Birch's son Laurence visited several times a week, and Margot wasn't to mind him – he was much nicer than he seemed.

Had Margot any plans? Mrs Birch had asked, discreetly avoiding the wedding-dress-sized elephant in the room. Margot had no plans. Neither did she have any cash until she could get to Coutt's on Lower Sloane Street, nor a change of clothes. Not to worry, Mrs Birch had nodded, and a few moments later a bone-china cup of tea sat on the chest of drawers beside a clean skirt and blouse that Mrs Birch had drawn from her collection of clothing left behind by previous girls.

Margot sat on the porridgy mattress, fiddling with the engagement ring that had belonged to her almost-mother-in-law, whilst at Claridge's a wedding breakfast for three hundred was right now going cold. It was dreadful, of course, but everyone would get over it.

And then she realised there was one person to whom she hadn't given a moment's thought – Hugo.

Breaking off one's engagement was one thing, but bolting twenty minutes before the wedding was another matter. Through all these months of preparation, the romantic feelings she'd hoped would grow simply hadn't, and yet she had a sneaking suspicion that Hugo would be fine.

*

'Bloody hell, love. You get lost on the way to Westminster Abbey?' Joan exclaimed. Mrs Birch had said she'd be sharing, but she hadn't expected it to be with Princess flipping Margaret in full wedding gear.

'Miss Stockton has had a bit of a day, haven't you?' Mrs Birch said.

Joan dropped her suitcase to the ground. 'You and me both.'

'It was quite possibly the worst of my life until Mrs Birch here rescued me,' the young woman said, sounding like the announcer on the radio news.

'She's rescued me, an' all,' Joan said. 'Saint Leonora, I reckon.'

'Absolutely,' Margot added. 'She should have a white charger.'

Mrs Birch blushed a little. 'Nothing saintly about taking someone in when they need a bed.'

The bride smiled. 'Looking like this, my best bet would have been a park bench or a police cell.'

'We'd still have been sharing, in that case,' Joan laughed.

Mrs Birch nodded. 'I can see you two will get on famously. I'll leave you to it while I get the dinner on. You must both be starving – I'll put you something by.'

Joan waited until Mrs Birch had gone, then nodded towards the empty bed. 'This one mine?'

'Unless you'd prefer the one by the window?'

'Nah, you're all right.' Joan plonked herself down, staring at her new room-mate's wedding gown. That hadn't come out of a catalogue, for sure. And the tiara looked real, not that Joan had ever got close to a genuine diamond. 'I'm Joan, by the way.'

The other woman smiled. 'Margot.'

'You had a change of plan, then?'

'I ran away. Never even made it to the church.'

Joan burst into laughter. 'Wait till your mam gets hold of you.'

'Oh, heavens. Don't.' Margot put her head in her hands.

'Yeah, well, don't seem likely she'll find you here.' She pressed her hands on the edge of the bed and bounced her knees.

'So why are you here?'

Joan shrugged. 'Same as you. Didn't work out with my bloke, fell out with my mum . . .'

Margot smiled. 'Small world, eh?'

'So, you going to wear that thing all evening?' Joan asked, gesturing towards the white gown, its hem tinged with street filth.

'That or these things Mrs Birch lent me.' Margot held up the shapeless wool skirt. 'Should stop me getting engaged again in a hurry.'

'We can do better than that.' Joan dragged her case on to the bed and pushed open the clasps, rooting around until she found a short navy shift dress with little cut-outs around the neckline. It was one Alf had bought her, and she doubted she'd want to wear it again. 'Here, you look about my size. You can have it if it fits.'

Her new roommate looked as though she might cry with happiness. 'Really?'

They were worlds apart, but Joan liked Margot already. 'Yeah, go on, so long as you let me fix your make-up. You ain't coming to the pub tonight looking like that.'

9

The smell of burnt toast and boiled eggs climbed slowly up the stairs as Margot listened to the morning rush hour on the landing below and Joan's light snores across the room. They'd been late in last night, coinciding with a bespectacled, studious-looking type leaving Mrs Birch's parlour. She had introduced herself as Hillary before scuttling away, a Dostoevsky volume tucked under her arm. Miss Stevenson the civil servant, presumably.

Margot sat up slowly, registering the three port and lemons Joan had bought her at the pub around the corner. Well, one port and lemon. She and Joan hadn't bought another drink for the rest of the evening. There had been a moment when a couple of young men talking to Joan had locked horns, but Joan had grabbed Margot by the hand and for the second time that day she had fled, this time in fits of laughter as they ran back to Ludlow Gardens.

This morning, however, she was faced with the reality of not only an empty purse, but no purse at all, and rent to pay. She looked across the room at the crumpled pile of ivory silk and net – it had cost more than most of the girls here probably earned in six months, but Margot couldn't even buy a bus ticket with it. She and Joan's navy dress needed to take themselves to the bank.

One strong cup of tea later, Margot marched past Victoria coach station in her ivory satin wedding shoes, pausing as she spotted a copy of that morning's *Standard* dropped on a bench. She flicked through, finding a small piece about the society bride who had left guests at the Brompton Oratory horrified. Apparently, the bride had yet to be located and the groom had departed on honeymoon without her. Let them all stew, Margot fumed as she finally arrived at Lower Sloane Street and skipped up the steps to the bank.

'I'd like to make a withdrawal, please,' she told the bank teller.

The young man glanced across to his manager. 'Take a seat, Miss Stockton-Jones. I just need to . . .' the clerk said, blushing as he jumped up from his seat.

'Is there a problem?' she said as the older man sat opposite her.

'I'm afraid this is rather embarrassing. It seems your account has been frozen until certain matters are resolved.'

She sat back, folding her arms. 'You mean until I apologise for missing my wedding?'

He frowned, drawing his receding hairline a little lower. 'I can offer you the use of our telephone, if that helps?'

'Thank you, but I won't be forced into an apology.'

'Then I'm afraid there is little I can do.'

'But I haven't a penny on me,' she said, determined not to cry.

He hesitated, fumbling in his trousers pocket. 'I have a few shillings . . .'

'You're kind, but no. If I must learn to stand on my own two feet, I may as well start now. You may pass that on, if you wish.'

As she left the bank, Margot assessed the few options left to her, the closest of these being a ten-minute walk away in Chelsea, and so she made her way towards the King's Road.

It took a few bangs on the door of the pastel-pink mews house before Diana appeared, wrapped in Margot's silk kimono and looking like she had slept under a pub table. 'Escargot! You're alive.'

She swept Margot inside. 'You've caused a frightful stink, old girl.'

'I don't know what came over me. I just suddenly couldn't do it.'

'Common sense,' she said. 'That's what came over you.'

'Oh God. Poor Hugo.'

'Hugo will be fine. Anyway, you missed a cracking spread at Claridge's.'

'The reception went ahead?' Margot asked.

'Your pa didn't want to waste all that food and drink. Even if neither the bride nor groom was there. Hugo bolted off to Italy, on your honeymoon. With that friend of his. You know, I've always thought that friendship a little odd.'

Margot had, too, when she allowed herself to think about it, but she genuinely did want Hugo to be happy, so good luck to them. 'At least the holiday won't be wasted.' She plonked herself on the faded chintz sofa, shifting to remove a gin bottle stuffed behind a cushion, and folding a handmade gold dress she was sure had belonged to Diana's old flatmate Nancy. 'What am I going to do, Di?'

'Well, you can't move back in here,' she said, lighting a cigarette. 'I've got a new girl arriving tomorrow.'

'You didn't hang about.'

'You were supposed to be married.' She clapped her hands together. 'Oh, Marge, you missed a great night. We all decamped to Quaglino's.'

'You went to Quag's without me?' Margot was horrified – the fashionable restaurant in St James's was absolutely her favourite place for dining and dancing.

'You'd run away, remember? Anyway, I met this friend of your brother's there – Cosmo said she needed somewhere to stay, so . . .'

She sighed. 'It's all right. I understand,' she said, absolutely not understanding how Diana could have let out her supposedly best friend's room on the very day that friend had become essentially homeless. And certainly not to some acquaintance of Cosmo's – the girl was probably a stripper, at best. At least she'd have fewer clothes for Diana to pilfer. More than once over the years Margot had wondered at their friendship, and whether she and Diana had stuck together merely out of con-venience. She was beginning to realise she'd probably been right. 'I'd better get my things, then.'

'I'll help you pack. Sooner the better, though,' Diana went on. 'Your mother's been telephoning. I wouldn't put it past her to come and knock the door down.'

'Did she sound worried?'

Diana laughed. 'About the embarrassment, most likely. She couldn't even pick you out in that end-of-year school photo, remember?'

'Gosh, yes. I'd forgotten that.'

'At least your brother gives two hoots.'

'Cosmo probably thinks it's all terribly funny.' Margot

could imagine her elder brother relishing the drama, maybe even a little peeved that his straight-laced sister had outdone him for once.

'Actually, he doesn't. He wants to take you out to dinner.'

'The last thing I need right now is to cavort around with Cosmo's set.' Margot found Cosmo's friends, a mix of Old Etonians, studiedly artistic types and brash new money, pretty ghastly en masse. 'I do feel bad for Pa, though,' she said.

Diana pressed a hand on hers. 'Don't. Anyone can see marriage to Hugo would have been a disaster. Including your father.'

'So why didn't I see it?'

'Probably because marrying anyone would have got you away from your mother. So, what *are* you going to do?'

'Beg on the streets, at this rate. They've frozen my bank account. I literally have the clothes I ran away in and this borrowed dress.'

Diana rubbed the navy crepe fabric between her fingers. 'Nice. Very modern. Where'd you get it?'

'The girl I'm sharing a room with.'

'Sharing a room?' Diana's eyes almost popped out. 'Where?'

'A boarding house. In Pimlico.' She waited patiently whilst Diana recovered from a fit of convulsive laughter. 'Actually, I rather like it there,' she said defensively. 'The trouble is I've nothing to pay the rent with. Di, you couldn't loan me a bit, could you? Until I get a job—'

'A job?'

'What's so funny?'

'You're about as employable as I am. Which is a shame, because no one is going to marry either of us.'

'Oh, I'm sure my bolting will have made everyone forget your little dalliance with the gardener last summer.'

Diana grabbed the gin bottle and poured a slug into a dirty glass on the coffee table, knocking it back in one mouthful. 'Don't you believe it. Anyway, what sort of job are you after?'

'I don't know.'

'Well, what are you interested in? Other than dreary art galleries.'

'Art is not dreary.'

'The only point of art, as far as I can see, is in paying for this place.'

'Diana, you're such a philistine. Your family owns one of the most prestigious galleries in London, and you don't know a Turner from a Titian.'

'A what from a what?' she frowned, leaning back languidly on the sofa.

'Exactly. And you're meant to work there,' she added, knowing full well that if Diana turned up for even one hour of her nominal two days' work at Viner's, it was a miracle.

'Then maybe *you* should work for Daddy instead.'

'At Viner's? You think they'll let me through the door, after yesterday?' The thought of a job at the gallery, surrounded by art all day, suddenly made Margot excited about the possibilities life might now offer. One of the brightest girls in her year, Margot had been encouraged to apply to Oxford, but was talked out of it by her mother. Perhaps this was her chance to make up for it.

Diana patted her hand. 'You leave Daddy to me.' She took a few pound notes from her handbag and held them slightly out of Margot's reach. 'It's just a loan. I was rather down at the roulette table last night and had to borrow a few quid. I'll need it back pronto.'

'Of course. If you pass these on.' Margot found some paper and scribbled a note to her parents, explaining that she was disappearing for a little while, and not to worry about her. A second letter addressed to Hugo told him how terribly sorry she was. She slipped her engagement ring into the envelope with it and gave both letters to Diana.

Twenty minutes later Margot stood on the King's Road clutching a suitcase containing her worldly goods. She raised her hand to hail a cab, but wasn't that her old life now? And besides, she wasn't sure how long the money Diana had lent her would have to last. For the first time ever, Margot climbed on to the back of a red London bus.

'So it's all very straightforward really,' the woman told Joan, running her eye once more over the potential new recruit.

Brenda Mason had risen through the ranks at Henrietta's House, from hostess to sleeping with the boss, marrying the boss, burying the boss and taking over Henry's, as it was known everywhere from the Houses of Parliament to the Garrick to Kensington Palace. Now in her fifties, Brenda ran a tight ship that she skippered expertly through the muddy waters of sex, wealth and champagne.

As Margot had set out that morning, so Joan too decided to start job-hunting. Aim high, she'd told herself as she'd turned into Berkeley Square and made her way down the canopied steps to one of the classiest clubs in London. Henrietta's House often featured in gossip magazines for its celebrity parties and minor-royal shenanigans and was the favourite haunt of East

End boys who'd terrorised their way to the top of the food chain. She'd clear tables in a Soho dive if she had to, but champagne hostess was more what she was after.

'No pocketing the tips,' Brenda went on, tapping a red fingernail on the white damask tablecloth, 'and no accepting payment for extras. Understood?'

'Understood,' Joan said. 'So, have I got the job?'

Brenda folded her arms across her tight black satin blouse. 'I'll try you out for a week. Starting tomorrow. Uniform provided, and we have our own make-up girl and hairdresser. The more drinks you sell, the more you earn. And that's on top of your wages, paid every Friday.'

Joan looked at the figure Brenda scribbled down for her. It would have taken weeks to earn that at the dry-cleaner's. She glanced across at the cleaning woman mopping the dancefloor, who could so easily have been her mum. She'd show 'em – Ma, Alf, the girls in her class at school, parading wedding rings and prams as though they'd won the Pools. 'I reckon that'll do,' she said.

'Hard work and discretion,' Brenda said. 'That's all I ask. Got it?'

'Got it,' Joan said.

Brenda narrowed her eyes. 'Let's hope so.'

10

Margot trudged up the front steps of 31 Ludlow Gardens a few days later, feeling utterly sorry for herself after a fruitless day's job-hunting. She had paid Mrs Birch a week's rent from the money Diana gave her, but as yet had no plan for how to pay any more. Maybe her landlady needed help around the place? She squeezed past Linda, engaged in a coin-hungry telephone argument with her fiancé, and knocked on the parlour door.

She was surprised to find Mrs Birch sitting in her armchair listening to Beethoven on the Third Programme and scratching away with a pencil at a leather-bound book. Her pinny had been exchanged for a floor-sweeping silk dressing gown, her long grey hair caught in a scarf. With her striking, slightly masculine profile, she looked like an *enfant terrible* of the twenties.

'May I see?' Margot asked.

She lifted the book to show Margot a sketch of a Michelangelo drawing, taken from memory. 'Any good?'

Margot would say so. She had spent hours in the National Gallery and the Portrait Gallery examining their collections whilst her mother shopped, and liked to think she knew quality when she saw it.

'I studied art in a former life,' Mrs Birch explained.

Margot glanced at a framed oil in the style of Rubens. 'You did this?'

Mrs Birch shook her head. 'It's by an old friend of mine. He reproduces Old Masters for private clients, film sets, that sort of thing. Or used to. I've no idea these days.'

'You're no longer friends?'

'In spirit, we always will be. We were students together at Chelsea. You've met old Mr Lyov?'

Margot recalled the elderly gentleman who appeared every few days with books or flowers for Mrs Birch. 'Yes, of course.'

'Lyov was our art professor. Since his wife died, he comes here for company and, well, for my sympathy. It's certainly not for my cooking.'

'Sympathy?'

'I'm not sure I should really say, but I trust you, Miss Stockton. You see, dear Lyov left behind several members of his family when he escaped the Revolution. He's desperate to contact his sister, who is terribly ill, but we're not exactly on the best of terms with Russia.' How could Margot not have noticed that the world had nearly come to an end the year before over the placement of Russian nuclear missiles in Cuba? London was still rife with rumours of undercover Russian spies, and there were plenty who kept their understairs cupboards stocked in case Khrushchev pressed the button. 'It helps Lyov to talk about his family in a safe place, without being accused of being a communist. And to talk about art – it distracts him from his problems.'

Margot looked around the room, at the shelves crammed with Tolstoy and Trollope, Brontë and Byron, the well-thumbed art books littering every surface. 'So did you have a career in art after you graduated?'

Her landlady's face clouded slightly. 'For a time.'

'As an artist?'

'Sadly not. I was unable to complete my studies. My father was ill and I looked after him.' She nodded towards a framed photograph of a couple in austere Victorian wedding attire. 'Albert and Rose, my parents,' she explained. 'Albert was a Fleet Street printer, but still found the money to educate me, even bailed me out of prison when I thought it was a good idea to go on a Suffragette march as a teenager.'

'And was it? A good idea, I mean.'

Mrs Birch sat a little straighter. 'It is always a good idea to fight for one's rights, as my parents taught me. Never forget the struggle that gave you your vote, young lady.'

A vote her own mother refused to take up, Margot mused, pronouncing that politics was for men. 'Mrs Birch, talking of struggling, I need to ask you something.'

'Yes?'

'It's rather tricky, but I haven't found a job yet, and I'm worried about paying the rent. Do you know of anyone who needs a cleaner, or dog walker? Anything, really. I've a friend who might know of something at a gallery, but . . .'

'An art gallery?' Leonora sat a little straighter.

'Yes, her family owns it, but it's an outside chance, and I'm going to run out of money soon.'

The door opened suddenly, and Laurence Birch appeared, his narrow knitted tie loosened and shirtsleeves rolled up. 'Can't you just ask Daddy to top up the trust fund?' he said, tapping tobacco into his pipe.

Margot had met Laurence a few times in the hallway, and each time he had pointedly ignored her. Quiet, serious Laurence Birch was hard work – a journalist, his mother explained proudly, on a left-wing national newspaper – and clearly considered her flippant and spoiled. In turn she found him a humourless, inverted snob whose pipe-smoking was a ridiculous affectation in a man no older than herself.

'Laurence, dear, please don't be rude. Margot is part of this household now.'

'Really? Or is she just slumming it from Kensington until Daddy drags her back to the stately home? She's not one of us.'

'One of us?' Margot retorted. 'Where did you learn to talk like that? At the workhouse? On the picket line? Or was it at university?'

Mrs Birch laughed, clapping her hands together. '*Brava*, Margot. Laurence, perhaps you would like to tell our guest where you took your degree?'

Laurence coloured a little before muttering, 'Oxford.'

'Oh, how splendid,' Margot replied sarcastically. 'Were you in the Bullingdon Club? Did you debate Marx whilst wearing a tuxedo?' The more she looked at him, the more she saw Sebastian Flyte with an enormous chip on his shoulder.

'Well, at least I wasn't in the Pony Club.'

'That's quite enough. Margot has just asked if I can find her any skivvying work, so I think we can dispense with the silver-spoon talk.' She widened her eyes. 'I have an idea. Is there any work going at your newspaper, Laurence?'

'Not unless she can make tea, which I very much doubt.'

'Thank you,' Margot said, 'but I'd rather mop floors than make your tea.' She glanced at the clock on the mantel. 'I think I'll head up and see Joan before she goes out. She's teaching me to eat jellied eels and say "cor blimey".'

'Oh, the showgirl,' Laurence said sniffily.

'She's a waitress, and it's jolly hard work, actually.' Margot stood, her gaze now level with Laurence's. 'And now, if you'll excuse me, I have to polish my tiara,' she said, painfully aware of the actual tiara tucked in her underwear drawer. And as Margot made her way up the stairs, she heard Mrs Birch despairing at her son being a stuck-up bore.

'Gawd, look at you,' Joan said from within a fug of nail varnish and hairspray. 'Long day?'

'You could say that.' Margot slipped off her shoes and rubbed her feet, aching from the miles they had pounded on the London streets.

'What you going to do tonight?' Joan asked, pausing as she applied a second coat of Revlon Stormy Pink to her toenails.

Margot shrugged. 'Count bedbugs.'

'You need to get out, girl. You can't stay stuck here on your own while I'm working.'

'Maybe.' She might be down to her last shillings, but not once had Margot missed the endless dreary suppers with friends of her parents, or damp country-house parties where she had to pretend to like slobbering Labradors and coo at ghastly children who should have been locked in the attic. She'd had more fun with Joan over the last week than she'd had for years.

Joan pulled her foot close and blew on the pear-scented varnish. 'Why don't you take that son of Mrs Birch's out for a drink and see if you can get him to crack his face? You'd think he was fifty-three, not twenty-three. Linda says he's very political – a socialist, socialite . . . it's sapped his sense of humour, anyway.'

Margot shuddered. 'No, thanks. I might see if Hillary fancies the pictures this evening. There's a French film on up the road.'

'Hillary?' Joan screwed up her nose. 'That one would only fancy a night in with her book and her slippers. You could take Linda out, but you'd have to listen to her bang on about Dreary Derek all evening.'

'Linda's all right.'

Joan stared at her. 'Linda is the most boring person ever to walk this earth. Her idea of excitement is a new episode of *Coronation Street*.'

'She means well,' Margot tried.

'Oh, by the way, this came for you,' Joan said, pulling an envelope from beneath a pile of discarded hosiery.

Margot took it from her, recognising Diana's handwriting. *How about lunch?* the letter inside read. *I have news about the gallery. Stockpot, King's Road tomorrow, one p.m.* She looked up. 'I might have a job,' she said, smiling.

Joan screwed the lid back on the nail polish and threw it across to Margot. 'Get some of that on. I'm working tonight, but let's go dancing tomorrow to celebrate.'

'Dancing? Where?' Margot loved their evenings out at Soho coffee bars that served all-day breakfasts until midnight, Formica tables pushed to one side for dancing whenever the Beatles came on the jukebox.

Joan leapt up, pulling a thigh-high silver shift dress from a carrier bag on the floor and holding it up to her. 'Somewhere I can wear this,' she said. 'Bought it on Carnaby Street with my first wages. What do you think?'

Margot thought it looked as though Joan had forgotten to buy the matching trousers. 'My mother would hate it,' she said. 'It's perfect.'

11

Joan grabbed her costume from the rail and pushed through to her space in the Chicken Coop, as the girls' dressing room was known. It wasn't a bad nickname, Joan thought as she listened to the clucking and bitching, the air thick with powder and sweat.

'You're late,' her neighbour Vera said, chin pushed towards her mirror. 'Brenda's kicking off.'

'Bus didn't come,' Joan replied, stripping down to her underwear.

'Broomstick broke down, more like.' Vera tied a black lace choker around her neck and sat back to admire the effect.

'Good job I nicked yours, then, isn't it?'

The first shift was about to head back for their fag-and-sarnie break, and so Joan quickly pulled on her fishnets and squeezed into the tight black corset. She might be the new girl, but she was an instant hit with the customers. By the end of her first night she had sold more watered-down champagne than any of the others, and turned down invitations to a country-house weekend, Goodwood and the Henley Regatta.

'Get a move on, ladies,' Brenda shouted, her tight red shirt unbuttoned almost indecently low.

'Keep your hair on,' one of the old hoofers shouted back as the girls drenched themselves in perfume and scuttled away on high heels, their green-black feather headdresses and tailpieces trembling.

'Joan, shift it,' Brenda yelled.

'Just finishing my make-up,' she called back. It was the work of two seconds to create the black wingtip flicks Joan had tried to teach Margot yesterday. That girl needed taking in hand – she had potential. In Joan's experience, posh women either looked like farmers' wives or racehorses, and Margot was definitely a thoroughbred. She brushed white shimmering powder across her eyelids then smiled at her reflection. The girl had come a long way from Bethnal Green.

The club was packed, as usual, the low hum of laughter and conversation overpowered by the four-piece jazz band playing on the tiny, spotlit stage, the black and white of their tuxes the perfect backdrop to the singer's gold gown as Joan wove through the lamplit tables.

She was getting to know the regulars, and didn't bat an eyelid when she took the champagne order from a lively table that included at least one minor royal. There was plenty to tell, but who'd risk it? If you couldn't bag yourself a husband at Henry's, you could at least build a nice little nest egg.

She felt a hand on her arm and turned to the two young men in DJs, their tans telling of a winter away from the Big Freeze. 'Can I get you anything?' she said in the refined voice she was cultivating through mimicking Margot. Brenda liked her girls classy, and so they all spoke a slightly strangulated variation of a BBC accent.

'I should say so,' one of them quipped, slapping his lap with one hand. 'Let's see how hospitable you hostesses actually are, shall we?'

Joan sighed. It didn't happen that often here, and when it did, the girls had full permission to put a lid on any nonsense. Any whiff of sexual favours, and the vice squad would shut the place down. 'Sir, if that's what you're after, I'll order you a cab to Soho.'

The man laughed. 'I like it,' he said. 'She's got spirit.'

Joan smiled sweetly. 'She's also got a rather effective right hook.' She hesitated. 'Sir.'

'Don't mind him,' the other said. 'His nanny forgot to teach him manners.' He turned to his neighbour. 'How about apologising to the young lady, Dickie?'

The man stood unsteadily, leaning against his chair as he executed a low bow.

'Oh, sit down, you chump,' Joan said, 'before you fall down.'

'Perhaps an Alka-Seltzer for my friend here,' the other man said quietly, pushing his hand through his unruly dark curls, 'and I'll have a brandy before I take him home. I'm sorry about his behaviour,' he added, then frowned. 'Have I seen you here before?'

'I'm new,' Joan said.

He nodded. 'I ought to make the effort to get here more often, in that case.'

The compere had appeared now, taking the microphone and cracking a few jokes as the next act prepared to go on stage – a trio of French dancers wearing little more than diamanté-embellished lengths of string. 'I'd better get on,' Joan said, seeing Brenda watching her from the bar.

'Here,' the man said, pulling a card from his pocket. 'In case you fancy a cup of tea sometime.'

'Oh, we're not meant to—'

He held his hands up. 'I'm not asking you to. It's just a cup of tea.'

'Right you are, but if my boss sees me taking that, I'll be out on my ear.'

'Of course. I shouldn't have asked.'

She smiled. 'Sorry.'

'I shall just have to come again and hope you're on duty. Or . . .'

'Or what?'

'I usually have breakfast at the Marylebone Café on Mortimer Street. And if you happened to walk past any morning at around ten a.m., you might just find me there.'

She sashayed away, glancing back to see the man smiling at her. He was nice. Classy. She wouldn't mind having a cup of tea with him, if that's all it was. Alf would kill her if— If what? If nothing. She wasn't Alf's girl any more. She could meet whoever she wanted.

'That fella giving you bother?' Brenda asked as Joan handed the order chit to the barman.

'Just being friendly,' Joan replied.

'Good. Now get that bleeding champagne to table seven before they die of thirst.'

12

Margot sat on the top deck of the bus as the clippie worked his way along the aisle, handing out tickets. She loved listening to the conversations around her as bowler-hatted businessmen griped about Prime Minister Harold Macmillan, and women with stiff grey perms tutted at the length of girls' skirts. Margot tugged at the hem of the slightly-above-the-knee red woollen skirt Joan had lent her, crossing her legs demurely. Months of finishing school couldn't be erased overnight, it seemed, even though she realised more and more what she had been missing out on.

Suddenly, if Margot wanted to lie on her bed all evening reading Muriel Spark novels about girls in bedsits, there was no one to tell her that books made a girl dull – quite the opposite, in fact. As Margot had listened to Hillary's stories of university life on the way to the cinema last night, she realised that what actually made a girl dull was talking about point-to-points and ski seasons.

As the bus rattled along the King's Road, Margot looked for the mews house where in hindsight she had mainly squabbled with Diana about borrowed clothes and leaving Margot to pay the bill whenever they went out for dinner. She wondered whether Diana would stand her own lunch today – even at Stockpot prices, Margot was not in a position to be generous.

She was also not in a position to fall out with Diana: the Viner's job was her only lead.

The Stockpot was, as usual, packed, diners crammed in for a three-course lunch at the same price as a new paperback book. She spotted Diana waving a menu, and was irritated to see that someone had been put on their table – she didn't want to have to beg for a job in front of a stranger. But then the stranger turned and Margot recognised her brother. So that was why Margot had been invited for lunch – it was a ruse to lure her back into the family fold.

She slid on to the vinyl seat opposite Diana, dressed in black and dripping in jewels. 'You know it's lunch at the Stockpot, Diana, not Breakfast at Tiffany's?' Margot said.

'Darling sis, I've missed that wicked tongue of yours,' Cosmo laughed beside her.

She glared at Diana. 'Why didn't you tell me he would be here?'

Diana pulled off her sunglasses then reached across the table for Margot's hand. 'Now don't be cross, Escargot. Cosmo has been worried about you.'

Margot snatched her hand back. 'Worried he won't be able to dig the dirt on me, you mean.'

'Don't talk nonsense,' Cosmo said. 'I just want to know my little sister is safe.'

'Well, she is, so you can report back to Mother now.'

Diana sighed. 'I knew you'd be difficult.'

Margot turned to her brother. 'You've always adored a drama, Cos. In fact, it's usually you creating one. Well, this is my life, not a bit of gossip.'

'Diana tells me you're living in a boarding house.' He

paused as the waitress stood over them, her long black hair scraped into a sweaty ponytail and pencil hovering over her pad. 'Three cottage pies then treacle sponges all round, please,' he said. 'And bring us a bottle of the house paint-stripper, would you?'

'What if I want to choose what I eat?' Margot said, as the girl thumped three heavy glass tumblers on the table.

'Oh, for goodness' sake. I'd been looking forward to seeing you, but I'm not so sure now.' Cosmo pulled the carafe across and sloshed watery red wine into three glasses, pushing one across the table to Margot. 'Drink that. It might make you more agreeable.'

He picked up his own and downed it quickly, and Margot spotted the telltale signs that her brother was not quite as chipper as he made out. Cosmo had always been good at covering up life's bumps, but he was a moth to the flame, and the flame was decadence. The 'Playboy Earl' always made for good newspaper sales, even if he wasn't technically earl yet. He hadn't asked to be promoted to first in line after their elder brother died in a riding accident, and neither of them had asked for parents who dealt with it by moving abroad, leaving their remaining offspring to languish in draughty boarding schools where Margot came top of the class and Cosmo was thrown out for running a gambling den in the fifth-year dorm. Frankly, things hadn't really improved for him ever since.

Diana held up her glass, widening her heavily made-up eyes. 'Well, this is going swimmingly, don't you think, Cosmo?'

At which point Margot realised exactly why Diana had invited her here. Diana had carried a torch for Cosmo Stockton-Jones ever since the three of them were in the Pony

Club together. Now that Diana had worked her way through most of the eligible men in London, and her parents' staff on the Oxfordshire estate, Cosmo had been thrust reluctantly back into the spotlight. If Margot weren't so dependent on Diana finding her a job right now, she'd lay it on the line about how Cosmo derided their childhood friend in private. Diana was as likely to land Cosmo as he was to take religious orders, but this was not the time to point it out.

'You know, I think I might leave you two to it,' Margot said, picking up her handbag from beside her. 'I have somewhere to be.'

Diana sniffed. 'You have nowhere to be, and we all know it.'

She sighed, defeated. Defeated and incredibly hungry. She had lost weight over the last fortnight, as her diet had deteriorated into toast and biscuits, and the waitress was already on her way with their food.

'Besides,' Diana said, 'if you do decide not to run away again, I have some news for you.'

'News?' she said, brightening.

'About the job. But I'll only tell you if you promise to come to Pa and Ma's annual house party in August.'

Margot felt her resolve slip. Despite the complications of avoiding Diana's father, she loved Charlwood, the Viner estate in Oxfordshire, where Diana had grown up and the two girls had spent whole summer weeks left to run wild by their parents. After all, if there were a job at Viner's, she would have to get used to being around Sir Edwin.

Diana beamed at Cosmo. 'You'll be there, won't you?'

He shrugged. 'You know me and a party.'

'So, Margot?'

'It's ages away. I'm not sure . . .'

'Too smart for you, are we, now you have your charming working-class friends at the hostel?' Diana sniped.

'Boarding house,' Margot said pointedly.

Diana waved her words away. 'Just say you'll come, and I'll tell you the news.'

Margot dipped her fork into the sludgy brown matter on her plate. 'Fine.'

Diana looked at Margot and Cosmo, waiting until she had their full attention. 'So, Pa has agreed to give you a job.'

Margot put her fork down, shocked at Diana actually coming good. 'Really?'

She nodded. 'He needs someone in the office, and I told him how you love dreary old paintings. You can start on Monday.'

'Bravo, sis,' Cosmo said, filling their glasses once more. 'First in the family to earn an honest living.'

'I don't know what to say. Thank you, Di. Truly. I'm delighted.' And she was: a job at Viner's was more than she could ever have hoped for. She was finally a part of the art world, rather than a mere observer.

Diana clapped her hands together. 'I'd say lunch is on you, then, Marge.'

Cosmo stepped in, seeing her discomfort. 'No, my treat. Least I can do.'

Margot watched him refill his glass and drink it down in one, seeing the brother who for all his faults and irritations was a little broken and very lost. She had always been the rock that steadied him, the one who had coped best after their brother's

73

accident, whilst he had unwillingly found himself next in line to inherit Blythmere and the ghosts that walked its now empty rooms.

How lucky she was to have a new life now, another chance.

13

Tuscany, August 1989

'So that, you see, is how I ended up living in Ludlow Gardens with a nightclub waitress.'

'A waitress who became a household name,' Phoebe added, which in Joan Carter's case included a husband who spent most of his life hiding out on the Costa de Sol, and a career that had put her at the centre of countless TV dramas and gossip columns.

Margot smiled. 'Joan always did like the spotlight. It's a shame she couldn't make it today. I think you'd like her.'

'She was invited?'

'Yes, but she's filming at the moment. Perhaps you'll get to meet her another time.'

'I hope so. And preferably when I'm not completely wrung out.'

'Forgive me. It's a bad time to be offloading all this history on you.' Margot frowned. 'Did Bruce really never mention Leonora?'

'Not a word.' She picked up the photograph again. 'So what is this all about?'

'Your uncle loved a puzzle, I believe.'

'He used to set them for me when I was a child. But please

don't tell me this is all about a puzzle? I'm not sure I have the energy.'

'Even if it helps you get to know your uncle better?'

Phoebe hesitated. 'I don't know. I'm already beginning to think I didn't know him as well as I thought.'

'I'm sorry.'

She scrubbed at her eyes, pushing back the tears she'd held at bay all day. 'I can't believe he'd plan for us to have this conversation on the very day I buried him.'

'It's hard, I know. But maybe it's because he really needed you to listen.'

Phoebe detected an urgency in Margot's voice. 'He's dead. What can be so important?'

'That's for him to tell you.'

She groaned. 'I can't cope with riddles right now. Can we do this tomorrow, maybe, when I've had some sleep?'

Margot shook her head. 'I have to leave tonight.'

'He's really put me on the spot, hasn't he?'

'Look, I don't want to force anything on you. Maybe this can wait a few months, I don't know.'

Phoebe was being given a way out, if she chose it, and yet she knew Margot was right: Bruce would never put her through this unless it mattered. 'I'm sorry. You came all this way to help Bruce – the least I can do is listen.'

'You're sure?' As Phoebe nodded, Margot drank back the last of her brandy. 'Tell me, how much do you know about what happened with Edwin Viner and your uncle in 1964?'

'Not much. It was a taboo subject in my house.'

'I'm not surprised. Your uncle was barred from discussing it. As was Leonora.'

'Leonora Birch was involved?'

Margot smiled. 'Leonora was at the heart of it.'

'So why didn't Bruce just put me in touch with Leonora, instead of sending you here?'

'I don't know. I haven't been in touch with Leonora for years. We wrote to one another for a time, and then suddenly the letters stopped. When I received Bruce's invitation to the funeral, I half-hoped she would be here too, but it seems not.' She hesitated. 'They were more than just old friends, your uncle and Leonora.'

Phoebe's eyes widened. 'Oh. You mean they were lovers?' How could Bruce have kept such a thing from her?

Margot nodded. 'Over many years.'

'But I've been coming to Villa Clara since 1971, and there was definitely no Leonora on the scene.'

'So you've never seen any of her paintings here?'

Phoebe shook her head. 'Not that I know of.'

Margot sighed. 'Shame.'

'So where did she go? Did they separate?'

'I don't know, but something must have happened to keep her from him.'

'Something to do with Viner?'

'Perhaps.'

Despite herself, Phoebe felt her curiosity piqued. 'Am I correct in thinking we have a case of *cherchez la femme* here?'

Margot glanced around the studio. 'Doesn't everything boil down to that in the end?'

'Now you really do sound like Bruce.' A breeze drifted through the open door and Phoebe rubbed at the raised hairs on her bare arms. 'And what of Viner? He must be an old man by now.'

'He is. Still advising on the Royal Collection, though. Still director of his gallery.'

'Still Bruce's nemesis?'

Margot smiled. 'Perhaps, although he too kept his silence about what really happened back then.'

'What did really happen?'

'See? You're intrigued. Bruce said you would be.' Margot reached into her handbag and pulled out a letter. 'You've heard enough from me. Read this. He can explain it so much better than I.'

'Thank you,' Phoebe said, taking the thick vellum envelope from her. She could almost hear Bruce's deep chuckle, see him rubbing at the thick, greying beard as the bait was taken – almost taken, she corrected herself.

'And now I must go. I shall be out of the country for a while.' Margot took Phoebe's hand. 'I hope you'll do this. When you feel ready.'

'*If*,' Phoebe added. 'Right now, I have a failing museum in London to deal with, and a money-guzzling, leaking old pile, a thousand miles from home.'

'Fair enough. *If* you're ready. It may even help how you are feeling without Bruce. And if you do find Leonora, please tell her I would love to see her again.' Margot kissed her on each cheek, leaving a cloud of Chanel No. 5 hanging in the air as she let herself out of the studio, her silhouette quickly swallowed by the inky darkness outside.

Phoebe waited until Margot's footsteps had faded to nothing, then looked at the letter. Her name had been written carefully in ink across the envelope by Bruce, and she welled up at how much it must have mattered to him, that he had asked Margot Stockton all the way here to talk to her. It would cost Phoebe nothing, other than a few minutes of her time, to see what he wanted, and so she sliced through the top of the envelope with a silver letter-opener and pulled out a sheet of paper.

My dearest Phoebe,

If you are reading this letter, then I am already attempting to negotiate my way through the pearly gates and must trust you to pick up this story where I left off many years ago and see it through to its conclusion. It began, as so many stories do, with a woman, and ended with reputations destroyed and wrongs unrighted.

I have no right to hope you have either the time or the energy to follow the trail I have set for you, but perhaps in doing so, you will come to know me a little better. There are things I would love to have shared with you, and I hope you will come to understand why I could not.

I say this story started with a woman, but in fact it was two women. The first is an old friend of mine, and the second is an old friend of yours. Go to the easel beneath the window, my dear girl, and say hello. This story begins with both of them, right here at Villa Clara, fifty years ago.

Phoebe made her way across to the window, moonlight throwing a blue cast on the velvet cloth draped over the easel. She lifted the heavy fabric, pulling it slowly away as first one corner of a heavy, ornate gilt frame was revealed, then a chequerboard floor and elegant table legs, and finally a seated woman, the quill in her hand poised above a sheet of paper. It was identical to the painting that hung in her museum. Identical in all but a few details, Phoebe realised as she looked carefully.

Unlike Phoebe's painting, where the candle had burned out, here the candle on the desk had not yet been lit, and instead of a map on the wall behind the woman, there was a framed drawing. She looked closer, recognising it as a Leonardo da Vinci sketch of the hindquarters of a horse. It had come to auction around fifteen years earlier, to a great fanfare.

She took the painting from the easel and placed it on Bruce's bench, switching on his Anglepoise work lamp. Phoebe thought back to the game in which Bruce used to test her on country, date, artist, medium, rewarding correct answers with paper-wrapped sweets he would throw across the studio for her. She remembered the tortuous journey to her identifying an early sixteenth-century Mannerist portrait of a woman in a green gown, only for Bruce to present her with an identical painting and ask her to spot the original. Finding a faded exhibition label from Paris attached to the back of the second version, she had shouted, 'This one!', to be told Bruce had painted it himself, over an old canvas with ready-made provenance stamped on its back. He really was the best.

Using a magnifying glass, she examined the letter being written by the subject, but the writing was too small to read. So why a letter? Unable to find anything else obvious, Phoebe turned to the frame, clearly one Bruce had repurposed. Apart from a few scratches, there was nothing unexpected, and so she flipped the painting around. And there, tucked into the back of the frame, was a black and white postcard of Ventimiglia, the coastal town that sat close to the border with France. Its postmark was dated 15 September 1939, and it was addressed to Bruce at Villa Clara.

E and I have finally made it back to London without killing one another. He is a frightful loser, in love as in everything else, said the author. *The news from Ventimiglia is the worst possible, however – she has been taken. All love, as always, until I can return. Your Nora.*

'She has been taken.' What was meant by this?

She took Bruce's notebook dated January to December 1939. Clipped to the page marked 8 September was a receipt for *custodianship of painting of a woman, for verification and valuation in London by Edwin Viner on behalf of Messr. Bruce Cato*, signed by Viner, countersigned by Bruce and witnessed by Leonora Birch at Villa Clara, San Gimignano.

14

Leonora looked around in vain for a porter to help with her luggage as Edwin marched ahead along the crowded platform, his trilby surfing the wave of passengers searching for their carriage on the Paris boat train. If Edwin knew how close she was to calling off their affair, then perhaps he might have been a little more attentive to his assistant, but that simply wasn't Edwin's way.

She had travelled barely a mile by hackney cab to London's Waterloo Station, and already she was irritated and overheated. Her tight-waisted knee-length navy suit was ideal for the Viner's showroom on Bond Street, but far too uncomfortable for a journey across Europe. She longed to rip at the polka-dotted cream silk pussy-bow at her throat, to kick off the new shoes rubbing at her heels and wrench the pillbox hat from her hair. Being personal assistant to one of London's foremost art dealers came with an expectation of sartorial discomfort that Leonora found intolerable. Oh, for her student days, a decade and a half ago, when she had wafted around Chelsea School of Art with no girdle, a paint-flecked smock and flat brogues.

Close to choking in the muggy, smut-filled air, yet again she wondered why she had agreed to this Italian trip. What species of idiot headed towards the eye of a storm, with Hitler poised to unleash war on Europe?

The species of idiot who had missed out on a scholarship to Italy as a student, and who couldn't quite let it go.

'Miss Birch, really, must you dawdle?'

She glanced at her trunk. 'Well, if someone were to help me with this, I could move a little faster.'

Edwin sighed, clicking his fingers at a passing porter, who immediately brought a trolley. 'You see, it's not that hard, is it? Now do hurry. We have a dinner reservation in the dining car. That chateaubriand will not eat itself.'

She hesitated, hearing a newspaper vendor hawk the evening edition. It seemed Hitler's threats to invade Poland were more real each day, and again Leonora considered the wisdom of travelling into the bosom of Germany's nasty little gang of Fascist friends. 'Edwin,' she said, catching up with him as he began climbing the carriage steps, 'do you really think this trip is wise?'

He sighed. 'No first names in public. You know the rules. And Miss Birch, we've been through this.'

'But what if Hitler does invade Poland whilst we're abroad?'

'We'll be in Italy, not Poland.' Edwin tightened his already narrow lips. 'We will only be a week. Two at most. And if this painting my contact has is what I think it is, I'm prepared to outrun the Nazis to bring it back to London.'

'Is a painting worth the risk?'

'You should know better than to ask that.'

Behind her, a whistle blew shrilly. 'Last call for the Paris boat train,' the guard shouted.

Edwin held his hand out to her. 'Now are you coming, or do I have to drink that bottle of champagne all on my own?'

'Leonora, I asked whether you plan on eating any of those oysters.'

She looked down at the silver platter of slimy, gelatinous molluscs arranged on a bed of crushed ice. She should be relieved they were finally in Paris, the first stop on their way to Italy, but had been unwell for most of that day. 'Perhaps you should have them,' she said, feeling queasy once more as he tipped them into his throat.

'Waste not, want not, as Nanny used to say,' Edwin replied, dabbing his chin with a starched white napkin.

'You'd hardly think there's almost a war on, would you?' she said, her gaze wandering across the revered Paris restaurant, the other diners also dressed as though nothing had changed.

They had spent the afternoon perusing the Louvre and buying Leonora's elegant satin gown, which suited her tall, slender frame and Edwin's idea of how a mistress in Paris should appear. She was clearly not the only one of those, she mused, looking at the bored, diamond-clad young women sitting across from their elderly patrons, dressed in the latest Chanel or Balenciaga. If the designer boutiques were anything to go by, Paris was preparing for a party, not a war, as clothes and jewellery were scooped into shopping bags and champagne sales apparently at an all-time high. The presence of refugees from further east and from the aftermath of the Spanish Civil War seemed to make no difference to the mood of the city.

She recalled Edwin's meetings that afternoon with two wealthy Jewish families dissolving their art collections before leaving for America. Leonora had been sickened by his opportunism, but he insisted another dealer would offer them even less for their Rubens and Giotto masterpieces a few days later. She really did have to end this relationship, sooner rather than later.

'War will never make it past the Maxim's doorman,' Edwin said. 'Not even in a dinner jacket,' he added, brushing crumbs from the black satin lapel of his own evening attire.

Leonora looked at him, his aquiline features softened in the candlelight so that for a moment she remembered how handsome he was, and why she had finally allowed herself into his bed. She was a thirty-six-year-old unmarried woman, after all, her one great chance almost half a lifetime behind her. She had begun to wonder whether she was capable of falling in love again. Bruce Cato was an impossible act to follow.

She leaned across the table towards Edwin, the heavy orchid corsage at her breast brushing the white damask tablecloth. 'I think that's the Duke and Duchess of Windsor over there,' she whispered, nodding towards a table partially hidden by a screen, waiters and sommeliers hovering nearby.

Edwin dropped his napkin on the table. 'Really, Leonora. You can be terribly common sometimes.'

'Don't pretend you're not curious,' she replied curtly. 'I expect you know one another already, though. Did you and the Duke go to school together? Play polo?' She knew she was being childish, but she'd not slept a wink on the boat train, kept awake by a combination of seasickness and Edwin's infernal snoring in the bunk beneath her. One night in Paris, and then they had to do it all over again tomorrow, with the long train journey across the border and on to Florence. How did women remain married to men all their lives? she wondered.

'Leonora, don't make me regret bringing you. This was an opportunity to spend some time together away from London.'

She raised her eyebrows. 'Where I can't put off the Honourables queuing up to be Lady Viner?'

'If you're going to be snippy, you can find somewhere else to stay tonight. I am not wasting the Ritz on a grumpy secretary.' He glanced at the eau-de-nil halter-neck Maggy Rouff evening gown fresh off the Champs-Élysées, the perfect foil to her red hair. 'Nor that dress.'

She sighed. What was the point in sniping? They were stuck together for the next fortnight. Besides, she longed to visit Italy. She would be nice to Edwin, be nice to this friend of his in Tuscany, and imbibe as much art and red wine as she could before Mussolini kicked them out.

'Fine,' she said. 'Why don't you tell me all about this dealer we're visiting? Why do I know nothing about him?'

He brightened. 'Well, for a start, he's more than a dealer. He and I prefer to work directly with one another.'

'More than a dealer?' she asked, curious now.

Edwin paused as the waiter refilled their glasses and cleared away the shucked oyster shells. 'He's a restorer too. A fine craftsman in his own right. He looks out for pieces for me over there, and undertakes repairs when necessary. Old Masters are his speciality.'

'How interesting. We had to study and copy the techniques of the Old Masters when I was a student. I'm afraid I was rather dreadful at it, but there was one fellow in my year who could produce work so authentic that even Professor Lyov struggled to tell the original from the copy.'

Edwin chuckled. 'If one were less honourable, one might be tempted to take advantage of such a talent.'

Leonora sat up straight. 'Edwin!'

He shook his head. 'I merely meant that in my business one must be wary of the unscrupulous.'

'And this work your contact has found – do you know what it is?'

'I know what Perry thinks it is.'

'Perry?'

'We discovered at school that his middle name was Peregrine. The nickname rather stuck.'

'How utterly hilarious.' She could only imagine the boarding-school dormitory japes, and braced herself for meeting yet another chinless, entitled bore.

'Anyway, I've already said too much. Dessert?'

As Edwin buried himself in the menu, Leonora's thoughts returned to the precarious state of the Continent. 'Edwin, you do think we'll be all right, don't you? I heard someone on the train saying that they're going to start conscripting for the army at home – Chamberlain obviously thinks something is about to happen.'

'Dear girl,' he said, taking her hand across the table, 'do you see the Duke and Duchess fretting? Have we been barred from catching a train into Italy? No. Trust me. We are safe.'

15

Leonora had expected the crossing into Italy to be complicated, but still it was a shock to be taken off the train at the border station of Ventimiglia, their tickets and passports checked whilst passengers on the opposite platform sweated under the scrutiny of Mussolini's police. Weeping children clung to parents dragging heavy suitcases, desperate to escape Fascist Europe, while she and Edwin were heading there to chase a painting. She suddenly felt ridiculous.

She supposed they must look unlikely spies, Edwin in his three-piece linen suit and she perspiring under the brim of her straw hat. For long minutes she stared at her passport clasped in the hand of the guard, who looked like he had been conscripted from a high-security prison. Her ability to return home to London lay most literally in this man's grasp.

Eventually they were waved through to the Florence train, a long vehicle of third-class carriages. She had bought panini and ripe peaches from a stall at the station, but in the heat of the stuffy carriage, heavy with cigarette smoke and the clucking of hens penned in a basket on the ground, neither she nor Edwin were hungry. Leonora spotted a small, grubby girl clinging to her mother's legs, her hungry eyes transfixed on the sandwiches, and offered them to her. Mother and daughter devoured the sandwiches silently whilst others looked on, waiting to pounce on any dropped crumbs.

As Edwin closed his eyes to veil himself from the surrounding proletariat, Leonora watched the Italian countryside unfold. She had so nearly come here fifteen years ago, pipped to the post for the prize that would have sent her to study at the British School in Rome. Perhaps being a woman had made a difference, but in truth the fellow student who had won the scholarship was by far her superior. Bruce Cato had been her friend – more than that, in fact – and losing out to him had been a double blow, as it had nipped their romance in the bud. He had asked her to come with him to Rome, but her sick father needed her. Some things were just not meant to be. She wondered what had become of Bruce. Certainly she had never come across him in London artistic circles, but probably that was just as well. Her heart had been broken once; twice might just be too much.

Leonora concentrated on the view, drinking in the corrugated fields of vines, tall cypress trees and dusty-green olive groves, the landscape that had inspired artists from Leonardo to Raphael. How many hours had she spent in the studio studying the works of these great masters, trying to analyse the essence of their genius? Still the smell of linseed oil and white spirit took her straight back to a time of possibility, when she might have become something more than assistant and mistress to someone whose appreciation of art was its monetary value. Shame on you, Leonora Birch, she chided herself. You could have been so much more.

The taxi waiting for them was no more than a horse and cart into which their luggage was squeezed amongst crates of pungent tomatoes by the gnarled old farmer, who urged the skinny nag into action with a flick of his whip. Here in the country-side, the grip of Mussolini seemed weaker, and as the creature clip-clopped past olive groves, swatting flies with its tail, occasional graffiti denouncing Il Duce was the only reminder that Italy was on the brink of catastrophe.

As they rode deeper into a landscape littered with desiccated sunflowers and fruit-laden vines, she closed her eyes, a poppy-coloured lightshow flashing through her lids as the warm Tuscan air tugged at the pins in her coppery-red hair, which brushed in gentle waves against her long neck.

They were eventually deposited, dusty and sweaty, at the gates of an old hilltop villa, a four-square stone building with tall, shuttered windows and topped by a shallow terracotta-tiled roof. A short distance away stood a medieval watchtower, squatly keeping guard. The villa was tired, shabby, vines creeping across its façade, and possibly the most beautiful building Leonora had ever seen.

'This is it. Villa Clara,' Edwin said, clambering out of the cart. 'Old wreck, but Perry loves it.'

A stooped woman in peasant dress and a pinny watched them descend, her hand raised against the low sun as she gestured for them to follow her.

'Where's the man to collect the bags, Marianna?' Edwin called after her, then reluctantly lifted his case from the ground. He stared at Leonora. 'Are you waiting for your trunk to grow legs?' he said as he slung his jacket over his arm and headed off behind the housekeeper.

Leonora's Italian was rusty, especially in the face of the woman's thick dialect, but she understood enough to discover that her room was thankfully at the opposite end of the house to Edwin's. The terracotta floor proved a perfect antidote to the raging heat as she slipped off her shoes, and she pushed open the shutters to reveal a watercolour vista tinged with bronze and gold as the late-afternoon sun coloured the Tuscan hills.

She looked around the bedroom, its Persian rug, rustic oak furniture and heirloom crochet bedspread so different from Ludlow Gardens, with its dreary anaglypta and city-smudged windows. A vase bearing a burst of rosy-orange dahlias sat on her bedside table, and she smiled, remembering how Bruce used to buy them for her, saying they reminded him of her hair.

Works of art were crammed into every spare inch of the rough, white-washed walls, and whilst she didn't recognise many, there were some that surely shouldn't be relegated to a spare bedroom: a Piero della Francesca annunciation scene, Botticelli nymph, even a sketch by Modigliani. What collector hid such treasures in a guest room? Maybe there was more to this Perry than a weak chin.

16

Leonora jumped as the housekeeper called her down to dinner. She had lain on the bed just to rest her eyes, but must have slept for at least an hour. She scrambled into a floor-length emerald-green gown she had bought in Paris, amused by its butterfly print and playful twist at the neckline. In the simple, beautiful setting of the Tuscan villa, it needed no jewellery, and so she wore her hair loose and just a smear of cherry-red lipstick.

A brief pause outside Edwin's bedroom door offered a reprise of the snoring that had plagued her since they left London, and she made her way outside alone, stopping to smell the jasmine spilling across an arched, torchlit walkway. The terrace boasted a long table beneath an ivy-covered pergola, candle lanterns casting islands of light across the roughened wood. Three glasses of champagne waited on a silver tray, and she took one across to a low stone wall looking out on a formal garden littered with classical marble statues, the nearby watchtower glowing golden in the evening light as starlings darted across its bulky form.

'It's a piece of heaven, isn't it?'

Dragged from her reverie, Leonora turned to face the man silhouetted by light from the house. She blinked, confused for a moment by the familiarity of his deep voice. Maybe it was the champagne, the heady scent of rosemary, or the heat, still fierce even though the sun had almost dipped beneath the horizon. Maybe it was an echo of her own recent thoughts. 'I'm sorry,' she said, trying to make out his features as she held out her hand. 'I'm Leonora Birch.'

He took her hand in his, turning so that he was illuminated by the glow of the torchlight, his face breaking into a smile. 'I know exactly who you are, Nora,' he said.

She jumped as though she had received an electric shock, her body reacting involuntarily to the once-familiar nickname. 'You?'

'I believe so.'

'I don't understand,' she said, her voice a little louder this time as she struggled to accept it really was Bruce Cato standing there before her. 'Are you a guest here too?'

'Hardly,' he laughed. 'I think you'll find you're my guest.'

'Then who's Perry?'

Bruce hesitated. 'Ah yes. Bruce Peregrine Cato. At your service.'

'Peregrine?' She couldn't help a snort of laughter. 'You told me you were a grammar school boy.'

'You think your father would have let me near his daughter if he knew I'd worn a top hat to school?'

'Probably not.'

'But my politics were genuine. Still are. One can't choose one's background. So what are you doing consorting with the likes of Viner?'

She shrugged. 'It's work. I gave up painting—'

'Shame. Lyov always thought you were better than me.' He smiled. 'I miss that old devil. Do you still see him?'

'Lyov? I often visit him and his wife. He still talks about you.'

Bruce laughed. 'About how much trouble I was, I expect. Don't think he ever forgave me for pulling that trick with the Walton Prize.'

'Lord, I'd forgotten that. Trust you to try to catch him out with a reproduction. But of course he forgave you. He still maintains he's never known a student so talented as you.'

'I'm sorry you stopped painting, Nora.'

She shrugged. 'It would have been a hard career for a woman.'

'Perhaps.' He tipped his head on one side. 'I never forgot you, Nora.'

She held a hand up as he took a step closer. 'No. No, Bruce.'

'I'm sorry. I've had time to prepare for this, and now I've ambushed you.'

'You knew I was coming?'

'Of course. Who do you think organised your train tickets?'

'Clearly not Edwin,' she said. 'The last person I expected to see ever again was Bruce Cato, and now here you are.' Looking even more handsome than she had remembered.

'And here you are. You were beautiful as a girl, but now . . .'

'Bruce, don't.'

'Nora, I wish you'd come with me back then. I wish things had turned out differently.'

'Things turn out as they are meant to. My father was ill, and I had no choice.'

He looked at her. 'And now . . .'

She shook her head. 'He went on for another four years after you left.'

'I'm sorry.'

'Don't be. I just hope you've had a good life, found someone to love you,' she said, glancing to see whether he wore a wedding band and feeling an involuntary flicker of hope that there was none.

'A good life, yes. But love?' He shook his head. 'How could I have wanted anyone else after you?'

'Don't be silly, Bruce. We were young.'

'Old enough to know we loved one another.'

She sensed the conversation was about to take a dangerous turn and so she leaned on the balustrade to watch the last inky-red rays of sun shrink into a night sky so deeply blue that she suddenly longed to paint it. 'I'm glad you've made a life with your art.'

'I'm lucky. I get out of the studio too. Going to estate sales, digging through flea markets on the off chance of finding a Titian hidden amongst old newspapers.'

'I can imagine. And what is this mysterious work Edwin has travelled across Europe to see? Did that come from a flea market?'

'Not exactly. I'll show you in the morning, when the light's better. It's worth the wait, trust me.'

He placed his hand beside hers, and she noticed the paint beneath his fingernails and embedded in every callus, the whisper of white spirit, and she was taken back to parquet-floored studios with tall, north-facing windows, the hush of concentration at easels as time took on new dimensions and hours seemed like minutes. For a second their little fingers brushed against each other before she pulled away.

'Nora,' he said quietly, 'I never stopped loving you.'

Her stomach flipped as she recognised the intimacy in his voice, years of loneliness stirring feelings she had tried so hard to suppress. 'Bruce, it's been a long time.'

'I know. And I've missed you every single day.' He glanced towards the dining table, a vase overflowing with fire-coloured dahlias at its centre. 'Your favourites,' he said, 'unless you've changed your mind about those, too. Did you like the ones in your room?'

She smiled, touched that he had remembered such a tiny thing. 'They're beautiful. And I missed you too, but circumstances were against us.'

'And now they have changed.'

Leonora jumped at the sound of footsteps, moving away from Bruce as she saw Edwin standing behind them in full dinner attire, in contrast to Bruce's simple cream linen shirt and trousers.

'Ah, so I see you two have made friends,' he said, coming across to slap Bruce heartily across the shoulder. 'How are you doing, old chap? And what do you make of my lovely assistant?' he added, looping an arm around Leonora's waist.

Bruce's eyes widened. 'Oh. That kind of assistant,' he said tightly, and as he led them to the table set for an al fresco dinner, Leonora wished she could slip into the dark shadows at the fringes of the terrace and never be seen again.

17

Leonora had left the men talking late into the night, so was unsurprised to see no sign of Edwin at breakfast, where last night's supper of mountain lamb had been replaced with warm ciabatta, home-made preserves and ripe figs. One of the three places set showed evidence of an early riser who had already left the table.

She helped herself to freshly squeezed orange juice and coffee from the enamel espresso pot, taking it black in the hope of easing the slight headache and nausea from two glasses of champagne on an empty stomach the night before. As she felt herself recover, she listened to the cicadas trilling, took in the church towers marking distant hilltop villages. No wonder Bruce had never come back to London.

Thinking back to their conversation, she wondered where it might have led, had they not been interrupted. Bruce Cato still loved her, and unless she had suddenly developed a heart condition, the palpitations she had suffered all night indicated she still loved him.

There was, however, the small matter of Edwin.

Edwin had always been a bad idea, but she'd been lonely after her father died, rattling around the empty Pimlico house after years of attending friends' weddings then christenings. They both knew the liaison was going nowhere, but it was a

diversion. Until now, when it had become an albatross overnight, making her look like some cheap secretary on the make.
She would end the affair today, even if it meant a ghastly
atmosphere and an insufferable journey home.

She stood, tugging her slim white linen skirt back over her
knees and putting on her large, white-framed sunglasses. This
bright light did nothing for one's crow's feet, but the horse had
not quite bolted from the stable, and so she took out her compact and dabbed on some red lipstick, pinching her pale cheeks
that had yet to catch the Italian sun.

Signor Bruce was in his studio in the watchtower, Marianna told her, pausing in her sweeping of the terracotta-tiled
hallway, and so Leonora picked her way across the scrubby
courtyard, scattering indignant hens in her path.

It was the smell that hit her first, linseed oil and turpentine,
sable and cedarwood, dust-sprinkled light slicing through the
windows on to a series of works in progress on easels, others
stacked against the walls. The crackle of a gramophone broke
through the chattering cicadas, twenties dance music playing
to the empty space.

Bruce was humming loudly, his back to her as he washed
brushes at a long trough sink across the room. He hadn't heard
her, and so she tiptoed across to a portrait of a woman, her
peach-like flesh in contrast to her sober seventeenth-century
black gown and lace cap. Was this a restoration job? she wondered. It was possible, but the entire canvas had been worked,
and the cracks one would expect on a painting of this age were
absent.

'Still wet,' a voice said, and she turned to see Bruce rubbing
at a paintbrush with a rag.

'Rembrandt?' Leonora said, avoiding the Edwin-shaped elephant in the corner.

He shrugged, wiping his hands on the faded linen shirt he wore loose over peg trousers that Leonora swore she remembered from the previous decade. 'Rembrandt via Cato. Well, entirely Cato, if you must know.'

'It's a copy?'

She looked around the studio. 'Are all these copies?'

'Some. Most are restorations. Although the way things are, I'm not sure I'll complete them before we find ourselves at war.'

'It's hard to imagine when you're tucked away here,' she said.

'Until you hear Mussolini's Folgore fighter planes on their practice missions overhead. Or go into town and see some poor farmer's boy flogged by blackshirts for refusing to pledge allegiance.'

'Aren't you frightened?'

'No more so than I would be in London, if Chamberlain declares war on Hitler. Nowhere in Europe will be safe. I may as well stay here, a mile up a rutted track, and take my chances.'

She leaned closer to examine the details of Bruce's brushwork. 'How on earth do you make it look so authentic?'

'I buy up poor-quality paintings of the relevant period, keep the frames and strip the canvases back to the ground layer. I only work in materials available at the time of the painting I'm reproducing, and you know as well as I do about replicating the brushes an artist might have used.'

'So what will you do with it?' she said, gesturing to the portrait.

'Well, it'll be baked in the oven to dry the paint off first, but this one is for Edwin.'

She raised her eyebrows at him. 'Edwin deals in fakes?'

Bruce laughed. 'Not exactly. And I wouldn't call it a fake, so much as a copy. Fine line, but an important distinction.'

'Then Edwin deals in copies?'

'Edwin has an American client who commissions high-quality copies of Old Masters for his Texas ranch.' He held a hand up. 'Everyone is a winner: the American has walls full of paintings and drawings to show off to his friends, whilst Edwin and I make a small living from it.' He gestured to a half-finished *Mona Lisa* propped against the wall. 'That one's for a film production company. The reclining Venus over there is for a client who lost the original in a house fire.' He frowned. 'You don't approve?'

Leonora couldn't help a sense of unease that Edwin was trading in copies, and that this was the first she had heard of it, but if everything was above board, what could be the harm? 'It's not for me to judge.'

He glanced at her. 'Nor for me to judge your dealings with Edwin.'

She hesitated. There was no point in denying the affair – why should she? She had done nothing wrong, only a little foolish. But where Bruce had sold out his talent to an American, she had compromised her dignity, which was far worse. 'It's just a silly fling,' she said now, desperate to justify herself.

'Nora, what you do is your business.'

'I know that,' she snapped back. 'But I also know that these last years since Dad died have been difficult and lonely. I'm not exactly on *Tatler*'s eligible virgins list, and I've come somewhat adrift from our old set. The fine young socialists who used to visit Dad see me as a class traitor.'

'I understand. But Edwin?' he said, holding his hands out in disbelief.

'All right. I know. It's utterly ridiculous. The man is a pompous bore.' She smiled. 'And I really do mean boring.'

'Oh Nora, I wanted better for you.'

'Well, this little liaison has run its course, so let's hope something better is around the corner.'

'I'm glad,' he said. 'I mean that it's run its course. I don't like to think of you with Edwin.'

'Trust me. Nor do I.' She trailed a finger along the frame of the Rembrandt. 'So now you know all about my tawdry love life, it's only fair you tell me about your own.'

'It's had its share of tawdriness.' He shrugged. 'There have been a couple of dalliances, but I'm contented here, if a little lonely. I have Villa Clara, my work . . .' He stood a little closer, taking her hand. 'Nora, I'm sorry things have been hard for you. I wish . . .'

As he hesitated, she looked closely at him, searching for the boy she had known in different times. 'Wish what?'

She watched him, remembering the warmth she had felt for him when they were young. Had it been simply a childish infatuation? And if so, why was her heart beating faster? She, Leonora Birch, who was impervious to such things?

'I don't know. But if you ever wanted to take a break from London, from Edwin, you could come here. Stay for as long as you like. It should have been you on that scholarship, after all, not me.'

'No, it was right that you came here. Look at you,' she said, admiring his deep colour, the beard he had allowed to grow. 'You're part of the landscape now.'

'I thought you'd broken my heart,' he said quietly, 'but maybe there's still time to repair it.' There was a brief silence, comfortable and yet heavy with possibility, until Bruce glanced at the paint-spattered watch strapped to his wrist. 'We should go,' he said. 'I told Edwin to meet me in the drawing room. Join us?'

'Of course, unless you're planning a duel to the death.'

'Well, now you mention it . . .'

An ornate vaulted ceiling straddled the drawing room of the Villa Clara, punctuated with splashes of bare brick where the plaster had yielded to time and damp. Old tapestries and a few paintings in the modern style were complemented by worn rugs stretching across the terracotta tiled floor. Edwin threw down his days-old copy of *The Times* and jumped up from a threadbare settee to greet them. He had, Leonora was relieved to see, finally relinquished the Savile Row three-piece pinstripe in favour of a cream shirt and matching loose trousers that made him look as though he were fresh from the cricket crease.

'Ah, at last.'

'Apologies,' Bruce said. 'I was finishing up in the studio.'

'So,' Edwin said, rubbing his hands together, 'where is this treasure you've uncovered?'

Bruce inclined his head towards an easel in the far corner of the room, covered with a white linen sheet. 'I discovered it in the basement of a palazzo in Venice,' he explained, leading them towards it. 'The owner had died, and the family wanted rid of everything. I found this amongst some rather second-rate landscapes, so filthy it was almost impossible to make out. It took me two months to clean it up, but I think you'll agree it was worth it.' Bruce put his hand to the sheet then hesitated. 'I should say, Edwin, that I am almost one hundred per cent certain this is an original. And less than one per cent certain I would sell it.'

'Not sell it? Don't be absurd.'

'I mean it,' he said firmly. 'No painting's worth is limited to its price, and this is one I'm not sure I want to part with, except on loan to a public gallery.'

Leonora saw Edwin's irritation, the bristling of the pale, pencil-thin moustache as he found a placatory smile with which to soften the atmosphere. 'Of course it's up to you, Perry, but since you've dragged me halfway across Europe, perhaps you'd be good enough at least to let me take a look?'

As Bruce pulled the sheet away, Leonora heard her breath catch, and Edwin, for once speechless, whistled in disbelief. To view the painting, no bigger than a folded newspaper, felt like an invasion of privacy as a young woman sat at a writing desk, dressed in a cobalt-blue gown, her pen poised over a sheet of paper beside a candle that had burned down to nothing in its pewter holder. It was extraordinary in its simplicity, the brushwork deceptively quick, and yet saying everything. The expression on her face was so clear, such a snapshot of a living, breathing woman, that it could have been a photograph.

It was exquisite, perfect, impossible.

She looked at Bruce. 'Is it what I think it is?'

He smiled. 'That would rather depend on what you think it is.'

'Well, I know what I'm looking at,' Edwin said, standing back and smoothing his moustache as he examined the painting from further away. 'But it can't be possible, surely? There are only three dozen of these in the entire world.'

'That we know of,' Bruce said. 'Records show that a handful more may never have been found. Look at it. The colour, the composition, the subject, the light . . . Nora, do you see?' He took her hand and pulled her closer to the easel, their fingers touching for a little longer than necessary. 'How many times did we have to copy his work when we were students?'

She looked at him. 'I can't believe I'm saying this, but I think you've found one of the lost Vermeers.'

18

Over the following few days, Leonora searched Bruce's library for references to the missing Vermeers, several times coming across a 1696 Amsterdam auction of twenty-one Vermeer paintings owned by Jacob Dissius, a Dutch printer whose wife's family had been patrons of the Delft artist. A transcript of the sale catalogue had allowed identification of twenty works known to be in circulation. The twenty-first, listed simply as 'Girl at a Desk', was believed lost or destroyed.

As Leonora's conviction that the painting was genuine grew stronger, so too did the pull between herself and Bruce. Edwin had been neither surprised nor hurt at her breaking off their relationship, such as it was, but furious at losing to Bruce. She should have known: Edwin would throw his newspaper on the fire rather than admit to being unable to finish the crossword.

Meanwhile, Bruce and Leonora strolled in the olive grove or spent time in the studio, where they began preparing pieces for the journey back to London. With the postal service almost entirely corrupt by now, and ships about to be requisitioned for war, Leonora and Edwin would only take a collection of small yet beautiful drawings Edwin had commissioned for a client, which could easily be stored in their luggage.

Bruce showed her how he had made the drawings, collecting oak galls from the grounds of Villa Clara, and crushing them with gum arabic, rainwater and iron sulphite to create an ink that oxidised and instantly appeared aged on the paper. She had been stunned by his Raphael sketch for a well-known larger painting, and by a sleeping woman, inspired by an existing drawing of Rembrandt's mistress in the British Museum. Bruce had also produced a Dürer drawing of a hand, executed on pages taken from a centuries-old book he had found in an antique shop. Allowing the original drawings to be kept in storage to avoid damage, these works were an artform in themselves, to be displayed and enjoyed by their owner.

Even at Villa Clara, it was impossible to ignore the gathering storm clouds, and almost daily Marianna the housekeeper arrived with stories of violence in the villages and towns, military brigades stamping out anti-Fascist demonstrations with arbitrary arrests.

'Come back with us,' Leonora pleaded with Bruce one evening.

He shook his head. 'I can't abandon Marianna and her family – this is their home too. Nor can I just leave the studio – there are some valuable pieces in there.'

'Then I'll stay too.'

'You can't.'

She felt her heart sink. 'Because you don't want me here?'

'No, Nora, you fool. Because it could be dangerous and I won't lose you a second time. Things need to blow over in Europe before you and I can live here together.'

'Blow over or blow up?' She sighed, fearing that Chamberlain's 'peace in our time' was a ridiculous fantasy, along with the life she was already imagining here with Bruce.

He took her hands. 'Nora, I love you. I want you here with me, at my side, as my wife—'

'Your wife?' she spluttered.

He winced. 'As proposals go, that was clunky.'

Leonora fixed her eyes on his. 'Are you asking me to marry you, Bruce Cato?'

'Are you asking me to ask you?'

'I have never asked for anything in my life.'

'You always were a difficult woman, Leonora Birch. And yet I still want to marry you.' He smiled. 'So will you?'

She took a step towards him, placing her arms around his neck, relishing the sense of homecoming as he wrapped his arms about her waist. 'What do you think?' she said.

A thunderous downpour had forced them all indoors for dinner, as waves of torrential rain pounded the terrace, flashes of lightning bouncing off the cut glass. The atmosphere was similarly static inside, Bruce barely able to take his eyes off Leonora's one-shouldered black chiffon gown, whilst Edwin shot dagger-like glares across the table.

'You must let me take your painting back to London to have it assessed properly,' Edwin said briskly. 'There's a chap over in America – Burroughs – he's developed a means of looking at the layers of a painting by creating a shadowgraph. An X-ray, if you will. It will help determine whether this really is a Vermeer.'

'I am already almost certain it is,' Bruce said.

'You're a scientist now, are you? Let an expert see it, Cato, for God's sake. Do you really want a work as important as this sitting in a leaky ruin, seen only by your housekeeper and your . . .' He hesitated. 'Your mistress?' he added, waving a hand towards Leonora.

'Fiancée,' Bruce countered. 'If, and I do mean if, it is genuine,' he went on, 'I want it in public galleries, to be shared with as many people as possible, instead of stuck in the bank vault of one of your clients.'

'I hardly think the galleries of Europe are a solid bet at the moment,' Edwin said, 'unless you like a little Nazi with your art.'

'Edwin has very helpfully been repatriating Jewish art collections from Paris to Mayfair,' Leonora put in, screwing up her napkin.

'Better in my hands than Goering's,' Edwin said. 'I hear he's quite the collector. Those works would have been in Hitler's drawing room straight after the Germans' arrival in Paris.'

Bruce stared back at his old school friend. 'You always were an opportunistic little shit.'

Edwin laughed heartily, lighting a cigar. 'Very good, Perry. Just as well for you that we're no longer in the quad, or you'd find yourself tied to a drainpipe.'

'Perhaps you'd care to leave my trousers on this time,' Bruce said coldly.

'Oh, grow up. Your parents sent you to that school to toughen you up, just like the rest of us.'

'They sent me there for an education, and I certainly received one – into how utterly entitled your class is.'

'Entitled enough to dally with another chap's woman?'

'Gentlemen, please,' Leonora said.

Edwin turned to her. 'You needn't play the innocent. Frankly, it's poor form to play away on another man's expense account.'

'Bruce and I are old friends. I didn't plan this . . .' Leonora began as a crack of thunder rumbled across the hills outside, setting the glassware trembling.

'Save your breath, Miss Birch. Do you honestly imagine I was going to make a wife of my secretary?'

Leonora felt her cheeks burn with anger. 'I am your researcher, not your secretary, Edwin.'

'Just as well, because your typing is atrocious.'

'Perhaps you'll move on to Miss Stevens now. You certainly didn't employ her for her typing skills.'

'Nor you for your bedside manner,' he countered.

'That's enough,' Bruce said. 'You're talking about the woman I'm going to marry, Viner.'

Leonora felt the colour rise to her cheeks. 'That woman,' she countered angrily, 'has a name and she's sitting right here.'

'I'm sorry,' Bruce said. 'You see, Viner? Some of us are capable of respect.'

'Oh, I respect you, all right,' Edwin countered. 'The best forger this side of the Mediterranean.'

Bruce slammed his fist on the table as a sheet of rain lashed the windows. 'How dare you? That would imply intent to deceive. I am a copyist, and an artist in my own right.'

Edwin sighed. 'Whatever you say, old chap.'

They were interrupted suddenly by the sound of the front door slamming, as a woman's voice broke into long, keening wails.

Bruce leapt up from the table. 'That's Marianna.'

Leonora and Edwin followed him to the hallway, where the housekeeper sat on the ground, her teenaged son's bloodied head in her lap, whilst his girlfriend held his hand.

'What's happened?' Leonora asked, shocked at the amount of blood leaching into the rough bandage.

Bruce spoke to the tear-stained girl, trying to make sense of her garbled sobs. It seemed a truckload of military police had arrived in the village after dark, having heard an anti-Fascist group was hiding out there. Soldiers had pulled out every man under the age of twenty-five and beaten them in the rain-soaked square, before choosing two prisoners at random. They would return the next night and burn down every property if the prisoners did not confess. Marianna's son, who had been acting as a courier for resistance groups based in Rome and Turin, had been spared this time, but the net was closing.

'That settles it,' Bruce said to Leonora and Edwin. 'I'm putting you both on the train to the French border tomorrow morning. You can't be here if the guards come.'

'What will happen to the boy?' Leonora asked.

Bruce handed Marianna a glass of grappa, and they watched her pour the liquid into her son's mouth, waiting a tense moment before he relaxed a little. 'He'll be safe here tonight, then we'll move him and the girl tomorrow. I have friends in the mountains.' Bruce ran a hand through his dishevelled hair, concerned, she could tell, beneath the veneer of practicalities.

'And what about us?' Edwin asked, leaning against the wall. 'Who's going to take us to the station in the morning if the whole village is panicking about witch hunts?'

Leonora shot him a filthy stare. 'How can you think about yourself when this boy is bleeding all over the floor?'

'Edwin's right, though,' Bruce said. 'I'll take you myself in the car.'

'Come with us, Bruce, please,' Leonora begged. 'There's nothing heroic about holding the fort in a burning house. Look at our dear friend Lyov – he knew when to leave Russia.'

'Maybe I will leave too. Just not yet. I need to make plans. Besides, the military police are unlikely to find their way here for a while.'

'Where there's a prize expatriate Englishman waiting to be made an example of?' Leonora said, rinsing the bloodied cloth in the bucket and handing it to Marianna. 'Things will only get worse when war breaks out.'

'There's no guarantee Italy will fight,' Bruce said uncertainly. 'It's all just posturing for now.'

'Well, I think this all settles one thing for sure,' Edwin said.

Leonora turned to face him. 'And what's that?'

He glanced towards the drawing room. 'The Vermeer is coming with me.'

The next morning they placed the painting, wrapped earlier by Bruce in a soft blanket and tied with string, beneath a false bottom in Edwin's suitcase, whilst the drawings were packed into Leonora's. Although she was anxious to return to the familiarity of London, as she watched the cases loaded into the Alfa, it was unbearable to think that war and politics might tear her and Bruce apart once more.

'It will be all right, Nora, I promise,' Bruce said, taking her hand.

'I wish I could believe you.'

He brushed her lips with his thumb. 'I'll find you again, Leonora Birch.'

'You had better,' she whispered.

As they drove in silence, taking back routes in order to avoid roadblocks, it became increasingly impossible to imagine that she would be returning to Villa Clara any time soon.

If the chaotic scenes at Milan central station weren't enough to convince Leonora they were leaving not a moment too soon, then the armed guards on board the train to the French border silenced even Edwin. In just a fortnight, the world had changed dramatically.

Every ten minutes, it seemed, they were asked to show their tickets and papers to uniformed men with German Shepherd dogs on leashes. At every station, more people fought to board the train, whilst others were marched off at gunpoint, and as they passed through the port of Genoa, the sleek grey battleships dotted across the shimmering Mediterranean were a stark reminder of the war games being played out on the Polish border.

A young pregnant mother with an East European accent and a toddler clutched to her called out in desperation for anyone in the cramped, sweaty carriage to let her sit, and as Edwin studiedly re-examined the cricket scores in his fortnight-old newspaper, it was Leonora who gave up her seat. As she stood, trying not to focus on her travel sickness, she listened in to the muttered conversation between two young Frenchmen returning to fight, unconvinced by their confidence that France would hold firm against a German invasion.

The train's brakes suddenly kicked in violently, and Leonora grabbed hold of an overhead strap as bags fell from the luggage racks.

'Where are we?' someone shouted in Italian. 'This is not Ventimiglia.'

She peered past the shoulder of a stout middle-aged woman pressed against her. They were pulling into a small seaside station, its platform lined with a reception committee of army, police and blackshirts.

'Edwin,' she said, looking down. 'This is San Remo. Why have they stopped here?'

'How the devil should I know?' he replied, dabbing a handkerchief across his damp brow.

The carriage door opened and an officer demanded that everyone disembark with their luggage.

'They can't do this,' Edwin muttered, refusing to move.

'For God's sake. They can and they have.'

He got up wearily. 'I'll be having words at the Embassy when we get back.'

Eventually Leonora and Edwin stood side by side on the sun-drenched platform amongst the long line of anxious passengers as the officer in charge shouted his orders.

'You speak Italian. What's he saying?' Edwin whispered.

'He wants all the men to take their luggage to the ticket hall,' she whispered. 'They're looking for political activists.'

'I'll not do a damn thing he tells me to,' Edwin spat. 'And they needn't think they're getting their hands on my suitcase.'

Leonora felt sweat breaking out on her back and behind her knees. Her feet burned as heat from the sun-cooked concrete bled through her shoes, and she fanned herself with her papers. 'Just go or we'll be here all night. The painting is well hidden.'

'I've had enough of this,' Edwin said suddenly, taking a step forward. 'Now look here,' he said to the officer, 'I know people – important people—' Before he could finish, however, one of the soldiers pressed the barrel of his pistol into Edwin's forehead. Cowed at last, Edwin grabbed his suitcase and marched away.

Leonora sat on her suitcase with the other women and let her gaze drift towards the French border a few kilometres away, a nominal line cut through the mountainous range clinging to the coastline. She had been right: this entire trip was utter folly.

As the afternoon wore on and children became more fretful, a stream of vehicles came and went from the station concourse. 'My husband,' one woman shouted as she broke through and ran towards the exit, causing a stampede as others hurried to see what was happening. Leonora watched in horror as the wife was knocked to the ground with a blow from a truncheon. The silence that hung over the chastened passengers who returned to their places was punctuated by the bickering of seagulls and shouts emanating from the ticket office as the searches continued.

Shadows had lengthened along the platform by the time the male passengers began to return. Reunions were brief and cautious, and those whose loved ones had not reappeared were given the choice at gunpoint of getting on the train or joining their menfolk, so that young mothers were torn between their husband and their child, elderly women forced to weigh up what they had to lose.

'Edwin!' Leonora called out as he reappeared, his expression thunderous. He pushed his way into the carriage and on to a seat, his shirt collar grimy and blond hair tousled. 'What happened?' she asked. 'Did they hurt you?'

'I'd have liked to see them try,' he snorted as the train jolted and sooty steam drifted in through the open carriage windows.

'Well, at least we'll be on our way soon.' She glanced at his suitcase. 'And with our cargo intact.'

'You stupid woman,' he said, shaking his head.

'What do you mean?'

'They went through every pair of underpants, every book. Anything of value, they took it. This wasn't just about activists. This was organised robbery.'

'But your suitcase has that false bottom. Surely that was safe?'

He shook his head, staring out through the window. 'They've taken her,' he said. 'The Vermeer has gone – to sit in a pathetic little mayor's office, or some Mamma's poxy apartment as a gift from her thuggish son. And you know the worst of it? They don't even know what they've stolen.'

'Oh, Edwin. I don't know what to say.' For a moment she imagined she saw tears in his eyes.

'Before I even had the opportunity to verify its existence.'

Of course. That was what had upset him: Edwin Viner, rescuer of a lost Vermeer, hero of the art world. Edwin no more cared about the artworks that passed through his gallery than he did about the staff who worked there. They were mere signposts of his career, notches on the bedpost. He sickened her. So much so that the lurch of the train finally leaving the station was enough to send her fighting through the packed carriage towards the primitive bathroom.

Had Leonora imagined things could not possibly have become any worse, notwithstanding the chaotic train journey across France and fight to get on to a boat train from Calais, one week later, as war was officially declared, in a small consulting room near Victoria Station she received news that would alter the path of her life for ever.

19

It seemed impossible, as Phoebe sat in Bruce's tranquil studio examining the postcard once again, to imagine the war had ever reached this corner of Tuscany. And yet, according to some at his funeral, Bruce Cato had played his part in it. He used to tell Phoebe how he had removed valuable works of art from their frames and hidden them in the cellar, and knowing the Germans would loot anything of value, filled the empty frames with reproductions. He was chuffed by the idea of these poor-quality Old Masters now hanging in private homes, peopled by the faces of characters from the local village.

But what of the years after the war? . . . *until I can return. Your Nora.* Why did she not return? Her photograph still sat on Bruce's desk fifty years later, and she was clearly in his heart, but what had come between them? Phoebe knew Viner had married an actress of impeccable stock, making them the 'it' couple for many years, so it was not that Leonora had stayed with Edwin. And then in the early fifties Bruce married a Rome art dealer with a temper only marginally shorter than their marriage. If there had been relationships in the years following the divorce, he had kept them quiet.

Bruce had led Phoebe to uncover a love triangle and a lost painting, but why? Was it connected to the longstanding enmity with Edwin Viner? And did she even have the energy to find out?

She turned the painting over and ran her hand across the back, pausing as her fingers found a tiny, tarnished brass plate. She rubbed her sleeve across it until she was able to make out the letters engraved there:

Andrei Lyov,
Antiquarian Prints, Books and Fine Art
11 Cecil Court
London WC2

She knew Cecil Court, of course, the tiny Covent Garden alley crammed with booksellers and antique shops where one could buy anything from military medals to silver snuff boxes. Lyov . . . the same name as the art professor Margot had mentioned, mutual friend of Bruce and Leonora.

Phoebe jumped as she heard the door open.

'Hey,' Stefano said. 'I wondered whether I'd find you hiding here.'

'Not hiding, just . . .'

'It's OK,' he said, loosening his black tie as he perched on the sofa. 'I get it.' He nodded towards the painting as she put it back on the easel. 'What are you doing?'

'Bruce has set one of his little treasure hunts.'

'Seriously?'

She handed him the letter. 'He left this for Margot to give me. And,' she added, 'that painting. There's an address on the back.'

Stefano read the letter and handed it back to her. 'Are you going to do it?'

'I'm a bit old for treasure hunts.'

'But it must have been important to him?'

'I guess.'

'So how are you feeling?'

She shrugged. 'Ask me in six months.'

'It's tough. I can't believe he's gone either.' He glanced around. 'I feel like he's going to walk in at any moment.'

'To make us study Dante with him!' she laughed.

Stefano smiled. 'I wish I'd appreciated his extra-curricular lessons more at the time.'

She swatted at his arm. 'You just wanted to be out catching lizards.'

'I didn't care what I was doing, as long as it was with you,' he said, then looked away. 'Did you ever get to explore up there?' he asked, glancing towards the trapdoor in the ceiling.

'No. Never been a fan of rats.'

'Not tempted now?'

She shuddered. 'No, thanks. Especially not in the dark.'

'So what are you going to do with all this?'

'The studio?'

'The whole thing.'

'I don't know. I'd never planned on having the responsibility of this place. Not for a long time, anyway.'

'It's a lot, I know, but Villa Clara is a very special place.'

'With very special expenses.' She pressed her face into her hands and groaned. 'I can't even begin to think about it.'

'I'm here to help you, Phoebe,' he said. 'I know this place inside out, and its problems.'

She looked up at him. 'And the museum? What about the problems there? I can maybe keep it going into the new year, but then what?'

He hesitated. 'I know we'd said we'd talk about this properly in the office, but you should be aware that Bruce's finances weren't in great shape. Which is not to say we can't find ways to make things work in the short term.'

Phoebe sighed. 'It's that bad?'

'Bruce had let things slide, but once probate is through, maybe we can look at selling off some of the land to plug some gaps.'

'And how long will probate take?'

He shrugged. 'This is Italy . . .'

'So I really am stuffed.'

'We all are.'

She suddenly gasped. 'Your parents.'

He lifted his hands in an Italian shrug. 'I can't ask you to make decisions based on other people.'

'You don't think I'd throw your family out?'

'I hope not. But you have a life in London.'

Villa Clara was so much more than just a home to all of them, and suddenly she felt the weight of responsibility Bruce had carried all those years. 'Stefano, it would kill me to get rid of the villa. It's been my life.' She smiled. 'As has your family.'

'And me?' he said quietly. 'What am I to you?'

She threw an arm around his slim waist, enjoying the feel of his soft linen shirt under her hand. 'You're my oldest friend. You know everything about me . . .'

'And you know too much about me!' he laughed.

'Except why you didn't bring your girlfriend today?'

He shrugged. 'It didn't seem appropriate.'

Outside, Angelina began banging plates and glasses, a sure

sign that she was ready for the party to be over. 'We should help,' Phoebe said, unwilling to move.

'I suppose so. Take a minute. You buried your favourite human being today – Mamma can manage. And you'll stay for a while, now this bit's over?' he asked.

She shook her head. 'I need to be in London, but I'll come back as soon as I can. We can talk then about what to do.' She hesitated. 'I just remembered. You said something about the will, about a long-standing regular payment?'

'Yes. Bruce stipulated that it continue after his death.'

'Do you know who it's to?'

'It's to an L. Birch,' Stefano said. 'Mean anything to you?'

'It does now. Here, look at this,' she said, fetching the black and white photograph from Bruce's desk. 'Leonora Birch. Margot Stockton told me she and Bruce were friends before the war, but it seems they were more than that. Does she look familiar?'

He took the picture from her. 'No. But then my family only came here in the early seventies.'

'Why do you think Bruce was sending her money?'

Stefano shrugged. 'I don't know. I'll see what I can find out.'

'At least I know I'm not chasing a ghost,' Phoebe said.

He smiled. 'So you will do it? Follow the trail?'

She groaned. 'I don't know. I need to fix the puzzle of how to pay Tilly next month first.'

He pressed a hand on her thigh to push himself up, his touch so familiar. 'I'm going to chase off those stragglers so we can all get to bed.'

She watched him leave, then took one last look around before switching the lights off in the studio. As she wandered back across the courtyard, she imagined she heard Bruce's voice in her ear: 'So, dear girl, are you going to take the bait?' She turned around, half expecting to see him walking beside her, cigar smoke pluming into the night, but the only other sign of life was the moths dancing in the lamplight.

20

'Pheebs, you need a break.'

She looked up to see Tilly at the door. 'I know. But I'm trying to get these figures ready for the bank manager.'

Tilly put a mug of tea on the desk and glanced at the spreadsheet open on Phoebe's computer. 'Wow. That's a lot of red.'

'At least one packet of Ibuprofen's worth.'

'Why don't you let me have a look? Creative accounting is one of my more underrated skills.'

'I don't know . . .'

'Do you want this loan or not?'

'Honestly? I'd rather we didn't need one.'

'Well, we do, so let me take over.' Tilly sighed. 'Listen, you've been doing this since nine this morning. In fact, since you got back from Italy last month. You need a break. I've been dusting exhibits since nine – I need to use my brain.'

Phoebe hesitated.

Tilly pointed to the window. 'It's a nice day out there. Get some fresh autumn air.'

'I can't just take an afternoon off.'

'Then do something useful.' Tilly's eyes widened. 'I know.

Why don't you follow up on that letter from Bruce? Go and visit the shop? You can count it as work if you look at what they've got in there.' She nudged Phoebe. 'Come on. You must be a bit curious? I don't know how you've held out for so long.'

'Because I have a museum to keep going. Bruce should have known I can't just drop everything on a whim.'

'Then I'm telling you to. Go on, shoo! Before you burn out.'

Tilly was right, but even so, it felt like playing truant as she let herself out of the front door. A browse through an exhibition of works by modern Italian artist de Chirico at the Royal Academy served to feed her soul, whilst reminding her that Bruce had been sent to Rome as a Royal Academy prize-winner. No doubt his name had been removed from the roll of honour following the trial in 1964, and it suddenly hit her how hard it must have been for him to have his reputation sullied. Was it really too much to ask, for her to follow up the lead he had dropped for her?

Half an hour later she made her way across a traffic-clogged Trafalgar Square, passing the long-standing anti-apartheid vigil outside the South African embassy. She glanced towards the National Gallery, where pennant banners advertised an exhibition of drawings by Italian Masters from the Royal Collection, works that had perhaps once fallen under the care of Sir Edwin Viner during his time as advisor to the Queen. A surge of anger that Viner had survived whatever happened in that court room whilst Bruce was ridiculed even by his own family helped quicken her pace as she headed through London's theatreland, towards the shop whose nameplate she had discovered in Bruce's studio.

Cecil Court was a narrow pedestrian street straight out of a Dickens novel, where dusty-windowed antiquarian retailers nestled side by side. Number 11 sat pressed between a bookshop and a purveyor of military medals, its smut-dusted window displaying everything from medieval maps to Georgian miniatures.

'With you in a moment,' came a man's voice from the back room as Phoebe entered, giving her time to take in the framed prints and paintings squeezed side by side on the vermilion walls. Had Bruce come here to buy, or perhaps to sell on works he had come across himself? Eventually a tall man with the air of a consumptive Tolstoy aristocrat appeared, complete with a shock of thick white hair and faded corduroy jacket. 'Sorry about that. Was about to take a rather special School of Piranesi to the post office, but I'm darned if I can find it.'

Phoebe nodded towards a brown-paper-wrapped package sitting on the counter beneath an out-of-date *Miller's Antiques*. 'Would that be it?'

'You angel,' he sighed. 'I've a New York grande dame breathing fire down the telephone about this.'

'It's genuine?' Phoebe asked.

He stiffened instantly. 'Of course. I have the Lyov reputation to think of. My father was a professor of painting at the Chelsea School of Arts,' he added grandly.

'Valentin Lyov is your father?'

'Was. He would have been over a hundred now. You know of him?'

'He taught someone I know, many years ago.'

'He'd have been happy to meet you, in that case,' he nodded.

'Was this his business before yours?'

His dark eyes widened in horror. 'Goodness, no. He loathed dealers – called them the vampires of the art world.'

'But you're one of the good ones?'

'I like to think so. And on the understanding that I will only sell you something with an impeccable provenance, can I help?'

'I'm not sure,' Phoebe said.

He held up a forefinger. 'Are you a drawing or a painting sort of person?' he asked. 'Or perhaps you're more of a reader.' He picked up a tatty-covered book from the counter. 'First edition George Orwell.'

'Thank you, but I'm not buying. I was . . . well, I suppose I was sent here.'

He pressed a long, slender hand against his chest and feigned shock. 'You're not the art police, are you?' Intelligent and playful, this son of Valentin Lyov was exactly the sort of person Bruce had been drawn to.

Phoebe laughed. 'Definitely not. But I am Phoebe Cato – Bruce's niece?'

His eyes widened. 'Bruce Cato? Ah yes, you run the museum over the way in Bloomsbury. I've been meaning to visit, but . . .' He waved around. 'This place is a demanding mistress. How is your uncle?' he went on. 'Still raising hell?'

'He passed away. A few weeks ago.'

'I'm so sorry. We lost touch years ago, but I have happy memories of him. He will leave a large gap in this world.'

'He certainly will. Mr Lyov—'

He held a hand up. 'Andrei, please. Any niece of Bruce Cato is a friend of the family.' His eyes widened. 'In fact, you must come to dinner. My wife will love to meet you. And Irina, Father's youngest sister. She came here twenty-five years ago and claims still not to understand a word of English. But every time I complain about her, the old bat glares daggers at me.' He shook his head. 'I digress. So what brings you here?'

'Margot Stockton. I met her at Bruce's funeral.'

His face lit up. 'Dear Margot.'

'Indeed. She gave me a letter from Bruce, asking me to discover the truth about something that happened a long time ago.'

'How very intriguing.'

Now she was here in Cecil Court, telling Andrei about it, she couldn't help a little frisson of excitement at meeting someone from Bruce's past, through his own engineering. Damn him for knowing her so well. 'Although I have no idea why I'm here, what he wants from me.'

'So how exactly did you find me?'

'Margot also pointed me towards something in Bruce's studio.' She hesitated. 'A Vermeer. Well, a copy of an imaginary one he painted for my eighteenth birthday. Your address was on the back of the frame.'

'That makes sense. Bruce bought a lot of old frames from me. So what did this painting tell you?'

'It told me there was some kind of romance in his life, before the war.'

He nodded. 'Leonora Birch, of course.'

'And that she left Villa Clara in 1939, with Edwin Viner.'

'Viner.' Andrei shuddered. 'Goodness, Father disliked that man. Called him a crook in duke's clothing.'

'Any particular reason?' Phoebe asked. For years, she had endured either Bruce's anger at the sound of the man's name, or sycophantic praise from her parents. Suddenly, however, here was someone with a different view.

Andrei laughed lightly. 'Many, but the way Viner treated Leonora was enough. She was a great friend to my family, you see.'

Phoebe couldn't imagine Bruce had intended her to catch up on Lyov family gossip, and a more pressing question hung over her. 'Andrei, why do you think Bruce sent me here?'

'When you arrived, I asked you how I could help, and now I know.' He smiled. 'Why don't you take a look around? See if anything catches your eye.'

'I'm really not here to buy.'

'Who said anything about buying?' He immediately began busying himself flicking through an order book, leaving Phoebe to wonder what on earth she was doing here.

She dutifully browsed a rack of prints, and ran her eye across the walls, packed with framed oil paintings of varying worth. She tried to think as Bruce would, remembering how he used to try to catch her out, and yet ultimately always wanted her to win. She suddenly spotted a painting, high up on the wall, in which the da Vinci-style landscape featured Italian hills and olive groves, a meandering river leading towards a distant villa. And yet the colours were too bright for its period or even its frame, the texture puzzling. And then she saw it.

'May I look at this one?' she asked.

'Of course.' Andrei fetched a pair of steps and took it down, handing it to her.

'That's Villa Clara in the distance,' she laughed.

'*Brava*, my dear.'

She placed the piece on the counter, examining it closely.

'It's painted on paper,' she said. 'Should I try to remove it, do you think?'

'Here.' He handed her an artist's scalpel, and she began delicately slicing the edges of the paper landscape.

Phoebe carefully peeled away the top layer to reveal an oil painting beneath. She recognised instantly the now familiar latticed window, the blue and white tiles and the rug spread across a table, the bottom lip bitten in concentration. 'Bruce's Vermeer – again.'

'He sent it to me a few weeks ago, hoping you might find your way here.'

The painting was identical to that in the watchtower at Villa Clara, except that the candle at the desk had now been lit, and the artwork on the wall was a sketch Phoebe recognised as the figure of St Barbara in Raphael's celebrated painting the *Sistine Madonna*.

She turned it over, finding a letter tucked into the back of the frame. 'It's addressed to Leonora Birch,' she said, then scanned the text quickly. 'It's from a firm of London lawyers. Dated October 1939. An injunction against her.'

21

London, October 1939

'Edwin, I need to talk to you.' Leonora stood at the heavy oak door to his office, aware of the new junior assistant Ursula Knight staring at her. It was commonly accepted that one did not just barge into Sir Edwin's office.

He looked up from his desk, his white-gloved hand pausing mid-air as he held a magnifying glass to a charcoal sketch. 'I'm in the middle of something,' he snapped. 'And what have I said about addressing one another?'

She sighed. 'Very well, I need to talk to you, *Sir* Edwin.'

'Can it wait? I've had non-stop interruptions all day, what with those wretched air-raid busybodies telling us when we can switch the lights on. They're now demanding we put bloody tape across the gallery window.'

'There is a war on, unless you hadn't noticed.'

'How could I fail to, when there's a blockade on art works arriving from the Continent?' He shook his head. 'At least with my heart condition I can keep the boat afloat here, once the War Office has poached all my porters and secretaries.'

Heart condition? No doubt some Harley Street Old Boy had written a sick note to Churchill for him. She herself would have signed up for the Wrens or the WAAF like a shot, but her visit to the doctor had rather put the kibosh on that. 'Anyway, I haven't come here to talk about the war.'

'Good, because I need you to finish the paperwork for that Cézanne we sent back from Paris.'

She closed the door behind her and took the seat across from his desk, wincing as the waistband of her slim tweed suit skirt cut into her. This really was a conversation that could wait no longer. She took a deep breath. 'I'm pregnant,' she said.

He looked up, placing the magnifying glass on the green leather desktop. 'What on earth are you talking about?'

'I am with child. Your child.'

She watched as what little colour was in his sallow cheeks drained. 'Don't be ridiculous.'

'Did they not teach you biology at Eton? Believe me, I wish I weren't, but facts are facts. And we need to talk about it.'

'We need do nothing,' he snapped. 'If you have got yourself pregnant, I hardly see what that has to do with me.'

She tightened her lips. 'Well, I seem to remember it was you in bed with me in Le Touquet and Paris. Not to mention your London flat several times last summer. Forgettable though these events were. So I rather think it does have something to do with you.'

For a long moment he stared at her, his jaw working and fingers tapping on the desktop. 'You will not pin this on me, Miss Birch. For all I know, you could have lovers right across London.'

'Do you honestly think I could be bothered?'

He folded his arms. 'I imagine it's money you're after. To get rid of it.'

'I'm not getting rid of anything,' she replied. She had thought of little else for the past twenty-four hours, but it was not until she heard herself say these words that she realised she would keep the baby, whatever Edwin's reaction. Thirty-six years old, her opportunities for motherhood were limited.

'You want to blackmail me? Make me marry you, perhaps?'

'I have no desire to marry you, trust me. I just want you to know. You have the right.' She made a quick mental calculation. 'I imagine you won't want me on the gallery floor when I start showing, so let's say I begin my maternity leave at Christmas and return three months after the baby is born, when I will find a nanny. The beginning of September next year? That should do it.'

He shook his head. 'Are you completely mad?'

'Because I'm pregnant, I must be mad?'

He leaned closer to her across the desk. 'Would you please keep your voice down?' he hissed, a vein throbbing angrily in his temple.

'Listen, Edwin,' she retorted, 'this is not ideal for either of us, particularly me. As you know, Bruce and I had hoped—'

'Oh, of course. Bruce Cato. He's found out you're carrying his child and wants nothing to do with you, so you're trying to trap me.'

Damn him. Edwin Viner would not see her crumple. 'This is not Bruce's child. I wish it were. And thanks to our carelessness, it is impossible for me to be with Bruce. I would never expect him to bring up your child. I want neither your hand in marriage nor your money. Simply for you to agree the terms of my future employment.'

He stood suddenly. 'I don't think there is any point carrying on this conversation, Miss Birch. In fact, I don't think there is any point in your carrying on working here. Viner's cannot be seen to employ women of loose morals.'

She felt her stomach flip, wondering suddenly whether her unborn child was kicking against its father's behaviour – please God let it be nothing like Edwin. 'You're sacking me?' she said. 'You can't do that.'

'Is it your name above the door outside? No. It is mine. And I have every right to sack you. Now please clear your desk, Miss Birch. I want you out of the building by lunchtime.'

'But I have a child to think of. Our child. I need an income. How am I to survive?'

'That is your business. Now, if you don't mind, I have an appointment at the Palace in one hour.'

'No, Edwin,' she said, as he pulled her towards the door. 'I don't want to do this, but you are forcing me. Throw me out, and I'll tell the world about your child.'

'You will tell no one anything. Leave this office instantly.'

'Then I'll instruct my solicitor to fight you.'

His face clouded over instantly, all pretence at civility dissolved as he whispered close to her cheek. 'And I will instruct mine to destroy you.' He held the door open for her. 'Goodbye, Miss Birch. I trust we will never meet again.'

22

'Viner, of course,' Andrei said, returning the letter to Phoebe. 'I had no idea he'd turned on her quite that viciously. I wonder if Laurence did.'

'Laurence knew who his father was?'

'Leonora believed in being honest with her son, however painful.'

'It seems ridiculous, but I did wonder whether Laurence might have been Bruce's son.'

'You think Bruce wouldn't have been there for his own child?'

'I know. You're right. Was she ever tempted to break her silence about the pregnancy?'

Andrei shook his head. 'According to that injunction, she would have lost everything. At least as things stood, Leonora had the house in Ludlow Gardens.' He sighed. 'Such a waste.'

'In what sense?'

'She'd been a very talented artist in her own right, once upon a time. Becoming a single-parent landlady was probably not her plan.'

'And is that what drove them apart?'

'It's what drove Leonora to break off their engagement. She couldn't bear the thought of Bruce bringing up Viner's child.'

'But Bruce would have loved any child.'

Andrei held his hands up. 'I know that. You know that. But Leonora was proud – and incredibly stubborn.'

She smiled. 'That would have made two of them.'

Andrei looked up as the bell over the door rang. Lowering his voice, he said, 'I ought to play shopkeeper.'

'Of course. I've taken up too much of your time. But can I ask you one more thing?'

'Fire away,' he said, waving to the elderly gentleman heading towards a cabinet of silver trinkets.

'Leonora said in her postcard from Ventimiglia that "she is gone". Did she mean the Vermeer they were taking back to London?'

'I imagine so. It was stolen by Fascist guards at the station.'

'And was it actually a Vermeer?'

'That, we may never know. But certainly Leonora believed it to be.'

Cherchez la femme . . . 'Do you think Bruce wants me to find her?'

'Leonora or the painting?'

'Exactly.'

'I don't know. But you want to, right? You came in here looking as though you were on an errand, and now I see a fire has been lit.' He smiled. 'Take the painting,' he said covering it in bubble wrap and handing it to her. 'Look carefully. And if it does lead you to Leonora, please tell her to come to dinner,' he added before Phoebe walked back into the brightness of the real world, the painting tucked under her arm.

23

London, July 1963

Leonora enjoyed the early-afternoon lull, when no one needed coins for the meter or matches to light gas fires, and she could take time to read a book or listen to the afternoon concert. Small pleasures, but pleasures all the same.

She sometimes wondered what would have happened if she had met someone else, but in the early days she was too busy with nappies, chasing around after her young tenants with jobs and hairdressers to get to, important jobs in Whitehall as the war took hold, things to talk about other than weaning and croup. It at least distracted her from the pain of losing Bruce for a second time.

If it hadn't been for Edwin . . . in so many ways. It still broke her heart to think of the painting languishing in some dingy office or rotting in a cellar. If only she had taken it in her suitcase; if only Edwin hadn't made such a fuss at the station. All spilt milk now, she supposed, but some spills could never be completely mopped up, and this one was so catastrophic that neither she nor Edwin had ever spoken of it. Who, after all, would want to be remembered as the people who lost a Vermeer?

Instead she focused on what she did still have: her home, the stream of young women who filled it with chatter and laughter, and of course Laurence, who had promised to pop by later. The place was even more of a mess than usual, books and newspapers strewn liberally, but he would be the last to mind: 'Housework is institutionalised misogyny,' her son claimed, although to her knowledge he had never picked up so much as a dishcloth. She put this down to his father's genes, grateful it was the only characteristic he had inherited from Edwin, other than the nose designed for looking down at others.

She had been straight with Laurence about his parentage, as soon as she deemed him old enough to understand. To her relief, he had shrugged it off: she was his mother, and that was all that mattered. And he was her son, which was why she worried about the meetings he and Andrei attended with the other angry, educated young men they hung about with. After all that fuss about Cuba and the Russian missiles last year, things could easily be misinterpreted. Besides, Leonora herself didn't need any more ammunition for that awful Mrs Risley next door, who could make gossip out of a sermon and had as good as called Leonora a brothel-keeper the other day.

How things come and go, she mused, and now it seemed Edwin had reared his ugly head once more. It was a small world indeed, in which Margot now worked for the very same gallery where Leonora had once been employed. And for the same boss. Life could become interesting.

Margot was an interesting one in herself: Linda had left the *Evening Standard* lying around, and amongst the tittle-tattle about Princess Margaret and the price of coal, Leonora had seen a small feature about a society wedding that ended in chaos. The Runaway Bride had hit the papers for a few days, until Margot Stockton-Jones was spotted safe and well in a café on the King's Road. There was nothing the papers disliked more than a dull ending.

As for the other new lodger, Leonora already had a feeling Joan might be trouble, but she couldn't help being drawn in by her infectious laughter and talent for mimicry of everyone from Cilla Black to David Frost – even of Laurence, who definitely needed to take himself less seriously. She did worry about Joan working in the nightclub – men were men, whether they'd been drinking brown ale or champagne – but suspected the girl could look after herself.

The two young women would be good for one another – Joan would show Margot a bit of life, and, well, it wouldn't hurt for a bit of finishing-school manners to smooth the edges off the girl from Bethnal Green.

She looked at the clock and realised she needed to get going. As she stood, she caught sight of her reflection in the mirror above the old fireplace. Who are you? she asked herself, unrecognisable from that slender young creature she had once been, her copper hair now faded to the colour of a squirrel's brush and posture defeated by years of stooping over a bucket.

She stood a little straighter, remembering the woman who had once worked at Viner's Gallery, where young Margot had become her unexpected ear to the ground. I am Leonora Birch, she told herself, a very patient woman with a very long memory.

24

Margot loved the peace of the gallery early in the morning, when she could enjoy undisturbed the Old Masters illuminated by small spotlights. Viner's had been a London institution ever since Thomas Viner had established his Bond Street gallery in 1829. With its name a guarantee of discretion and infallible provenance, dozens of works hanging in national collections around the world had passed through this building.

The current exhibition of Renaissance drawings from the Florence school had been arranged, thanks to Margot's suggestion, according to the material used – chalk, charcoal, graphite, ink. 'You're a natural,' Sir Edwin had said to her as the opening-night crowd sipped champagne, charmed by Margot's discreet manner and impressive knowledge of the works for sale.

Already Margot had the uncomfortable sense that Sir Edwin's sights were rather firmly fixed on her – ever since the summer that she and Diana had left Roedean aged eighteen, he had been one of those fathers they jokingly called NBLAWs. So far, however, Margot had managed to sidestep this Never Be Left Alone With's attention. She was grateful for the opportunity, as they said, and would soak up everything she could learn about the business, whilst keeping her employer at a safe distance.

Already she had done everything from liaising with the company who crated up works for transportation around the world, to accompanying Sir Edwin on meetings with experts from the Courtauld Institute and British Museum. He had shown her how to trace a work's provenance through accompanying paperwork and the Viner's library of artist *catalogues raisonnés*, which were scoured for lists of currently verified works.

Take the Raphael sketch that was the undoubted star of the show, a drawing that had been brought to Sir Edwin by an anonymous seller. This particular work was remarkable, Sir Edwin had explained to Margot, in that it was one of three sketches by Raphael for a well-known painting on display in Germany. For this beautiful close-up sketch of the gently inclined saint's face to have arrived on the market was nothing short of miraculous.

Margot had been fascinated by the process of uncovering the life history of the Raphael drawing. It seemed the work had at one time been part of the Royal Collection, sold by the Prince Regent George IV in 1787 to settle enormous debts: a label on the back of the frame stated 'GIVR Carlton House Library', thus proving its one-time residence in the Prince's Mayfair mansion. An auction catalogue showed the work as having later been sold to a French count whose head was removed six years later, courtesy of Madame la Guillotine, and his home destroyed, along with his prized art collection. The count may have already sold the work on by the time the Château d'Aubois burned to the ground, or perhaps a *sans-culottes* peasant with an eye for art had taken the Raphael. Whatever the case, the sketch, having been missing for all of the nineteenth and half of the twentieth century, was now for sale again, for the equivalent of the original royal debt. Margot could not believe she had wasted so many years on an enforced husband hunt, when she could have been chasing artworks instead.

On Sir Edwin's insistence, his Head of Paintings Ursula Knight had taken Margot to a client meeting at a Jacobean country house in Sussex where Margot was embarrassed to be greeted warmly by the owners, with whose daughter she had gone to finishing school. This had done her no favours with Miss Knight, who set Margot the homework of tracing the lineage of a supposed Poussin being flogged to pay for the new roof. Using the documentation available, Margot had searched exhibition and auction catalogues at the V&A, and with her perfect French had telephoned an art dealer in Paris, through whose doors the painting had passed in the twenties. Sir Anthony Blunt, an acknowledged expert on Poussin and Director of the Courtauld, had also agreed to look at the painting, proclaiming it to the best of his knowledge an original.

A few days later, Miss Knight read Margot's notes through her wing-tipped spectacles, whilst Margot waited nervously for her verdict. Miss Knight simply looked up and nodded. And that was it: no fuss, but Margot suddenly found herself invited to examine a new acquisition or passed trade magazines containing articles Margot might find useful. She had passed a test.

'Margot?'

She turned around, embarrassed to be caught daydreaming by Miss Knight, whose pencil-tight black suit surely never allowed for a moment's reverie. Margot often wondered whether there was a gentleman friend in the picture, but it was impossible to imagine this terrifying woman in her forties donning a pinny and rustling up a shepherd's pie for anyone. 'Sorry. Yes?'

For once, Miss Knight sported agitated pinpoints of bright colour on her cheeks. 'Sir Edwin has chosen today, when we have the director of a prestigious American museum coming to look at the Raphael, to decide to sack his secretary.'

'What has this one done?'

'Apart from the precisely nothing she does every day, I have no idea. But she's clearing her desk as we speak. Which means, Miss Stockton, we must rally before he pulls in that daughter of his to help. She covered for two days before Christmas, and it took me until Easter to clear away the magazines and ashtrays.'

There was an understanding that Diana worked at Viner's two days a week to justify the trust fund and Chelsea house, but so far Margot had only seen her there long enough to beg a car off her father and badger Margot about the Charlwood house party. 'It'll be such fun!' she'd quipped whilst Margot tried to type out reports written in Sir Edwin's idiosyncratic handwriting. It would not be fun, Margot was convinced. She had no desire to find herself stuck between Cosmo and Diana, nor to be cornered in the library by Sir Edwin.

Ursula Knight narrowed her eyes. 'Miss Viner is a friend of yours?'

'We were at school together,' she said, almost apologetically. Increasingly, Margot wondered how their friendship had survived this long.

'It takes all sorts, I suppose. Anyway, I shall be busy upstairs sorting out this mess. Sir Edwin wants you to bring up the Corot landscape that came in last week.'

Margot had only once been trusted to go down to the storeroom, and as she made her way into the gloomy basement, Bob, Viner's maintenance man, looked up from his workbench where he was making replacement stretchers for canvases. 'What can I do you for, love?' he said through the cigarette clamped between his lips.

'Sir Edwin wants the new Corot from the storeroom, if you don't mind?'

Bob nodded. 'Lovely one, that. Come on, then. Follow me.' He fiddled about with the triple locks on the heavy steel door, switching on the strip lights to reveal a cave-like space where paintings and framed prints were stacked against the walls, and drawings kept in wide, shallow drawers. While Bob climbed a stepladder to search for the painting, Margot glanced around, spotting a tall wooden cupboard, a heavy padlock securing its doors. 'Why the belt and braces?' she asked.

Bob turned to the mahogany cupboard. 'Oh, that. Only the boss has access.'

'Why? What's in there?'

'The Villa Clara Collection,' he whispered. 'Stuff he bought in Italy before the war. That Breughel he sent to Sotheby's last week – that was a Villa Clara picture. Anyway, it's the Corot you're here for, not gossip. This it?' He passed her a darkly atmospheric landscape of winter trees lining a rutted track.

'It's beautiful,' she said, almost able to smell the incoming rain and sweet mulch of rotten leaves.

'They should get a good few hundred, even thousands, for it.'

Margot smiled. 'You should be on the gallery floor, Bob.'

He shook his head. 'Nah. I'm happy down here, with my own private art gallery. And,' he added, winking, 'no one telling me I can't eat my sarnies on the posh carpet.'

'Sir Edwin is lucky to have you,' Margot said.

'You remind him of that when it comes to handing out Christmas bonuses. And from what I hear, he's lucky to have a bright young woman like you working for him. Just . . .' He frowned.

'Just what?'

'Just watch out for yourself. And tell him Bob reckons that painting's a good 'un.'

She glanced once more at the padlocked wooden cupboard as she followed Bob out. If treasures as precious as this Corot were kept on the shelves, what could possibly be locked in there?

25

Once a week Leonora cooked up a Sunday roast. 'All part of the rent,' she would insist when Linda fretted about not being able to afford bed *and* board. It gave her a chance to see how things really were at Ludlow Gardens. And to ensure that Valentin Lyov, widowed these last ten years, got at least one square meal a week. Today, however, her dear old professor had telephoned to say he was busy, and although Leonora was concerned about his tone, lunch had all the same been a jolly affair, despite her cooking the chicken to near obliteration and Joan's merciless teasing of Linda's gentleman friend Derek. The poor man had spent the whole of lunch the colour of cranberry sauce.

She had a tongue on her, that one, especially to Hillary. No doubt just insecurity and a touch of jealousy as Margot and Hillary's friendship grew, but still. It was quite a relief when Joan disappeared to get ready to meet someone in town that evening. A gentleman, judging by how long it had taken her to get ready, but then Joan dolled herself up even to put out the empty milk bottles.

Margot had meanwhile taken Hillary to the National Gallery after lunch. Miss Stevenson was the perfect tenant, but so terribly serious, always at her books when she wasn't at work or evening classes. A stomp around town in the sunshine would do her the world of good.

Leonora had a sudden yearning to exercise her own brain. Perhaps she would pick up the Caravaggio biography Andrei had brought her, or do some sketching. Once she had slept off lunch in her armchair.

She jumped at the sound of the front door banging closed, smiling as she heard Laurence chatting to Linda and Derek, off to see *The Great Escape* at the cinema. Not a natural conversationalist, he always made an effort with her tenants. Everyone other than Margot. Perhaps there was still work to be done.

'Ma,' Laurence said now, hugging her briefly before falling into the opposite armchair. 'Look who I found on his way here,' he said, ushering in an old gentleman with a George V beard, three-piece suit and silver-topped walking cane. In the forty years Leonora had known him, Valentin Lyov had not changed one jot, an aspic-preserved relic of the Russian Empire.

'Lyov, we missed you at lunch.' Leonora planted three kisses on his white-whiskered cheeks, in time-honoured fashion, and he smiled, his eyes glinting through round, wire-rimmed spectacles.

'I am sorry. And how is my favourite pupil today?'

'Your pupil is sixty years old, with backache and an urge for a drink.'

He smiled, producing a bottle of vodka from his battered Gladstone bag. 'I have just the thing.'

Leonora took the old professor's hand and led him to the sofa while Laurence poured their drinks. 'And now, dear Lyov, tell me how you are.'

He drank down the vodka Laurence handed him in one gulp. 'The world has gone mad. I went for my usual walk across Regent's Park this morning, and I swear two men were following me. Me! A retired art professor.'

'It's paranoia about your being Russian,' Laurence said, sitting down heavily. 'Reds under the beds, and all that.'

Lyov raised his hands in despair. 'Are people really so stupid? Do they not know the Bolsheviks terrorised my family?'

Leonora patted his arm. 'You cannot let this get to you.'

'Easy for you to say. You do not have "spy" whispered behind your back. "Communist", for pity's sake. And in the meantime, my youngest sister is stuck in St Petersburg.' He shook his head. 'I received word today she is ill. Very ill. Queuing for cabbages in the snow while she coughs herself into an early grave. I need to bring her to London, where she can receive proper care.'

Leonora took his hand. 'There must be something we can do. Get money to her, perhaps?'

'It's almost impossible to get anything in or out of the Soviet Union,' Laurence said quietly. 'Relations have never been worse, especially now our own Secretary of State for War has been sharing a mistress with a Russian naval officer.'

'Men can be so stupid,' Leonora tutted. 'Laurence, can we write to somebody? Does your newspaper have a correspondent over there?'

'It doesn't quite work like that, Ma.'

'Well, then, we engage one of these wretched Cambridge spies,' Leonora said. 'Burgess and Maclean could do something useful, for once.'

They all looked up as the front door banged closed and

the sound of conversation drifted in from the hallway. 'That's Margot,' Leonora said.

'Oh, jolly good,' Laurence sniffed. 'She can teach us how to groom a pony. That'll help.'

Leonora pointedly ignored him. 'She and Hillary have been to the National Gallery.'

'To see all the artworks her family have loaned?' he quipped.

'Why don't you ask her yourself?' Leonora said to Laurence, who began fiddling with his cigarette case as Margot appeared.

'Ask me what?' she said, her expression challenging as it landed on Laurence.

Leonora smiled. 'Laurence wanted to ask whether you and Hillary would care to join us for a glass of vodka?'

Hillary shook her head. 'Not for me.'

'Sherry, then?' Leonora enquired. 'Did they let you drink that at Girton College?'

'I'd rather have a cup of tea,' Hillary said, pulling a Virginia Woolf first edition from Leonora's bookcase.

'Perhaps Laurence could make it?' Margot said, dropping on to the chaise longue. 'If he knows how.'

'Good idea,' Leonora said.

Laurence sighed. 'Fine. I'll telephone Margot's butler for advice.'

'Cook,' Margot shouted after him. 'Our butler never makes tea.' She looked around the room. 'We don't have a butler, by the way,' she added. 'Just . . . well, help.'

But not a bean for a daughter refusing to play the game, Leonora thought. 'Margot, why don't you tell Professor Lyov about your new job? She is working at Viner's,' Leonora explained, raising her eyebrows as a warning not to launch into his well-worn rant about art dealers, and Edwin Viner in particular.

Lyov nodded discreetly to Leonora. 'Please do, Miss Stockton. I need a distraction.'

Margot's face instantly lit up. 'Oh, I love it there. So much to learn, and I spend my entire day surrounded by works of art.'

'What more could one want from life? Leonora tells me you are already something of an expert?'

She blushed slightly. 'Hardly. Self-taught till now. But I read everything I can get my hands on.'

'Then you must come and see my collection of art books some time. I imagine you are learning a lot at the gallery?'

'I'm mainly just doing secretarial work – typing, proof-reading catalogues, that sort of thing – but yes, I do get to see the artworks up close.' Her eyes widened. 'We had a Raphael drawing in last week – a sketch of Saint Barbara.'

Something nagged at Leonora, an itch she couldn't scratch. 'Saint Barbara?'

'Yes. A sketch for the *Sistine Madonna*. An old acquisition of Sir Edwin's.'

'It's genuine?' Lyov asked.

'We believe so. The provenance is impeccable and the paper has been dated to within twenty years of the author's signature and date. It's on display in the gallery now, in fact, before it goes to an American museum.'

Leonora smiled thinly, trying to concentrate above the voice hovering at her ear. 'Well, in that case it must be genuine. Clever old Edwin.' She had kept a close eye on Viner's catalogues over the years, where every few months another unknown gem hit the saleroom. Leonora was not sure how he did it, but Edwin had connections somewhere.

Margot turned to Leonora. 'You know Edwin Viner?'

'I did once.' Which was all Margot needed to know for now, and so she deftly changed the subject. 'But we were talking of Lyov's family before you arrived, ladies. He has had a difficult day.'

'I'm sorry to hear that. What has happened?' Margot asked.

'My sister in St Petersburg is gravely ill.'

Leonora watched as Hillary's attention was drawn from the book she had been perusing. Of course. The answer to Lyov's problems could well be under her own roof. Civil servant? Leonora suspected her tenant was rather more than a Foreign Office typist, with the Russian lessons Hillary was taking after work, even though the girl already spoke German and French fluently. 'She needs to get out of Russia if she is to have the medical help she requires,' Leonora explained.

'That's terrible,' Margot said. 'Can she not catch a boat or something?'

Hillary turned to face the room, the book pressed to her chest. 'Not a chance. The latest government protocols have prohibited all movement in and out. Only yesterday the Kremlin reiterated their official position in a despatch to Reuters. The Foreign Office hasn't responded yet, but their reaction will be hostile, judging by today's statement from the US Ambassador's residence in Berlin.'

'Gosh, Hills. You seem to know an awful lot about this,' Margot said.

Hillary frowned, her mousy fringe covering her eyes as she clamped her jaw shut.

Leonora sat up straight. 'Hillary, what exactly is it that you do in that office in Curzon Street?'

Immediately, the well-trained shutters slammed closed. 'I can't say, but I may know someone who can help Mr Lyov's sister.'

Valentin Lyov's eyes misted over with tears as he came across and pressed Hillary's hands in his own. 'It would mean the world,' he said.

Hillary, not a natural receiver of physical affection, stepped back awkwardly, adjusting her glasses. 'As far as you all know, I've said nothing, but I will see what I can do.'

Leonora slapped her hands on her thighs. 'Well, this is splendid. How terribly cloak and dagger.'

The door pushed open and Laurence appeared with a tray of tea things. 'What did I miss?'

Margot smiled. 'Nothing that should be heard in the servants' quarters. Now perhaps you'd care to pour Hillary's tea?'

Leonora watched Laurence's irritated flush as he sloshed tea from the pot into Hillary's cup. He had gone his whole life being taken seriously – top of the class, double first from Oxford. It would do Laurence good to be brought down a peg or two by Margot. In fact, she thought as she caught Margot glancing across at him, it might just do them both good.

26

Phoebe threw her jacket on the armchair, kicking off her loafers as she went to the tiny kitchenette and opened the fridge. A cracked heel of Cheddar, bendy celery and half a tin of beans, which she threw into a pan, slotting two nearly furry slices of bread into the toaster.

She really ought to learn to cook now James had gone, but she had been spoiled by the Thai curries he had learned to make on his gap year. A gap year that stretched into a decade of lazing on the sofa or going for long, boozy lunches that he claimed were 'networking'. Networking for what? she had always wanted to ask. Networking for Phoebe's replacement, it had turned out.

As she looked around the flat, she wondered where, other than the fridge, James had made his mark. Everything here was hers, from the shabby leather sofa to the artworks she had collected at markets in Italy with Bruce. The books: hers. Vintage crockery and glasses: hers. Name on the lease: hers. Massive red wine stain on the carpet: James's. Even so, his absence made the place seem smaller, sadder. She would get used to it, she supposed, but did she want to? The rent was crippling, there was mould on the bedroom ceiling and the commute across London each morning seemed to take longer and longer.

Maybe she could look for somewhere else, but she'd never find another flat in Notting Hill she could afford. Rents were rocketing as developers bought up gentrifiable villas, and now nearly thirty, she was completely over the whole flat-share thing. If the museum really did fold, she couldn't afford the rent she was already paying. Let alone maintain a villa in Italy. She supposed this was what one termed a 'turning point', and she missed having Bruce's ear. 'Don't give up yet, old girl,' he'd have said.

She might not have Bruce, but she did have something of his to distract her, thanks to her visit to Cecil Court, and so she laid the Vermeer copy on the table. Was she looking for a missing woman or a missing painting? Was this a treasure hunt or witch hunt?

'Look carefully . . .' Andrei had said. She dug around in the drawer of an old sideboard and pulled out a magnifying glass, taking it across to the table. She examined once again the artwork within an artwork, certain she was looking at a Raphael. Her eye suddenly landed on a spot on the tiled floor of the painting, where a sheet of paper had been crumpled and thrown. How had she missed it? It was hard to make out, but yes, there was writing on it, an address just visible to the naked eye.

The Hon. Cosmo Stockton-Jones, she read, *13 Marlborough Mews, Marylebone, London.*

Another Stockton? She racked her brains for what little she knew of Margot's private life, recalling that she was of aristo-cratic stock, younger sister of a dissolute earl whose hedonistic lifestyle had peaked in the early seventies before drugs and racehorses put paid to the family fortune. Had Cosmo also been a friend of Bruce's? It seemed likely, knowing her uncle's fondness for interesting characters, but why had Margot not simply told her Cosmo was part of this unfolding story?

For a moment she felt a stab of irritation that no one would just tell her what they already knew, but then that was the game: Bruce had set it up, and everyone was playing by his rules. There was no choice but to do the same, if she were to follow Bruce's trail.

Phoebe was about to reach for the *London A to Z* when she became aware of an acrid smell from the kitchen. She rushed to the pan, but the beans were a blackened mess that would take more than bleach and a Brillo pad to remove. She had a sudden longing for Angelina's cooking, for rich pasta sauces and creamy lasagne, wishing she were at Villa Clara with Stefano and his family, instead of scrubbing together an existence in London. She hadn't the cash for a flight to Tuscany right now, but she would do the next best thing and call Stefano, topping herself up with one of their long chats. As soon as she had grabbed herself a takeaway.

27

London, August 1963

For all that she had lived in London since bursting into the world in the master bedroom at Percy Street twenty-five years earlier, Joan knew little of her birth city, she realised as she strode along Piccadilly. For residents of Stepney, anything west of Liverpool Street Station was a playground for tourists and the posh, where you went to serve in cafés or drive a taxi.

Until now. The previous afternoon, Joan and Margot had spent a happy afternoon in Carnaby Street, trawling boutiques where hems were as high as the prices were low. She looked down at her new cream shift dress and the tortoiseshell belt around her hips. It suited her, and she knew it, as did all the stiff-suited gentlemen craning their necks as they passed by. Life was good, and so was her pay.

'Taken to this like a fly to muck, you have, my girl,' Brenda had quipped as she tucked an extra five quid in Joan's wages. From novice hostess to most bottles of champagne sold, Joan had pushed more noses out of joint in the chicken coop than Cassius Clay, and been voted the customers' Girl of the Month for the second time running.

And then there was that chap. He'd come back a couple of times, making a point of asking for Joan and introducing her to his friends, like they'd have the remotest thing in common with a waitress in underwear. But weren't times changing? The new aristocracy were Merseyside guitarists and stick-thin models from Clapham, and so she had taken him up on his breakfast invitation, adding a couple of coffee dates when she realised how well they got on. 'You're a breath of fresh air, Joanie,' he'd said last time. Well, he was too: courteous, funny, vulnerable. The business with Alf had left her bruised, and she was ready to spend time with someone different; someone who just wanted to be friends, who treated her like a lady, and not an accessory.

Alf who? she told herself as she smiled at the top-hatted doorman outside the Savoy Hotel and made her way into the crowded bar with its low-hanging cloud of cigar smoke.

'Joanie darling,' he said, standing and kissing her on both cheeks, an affectation that still took her by surprise: greetings in Percy Street were a barely visible nod or a clip round the ear. He was dressed in an open-necked, misbuttoned shirt and a shabby velvet jacket straight out of the family dressing-up box, his unbrushed curly dark hair well past his collar. 'I got you a drink.'

'What is it?' she said, turning the glass around in her fingers.

'White Lady. Lemon, Cointreau and gin. Perfect for that dress you're wearing. I wish I could persuade my sister to drag herself out of the thirties and have some fun with her wardrobe.'

Shuddering at the sudden vision of some country type in tweed and jodhpurs, hay in her hair, Joan took a sip, screwing up her eyes. 'Blimey,' she said. 'I'd rather have a port and lemon.'

He laughed. 'Joanie, you are just adorable.'

Was he teasing her? She hated the thought of being his pet from the wrong side of the tracks, but she sensed he liked her for who she was, and had few real friends amongst the public-school bores she'd seen him with at Henry's. Joan may not know a fish knife from a *flambée*, but she knew friendship was not a competition to behave the most obnoxiously – nor, she noted as he ordered another whisky, to drink the most. 'You'll become an old soak,' she said. 'My dad had a thing for the bottle. Makes a man ugly, booze does.'

'Also makes a man forget.' He sat up. '*You* make me forget, Joanie.'

What was it he needed to forget? she wondered. 'And you make me forget about Alf.'

He nodded. 'Good. You deserve better.'

Joan had surprised herself by confiding in him the story of her break-up with Alf, the way she had let herself be paraded around in new coats, shoes, dresses, the rumours about extortion rackets and worse, even though all she'd ever got from Alf was some line about 'import–export'. Besides, for all his cash, he would never have brought her here. Wide boys like Alf wouldn't get through the door – unless they bought the bloody door.

She took another sip of the disgusting drink. 'Maybe I don't want anyone else,' she said. 'Maybe I just want to have some fun.'

'Who needs love when you have friends? Not you, and certainly not me.'

'I want to see a bit of the world, you know?' she said. 'I'd barely left the East End before I got my job at Henry's.'

He suddenly sat up. 'How about I show you my world, and you show me yours?'

She frowned. 'You want to sing Cockney songs around the pub piano?'

'Maybe . . . I have an idea. Do you have plans for the Bank Holiday weekend?'

'I dunno,' she said, stirring her drink with a cocktail stick.

'You do now. You're coming away with me.'

'Away? Oh no, I think you've got the wrong idea . . .'

'Not *away* in that sense, I promise. There's a house party in Oxfordshire.'

'What? A party in a house?' Joan knew his type was different to hers, but she couldn't help the disappointment.

'A country house, darling. You know, like in *Brideshead*?' He waited for her acknowledgement, then tried again. '*Rebecca*?'

She'd no idea what he was talking about, but country house sounded to her like mud and lace-up shoes. 'I ain't got to ride any horses?'

'No horses, no stables, and I'll ask them to shut the dogs away. You just need a cocktail dress and a swimsuit. We'll take the Jag, have the roof down. Seriously, Joanie, it'll be fun. Some of my old school chums will be there. In fact, Sis has said she'll come too. You'll love her. She can be a stuffy old stick sometimes, but she's great fun underneath.'

'I don't know . . .' Sitting in a cocktail bar like this was one thing, but a stately home?

'Just one night. I promise. And no funny business. You can bunk up with my sister. Come on. It'll be so much more fun with you there.'

Joan narrowed her eyes. 'I'll think about it. If,' she said, 'you let me take *you* somewhere.' She gestured to his whisky. 'Drink up. We're going dancing.'

28

Technicolor reflections rippled across the rain-slicked Soho streets as Cosmo and Joan dodged gaggles of young people queuing to get into bars and nightclubs, whilst another type of clientele lowered trilbies over their eyes and disappeared down dark staircases, where posters advertised scantily dressed 'Girls girls girls!' The pavements were packed, the air thick with rock and roll as mountainous bouncers scanned the streets for trouble.

Joan recognised the dinner-jacketed ex-boxer outside the Flamingo, a cauliflower-eared friend of her dad's from the Dog and Duck. Grabbing Cosmo's hand, she talked their way to the front of the queue where photographers waited on the off chance of snapping a Rolling Stone heading into one of the club's infamous all-nighters.

''Ere, Cosmo, who's your new girl?' one of them shouted.

'I ain't no one's girl,' Joan snapped back, flashing a smile for the cameras as she took Cosmo's arm and they slipped through the door to the club. 'D'you get that a lot?' she asked.

He shrugged. 'Combination of being in one film and having a title. Seems to drive them crazy.'

The club was rammed with everyone from Black American servicemen looking for a bit of jazz to remind them of home, to slim-suited mods sporting pale-lipped girlfriends with pixie haircuts and sweeping false eyelashes. Gangsters rubbed shoulders with jazz afficionados, and the atmosphere crackled with the possibility of danger. She'd brought Margot here the previous week, and her room-mate had looked as though she might have a heart attack – dancing at the Flamingo was a far stretch from a debutante ball.

A pall of cigarette smoke hung across the gloomy basement, occasionally morphing into something headier, and several times they were offered what looked like coloured sweets. 'You can't buy booze here, so people bring their own entertainment,' she told Cosmo, steering him away. 'Wait here – I'll get some drinks.' When she returned a few minutes later with two lemonades, Cosmo was deep in conversation with a man in a black turtleneck sweater and heavy tortoiseshell glasses.

'Joanie, meet Pip,' Cosmo said. 'He's just set up his own film production company.'

'You're in the movies?' Joan said, her voice rising an octave.

The man shrugged. 'Well, more kitchen sink than Hollywood,' he said in vowels from which the public school had been usurped by a Cockney accent that made Joan want to laugh. He paused a moment as he ran his eye across her. 'You ever done any acting?'

'Only acting up, if you believe my mum.'

'Didn't I tell you she's the real deal?' Cosmo said, then turned to Joan. 'Pip's always on the lookout for new faces.'

The other man reached into his back pocket, handing her a card. 'Come to the office for a chat. It's just up the road.'

Conversation soon became impossible, as the house band arrived from their previous gig, instruments carried across the heads of the cheering crowd and on to the stage, where they performed a brief sound check before piling straight into their first number. 'Hey hey,' sang Georgie Fame from the keyboard as his sax players lined up in their matching jackets and ties. Cosmo was no dancer, Joan discovered, happy to watch as Joan joined the melee on the dancefloor. She felt her body give in to the irresistible beat, hips swaying and hair falling across her face. She felt as though she had drunk a whole bottle of champagne, high on being just a girl moving to the music.

'You want to dance, miss?' a young Black serviceman shouted above the music. He was handsome, his smile broad and hair smoothed into stiff, Brylcreemed waves.

Joan let herself be led in the complex routine, laughing every time she missed a turn or switched the wrong way. He didn't seem to mind, patiently picking up where they had fallen apart. She sensed he missed his music and his old life. Probably his dance partner, too.

As the song morphed into another, a sudden whisper shimmered across the dancefloor and Joan felt the atmosphere shift as a procession of well-dressed men worked their way through the crowd, lions unsettling the grazing beasts as they set up camp. Their leader sat at their centre, his blond hair perfectly smooth, piercing-blue eyes narrowed as his flunkies fed him cigarettes and joshed about with the cockiness of the school bully.

Alf.

'You all right, miss?' the GI asked.

'Just seen someone I know.'

'We can leave it there?' he said, spotting Alf making his way towards them through the parting crowd. 'I don't want to make trouble for you.'

'I can dance with whoever I like,' she said, but the spell was broken.

Alf stopped in front of the GI. 'Who gave you permission to dance with my bird?' he said.

The serviceman held his hands out. 'Hey, man. We were just dancing.'

Joan put her hands on her hips. 'I'll dance with whoever I like. And I ain't your bird.'

'Joanie, come on.' Alf took her hand. 'Sit with me and the boys.'

'Get off,' she said, pulling away as the house lights went up and the band slipped into a quiet instrumental number while the dancers stopped to watch the new entertainment.

'I don't think the young lady wants to come with you,' said the serviceman gently but firmly in his soft Jamaican voice. 'Why don't you leave her be?'

Alf took a step closer to the man. 'And why don't you get your hands off my girl?' he said, his fist moving so quickly that the GI never had time to see the punch that cracked his nose. The man dropped to his knees and Joan crouched next to him as women's screams cut across the band's attempts to keep playing.

'What d'you go and do that for, Alf?' Joan said, handing the GI a handkerchief.

'I was protecting you,' he said, adjusting the cuffs of his jacket.

'I don't need protecting. Go and protect your fiancée instead.'

'Baby,' he said, holding his hands out to her, his blue eyes softening in the way that always made Joan melt. 'Mum and her cousin in Wicklow set us up. I never even met Siobhan before she arrived. She was as unhappy about it as I was. Got herself back on the next boat.'

'I don't believe you,' she said, even though she wanted more than anything to believe him. He was her Alf, and she loved him. Despite that horribly accurate right hook.

'When have I ever lied to you, Joanie?'

'Only every time you open your mouth,' she snarled back.

'Joanie, we're meant for each other. You know it.'

'I know I never want to see you again,' she snapped, resisting the urge to jump into his arms.

As Alf took a step forward, she felt a hand on her shoulder. 'I think this conversation's over, don't you?' Cosmo said to Alf.

'What the hell, Joanie?' Alf said. 'You got them lined up?' He pointed at Cosmo. 'I don't take no orders from some posh boy.'

Joan pushed between them. 'Then take them from me, Alf. Clear off.'

She was suddenly blinded as the flash of a camera bulb exploded nearby. Bloody great: she'd thought she'd make the front page for being on the arm of Cosmo, not for starting a nightclub brawl. 'You can clear off, an' all,' she shouted at the photographer, poised for his next shot.

'Joanie . . .' Alf cajoled.

She glared at him, fighting her own smile. He had her, and he knew it, but she wasn't going to give in without making him work for it. 'I ain't your Joanie. And you make sure you give this fella some cash to get his uniform cleaned.'

Alf hesitated before dropping a pound note on the floor.

'Don't come sniffing around again, Alf Jackson. I'm not interested.'

'I don't believe you, Joan Carter.'

'You'd better.'

'I ain't giving up,' he said before calling to his men. 'Time to go, lads. Show's over.'

'Are you all right?' Cosmo asked as the lights dimmed once more.

'Better than this poor bugger with a broken nose,' Joan said. She turned to the soldier. 'Another dance?' she asked, but he shook his head, muttering about getting back to the base.

Cosmo laughed. 'I can see life is going to be rather more exciting with you around, Joan Carter.'

29

It was five thirty and Leonora should have been thinking about supper. Instead she found herself sitting with the latest copy of *Art World*, rereading a feature about the recent sale of a work by Breughel through Viner's. It was believed to be a preparatory sketch, long since lost, for the famous *Artist and Collector* drawing of 1604. And yet here it was, brought to Viner's by a private client and reaching a record price when subsequently sold at auction.

Not extraordinary in itself, for hadn't she herself handled forgotten works sourced from country-house sales or inheritance dispersals? And yet after a quarter of a century, she recalled Bruce telling her about a Breughel he had created for a private buyer of Edwin's in the mid-thirties. Was it too much of a coincidence to imagine that not only had Edwin bought Bruce's version of Breughel's *Artist and Collector* long before the war, but that the original had also turned up at Viner's? Yes, it bloody well was.

It seemed she had more immediate concerns, however, as Linda, first through the parlour door that evening, handed Leonora a newspaper she had picked up on the bus on the way home. 'You ought to see this, Mrs B,' she said. 'But don't say I said anything, will you? I don't want to get no one into trouble.'

'Linda, if there's something I need to know, it will find me soon enough,' Leonora sighed, waving the girl away and spreading the crumpled newspaper across her lap.

She soon realised that Linda had most definitely wanted to get someone into trouble. The *Daily Express* had excelled itself with a series of photographs of a blonde nightclub hostess and earl-in-waiting engaged in a messy Soho brawl involving a gangster and a broken-nosed GI. Nothing new under the sun, except that this nightclub hostess lived under Leonora's roof, and the earl-in-waiting happened to be the brother of that hostess's room-mate.

Had all this anything to do with the hundred red roses delivered for Joan by some scar-faced, bald-headed goon in a sharp black suit that morning? They were, at least, a lot easier to deal with than the kitten the same man had brought to the front door in a basket a few hours later, a large bow around its neck. It might not have had a return label attached, but Leonora had despatched both man and feline briskly. The last thing she needed was gangsters on her doorstep.

'Miss Carter?' she called out as she heard Joan arrive home.

'All right, Mrs B?' Joan said, poking her head around the door. 'Here. I brought you back some leftover profiteroles from work. None of the girls would touch them. Worried about their figures.' She bit her lip. 'Oh, I didn't mean . . .'

'Thank you, Joan,' she said tightly. 'Now sit down. I need a word.'

Joan sat up straight, hands pressed on her bare knees. 'It's not the rent, is it? I thought I'd paid a month in advance?'

'Perhaps you can explain this?' she said, passing the newspaper across. She watched as Joan flicked through, stopping as she reached the feature about the nightclub fight.

'I look rather good, don't you think?' she said, pointing to the shot of herself smiling outside the club. 'That white dress photographed really well.'

'Maybe. But really, Joan, scrapping with gangsters?'

'It was just a night out that got a bit silly. It won't happen again, I promise.'

Leonora was not convinced, however – she had to nip this in the bud. 'Joan, people talk. Neighbours talk.'

'Talk about what?' said a third voice.

They both turned, to see Margot in the doorway.

Joan smiled sheepishly. 'Got myself in trouble.' She held the paper out to Margot.

'Page seven,' Leonora added helpfully.

They waited as Margot found the page then looked up, her brown eyes wide. 'Joan, what have you done?'

Joan folded her arms. 'It wasn't my fault Alf took against that soldier. Alf's my old boyfriend,' she added helpfully.

'That's my brother,' Margot said, pointing to the mop-haired young man entering the Flamingo.

Joan took the paper from her. 'Cosmo's your brother? Why didn't you say?'

'How could I? I only knew you were stepping out with someone from Henry's.'

'He's a client at the nightclub?' Leonora slapped her palm across her forehead. 'Oh, Joan. Really. You know what people will say about you?'

Joan folded her arms. 'Henry's isn't that kind of club. And I ain't that kind of hostess.'

'I know that,' Leonora said, collapsing back into her chair, 'but the newspapers don't. "Showgirl" – that's what it says there. Yet another euphemism for we all know what.'

Joan stood up. 'That's not fair. I ain't done nothing wrong. We're just friends.' She looked at Margot. 'In case you hadn't noticed, he doesn't have too many of those. At least, not real friends. You've met those toffee-nosed hooligans he hangs around with?'

'Well, yes. But Joan . . . Ever since he was in that stupid film—'

'What stupid film?' Leonora asked.

Margot sighed. 'Some arthouse nonsense his friend made. It caused a stir for about two minutes because some poor woman took her clothes off and because Cosmo has a title. And now each time he scrapes his car or falls out of a pub drunk, the papers are all over him. He doesn't need this.'

'And neither do I,' Leonora said. 'Joan, keep your friend-ships more discreet, please. You've seen what's happening to those two girls who hung around with Profumo. It never ends well for the women, trust me.'

'I ain't no Mandy Rice-Davies,' Joan retorted.

'So let's not help people assume you are. Now go and pour me a gin and tonic. I don't care where the sun is in relation to the wretched yardarm.'

As Joan huffed her way out, Margot stood, pulling her bracelet-sleeved jacket back on. 'I need to see Cosmo.'

'Of course,' Leonora said, 'but before you go, I want to talk to you about something.' She took the magazine she had been examining before Linda dropped her bombshell. 'What do you know about this work?' she asked quietly, pointing to the Breughel drawing uncovered by Viner's.

Margot sat beside Leonora on the throw-covered sofa and took the magazine from her. '*Artist and Collector*? Sir Edwin sent it to auction a week or two ago.'

'Did you have a chance to see it?'

Margot nodded. 'Only briefly, but yes. It was beautiful. In good condition, bar a little watermarking. A museum in Vienna bought it.' She frowned. 'Why are you interested?'

Why indeed? But it was too soon to reveal her cards. 'The article here talks of an anonymous private seller. Do you happen to know who that might be?'

'Oh, I'm not sure I'm allowed to talk about that sort of thing.'

Leonora looked directly into Margot's deep-brown eyes. 'My dear, I promise I wouldn't ask you this if it weren't important.'

'Why? What does the Breughel have to do with you?'

'A great deal, I suspect.' More than just suspected: Leonora knew. 'Margot, where did Edwin Viner obtain that drawing?'

She watched as Margot bit her bottom lip, the playing out of her divided loyalties until the young woman looked Leonora directly in the eye. 'Please don't say anything to anyone. I could lose my job. As could the person who told me.'

'I promise,' Leonora said.

Margot sighed. 'The Breughel belonged to Sir Edwin, not a client. It was part of his own personal collection.'

'So why not just say so?'

'I don't know. This collection . . . well, it's kept in the basement. He calls it the Villa Clara collection.'

Leonora felt the blood drain from her face. She had not heard that name in twenty-five years, and now here was Margot, speaking of it in terms of Edwin's private art collection. 'Villa Clara,' she said quietly.

'You know what Villa Clara is?' Margot said.

Leonora nodded. 'Oh, I know all right.' How to describe

the place where she had rediscovered the love of her life, only to lose him once more? 'A mutual friend of Edwin's and mine lived there.'

'Oh. I assumed Sir Edwin had perhaps bought up an Italian collection on one of his visits.'

'You'd be not far off the mark, but perhaps not in the sense you imagine.'

Margot frowned. 'You told me that Sunday afternoon with Lyov that you'd known Edwin Viner a long time ago. What exactly is your history with him?'

Leonora sighed. There was no point hiding the truth any longer. 'I too worked for Sir Edwin, at Viner's. Before the war. Before . . . well, before Laurence was born.'

'But why didn't you tell me?'

Leonora hesitated. 'I didn't want to eclipse your success at getting the job at Viner's. One that will set you up for a stellar career, I'm sure.'

'Do you think so?'

'I know so. I see in you the fire and passion I had at your age. And in your case, I hope Sir Edwin will be a stepping stone rather than a drawbridge.'

'What do you mean?'

She sighed. 'Let us just say that life had alternative plans for me.'

'Oh. You mean Laurence? But could you not have gone back to work at Viner's after he was born?'

Leonora let out a bitter laugh. 'I think not.'

'Really?'

'I know Edwin rather too well, and I also know he's not entirely what he seems.'

'Now that I can believe.'

Leonora felt a flicker of hope that Margot might have seen past Edwin's veneer. 'What makes you say that?'

'Well, the turnover of female staff, for a start.'

She sighed. 'Still?'

Margot nodded. 'We travel in pairs when he's around. And the secrecy – there are some transactions only Ursula Knight is party to.'

'Deadly Knightshade? Good Lord. She's still there?'

Margot laughed. 'That is the best nickname.'

Leonora narrowed her eyes. 'So . . . what is this Villa Clara collection?'

'They're drawings locked in a cupboard in the storeroom,' Margot said. 'Only Sir Edwin knows what's in there. In fact, only he has the key.'

'I bet he does,' Leonora said quietly.

'Mrs Birch, is there anything I should be aware of?'

She took Margot's hands. 'I can trust you, can't I?'

'Of course.'

'Very well. I strongly suspect Edwin is playing the art market for a fool, and at the expense of a friend of mine. I would never ordinarily ask you to go behind your employer's back, but if anything – and I mean *anything* – comes up for sale from the Villa Clara collection, I need you to tell me.'

'Tell you about what?' Joan said, appearing with a tray with three gins.

'Margot must tell me if she catches you behaving in such a manner as to bring this establishment into disrepute.'

'You do talk posh sometimes, Mrs B.' She placed the tinkling glasses on a coffee table. 'I promise I'll live like a church mouse from now on.' She tilted her head, listening as the front door banged closed. 'Speaking of which, that sounds like Pillory back from work.'

Margot cuffed her. 'Hillary is only ever nice about you.'

'Because she's desperate for me to give her a makeover,' Joan said. 'Difficult when she never takes that duffel coat off, though.'

'Joan,' Leonora snapped. 'That's enough.' She knew Joan was frightened of being left behind by Margot and Hillary's friendship, but this was becoming tedious.

'I was kidding. Just wish I were clever too.'

'You're perfectly clever, Joan,' Leonora said. 'Just lacking in common sense sometimes.'

They all looked up as Hillary poked her head around the door. 'Come and join us,' Leonora said.

'Righto.' Hillary unwrapped her striped university scarf from around her neck and perched on the arm of the sofa, a safe distance from Joan. 'Mrs Birch,' she said, 'I think I might have news for your friend Lyov.'

Leonora clapped her hands together. 'Oh, that's marvellous.'

'Tell him to be at the Regency Café on Friday morning at ten – a contact of mine will be there with information about his sister.' She hesitated.

'But?' Leonora said.

'If this contact were seen to meet Lyov alone, people might jump to conclusions.'

'Your colleague can't have breakfast without a Cabinet meeting being called?'

'Breakfast with a Russian?' Hillary said, eyebrows raised.

'But if the café were busy, and he had to share a table with a couple of people already there together . . .'

Leonora nodded. 'I see. In which case, I will be there with Lyov.'

'Are you sure?' Hillary asked.

Leonora was not sure – the whole thing seemed a little dangerous – but Lyov was her friend. She would do this for him. And in the meantime, it seemed the net was finally closing on Edwin Viner.

30

'Sorry, Marge,' Joan said, plucking the lemon from her drink. 'I really didn't know he's your brother.'

'I believe you.' Margot sighed, leaning back to let the pub landlord run a sopping-wet cloth across their table. Now she'd got over the shock of seeing Cosmo's face plastered across the popular press, she couldn't be angry. Joan probably was good for him.

'Anyway, Cosmo introduced me to this bloke – he's in films. Wants me to go to his office for a chat.'

'Does he now?' Margot raised an eyebrow, all too familiar with Cosmo's crowd, who flitted from producing films and driving fast cars to getting drunk with Lord Snowdon.

'Probably come to nothing.' Joan looked away, pretending to watch a card game about to blow up a few tables away.

'You won't know unless you find out.' Margot smiled. 'Perhaps I could come with you? Don't want anyone taking advantage of you.'

Joan laughed. 'I'd like to see them try.'

Given the newspaper photographs, perhaps Joan could indeed look after herself. 'What did happen at the Flamingo?' she asked.

Joan shrugged. 'I just danced with this GI. Nice bloke, great dancer. No one cares who you are or what colour you are at the Flamingo. That's why I like it.'

Margot shuddered as she recalled the time that Joan had taken her to the packed, marijuana-infused basement, imagining that any moment the police might raid it. No wonder Cosmo had been drawn there.

'It was just wrong place, wrong night. Alf always was protective.' Joan looked up, her cheeks colouring slightly to match her rose-pink bouclé dress and matching satin headband. 'I know you think he's bad news – a spiv, gangster, everything my mum called him.'

'I know I think you're not over him.'

She nodded. 'Oh Marge,' she said, pulling out a packet of cigarettes. 'I can't stop thinking about him.'

'But he's with someone else.'

'That's just it. He says he's not. Why would he send me all those roses, otherwise?'

Margot and Joan had begged as many jugs and coffee pots and vases as Leonora owned, just to house the things, which now graced every room in Ludlow Gardens. Shallow gesture or heartfelt plea? Margot was not convinced. 'And you believe him?'

'His mum and her cousin in Ireland set it up.' Joan blew a plume of smoke towards the nicotine-stained ceiling. 'And now it's off. He wants me back.'

'And you want him?'

'Maybe. But he needn't think I'll come running,' she said, a faint smile on her lips. 'So what about you? Any eligible bachelors in the picture?'

'Definitely not. I want to focus on my work. It's the first time in my life I'm doing what I really want.'

'I can see you with your own gallery one day: "Stockton Fine Art".'

Margot laughed. 'I don't know about that.'

Joan leaned closer across the table. 'Here, didn't you say Mrs Birch worked for Viner's back in the day?'

'Apparently. But there's no love lost there, as far as I can tell.'

'What's he like, then, your boss?'

'Sir Edwin? Bit of a creep but an undoubted expert in his field. I went to school with his daughter, Diana. In fact, there's a party at their place in Oxfordshire next weekend. Cosmo is going too.'

'I'll see you there, once I've bought myself a swimsuit. Cosmo invited me. Said they wouldn't mind.' She frowned. 'Think it'll be all right?'

'It'll be a relief to have you there – they're a stuffy bunch, apart from Diana.'

'And your boss won't mind me gate-crashing?'

Margot glanced at Joan's long bare legs, the twinkly blue eyes. 'I'm afraid he'll be only too delighted. Diana, however, might be less than thrilled. She's had a crush on my brother since we were children. It's all rather embarrassing, and Cos isn't remotely interested.'

Joan stubbed out her cigarette in the overflowing glass ash-tray. 'Should make for an interesting weekend, then.' She lifted her head, looking across the sea of heads at two newcomers pushing towards the bar. 'Talking of interesting, here's young Mr Birch. Reckon we can persuade him to buy us a drink?'

Margot followed Joan's gaze. 'Oh no,' she said, her heart

sinking at the thought of another sparring match. 'I don't think he'd want to sit with us.'

'Maybe not with me.' Joan winked. 'I should clear off and leave you two to it.'

'What are you talking about?'

'Oh, come on, Marge. The way you two bicker, you might as well just have done with it and hook up.'

'Don't be ridiculous. That man is a pompous idiot.'

'Only because he likes you and he's scared to let it show.' She leaned forward. 'And I've seen the way you look at him when you think he's not looking.'

Margot felt herself bristle. 'Joan, honestly. Let's just finish these and head back. I've got an early start tomorrow.'

But Joan had already shimmied through the crowd and was tapping Laurence on the shoulder. From his expression, he was even less keen for an encounter than Margot, but she painted on a smile as Joan dragged the two men to the table with a fresh round of drinks, Joan sitting beside Andrei, so that Laurence was forced to squash next to Margot.

As Andrei began relating some story of the Cecil Court shop and a would-be seller who had claimed a sketch clearly done by a three-year-old on cartridge paper was a genuine Picasso – 'there was even a jammy fingerprint in the corner!' he laughed – Margot tried to rid herself of Joan's words. Of course she and Laurence didn't like one another – quite the opposite, in fact. As though to prove the point, she tried not to breathe in the scent of his hair oil, horribly aware of the bare flesh of her arm as it accidentally brushed his shirtsleeve.

Andrei and Joan began laughing at a private joke, and Margot and Laurence were forced either to sit in silence or attempt conversation. 'Good day at work?' Margot said, as he asked the identical question. There was a moment when she thought he might laugh, but the steel-grey eyes looked away almost immediately.

'So,' she tried again, 'how was work?'

'I'm not sure my line of journalism is really your thing,' Laurence said.

'You might be surprised.'

He raised one eyebrow and took a long sip from his pint. 'I doubt it. My newspaper challenges what you might describe as your lot.'

'My lot?'

'The titled classes who sit in the House of Lords and pass laws for people whose lives they can't even imagine. Who care more about their horses than their staff and want things to stay exactly as they are.'

'You think I'm like that?'

'Your father's an earl, isn't he?'

'How do you know?'

He shrugged. 'It's my job.'

'What, to spy on me?'

'I care who lives in my mother's house, you know?' he said. 'And you might be having a splendid time now, but you'll be off as soon as you're bored. Like . . . I don't know . . . Marie Antoinette with her toy farm.'

'You really are a rude man,' Margot retorted, stung by his words. 'You've looked me up in *Debrett's* and think you know it all.'

'I know you only got your job because you played polo or went skiing or whatever with the boss's daughter.'

'And you got your job because you were lucky enough to have an education, to have a parent prepared to make sacrifices so that you could be whatever you wanted.'

'I got my job through hard work. Not Daddy's connections.'

'For your information, I got the job because I know what I'm talking about. And not because I went to a fancy university – education is wasted on girls, don't you know? I had to educate myself. And,' she said, aware that Joan and Andrei had stopped talking, 'I'm good at what I do.'

'This is true,' Andrei said, nodding. 'She has spent many hours with my father, going through his library. Picking his brain.'

'And she's out at galleries every weekend,' Joan chipped in.

Margot sensed she had the edge on Laurence as he looked away, twisting his beer glass between the palms of his hands. 'I want to earn my place in this world,' she said, 'which is a damn sight harder for a woman. Ask your mother.'

He looked at her. 'You don't know anything about my mother.'

Joan chuckled. 'I know she runs around after you, Laurence Birch. Bringing your washing for her to do, at your age?'

Laurence frowned. 'I work long hours. There's not always time to do it myself.'

'Or to cook your own dinners in that flat you two share?'

Andrei held his hands out. 'Leonora likes to look after us.'

'Does she really?' Margot said. 'Leonora Birch is a highly intelligent woman with better things to do than wash your underpants.'

'She was also a fine artist in her day,' Andrei threw in.

'With a career at Viner's,' Margot added.

'And do you know why she had to leave?' Laurence asked her. 'What Viner, this family friend of yours, did to her?'

Joan sat back and lit another cigarette, taking a puff before folding her arms. 'Reckon that's something we could try to find out at his house party.'

Laurence frowned. 'What party?'

'We're going to Viner's place for the weekend,' Joan explained.

'To Charlwood?' Laurence said. 'You wouldn't catch me within a mile of the place. Or that man.'

'You really do hate him, don't you?' Margot said. 'What did he ever do to you?'

Laurence stared at her. 'You really have no idea who you're working for, do you?'

Joan leaned closer over the table. 'So why don't you tell us, Laurence?'

Andrei shrugged. 'Yes, why not? I know – my father knows.'

Laurence scowled. 'Maybe. But it's not my secret to tell.'

'Then whose?' Joan pressed.

Margot watched Laurence hesitate, catching once more that peculiar familiarity about his features, the high forehead and deep-set grey eyes so unlike Leonora's. Until now she'd struggled to place this whisper of Laurence's paternal gene pool, but the truth suddenly struck her. No wonder Leonora's career had been cut short; no wonder she could barely speak Sir Edwin's name; no wonder Laurence was angry at a social class that closed ranks to protect itself.

She recalled Leonora's interest in the Villa Clara collection, and the suggestion that an old friend had been exploited. She thought of the locked cabinet in the Viner's basement and the trickle of Old Masters that appeared from within it. Maybe Leonora had not just been sitting in quiet defeat for all these years, but awaiting the opportunity to right old wrongs.

She glanced at Laurence now, but instead of seeing a prickly bore, she recognised the fatherless boy who had fought to prove himself. 'Everyone has a right to their secrets,' she said. 'And if Laurence wants to protect someone else's – well, I say good for him. I'll buy him a pint to prove it.'

He stared back at her, questioning whether she was teasing him. Their eyes locked for just long enough for Margot to feel the horror of an unwelcome blush, and she looked quickly away.

'A pint of champagne, in that case,' he said, as the whole table cheered the truce.

A light drizzle speckled in the glow of streetlamps as the four of them left the pub and Andrei shared his raincoat with Joan. Margot and Laurence fell into step behind them.

'You know he doesn't stand a chance with her?' Margot said. 'She's still in love with her old boyfriend.'

'That won't stop Andrei from trying.'

'Can't blame him. Joan is irresistible.'

'Not to me,' Laurence said. 'I mean, I like Joan, but . . .' He faltered into uncomfortable silence.

'Not your type?'

'Something like that.' Suddenly Laurence grabbed her arm, pulling her back violently as a black Morris 1100 veered a little too close to them. 'Thought he was going to ride the pavement there. Are you all right?'

Margot put her hand to her chest. 'Just a bit shocked.' She laughed. 'Will you lose your job for saving an aristocrat?'

He groaned. 'I really am a pig. I shouldn't have talked to you like that.'

'I probably goaded you,' Margot replied, aware of his hand still on her arm, his grip strong through the sleeve of her linen coat.

'Mum is a good judge of character, and she's very fond of you. Maybe it's time I put aside the class war.'

'For your mother?'

He half smiled. 'Can we start again? Go back to the bit before I called you . . .'

'Marie Antoinette?' Margot looked at him, seeing an awkward shyness instead of the usual antagonism.

'Touché,' he laughed. 'So how about it? No guillotines, just friends?'

They stood facing one another. 'Friends. I'd like that.'

31

It wasn't often that Leonora made it to the bustle of the West End, let alone the pavement opposite the gallery that had once been her place of work, but after her frank conversation with Margot, she needed to confirm with her own eyes what she already suspected.

Once Margot had worked out why Leonora left Viner's in 1939, there was no point holding back, and so she had told her young lodger everything: the theft of the Vermeer, the pregnancy and subsequent firing from her job, her broken engagement to Bruce, and the birth of her baby. Most importantly, she told Margot her suspicions about the Villa Clara collection, some of which she feared she had brought from Italy in her very own suitcase in 1939.

Soon after, Margot informed Leonora that a Rembrandt sketch of a reclining woman had gone up for sale, apparently on behalf of a French artist on his uppers. It was almost certainly a drawing of Rembrandt's mistress Hendrickje Stoffels, similar to one belonging to the British Museum. According to one of the porters at Viner's, it had in fact come from the Villa Clara collection. It seemed Edwin was having a clear-out.

From her vantage point, Leonora pretended to consult an *A to Z* whilst she waited to see if Margot, away on a consultation with Ursula Knight, was right and Edwin still left the gallery at 1.15 sharp each day for lunch at his club. Even though she was braced, it was a shock when he appeared. Carnation in buttonhole, long limbs striding in his Savile Row pinstripes, his oiled blond hair now grey and equine features irritatingly distinguished, he waited briefly for a break in the flow of shoppers before marching away.

Leonora crossed the road, pausing outside Viner's window, where a small, gilt-framed pastoral scene was discreetly displayed – a Fragonard, if she was not mistaken. Come on, Leonora, she told herself. Stop delaying. And with a final pat of her grey hair, she pushed the heavy glass door open.

The gallery floor was empty, other than for a young woman sitting at – or rather with her feet up on – her desk. 'Yes?' said the long-legged receptionist without dragging her eyes away from her magazine.

Where on earth was Edwin finding his staff these days, Leonora wondered, until the woman finally looked up, and Leonora found herself stared at by a pair of grey eyes almost identical to Laurence's, striking against the woman's raven-black beehive. This had to be the daughter, Diana, who had inherited not only her father's looks, but his ability to look at one as though there were a piece of rotten meat beneath his nose. Although she had seen Edwin's high brow and long nose in Laurence over the years, they were tempered by her late father's warm smile.

She chose to ignore the head-to-toe examination of her ancient suit, once a staple of her working wardrobe at Viner's. Even with the skirt taken up to the knee, it looked like something out of the dressing-up box compared to Diana's ruby-red shift with its matching nails and lips. Leonora pulled herself a little straighter. 'You have a Rembrandt drawing, I believe. Is it on display?'

'We only encourage potential buyers to browse,' Diana drawled, pulling a cigarette from her handbag and lighting it, so that Leonora had to bite her lip rather than tell the girl not to smoke in front of the artworks. She had no idea how this woman and Margot had become friends.

'How do you know my handbag is not stuffed full of twenty-pound notes ready to exchange for a rare drawing for my collection?' She watched the girl assess her, wondering how much hot water she might be in if she turned away a sale.

'Fine,' Diana Viner said, tilting her head towards a discreet corner of the gallery, almost an anteroom, where Leonora remembered bringing buyers desirous of privacy.

'Can you tell me anything about the work?' Leonora said.

Diana shrugged and handed her a small catalogue bearing the Viner's logo. 'It's in there somewhere. Ink on paper, I think – or maybe pencil – circa 16 . . . something.'

Leonora thanked her and made her way across the thick-carpeted gallery, keeping half an eye on the front door in case Edwin appeared.

The sketch was no larger than ten by eight inches, and yet in that small space and with such economy of line, the artist had created a scene of intense domesticity and intimacy, a pregnant woman taking a moment to close her eyes in her favourite chair. How could a few sparse lines of brown wash indicate the rosy glow of a cheek, the soft contours of a young figure? By the sheer artistry of the hand that had created them.

She let her mind drift back to where she had seen the drawing before, propped on an easel in an ancient watchtower in

Tuscany before being packed into her own suitcase; a commission for a private client, never to be sold as anything else. How dare Edwin treat Bruce like this, knowing he had no interest in the London art scene and would never discover the deception?

She dropped the catalogue on the desk. 'I have seen everything I need, thank you.'

'And will you be visiting us again?' Diana said, a thin smile on her face.

Leonora stared back at her. 'I certainly will.'

She barely heard the car horn blasting at her as she stepped out into the street, busy composing the letter she would write as soon as she got home. 'My dearest Bruce,' she tried out in her head as she marched towards the Tube station. No, too intimate: Bruce was married, and one did not address other women's husbands thus. 'My dear Bruce.' Yes, that was better. Formal, yet acknowledging their history. She quickened her step, her rage turning into something more constructive. Edwin Viner had better watch his back: Leonora was right behind him.

32

London, October 1989

The jam of courier bicycles and delivery vans, the office workers rushing for the Underground station at nearby Oxford Circus, all melted away as Phoebe turned off Wigmore Street, redbrick villas quickly replaced by the cobbled streets that had once housed their carriages.

Marlborough Mews was a peaceful oasis, the one-time stable doors punctuated by huge terracotta pots of lollipop-shaped olive trees. The only sound to break through the distant hum of traffic was a Simply Red album wafting from an open window, one James had bought for her birthday the previous year – hurrah, she muttered to herself. She was far from in the mood, after a gruelling afternoon with the accountant, but she would humour Bruce. Five minutes – ten at most – and she could get home and lose herself in a long bath and a good book. Besides, Stefano had asked her to report back that evening.

She spotted the elegant metal staircase leading to number 13, the flat above a black-painted garage door, a silver classic Jaguar E-Type parked outside, and it was a slim, fresh-from-the-shower gentleman who answered the door to her, a male version of Margot without the polished edges.

'Miss Cato! Sorry everything's a mess,' Cosmo said, indicating piles of dry-cleaning bags and unopened post. 'The help's away for a fortnight, and I clearly can't look after myself.' He frowned at Phoebe, his dark eyes twinkling. 'Would it be rude to drag her back from a family holiday, just to put my food shopping away?'

'You'd be advertising in *The Lady* next week if you did.' She glanced at the Selfridges Food Hall bags piled on the kitchen table, visible through a glass dividing wall. 'Maybe find the fridge instead?'

'Good plan, good plan.' He looked at his watch. 'Aperitif hour. Join me for a G and T? Well, T and T in my case. The G is only for guests these days.'

'Thanks, that would be great.' After all, she had time for a drink, didn't she? It would be rude to dash away too quickly, and now she had met him, she was intrigued to get to know Margot's brother a little better.

He fetched two tumblers, then dug around for tonic and ice. 'Don't know about you, but I'm peckish. Why don't you see what you can rustle up from that shopping?' He pointed with his foot towards a cupboard. 'Crockery in there. Stick it all on the coffee table.'

She was ravenous, she realised, and gratefully pulled smoked salmon and cold venison pie from one of the bags, plating them up with creamy French cheese and fresh figs. She really did need to up her game from cereal and tinned soup.

'Chin chin,' Cosmo said eventually, sitting opposite her in a vintage teak armchair straight from an interiors magazine. The whole apartment screamed taste and money, beautifully crafted mid-century pieces sitting alongside Chippendale treasures, and looked down upon by at least one Picasso, a Dame Laura Knight and a Henry Moore sketch. A framed poster for an obscure sixties arthouse film hung above the fireplace, and recognising his face on it, Phoebe recalled Cosmo's brief career as a movie actor.

'All twentieth-century art,' he said. 'The antique stuff went in the auction when the house was sold. Blythmere,' he explained when she didn't respond. 'Fine old Georgian pile built by the first earl, now a luxury hotel and golf club.'

'I'm sorry.'

'Don't be. It was in a terrible state – even if I hadn't cleared out the bank accounts, there wouldn't have been enough in the coffers to keep the roof on. Besides, it had bad memories.' He hesitated. 'We had an older brother, Margot and I,' he explained. 'Riding accident when he was eighteen.'

'That's dreadful,' Phoebe said, spotting a lifetime of coming to terms with grief.

He leaned forward, helping himself to a forkful of salmon. 'You can say that again. No wonder I went off the rails. Sis dealt with it all rather more politely – just didn't eat for about five years. Oh, and got herself nicely expelled from the fold when she did a runner from her wedding and joined the commoners.' He smiled. 'Quite the scandal in its day.'

Phoebe laughed. 'Margot jilted someone at the altar?'

He narrowed his handsome, crinkly blue eyes and waved his fork at her. 'Doesn't mention that on the *South Bank Show*, does she? It's how she met our Mrs Birch, however, so it all worked out in the end. But,' he added mysteriously, 'what exactly is the end?'

'Now you sound like Bruce!' she said.

'I shall take that as a compliment. So, what do you know so far?'

'Well, I know about Leonora Birch and the affair with Edwin Viner, the lost Vermeer, your sister moving to Ludlow Gardens . . .'

'And the Villa Clara collection?' He sat back, crossing his legs and jiggling one of his Moroccan slippers on the end of his toe.

'Villa Clara is the name of Bruce's home in Italy,' Phoebe said, confused.

'Exactly.'

'But I've never heard of any collection. What kind of collection?'

'That, my dear, is for you to find out.' Cosmo stood. 'Come with me.'

'Really? I ought to be getting back . . .'

'This won't take long.'

Phoebe could see there was no escaping, and so she followed him into a bedroom crammed with antique furniture, photograph albums, battered wooden nursery toys.

'Last of the salvaged goods from Blythmere,' he explained. 'I keep asking Margot to come and help me sort through, but she's always too busy.'

'What does this have to do with me?'

He nodded towards a pile of boxes stuffed with art books. 'From the Blythmere library. Margot insisted on hanging on to them.' He smiled. 'There may also, if you know what you're looking for, be something from a little further afield.'

'Cosmo, I'm not really sure I have time for games . . . even Bruce's. I have a ton of paperwork to get back to.' And, most importantly, her weekly phone chat with Stefano.

'I refuse to let you go home without a coffee, so you may as well browse those books while I make it?'

She smiled. 'Fine. And sorry to sound churlish. It's enough trying to get my head around losing Bruce, without him popping up everywhere.'

'You never know. Doing this might help you? Saying goodbye is a long process, trust me.'

'Thank you.' It struck Phoebe that maybe he was right: for Bruce simply to disappear felt wrong. This connection, although painful, at least kept him a little alive whilst she acclimatised to the new, Bruce-free world.

He winked. 'And don't forget: Villa Clara.'

As Cosmo left, she pulled one of the boxes of books across and sat on the floor. It was an impressive collection, alphabetised by the boxload, but Phoebe had no time to do more than flick quickly through each and discard it, focusing on artists Bruce had particularly loved, or who had worked in Tuscany – da Vinci? Nothing. Donatello? Giotto? No and no again.

What was Cosmo trying to tell her? She kept going, until she reached the box of books about artists from M–P. Villa Clara . . . Think like Bruce . . . And then she knew. She dug through the box, hoping her instincts were right, until she found a book about a seventeenth-century Flemish artist, a rare professional female working in a man's world, who predated Vermeer with her intricate still lifes commissioned by wealthy patrons: *The Life and Works of Clara Peeters*. She opened the book, to see

Villa Clara inscribed on the inside in Bruce's handwriting. A Villa Clara clue hidden in a book about a Clara.

Something had been placed between the pages, and she opened them to find a small, unframed canvas. '*Girl at a Desk*,' she said quietly, pulling it out carefully and dislodging a tissue-thin airmail envelope addressed to Villa Clara.

'*My dear Bruce*,' she read out loud, '*it has come to my attention that some of the drawings I brought back from Villa Clara in 1939 have come up for sale at Viner's, advertised as originals. Please advise how you would like me to proceed.*' Phoebe looked closely, seeing that '*Always yours*' had been replaced by a simple '*Regards, Leonora Birch*'.

'Now do you see?' Cosmo asked, standing in the doorway.

'Viner kept Bruce's copies and passed them off as authentic?' Phoebe had never particularly liked Edwin Viner, but he didn't strike her as an out-and-out crook. 'But his is one of the most respected galleries in London.'

'Was. It's going down the pan now the daughter has taken over – Diana is no more capable of running a business than an egg-and-spoon race. Anyway, Mrs Birch cottoned on. And when Margot was invited to a weekend party at Charlwood, Viner's Oxfordshire home, it seemed the perfect opportunity to find out more.'

'So what did happen at Charlwood?' Phoebe asked.

He smiled. 'Look closer at the painting.'

In this latest version, the painting within a painting depicted Breughel's famous *Artist and Collector*, and the candle on the desk had burned a little lower. As she looked closer, she realised the woman's pen was not now poised over a letter, but something quite different. She burst out laughing.

Cosmo peered over her shoulder. 'Our lovely Vermeer girl, about to read a *TV Times* from 1968,' he chuckled. 'And see who's on the front cover.'

'Who is that?' Phoebe asked, as she looked at the image of a bubbly blonde actress.

'Come on, Miss Cato, everyone knows Joan Carter. Where were you in the seventies when she was on every TV quiz show and sitcom? National treasure, our Joanie.'

Of course Phoebe had heard of Joan Carter – who hadn't? 'But what did she have to do with Margot and Leonora?'

'Believe it or not,' he said, 'she and Margot were room-mates at Ludlow Gardens. Joan and I became friends too.'

'Anything more . . .?' Phoebe asked delicately.

Cosmo laughed. 'Not a chance. She'd have eaten me for breakfast. Besides, she had a rather terrifying boyfriend. One did not mess with East End gangsters in those days.'

Phoebe smiled. 'I'm still staggered at Margot Stockton and Joan Carter being friends.'

'Opposites attract, I suppose. And it did Margot good to lighten up. She can be a frightful bore, given the chance.' He shook his head. 'Your uncle and I – we had some memorable nights out when he was over here in the early sixties. Did he ever mention how he got kicked out of a Mayfair nightclub with Sean Connery? Let me give you some advice: never get into a whisky-drinking competition with a Scot.'

'That sounds exactly like my uncle!' How good it was, she realised, to hear first-hand from someone who had known Bruce back in the day, adding flesh to bones she had thought she knew so well.

'I'm not sure Joan was that impressed. She nearly lost her job over it.'

'What was Joan's line of work?'

'Best hostess at Henrietta's House. Good thing Mother never met her – she'd have been furious.' He went across to a spindle-legged marquetry desk, rummaging in a drawer. 'Here,' he said, handing her a yellowed sheet of folded newspaper. 'What one might expect on a night out with Joan Carter in 1963.'

Phoebe opened the paper to reveal a double-page spread of photographs of a younger, achingly handsome Cosmo entering a Soho nightclub with Joan Carter on his arm, before the night degenerated into a brawl. 'I don't quite see what Joan Carter has to do with my uncle, though?'

'Joan Carter has everything to do with your uncle. I took Joan with me to Charlwood House in August sixty-three. Margot was there too. Leonora had asked her to keep an eye out for anything suspicious.'

'Items from the Villa Clara collection?' Phoebe asked. The Swinging Sixties, a nightclub hostess, a country estate and a whiff of unscrupulous dealing – even in Phoebe's current state of mind, it was impossible not to be curious.

'Possibly. I'm afraid I was more interested in drinking the bar dry that weekend than in researching dodgy artworks.'

'And did Margot uncover anything?'

'Margot would make a terrible spy. Skittish as a racehorse when under pressure. Our Joanie, however,' he added, 'was a different kettle of fish.' He smiled. 'You should meet her.'

Phoebe sighed. 'How did I guess you would say that?'

'Topolino.'

'Hey, Stefano,' Phoebe said later that evening, glad he couldn't see her frayed but favourite pyjama bottoms and stained Live Aid T-shirt. 'How's things at the Villa?'

'You know . . . the fig trees are bursting with fruit, the evenings are cooler, the olives nearly ready to harvest.'

She sighed. 'It sounds idyllic.'

'Then come and see for yourself.'

'I wish I could . . . there's so much to do here,' she said, picking at a loose thread on the sofa arm.

'How was the meeting with the bank?'

'On a scale of OK to catastrophic, it probably came in at a safe dreadful. I think I can kiss goodbye to the prospect of a loan.'

'I'm so sorry,' he said. 'I wish I could give you a hug right now.'

She smiled. 'I wish you could too.' As long as she could put something decent on and sort out her hair. Except that it was Stefano – it didn't matter, and he didn't care what she looked like. 'But hey, something interesting did happen today,' she said, then went on to tell him about meeting Cosmo, and the Joan Carter connection.

'I have no idea who you're talking about,' Stefano said, confused as ever by British culture. 'Are you going to meet her?'

'I don't know. She lives in Spain. Marbella, I think.'

'Spain isn't so far.'

'It is when the bank account is empty.'

'Come on, Phoebe. This is the first time I've heard you excited about anything for a long time. You should go. Bruce obviously wants you to. Besides, aren't you curious to see what she has to say?'

'I suppose so.'

'What if I lend you the money?'

'Oh, Stefano. I couldn't let you.'

'Nonsense. I want to. You can pay me back when probate comes through and you're swimming in cash.'

'What? Really?'

He laughed. 'No. But please, let me. For Bruce.'

'I don't know . . .'

'You can thank me by coming to visit on your way back.'

'Since when was Italy on the way back from Spain?' she laughed.

'Seriously. Have a couple of days in Spain, and I'll stand you the extra flight to Florence. It would be good to see you, and there's stuff here we need to sort out before winter.'

It was tempting, for sure. She hated this time of year in London, when the nights started getting darker. 'I suppose I could do with collecting Bruce's notebooks. See if I can identify the drawings that went through Viner's.'

'There you are. Sorted. I'll wire you some money over, and you let me know dates. And Phoebe . . .?'

'Yes?'

There was a pause, in which she could picture him frowning. 'I've missed you.'

She felt a smile stretch across her face. 'I've missed you too.'

33

Spain, 1989

With autumn chasing its tail, summer clung on ferociously as Phoebe watched the scrubby jacaranda trees and cacti rush past, dust kicked up by the taxi as it climbed the hills set back from the shimmering Spanish coast. Ever since the sixties the Costa del Crime had been a magnet to international police-dodgers taking advantage of a loophole to evade arrest in the UK and become lost amongst the dense tourist population in high-rise beach resorts. Phoebe paid the driver and climbed out on to the oven-hot gravel track, glad she had packed sundresses and sandals. She headed towards the entrance of the Villa Aphrodite, where plaster statues of its eponymous goddess stood guard atop the gates punched into a high-security wall.

Within minutes she had been buzzed in and escorted by the housemaid through a Spanish-style ranch house, its several hundred square feet of open-plan living space dotted with white leather sofas and fur rugs, the only furnishings that hadn't been gold plated to within an inch of their lives. She shielded her eyes as they headed through huge glass doors to a patio area with its own raffia-fringed cocktail bar and jacuzzi. Beyond a pool littered with lilos, sprinklers fed a constant stream of water across a green lawn, overlooked by a legion of Greek statues straight from the Argos catalogue outdoor-sculpture section.

'Over here, love,' a voice called out, and as Phoebe's eyes adjusted to the bright sunlight, she saw a deeply tanned woman waving from a sunlounger, her face obscured by a wide straw hat.

'Joan?' But of course it had to be: who else would lie beside a pool in full make-up and jewellery, a pair of gold high-heeled sandals complementing her plunging leopard-print swimsuit?

'Pleased to meet you, Phoebe Cato.' She took off her black sunglasses, light catching her shocking-pink nail polish and the diamonds clustered on her fingers. 'You look like you could do with a swim, my girl. How about you get your cossie on, and once you've had a cocktail and cooled off, we'll have a chat, eh?'

It felt ridiculously indulgent, especially since hearing from Tilly that the only visitors to the museum that day were a Canadian couple who had got lost on their way to the Tube. Their promise to tell friends in Ontario how much they enjoyed the Cato was sweet, but unlikely to yield the visitor numbers needed to pay next month's bills. However, as Phoebe plunged through the dappled surface of the water a few minutes later, with every stroke she felt the weight of the museum and of the crumbling Tuscan estate melt away.

'You look a different person already,' Joan said as Phoebe dried herself off.

'I just need my own swimming pool in London, and I'll be sorted,' she laughed, sitting on a lounger beside Joan.

'Surely you have one at Villa Clara?'

Phoebe rubbed her hair with the towel. 'No pool. Barely any decent plumbing.'

Joan looked horrified. 'What's the point of your own Tuscan villa if it doesn't have a pool?'

'That's the least of the problems at Villa Clara. It needs a new roof and complete rewiring before I can even think about anything else.'

'You got the budget for all that?'

'Nope.'

'Hm. Got yourself a bit of a white elephant there, my girl.'

'Tell me about it.'

'So what you going to do? Sell it?'

It sounded so sensible from Joan's lips, but her heart kicked in protest. 'I don't know that I could. It meant everything to Bruce. And to the people who live there.'

'Listen, darling, I know a dead duck when I see one. And I know when to cut my losses.'

'It's not that simple . . .'

'But you've got your museum too. Planning on keeping both going?' Joan sighed. 'Never mind me. It's your life. Your business. You'll know what's best, when the time comes.'

'I hope so.'

'Anyway, you didn't come over here to tell me all about your troubles.'

'Well, no . . .'

Joan rang a little bell, waiting for the housekeeper to appear. 'Two pina coladas, I reckon,' Joan whispered to Phoebe. 'Should loosen the tongue nicely.'

34

Oxfordshire, August 1963

Margot tightened her silk scarf around her chin, determined her blow-dry would last at least until she jumped into the Charlwood pool, a necessary antidote to the scorching sun and the dust kicked up by the Jaguar under Cosmo's erratic hands.

'All right, Marge?' Joan shouted to her from the front seat, one hand holding her sunglasses in place, her blonde hair whipping across her face.

'Just splendid,' she replied, looking out at the avenue of wispy silver birch she knew almost as well as the old game of avoiding being left alone with Sir Edwin in any of the many rooms at Charlwood. It felt like sweet justice that she was now planning her own unguided tour of the house. If there were anything suspect hanging on the walls of Charlwood, she would find it, and report straight back to Mrs Birch. She wondered whether she should have told Joan what was going on, but for the time being, she would play her cards close. Joan might prove a handy extra weapon later on, if she needed one.

Finally, the elegant Queen Anne house came into view, its graceful redbrick façade punctuated by tall, leaded windows and balanced by a deeply sloping roof from which dormer windows peeped. As they pulled up, Labradors scattered in a shower of gravel, and judging by the shrieking from the pool beyond a tall yew hedge, the party had well and truly started. Diana skipped down the front steps to greet them, her expression turning thunderous as Cosmo opened the passenger door.

Joan dropped her small suitcase at Diana's feet. 'You must be the housekeeper,' she said, running her eye along Diana's slim black dress. 'Stick that in my room, would you, love?'

'Look at that dreadful girl,' Diana said from her sunlounger, tipping her sunglasses to get a better view of Joan, who was squealing as Cosmo piggybacked her across the pool in a race against two other couples. 'How do you bear it? She has a voice like fingernails down a blackboard.'

'I rather like her, actually,' Margot replied, sitting up to take a sip of the gin and tonic brought to them by the ever-patient butler, a pushover when it came to Miss Diana. Not as much as the previous gardener had been, Margot recalled, spotting Henson's elderly replacement titivating the rose beds a little distance away. Poor Henson – he had fallen completely for Diana, who took the young man to her flat for precisely three days before she became bored and released him, unemployed, into the wild.

'Oh darling, I wish you'd give up all this common-people nonsense and come back to the flat. I miss you.'

'You let my room, remember?'

Diana flicked at a fly that had landed on her navy swimsuit. 'Only because I had to. Anyway, she moved out last week. Some people are just not equipped to live with others. She kicked up a fuss every time I had friends over or touched anything of hers. Honestly – who labels pints of milk or bottles of gin?'

'Poor you.' Margot remembered well the frustration of going to finish off leftovers, only to find Diana had got to them first, the new packets of tights that went walkabout.

'Surely he's not interested in her?' Diana went on, wincing at Joan's victory scream.

'They're just friends,' Margot said.

Diana dropped her magazine on the ground and turned to Margot. 'Friends? She got his photo splashed all over the papers the other day – and her own, of course. She's on the make. And besides, she's a . . . well, a nightclub hostess.' She shuddered. 'And we all know what that means.'

'Do we?' Margot challenged.

'Come on, Marge. They're all on the game.'

Margot shook her head. 'You have absolutely no idea about the real world, do you?'

'I know what it's like to earn a living,' Diana retorted.

'Two hours a week filing your nails at a desk in exchange for the trust fund?'

'You can talk.'

'Not any more. My trust fund has dried up, and you know what? I'm glad. I'm proud to go to work every day, to pay my rent and work out what's left after I've bought essentials.'

'Darling, you're in danger of becoming dull. I thought you'd liven the gallery up, but you take it so seriously. Always head down, working away. You'll never find anyone else to marry you.'

'I'm not sure I want to get married, actually.'

'Don't be ridiculous. It's literally the entire point of our existence,' Diana said, watching Cosmo climb out of the pool.

Diana had it bad, Margot realised, and her humiliation that

Cosmo was too busy chatting with the pool boy to notice her wave was painful to witness. 'Talking of work, while I'm here, do you think I might have a look at some of the Charlwood artworks? For work research.'

'Artworks? We're here to dance and drink champagne, not look at old pictures.'

'Diana, you are set to inherit two Reynolds, a Gainsborough and, if I recall, a rather fine Whistler. Please at least pretend to care.'

'I don't have to, with you here to do it for me.' She waved a hand dismissively towards the house. 'Help yourself. Pa's back tonight.'

'He's not here?' Margot asked lightly.

'Meetings in London. And Ma is in Juan-les-Pins with your mother.'

Margot groaned. 'No doubt having her ear bent about the runaway daughter.'

Diana shook her head. 'I reckon we'll be the bottom of the list. "Diana who? Margot who?"'

'Maybe you're right.'

'You know I am. Anyway, Pa will hardly mind you doing your homework – you're teacher's pet. Just don't go in his study or he'll hit the roof.'

'His study?' Margot held vague memories of a locked door on the first floor, admonitions from the housekeeper not to disturb Sir Edwin, in the days when she and Diana held hobby-horse races along the landing.

'Not even Ma is allowed in there. Only old Frostychops the housekeeper, and she'd die for Pa if he asked her to.'

'Why the secrecy?' Margot said casually.

Diana shrugged. 'Probably keeps his *Playboy* mags there. As long as he pays my Harrods account, he can hide what he likes. I've never seen anything, anyway.'

'You've been in there?'

'Barton hides her key inside the piano lid – thinks no one will ever find it there. Which is a fair assumption in this house.'

'But you did?'

'I followed her once.' She peered at Margot, her eyes narrowed. 'Anyway, why are you so interested? Casing the joint?'

Knowing Diana's bloodhound ability to sniff out trouble, Margot played it lightly. 'Absolutely. Looking for something to hang on the wall of the shared bathroom at Ludlow Gardens.'

Diana suddenly sat upright, peering across the glittering azure pool, where Joan was now being taught to dive by a man Margot recognised as a High Court judge Hugo had known. 'Looks like Cosmo managed to get away from Eliza Doolittle. He's going indoors.' She stood up, smoothing her swimsuit and slipping her feet into a pair of strappy gold sandals. 'I need to warn him about the dodgy plumbing in the en suite.'

Margot looked up at her. 'In the room that happens to be next to yours, I suppose?'

Diana frowned. 'Everyone has to sleep somewhere.'

'I know. Just don't . . . well, try not to have expectations. About Cosmo. I'm not sure a relationship is what he's looking for right now.' For all that he irritated her with his irresponsible behaviour, Margot was worried. There was something lost about her brother, an unhappiness that only Joan seemed able to alleviate.

Diana straightened her shoulders. 'Really, Margot. Cosmo is quite capable of deciding what he wants.' She flicked her towel across her shoulder and turned back to Margot with the mean smile she remembered from the days of Diana swapping allegiances in the school dorm, or the flat-sharing days when she'd been caught yet again borrowing 'just a fiver' from Margot's purse. How had their friendship lasted so long? Shared neglect and loneliness, she supposed.

'Cocktails at six,' Diana added briskly. 'And keep that friend of yours under control. I can't have her embarrassing the servants.' She paused. 'Although I don't suppose you remember what those are.'

35

By the time the sun had begun to sink in the cloudless sky, the blackbird's evening ballad obliterated by the record player Diana had rigged up outside, the drive was packed with shiny new cars and the terrace crammed with bodies gyrating to Ray Charles, champagne sloshing from glasses on to dinner jackets and itsy-bitsy cocktail dresses. Margot smiled as she watched Joan and Cosmo, who for once seemed to be enjoying himself without a glass in his hand.

Half of Diana's London crowd had turned up, eligible bachelors as far as the eye could see, yet despite the appearance of her flirty gold lamé cocktail dress, Margot felt disenfranchised from these people, with their talk of Ascot and Antibes, discussing Cuban cocktails rather than the Cuban missile crisis.

What would Laurence make of this? she wondered. So recently her nemesis, and now her . . . her what? Her friend, who had come to Ludlow Gardens straight from work four nights last week, to coincide with her regular post-work chat with Leonora. Who had whisked her off to the cinema and taken her to a talk at the London School of Economics. One thing was certain: she had never looked forward to seeing poor Hugo as much as she did Laurence.

Poor Hugo? According to a mutual acquaintance, Hugo was doing just fine, and had just bought a flat in Holland Park with his friend. At least she never had to wonder whether the marriage would have worked – it hadn't stood a chance, and now both she and Hugo were free to be their true selves. Maybe one day they could even be friends.

She glanced at her watch. If she were to explore Charlwood before Edwin returned, she needed to get on with it. She saw Joan peel away from Cosmo and Diana slip straight into her place. There would never be a better moment, and so she headed indoors, where the elegant wood-panelled entrance hall had become a temporary dancefloor to a handful of barefoot young women practising the Twist. Margot moved quietly through, bypassing family portraits of Victorian patriarchs through to the bewigged first Lord Viner, granted his title by Charles II.

The dining-room walls she had already scanned during a boisterous dinner-cum-bread-roll-fight, presided over by a rather poor portrait of Diana's mother, looking as though she wished the artist would hurry up so she could go to the bathroom. The drawing room offered only a selection of modern works from the St Ives artists – not Bruce Cato's usual fare.

Across the hallway, the hospital-crockery-green music room boasted both an elegant harpsichord, its raised lid displaying a bucolic portrait of Charlwood, and a polished black grand piano, home to a sea of family photographs and, with luck, the key to Edwin's study. She lifted the lid of the piano keyboard, reaching her fingers inside until there it was, almost out of reach.

The grandfather clock in the hallway chimed eight p.m. as Margot glanced up the wide wooden staircase. The dancers had left, and she had one chance to make it to Edwin's study at the far end of the long landing. She took off her slingback kitten heels and began climbing the creaking, uncarpeted steps. If asked, she could claim she was going to her room in the attic – relegated, she noted, from the Chinese Room beside Diana's, now assigned to Cosmo.

Her hand shaking slightly, she unlocked the study door and closed it behind her. Perhaps even the housekeeper hadn't been allowed in for a while, Margot judged, taking in the overflowing ashtray, scattered correspondence and dirty brandy glasses. She glanced at a few letters addressed to Edwin, mainly reports from conservators and curators, and a couple of bills from his Pall Mall club. A letter from a client in California contained a cheque for a recently purchased Michelangelo sketch – a definite Villa Clara candidate.

Margot was about to try the drawers of the desk when she heard car tyres on the gravel outside. She moved to the window, just in time to see Edwin storm out of his black Bentley, throwing the keys at a manservant. A white sportscar skidded to a halt beside Edwin's and a sharp-suited young man leapt out, yelling in gutter Cockney as he pushed his way into the house.

Margot quickly rearranged the desk as she had found it, and was about to leave when she spotted a partially open door leading to a vestibule no larger than a cupboard, a small curtain drawn across the facing wall. If this was the reason no one was allowed in here, she couldn't risk finding out. She locked the door behind her, hiding in the neighbouring bedroom just as Edwin thundered up the stairs.

'Don't you run away from me,' a voice called out as a second set of footsteps followed.

'And do not talk to me like that in front of the servants,' she heard Edwin hiss. 'If we must have this conversation, it can be in my study. And then I want you out, Jackson. Understood?'

As the study door slammed closed, Margot tiptoed to the landing, trying to make out the raised voices over the sounds of the party outside.

'You owe me,' the young shark yelled.

'Keep your voice down, man.'

'I'll keep my voice down when you pay me my grand.'

'I told you,' Edwin said, his voice wheedling now, 'until I get the money from the client, there's nothing I can do.'

'There's plenty I can do, though—'

'Hey, there's no need to resort to that,' Edwin said, his voice an octave higher.

'Then don't make me.'

There was a brief pause before Edwin continued. 'I have a suggestion. One that will make you three times what I owe you.'

'No more jobs until you cough up for the last one.'

'Wait until you hear what I have to say. Come, look at this.'

Margot heard the shuffling of feet and then the younger man's voice. 'A curtain in a cupboard? You take me for an idiot?'

There was a pause, and then Edwin spoke again. 'This, my friend, is possibly the most valuable thing you will ever set your thieving East End eyes on.'

'It's not even very big. Are you taking the piss?'

'I'm just saying that I have a client who will pay a king's ransom for this painting, and I need someone to get it to him. For a very hefty fee.'

'How much?'

'Three thousand.'

That seemed to have done the trick: the two men carried on talking, but as the dancing downstairs increased in volume, Margot could no longer make out what was said. It seemed Edwin's secret was possibly bigger than Leonora had imagined, or why would he have offered the price of a house, just to move whatever was in there?

36

'You said he was up to no good,' Joan said, taking a champagne coupe from a passing waiter. She'd probably had too many already, but, well, champagne was champagne, especially when it was free. 'What do you think's going on?'

'He wasn't exactly talking to Sir Anthony Blunt in there. And I bet you anything that whatever's behind that curtain is not on the books at Viner's.'

'Are you going back in there?'

'Not a chance,' Margot replied, stabbing at an olive in her martini with a cocktail stick. 'I only just got the key back before he came down.' She glanced up as Edwin appeared on the terrace, fiddling with the white shirt cuffs beneath his dinner jacket as he watched his guests dance beneath the fairy lights. 'And here he is now.'

'So that's the famous Edwin Viner,' Joan said. 'He's good-looking for an old bloke. I'll give him that. I can see why Mrs Birch fell for him.'

'And why she fell out with him,' Margot snorted.

There was a sudden break in the chatter as a white sports car swung around from the back of the house. The driver blasted on the horn then slowed down to point at Edwin before accelerating away. Joan felt her stomach lurch. 'Who did you say he was talking to upstairs?'

'I don't know. I just caught a surname. Now what was it . . .?'

'Come on, Marge. This is important.'

'Why?'

'Because I think I know who Viner's dealing with.'

Margot chewed on her lip for a moment. 'Jackson. He called the man Jackson. You know who that might be?'

'I bloody ought to. I was engaged to him.'

Joan waited a moment as Margot's eyes widened. 'You mean . . .'

She nodded. 'Alf Jackson. I'd know that car anywhere.'

Margot took Joan's hand. 'Do you think he'd tell us what's been going on?'

Joan took a cigarette from her tiny chainmail evening purse. 'Doubt it. I don't know what his line of business actually is. He keeps work and pleasure very separate.'

'And are you . . . well, pleasure again?'

Joan smiled. 'I never really wasn't. I just didn't want him to know it.'

'I'm pleased for you . . . I think?'

Joan gestured towards Diana, dragging Cosmo back to the dancefloor. 'It'll keep her off my back anyway. She as good as called me a tart, you know?'

'Ignore her. She's miffed because Cosmo's not interested in her charms.'

'Charms?' Joan snorted. 'Spells, more like. Can't *she* tell you what's in the study?'

'She's no idea. And no interest, to be honest,' Margot sighed. 'Plus she's barely talking to me.'

'You need someone to get in there?'

'Yes, but I don't know who or how.'

'Maybe I do.' Joan watched as Edwin spotted Margot and headed through the crowd towards them. 'Look and learn, girl,' she whispered.

'Margot,' he said, kissing her on both cheeks. 'How lovely that Diana brought you. Always a delight to have you brighten up Charlwood.'

'Always a pleasure to be here,' Margot replied tightly.

'And who is this lovely creature?' he asked, turning to Joan.

'Joan Carter. Pleased to meet you.' She put her head on one side and offered him the smile that guaranteed a twenty-quid tip at Henry's. They were all the same, these men with thoroughbred wives and fancy lives, when a pair of big blue eyes was trained on them. And from his reaction, she knew she had him.

Joan teased and flattered, giggled at champagne bubbles and asked how Sir Edwin could be old enough to have a daughter her own age? She danced with him, wagging her finger when his hand strayed too low. She told him stories about Henry's, paving the way to ask about his line of work.

'You sell paintings?' she asked. 'What, valuable ones? Oh, you know the Queen? I reckon you're making this whole art thing up. No? Then prove it.'

'That would be my pleasure,' Edwin replied, taking her elbow and leading her into the house. 'Let me give you a tour of the Charlwood art collection.'

'So what makes one old painting more special than another?' she asked, as they stood in a drawing room the same colour as the box containing the Blue Grass perfume Alf had sent her yesterday. Every piece of furniture looked as though it had come from a museum. How did the Viners relax? she wondered. Where were the tellies and Pools coupons? The fag packets and magazines, half-drunk mugs of tea? Give her Ludlow Gardens any day.

'That, my dear, is the million-dollar question. Is it the brushwork? The rarity of a piece? Maybe the romance of its conception? To me, it is its luminescence, the subtle play of chiaroscuro, the sense that one could reach into the painting and become part of it, as though one is witnessing the very psyche of the artist.'

Although Joan was irritated by his pomposity, at least he was trying to impress her, and so she kept pushing. 'Well, I'll have to take your word for it. They still all look the same to me.'

'I don't believe you,' he said, standing so close behind her shoulder that she could smell his cologne. 'How about this one? Surely this will melt your cold, heathen heart?'

They paused in front of a painting of a little girl. Quite sweet, she supposed, but nothing special – the sort of thing her gran might have had on the wall of her front room, if her old man hadn't been running a bookie's from it. 'I don't see it,' Joan said. 'Just some old-fashioned kid in a white dress. Could be a soap advert. Hope you didn't pay much for it.'

'Buy it?' he laughed. 'This is an original Joshua Reynolds, a portrait of my great-grandfather by the great master in the 1790s.'

'But it's a girl. It's wearing a dress and has a ribbon in its hair.'

'Oh, you dear sweet thing. Back in those days small boys were dressed the same as their sisters.'

Joan's eyes widened with shock. 'You'd get arrested for that now, outside a few particular clubs in Soho. And most of the blokes in there are probably coppers.'

He laughed, his hand landing lightly on her shoulder. 'Perhaps so. But the beauty of this portrait remains unaltered – look at the tendrils of hair catching the wind, the sweet expression, the finger pointing to who knows what? Is the child trying to show us our own lost innocence?'

'Probably its mum is just out of view with a bag of gobstoppers.' Joan turned to face him. 'Surely you've got something better?' She lowered her voice, tilting her head. 'Something really, really special?' *Come on,* she told him silently as she played her fingers on the sleeve of his dinner jacket. *You know exactly what you've got tucked away in your study.*

He hesitated, his desire to impress her fighting his instinct for caution, until he clearly decided she would not have a bloody clue what she was looking at. 'Very well. Come with me. But you are not – and I really do mean not – to tell a soul about this.'

'Well,' she said brightly, 'unless it's Paul McCartney served on a plate, I doubt I'll remember.'

He led her up the wide wooden stairs and along a gallery-like landing interspersed with more paintings, whose frames looked more interesting to Joan than their subjects. How Margot spent all day surrounded by these dreary things was beyond her.

They came to a halt and he slipped a hand inside his jacket pocket, pulling out a key and pausing for a moment. 'You know, you really are a most attractive young woman, Miss Carter. If you ever . . . well, if you ever felt like visiting me at the London flat, I'm sure we would get along famously. And perhaps take it from there? We could come to some arrangement, I'm sure.'

Could we now? Joan thought to herself, already tired of batting away such propositions from wealthy men old enough to be her father. Instead, however, she smiled sweetly. 'I'll think about it. Now are you going to show me this old picture or not?'

37

'So let me get this straight,' Leonora said, unsure she could believe what she had heard. 'Margot saw something hidden behind a curtain in the study, then overheard Edwin negotiating with a criminal.'

'That was my Alf,' Joan retorted, arms folded as she sat side by side with Margot on Leonora's narrow settee. 'He's a businessman, actually. And he's taking me out tonight. I might wear that new Mary Quant pinafore. And my white tights. Would you help do my hair, Marge?'

'Joan, please!' Leonora screwed her eyes closed against the headache that had now firmly taken hold, exacerbated by the sound of Linda's television blasting *Sunday Night at the Palladium* from upstairs. 'Can we please stick to the subject?'

'Sorry.'

'And what is it that Edwin said to this friend of Joan's?' Leonora tried again.

'It sounded like Edwin owes him money,' Margot said.

'For what?'

'I don't know. But Edwin offered him a lot more to pass another painting on to another client.' Her eyes widened as she nodded slowly. 'A *lot* more.'

'What are we talking here?'

'Three thousand pounds.'

Leonora let out a slow breath. Three thousand pounds? Just to deliver an artwork? A Rubens sketch had just been sold to Conalghi's for a third of that. Whatever Edwin was up to, it was not small fry. The Villa Clara collection was merely the tip of the iceberg. 'Joan, what does your businessman friend do exactly?' she asked gently. 'Might he be involved in the art trade somehow? Working for Edwin?'

She shrugged. 'I suppose.'

'So Edwin wants Alf to deliver this painting in the study for him. Did you get a chance to look at it, Margot?'

'Edwin came back before I could. It was too risky to try again.'

'Quite right. The last thing any of us wants is for you to lose your job.'

'I'd do anything if it helped you, Mrs Birch,' Margot said.

Leonora looked at the young woman's earnest expression, knowing that, yes, Margot probably would give it all up to help her. Never had she imagined that anyone other than Laurence would care so much.

'And I would too,' Joan countered, 'except there wouldn't be much point. All I do is smile in tights, really.'

'Well, thank you, Joan,' Leonora said. 'I'll bear that in mind. But what I really need is to know what Edwin's trying to get rid of, that he can't just put up for sale in the gallery.'

Joan brightened suddenly. 'I can help with that.'

'You know what the painting is?' Leonora asked.

'Not exactly, but Margot reckons *you* might.'

Margot nodded. 'You see, Joan managed to get into the study – with Edwin.'

'You didn't?' Leonora would never cease to be surprised by Joan Carter.

'Creepy, he was. Wanted me to go to his London flat. And we all know what for.'

'Oh Joan, I hope you weren't put in a difficult position.'

'He don't scare me. Besides, his daughter barged in before it got sticky – accused me of trying to get my claws into her dad. As if!'

'I'm afraid Diana has a bee in her bonnet about Joan,' Margot explained.

'But you had a chance to see whatever he's trying to sell on?' Leonora's efforts to remain patient were increasingly challenged.

Joan frowned. 'Well, it looked old. I mean, really old.' She scanned the walls of the room, settling on a painting of a vase of flowers Leonora had completed as a student. 'About that size, I suppose. No frame. Made it look like a tea tray.'

'Joan, really!'

Joan grimaced. 'Ask me to describe a pair of shoes or a handbag, and I'll tell you exactly where they were bought and when.'

'So this painting – what was it of?'

'A woman, sitting at a table. Long dress, fancy curls in her hair. Next to a tall sort of criss-crossed window.'

'A leaded window?' Leonora suggested. Something stirred in her, the memory of a long-forgotten image. 'To which side?'

After a moment's consideration, Joan plumped for the woman's right-hand side. 'Oh, and the floor was black and white. With a little border of blue and white tiles.'

'And what was she wearing?' Leonora asked, on the edge of her seat by now.

'Oh, that's easy. A long blue dress. But not just any blue. It was really bright, like . . . like the sky on a clear day at Brighton beach.'

'Indigo?' Leonora prompted.

'If you say so. And then she had this sort of yellow jacket, puffy, with a fur trim around the collar, on the back of her chair.'

The stirring became a flicker as Leonora pushed further. 'Good. And what was she doing?'

'I'll show you.' Joan pulled a chair out from the small table Leonora used as a desk. She arranged herself so that she was slightly side on to the table, her chin raised as she bit on her lower lip.

'Mrs Birch, are you all right?' Margot asked. 'You look like you've seen a ghost.'

Leonora's eyes swam and she clutched the arm of her chair. She was taken back, years, to a villa in Tuscany, to a moment when she thought that not only had she rediscovered the love of her life, but that he in turn had discovered something of immeasurable worth. Something to be shared with the world – to be celebrated, venerated, studied and gazed at with awe and tenderness.

'Oh my,' she said, pressing a hand to her mouth, tears springing to her eyes.

Joan looked alarmed. 'What did I do?' she said.

'I don't know.' Margot came over to Leonora, kneeling beside her. 'Mrs Birch, what's upset you?'

'After all these years,' she sobbed. 'I thought she'd gone for ever.'

'Who?' Margot asked.

Leonora turned to Joan. 'The girl, of course. Look.'

Margot frowned. 'I don't understand. What exactly is it that Viner has in his study?'

Leonora looked once more at Joan, who had perfectly reproduced the pose in the painting stolen in 1939 at Ventimiglia. Except that it had not been stolen, at least not by Mussolini's thugs. No, this thief was far more sophisticated, a master of the long game, lies dripping from his tongue as frequently as Bruce Cato's drawings passed through his gallery. As her shock at recognising the tableau turned to anger, she kicked herself for believing Edwin at the time, but why shouldn't she have? The circumstances were so terrifying, people dragged off at gunpoint to who knew what fate. The theft of a painting was an easy crime in comparison.

Leonora took a deep breath. 'If I am correct, Joan has just seen a painting discovered in a Venetian palazzo sale in 1939 by Bruce Cato, an artwork Edwin and I were bringing to London to safety. Except that it was stolen en route. Its value is beyond mere numbers.'

'What is it?' Margot asked.

Leonora hesitated. 'I have every reason to believe this is a Vermeer.'

Margot could not have looked more shocked if Leonora had tap-danced naked across the parlour. 'You mean Johannes Vermeer of Delft, sixteen thirty-two to—'

'Sixteen seventy-five,' Leonora finished. '*Girl with a Pearl Earring, The Milkmaid* . . . And now, finally, *Girl at a Desk*.

Catalogued as having been sold at auction in 1696 to a French collector and bought fifty years later by Count Niccolò da Minotto. It disappeared from sight for nearly two hundred years, presumed lost, until Bruce found it.'

'Did you ever tell anyone about this?' Margot said, but Leonora shook her head.

'I was ashamed, devastated to be involved in the loss of such a priceless work of art. Edwin and I agreed never to talk of it.'

'Which suited that bugger perfectly,' Joan said.

'So what are you going to do, now that you know?' Margot asked.

'What am I going to do?' Leonora stood, smoothing down the creases in her tweed skirt. 'I am going to have an early night and a jolly good sleep. Tomorrow I commence battle.'

38

Margot's fingers paused as she looked up from the sale entries she was typing, interrupted by a commotion in the gallery downstairs. Across the office Ursula Knight froze halfway through lifting a heavy volume from a bookcase.

'What on earth . . .' Ursula put down the book as footsteps thundered up the stairs, her cat's-eye spectacles bouncing at the end of the chain around her neck. She glanced at the closed door of Sir Edwin's office, where he was dictating letters to the new secretary, syllable by syllable.

'I tried to stop her,' Diana said, panting as she raced to catch up with the woman now standing on the threshold of the office.

'Well, really, this is most unusual,' Miss Knight said, formidable with her helmet of lacquered grey hair and the silk pussy-bow at her neck – more of a tiger-bow, Margot often thought. 'We cannot have people simply barging in here,' she said to the intruder. 'What is the purpose of this?'

'You really need to ask?' Leonora set her shoulders and stared back at her opponent, studiously avoiding eye contact with Margot as she waited for the penny to drop.

Antagonism turned to recognition and then shock as Ursula frowned, taking a step forward. 'Miss Birch?' She set her steely gaze on Diana. 'Miss Viner, you may go now. We cannot have the gallery untended.'

Diana pulled a face at Margot before reluctantly closing the door behind her.

'It's been a long time, Miss Birch.'

'Indeed it has, Miss Knight. Never thought you'd see me here again?'

'Not after . . .'

'After Edwin sent me packing? Really, let's not beat about the bush. We're both too old and wise for that.'

'And did you . . .'

'Have the child? Yes.'

'I'm sorry.'

'Why? I had a wonderful son, and you the opportunity to take my place. Look at you now, with your career – my career, as it happened.'

'Miss Birch . . .'

'Please, don't. I'd probably have done the same in your position.'

'You would?'

Leonora shrugged. 'Possibly. I just hope you've been rather more careful than I was. We both know what he's like.'

Margot watched as Ursula Knight straightened. 'I don't know what you mean.'

'Oh, please. Let's not pretend. Exactly how many secretaries has Edwin got through in the last twenty years?'

There was a pause, and for a moment Margot thought Mrs Birch might be thrown out, but then Ursula Knight broke into a thin smile. 'More than I have digits upon which to count them,' she replied.

'Miss Knight, there is something I need to discuss with Sir Edwin urgently – a matter of an artwork that seems to have ended up in the wrong place. I don't suppose you are able to let me see him?'

'You know I am not. However, if I were to leave the room briefly, for instance to visit the basement and ask Bob for his advice on something, then I cannot be held responsible for what happens in my absence.'

Leonora looked at her watch. 'If I remember rightly, Bob goes on his morning tea break at any moment. You'd better hurry if you're to catch him.'

'Miss Stockton, will you come with me?' Ursula said.

Leonora waved a hand dismissively. 'She can stay. We don't want it to look like an ambush.'

As Ursula left the office, Leonora smiled at Margot. 'Let's see what the old bastard has to say for himself, shall we?'

'What is it?' he called out irritably from the other side of the door, and for a brief moment Leonora wondered whether she should just flee. To do so would excuse Edwin from everything he had done, however, and so she took a deep breath.

Edwin stood up from behind his desk as the young secretary taking dictation jumped at the intrusion. Where had he found this one? she wondered, looking at her indecently short skirt and peachy complexion. At the school dance?

'What on earth is the meaning of this?' he stormed, his face clouding with anger in a reprise of the last time she had been in this room.

'You can leave,' Leonora said calmly to the girl. 'Unless, Edwin, you want her to hear what I have to say, which I highly doubt.'

'Miss Knight?' he shouted across the room, but Leonora shook her head.

'She's not there. I waited until she had left the office.' She looked at him. He had barely changed, still wearing his Eton tie and silk pocket handkerchief, but how must she look to him? Like the dirt beneath his shoe, just as she always had. 'You don't remember me, do you, Edwin? Even after you threw me out of this very room over twenty years ago?'

She watched the cogs of memory play out across his face, confusion turning to shock and then anger. He waved towards the young secretary. 'Get out,' he said, tensing when she hesitated. 'Now!' he roared, so that she scuttled away, blonde ponytail bobbing behind her.

'What is it you want?' he said eventually. 'Money, I suppose?'

'Not everyone is like you, Edwin. No, what I want from you will be much harder to extract.'

'Miss Birch, I warn you, you are trespassing and I will call the police if necessary.'

Leonora laughed. 'You won't want to when you've heard what I have to say.'

He came around from behind the desk and took her arm. 'You need to leave now.'

She tilted her head and smiled. 'Just like old times, isn't it, Edwin? Except that back then I didn't know you were a thief as well as a rotter.'

He dropped her arm, taking a step back and pointing at her. 'Enough, Miss Birch.'

'Oh, but I haven't told you why I'm here.'

'I don't care. I want you out.'

'Before I tell you that I know what really happened at Ventimiglia in 1939?'

He hesitated, his jaw working as he stared back at her, the sound of the street below breaking into the silence. 'You don't know anything.'

She took a step forward. 'That's where you're wrong, Edwin. I know everything,' she said quietly, jabbing at his chest with her forefinger. 'I know you kept the Vermeer. I know you have it hidden at Charlwood. And I know you're planning on selling it to some shady collector. I also know this is probably just the tip of the iceberg. What about those drawings we brought across in my suitcase? Reproductions created in good faith? I imagine you authenticated those somehow. You're a crook, Viner, and I intend to expose you. Call the police if you want – it will save me the bother.'

He pushed her hand away. 'You think they will listen to a deranged old woman with a score to settle? Don't waste your time – the Commissioner of the Metropolitan Police is a member of my club, and the Lord Chancellor and I were at prep school together. Go back to your little life and spare yourself the embarrassment.'

She pointed at him. 'Fool me once, shame on you. Fool me twice, shame on me. I see you, Edwin Viner,' she hissed, 'and soon so will the rest of the world.'

39

Spain, 1989

Joan held up her hands. 'Now I ain't no expert – you need Margot for that – but I know what I saw, even if it was twenty-odd years ago.'

Phoebe was unable to believe what she had just heard. Falsely authenticating Bruce's drawings was one thing, but this was full-on theft. If Bruce had not made copies, the subject of the last Vermeer may never have been seen again. 'But what did he plan to do with it? If it appeared on the open market, Bruce would have known.'

'Well, for a start, he tried to get my Alf involved. They did a bit of business from time to time.' Joan glanced at Phoebe. 'Just couriering, you understand?'

'And now Leonora had proof about the Vermeer, did she go to the police?'

Joan shook her head. 'No point. It was all Viner's mates at the top.'

'She must have done something, surely?'

'She certainly did.'

There was a pause, and Phoebe smiled. 'You're not going to tell me what, are you?'

'And spoil the game?' Joan glanced around the pool and gardens. 'Little bit of paradise here, isn't it?'

'It is.' The décor wasn't entirely to Phoebe's taste, but she had to agree that Villa Aphrodite had its charms.

'I wish your uncle had seen it. All this sculpture. Right up his street.'

Phoebe thought Bruce more likely to want a Henry Moore in his grounds, rather than a beauty pageant of fibreglass goddesses, but kept quiet.

Joan stood slowly, taking time to balance on her strappy heels. 'Here, why don't you go and take a look at my girls, as I call them, and I'll see what's happening with dinner?' She squeezed Phoebe's hand. 'You never know what you might find.'

'Do I have a choice?' she asked, but she knew the answer already: Bruce had set her up, and for once she didn't mind. Perhaps it was the change of scenery, the genuine indignation at how he'd been treated, but for the first time, Phoebe really wanted to know what he had left for her.

She tied a sarong around her waist and slipped on her sandals, crossing the grass to the first of the life-size statues, a woman balancing a flagon on her shoulder. It was a common representation of Dione, the goddess of water, made clear by the carving of her name into the plinth upon which she stood. Beside her was Tethys, mother of springs and rivers, then a rather buxom Rheia, who after some head-scratching Phoebe remembered to be a goddess of fertility. There was a theme here, and as she reached the next deity in line, she realised they were the seven Titan goddesses: Dione, Tethys, Rheia, Mnemosyne, Theia, Themis and, of course, the final one, Phoebe, goddess of the intellect, guardian of the oracle at Delphi.

She found her namesake and stood before her. 'So he's brought you into this too, has he?' she whispered, before running her eye across the statue and realising that they were all attached to cables, ready to light up at night. A hinged flap at the back of Goddess Phoebe's plinth had been designed to hide a circuit breaker, and so she lifted it, slipping her hand carefully inside and pulling out a cardboard tube.

A rolled-up canvas had been tucked inside the tube, and she laid it flat on a sunlounger. Vermeer's girl was still at her desk, and this time it looked as though there was a Rembrandt drawing on the wall as well as a calling card on the desk, on which Phoebe could just about make out a London address. Had Bruce left anything else for her? She shook the tube, and out fell an envelope, addressed to Mrs Leonora Birch at Ludlow Gardens and containing a sheet of headed paper from a now-defunct Fleet Street newspaper, dated Monday, 2 September 1963:

Dear Mrs Birch,

It has come to our notice from a member of the newsdesk that you may have information of interest to our readers. Given the high profile of the figure in question, I understand your need for discretion. Please do arrange a time to join Laurence in discussing this matter with me. We have provisionally made space for a feature on Sunday, 15 September.

Yours sincerely,
Geoff Pickles

Managing Editor
The Daily Bulletin

'Laurence?' she asked herself quietly, before the penny dropped. Of course: Laurence Birch. Leonora's son.

40

London, September 1963

'I just need my notebook,' Laurence said, leading Leonora towards his desk in the fug-filled newspaper office and sweeping aside sandwich wrappers. 'Sorry, it's a bit of a mess.'

'Darling, I'm not here to judge you on your housekeeping.'

'Mother, please . . .' He glanced at the shirt sleeved young men dotted around the open-plan space, feet up on desks or tapping violently at typewriters, cigarettes hanging from mouths. The nerve centre of the *Bulletin*, renowned for its exposés of government scandals, was not somewhere one would normally bring one's mother. The newspaper was the new kid on the block, squeezed on to Fleet Street amongst venerable old publications for whom it had quickly become an Establishment-challenging irritation. It had been Laurence's suggestion that the *Bulletin* might be interested in a story about fraudulent practice in the thick-carpeted inner sanctum of the London art world, and so here they were.

'Laurence, can we please go and see this editor of yours? I have Lyov coming for tea this afternoon. There is news about his sister.' After their meeting at the café with Hillary's contact, it seemed things were moving at last.

'Fine,' he said. 'Anyway, I've only got half an hour. It's nearly recess at the House of Commons, so a few of us usually nip over to a pub in Westminster to pick up the gossip.' Some had already been there, Leonora suspected, taking in the faint smell of stale beer.

Laurence tapped on the door of a glass cubicle filled with smoke, then led Leonora inside. 'This is Geoff Pickles,' he said, 'our managing editor. He's interested in running a story about Viner.'

'Mrs Birch, come on in,' said a bald-headed man through his fat cigar as he rose to greet them, his shirt straining against its buttons. 'That's a fine young man you've raised. Once we've located his sense of humour, he'll do all right here. Take a seat.'

'Thank you.' Leonora carefully set aside a pile of paper-work and perched on the edge of the greasy seat. She glanced at a set of proofs on Pickles' desk, red ink scrawled over them, the headline screaming the latest accusations against John Profumo, and a red cross marked heavily through a photograph of John F. Kennedy at a party, a blowsy blonde on his arm.

'Tomorrow's early edition,' Pickles explained. 'White House put the scuppers on that – seems the girl has Russian friends. Can I get you a drink?' He gestured towards the whisky bottle on a shelf behind him.

'A little early for me,' Leonora said politely.

Pickles laughed. 'Like son, like mother, eh?' he said. 'Bit more practice in the Punch Tavern will sort him out.'

'So,' Laurence said, bristling with irritation, 'perhaps we can decide whether this story is a goer?'

'Oh, I think we can already safely say it is: crooked aristocrat, stately home, art theft, and then this nightclub hostess,' Pickles said, tapping his pen on the desk. 'Wasn't she photographed with that earl's son in Soho recently? Some fight with a GI and a gangster, I seem to remember.'

Leonora sat up straight. 'That was a misunderstanding. You make it sound rather sordid. Miss Carter is a good girl,' she added, setting her crocodile-skin handbag on her knee.

'Course she is,' Pickles said, grinning broadly.

'And besides, the story's about Viner, not Joan.'

'We're just getting the full picture here.' He leaned forward over his desk. 'And now we need evidence. Can you give that to me?'

'I believe so,' Leonora said. 'We have a contact at the gallery, and I can prove that Viner has been passing off reproductions as originals.'

'How so?'

'Because I know the man who created them.'

'You're not tempted to go to the police?' Pickles said, relighting his cigar, the acrid smoke making her eyes water.

'If I could, I would,' Leonora said, 'but Viner has friends in high places. I guarantee nothing would stick.'

Pickles narrowed his eyes. 'Well, let's make sure we print something that *will* stick. I'm thinking a special in our Sunday edition.'

'And you won't mention my name?' Leonora said.

'Nor his, or our lawyers will be all over me. We'll let the public make their minds up about who it is. Shouldn't be hard to work out.' He pointed to Laurence. 'Birch, this is your scoop. I want you to write it. We need to publish hard, and we need to publish soon, before word gets out. You've got one week.'

Leonora felt a brief moment of panic: had this gone too far? After all, Viner was technically Laurence's father. They'd

234

discussed it at length, however, and Laurence was determined Edwin would not get away with theft and systematic fraud. This was not a patrimony claim; it was about justice for Leonora and for Bruce.

Pickles thumped his feet on the desk. 'So what do you say, Birch?'

'I'm only an assistant reporter,' Laurence said.

'Were. You just got promoted.'

Joan was nervous about introducing Alf to her Ludlow Gardens family. She'd only ever seen him surrounded by East End lackeys in dodgy pubs and smoky nightclubs. Today, however, he was respectability itself, booking out an entire restaurant and paying for everything, down to the dusty bottles of champagne dragged from the cellar of the Stepney trattoria. The owner must have been in debt to Alf, for the gingham-covered table was covered with fresh flowers, candles stuffed into wine bottles. He had even brought in a squint-eyed mandolin player, until Alf gave the man a fiver to clear off.

She quickly glanced at her left hand, recalling the evening that week when Alf had turned up on the stage at Henry's. If he hadn't bought champagne for every table and bunged a hundred quid at Brenda for the band to play 'I Only Have Eyes for You', Joan would have been shot. Instead, she was dragged onstage as he went down on one knee and presented her with the biggest diamond she'd ever seen. What could she have done, with the entire place yelling at her to say yes, Alf looking up at her with that cockeyed smile of his? Of course she said yes – she was Alf's girl, and now she was going to be Alf's wife. There was the small matter of telling her mam, and it would mean leaving Ludlow Gardens and her job – no Jackson wife would prance about in fishnets for the whole world to see – but not for a while.

She saw Leonora watching her now, knowing her landlady wasn't quite convinced about the engagement, but tonight was Alf's chance to prove himself. Margot had been cautiously pleased, whilst Cosmo wholeheartedly endorsed the engagement – 'Take a bit of joy where you can, Joanie,' he had said.

Then there was Laurence, sitting there in his rolled-up shirtsleeves and handknit tank top, staring at Alf as though watching a tiger in a zoo enclosure as he tried to piece together the story. 'So let's just go over this once more.' Laurence opened his notepad. 'You've known Viner for how long?'

Alf shrugged. 'Eight, ten years, I suppose. Took over the business from my dad. I'd met Viner once or twice before that, but Dad never told us much about what went on. I was just a courier when I was a kid – taking things here and there.'

'And now?' Laurence said, the end of the pencil between his teeth.

Alf laid his smooth hands on the table. 'This is off the record, right?'

Laurence was about to protest, but Leonora stepped in. 'We just need a broader picture of what he has been up to. No one will quote you, Mr Jackson, I promise.'

Alf fished a cigarette from the gold case in his breast pocket, leaning over as Joan lit it for him. 'Cheers, baby,' he said then turned back to the table. 'I have a network of contacts across Europe, dealing with connoisseurs and collectors. A few names as'd make you sit up, I can tell you. Supply and demand. Viner, well, he supplies the demand – creates it, even. He's got a collection of pieces he dips into, dozens of works that can't go on the open market. And when he can't find what they want, I help him source it, if you know what I mean.'

'I'm not sure I do,' Leonora said.

'Let's just say I'm often able to lay my hands on the kind of things money can't buy.'

'Lay your hands?' Leonora asked. 'Are we talking works of art here?'

Alf winked. 'No questions, no lies. But Viner, he sets it up and my company sources the goods then delivers.'

'Oh my goodness.' Leonora went pale, and Joan jumped in quickly.

'Like the painting I saw at Charlwood?' she said.

'Yeah. Except that one must be something special, given the money he offered me to shift it.'

'That painting,' Leonora said, 'belongs to a friend of mine. It was stolen by Viner while you were still in short trousers.'

'Listen, Mrs B,' Alf said, 'if that belongs to a friend of yours, I ain't touching it with a bargepole.'

'Thank you, Mr Jackson.' Leonora cleared her throat. 'As I see it, there are two issues here. One: the matter of the stolen Vermeer, and two: the distribution of the so-called Villa Clara collection.'

'Both of which,' Laurence added, 'are evidence of Viner's criminal activity, and the basis of my story.'

'What do we have so far?' Leonora said, pushing aside the unfinished bowl of tiramisu that was far too rich for her. 'Margot? You've been looking into the Villa Clara pieces?'

Margot, sitting beside Laurence, pulled a sheet of paper from her handbag, scanning the contents before passing it across the table. 'I have this list,' she said. 'I went through catalogues for the last thirty years and noted anything similar to the Rembrandt you recognised in terms of size and materials, and that came from an unknown seller.'

Leonora put on her glasses and took the paper from Margot. 'These are all strong candidates for being reproductions by Bruce. I brought three back from Villa Clara myself in 1939. There were no markings to allow them to be authenticated.'

'Strangely, they all had a full provenance by the time they went up for sale.' Margot held out her glass for a refill as the waiter came around the table with a raffia-covered wine bottle. 'Past owners, exhibitions, collectors' stamps . . .'

'So where did the stamps come from?' Laurence asked, pencil poised over his notebook.

'Viner,' Alf cut in. 'I've seen him do it.'

Leonora took off her glasses and leaned across the table. 'You've seen Sir Edwin Viner, adviser to the Royal Collection, deliberately falsify works of art?'

'He's got a box full of stamps – my old dad used to get them made up for him from a geezer in Deptford – then fake labels, things he's steamed off the back of old frames, invoices from a counterfeiter on the Isle of Dogs, stuff he types up himself on old receipts and what have you.'

'And where are these stamps kept?' Laurence asked.

'I don't know.'

Leonora turned to Margot. 'Any chance you can look for them?'

Joan watched Margot blanch. Breaking into the study at Charlwood had nearly finished off the young woman who had never even dodged a bus fare. 'I don't think we should ask her to,' she said gently. 'She needs her job, apart from anything else.'

Margot smiled gratefully. 'It's true, although I am beginning to think it's time to look elsewhere. I heard about a job going in a gallery off Piccadilly – the owner is a woman and is looking to expand. I'm not sure I can bear much more of Edwin, to be perfectly honest.'

'I'm not sure any of us wants you to,' Laurence said.

Oh yes, there were definitely developments there, Joan thought. Ludlow Gardens would be empty by the end of the year at this rate. Apart from poor Linda, of course, who would be saving up for her wedding for the next decade. And Hillary, unlikely ever to find a husband, wearing that duffel coat.

'I agree. You should get out, Margot,' Leonora added. 'Besides, once this newspaper feature is out, you may have no choice.'

Joan nestled against Alf's shoulder as she looked at the troubled expressions around the table. 'Do you think we've got enough to nail him?'

Laurence sighed. 'I don't know. If we could get Alf to go on the record—'

Alf held his hands up. 'Sorry, squire. No can do.'

'—or Margot can find concrete evidence that those drawings sold were copies . . .'

'That still leaves the painting,' Joan said. 'Are we going to just let him sell it?'

Leonora shook her head. 'I don't know.'

'You might not, Mrs B, but I do,' Alf chipped in.

'What do you mean, Mr Jackson?'

'I spoke to Viner this morning,' he said. 'Told him I'd take the painting and his three grand, as planned. Except I'd get it to you instead of his buyer.'

Leonora's face was a curious combination of horror and delight. 'I don't know . . .'

'But then he told me the deal's off. Reckon he's spooked. If you go to the police about that painting, I guarantee it'll have vanished quicker than you can say "old boys' network".'

Leonora sighed. 'That's that, then.'

'Not quite.' Alf straightened his shirt collar, stretching his neck. 'I've got an idea.' He smiled and tapped his nose.

'Alf, what are you thinking?' Joan asked, thrilled to see him in action.

Alf held up a hand. 'If you ask me, it's about time Sir Edwin got a taste of his own medicine.' He reached for the champagne bucket in the middle of the table, offering up the bottle. 'How about we all drink to the undoing of Sir Edwin Viner?'

Leonora smiled. 'I must write to Mr Cato and tell him,' she said, not fooling Joan for a second with her casual tone.

It took four days for Laurence to complete the feature, another two days for Pickles to edit it. The finished piece outlined the career of an unnamed man who had flooded the art market with high-quality copies that had potentially leaked into national collections. Laurence had interviewed former employees of the gallery, from young women who had been sacked for refusing to tolerate the unwritten parts of their job descriptions to a former porter at the gallery, who admitted to having packed up unregistered works after hours under the close supervision of Viner. None wanted to be named, but all were happy to spill the beans. Space had been booked in for the front pages in advance and Pickles was eager to see what Birch was capable of.

Margot was only too happy to assist, introducing Laurence to old friends such as Sir Roland Blackford, who had invited Viner to Norfolk to advise on a supposed Franz Hals painting he had inherited, only for there to be a break-in at the Hall three days later, the only item stolen being the Hals. Blackford knew of at least two others who had experienced similar.

They had done everything they could – it only remained to publish.

41

Tuscany, 1989

Stefano had been absolutely right: on the back of her brief stay with Joan, a couple of nights at Villa Clara had helped give her a little perspective. The shock of Bruce not being there was palpable but less violent, even though the enormity of what she was taking on hit her equally hard.

A series of storms had brought exceptional rainfall, causing damage to the roof of the main house, where a series of buckets remained in situ in case of further water ingress. A section of roof had collapsed above one of the guest bedrooms, taking with it great chunks of plaster and revealing worrying levels of rot in the timbers criss-crossing the ancient structure. 'The villa has stood for five hundred years,' Stefano told her. 'It'll take more than a bit of rain to see her off,' but she knew he was being optimistic. If she were in the market to buy an historic building, she would not touch this one with a bargepole. To appease her, he promised to arrange a structural survey, so that at least she would know the extent of any problems.

Swimming pool? she had thought to herself, remembering Joan's words as she swept broken plaster into a pile in the corner of the room. It was a pipe dream. Unless she gave up the museum, of course. The Americans had scheduled another meeting to discuss their offer on the lease, but if she gave up the Cato, what would be left for her in London? A soul-destroying round of job applications? Scrabbling together enough money to pay for the rent, whilst bleeding a fortune into the upkeep of Villa Clara?

It all boiled down to two answers: give up the museum and live in a ruin she couldn't afford to fix, or sell the villa and use the profit to patch up the museum finances until things started to level out. It was a question Stefano could not help her with: his heart was in Villa Clara, and she knew that his light-hearted comments about Phoebe coming out there permanently were in truth sincere. A truce had been called until probate was through, all decisions put on hold, and she had finally been able to enjoy this short oasis of time out from the real world, time in which she almost allowed herself to imagine not having to return to London, not having to say goodbye to Stefano.

And now her visit was nearly over. They had gone into San Gimignano that morning with a shopping list from Angelina for the last dinner before Phoebe went back the next morning. For a short while she had felt like just another tourist, as she and Stefano drank coffee in the square whilst bells from the many church towers pealed their cacophonous cries across the medieval streets. While they sat there, he talked to her about the breakdown of his relationship with Jocelyn, and when Phoebe had asked if it was the distance that had been the problem, he'd shrugged. She'd tried to be sympathetic, but couldn't help a little spark of pleasure in the departure of the irritating, perfect Jocelyn from his life.

He had left her briefly to do some errands, and wandering alone around the town, she had found herself standing in front of an estate agent's window. She had cast her eye over a dozen Villa Claras, noting with surprise the prices they were fetching, now that the North London literati was busy making its second home here. Checking Stefano was not in sight, she had popped inside, and persuaded by an agent keen to offer a valuation, she had taken a card. It was security, she had told herself as she dropped it guiltily in her pocket.

All talk of the future was barred that evening, as Phoebe dined with Stefano's family on the terrace, making the most of the last warm weather of the year and sharing stories of Bruce, toasting him with wine that would not make it to the inventory she needed to compile. She looked around the candlelit table, savouring this perfect evening with people she loved, and wishing she knew how to make the future safe for them.

'I don't want to go back tomorrow,' she said once the table had been cleared and the house put to sleep. She and Stefano sat on the balustrade together, looking out over the dark hills beyond, his jacket around her shoulders. Everything felt easier with him beside her. He was solid, reassuring, her best friend, and she would miss him.

'I wish you didn't have to.'

She sighed. 'Life. It gets in the way sometimes.'

'Then we mustn't let it.' He hesitated. 'And please, don't make any decisions yet. About the Villa, I mean.'

'I promised, didn't I?' Their hours of talks about what to do had ended in an amicable impasse, to be resolved only when probate was through and the full picture available.

'You did.' He sighed. 'Come back soon, Topolino.'

She batted at a moth drawn by the hurricane lamp beside

her, knowing it would be a while before she could allow herself the time or expense of another visit. 'I'll try. And in the meantime, will you look at getting someone in to open up the studio attic? I'm worried he's hidden some treasure up there that might save my life or get me into trouble.'

'Of course. As soon as I get a chance. I've got some overseas work trips coming up.'

'I'm sorry. I know you're busy.'

'We both are.' He smiled.

'And now I've got this silly hunt of Bruce's, on top of everything else.'

'It doesn't sound so silly.'

'I suppose not.'

'And it seems to have given you a new lease of life.'

She frowned. 'Really?'

'Of course. You've been so flat since Bruce died. He knew what he was doing, setting this up for you.'

'Manipulated from the grave,' Phoebe laughed. 'He'd love that.'

'And you think you can find something in those notebooks?'

'I hope so. He kept good records. I'm not entirely sure what I'm looking for yet, but at least having them in London will help. Even if they do take up my entire suitcase.' It had been strange going back into Bruce's studio and she hadn't wanted to loiter, picking up the notebooks and locking up after herself.

'So what's next? With the trail, I mean.'

'I need to find out whether Leonora did publish something about Viner.'

'I hope she did.'

'And there was an address on a calling card that Bruce had

incorporated into the painting hidden at Joan's. A lawyer's office in London. I guess I'll be paying a visit there, too.'

He squeezed her shoulder. 'He'd be proud of you, you know?'

She looked up. 'Do you think so?'

'Not everyone would have the energy to follow this through. It was a big ask.'

'That's what I thought at first, but actually I think it's helping me. Grieving someone like Bruce is hard, but this way, I feel he's helping me navigate it, giving me a reason to get up in the mornings.'

Stefano turned to face her. 'Has it been that bad?'

'Sometimes.'

'I hate to think of you being sad.'

She smiled. 'How can I be sad when I have a friend like you?'

They sat for a moment, looking at one another, and she felt a jolt, a shift in the air as suddenly he seemed different, or was it that she suddenly saw him differently?

A dull flash of light illuminated the skyline on the horizon, and a soft boom brought with it a breeze of cool air. 'We should go in,' he said. 'There's another storm coming.'

They hopped off the wall, and by the time Stefano delivered her inside the villa, fat drops of rain were pummelling the terrace. She hugged him goodnight before they kissed on the cheek and he ran under cover of his jacket towards his parents' apartment across the courtyard. Within minutes, whatever she thought she had imagined between them was washed away in rivers of rainwater.

42

It took her a few days of acclimatisation and catching up with Tilly about the museum before Phoebe could carve out time to investigate whether Leonora had indeed gone to the press. Another funding application had been turned down, and the Americans' offer upped in her absence, but she had also been offered a set of forged identity papers that had once belonged to a WW2 French spy and told a remarkable, tragic story of bravery that Phoebe longed to showcase. Such reminders of her original passion for the museum were helpful and confusing at the same time, and so it was with relief that she set aside an afternoon to search out the next stage of Leonora's story.

It was a long trek north-west up to Colindale and the anonymous-looking thirties building that held the British Library's newspaper archive. After working her way through the card indexes, she found what she was looking for, and it only remained to wait for one of the staff to sift through miles of print and microfilm and find it for her.

What did she have so far? she wondered as she opened her notebook and pulled out a pencil. Or rather who?

Bruce
Andrei

Cosmo

Joan

Four people, four paintings, four pieces of correspondence: the postcard from Ventimiglia; the injunction from Viner's lawyers; the letter from Leonora to Bruce; an invitation from a Fleet Street editor; and now the address of a London barrister.

Had Bruce meant for Phoebe to gather enough evidence to report Viner to the police? Or did he just want her to know what had happened? And what of Leonora? Where was she, and why had no one heard from her for so many years? Phoebe had taken a sneaky peek at the London telephone directory, but the only Mrs L. Birch she had found was a forty-six-year-old Laura in Richmond.

She considered again the miniature pictures within each painting: Leonardo da Vinci, Raphael, Breughel, and now Rembrandt. The candle in Joan's painting had burned down a little further than the last, suggesting a chronology to these drawings, which she would cross-check against Bruce's note-books.

A trolley trundled into the reading room and various large, leather-bound volumes were distributed amongst the other library users, until eventually a young man handed Phoebe a note. 'We've only got these on microfilm,' he said. 'They're ready at the desk for you.'

Phoebe gathered her things and collected the microfilms, waiting patiently whilst someone showed her how to load them into the viewer. She leaned closer to the machine, adjusting the brightness and focus as she wound forward to the front page of the *Bulletin* from 14 September 1963, where amongst the griping over a limping Tory government and a photograph of

Christine Keeler larking about in a bikini, it was impossible to miss a teaser for the Sunday edition the next day:

> **In the Frame:** Tomorrow, in a *Bulletin* exclusive, a former gallery assistant throws open the lid on the career of an internationally known Bond Street art dealer. From fakes and forgeries to a stolen masterpiece, learn how he has fooled the art world – and the Crown! – for over thirty years.

Phoebe sat back. This was fighting talk, even though Viner had not been named. Joan was right: Leonora Birch had been spitting mad. She quickly swapped film, fumbling as she impatiently loaded the *Bulletin*'s edition for Sunday, 15 September.

43

London, 14 September 1963

Leonora sat alone in her empty parlour, considering how life might change once the papers hit the newsstands the next day. Laurence and Margot had gone for dinner before heading to the Fleet Street office to see an early edition of tomorrow's *Bulletin*, and Joan was out somewhere or other with Alf. Linda had gone to look after her mother in Pinner after a hernia operation, and Hillary was on a night shift, having just had time to tell Leonora that Lyov's sister was on her way to Helsinki, the first stage of her journey to London.

An evening concert of Brahms was playing on the Third Programme, but Leonora could not relax. The opportunity to expose Edwin had been so tempting, but she wondered whether she should have dragged Laurence into a character assassination of his own father. Father? That was a joke. Even if Edwin had insisted, Leonora wouldn't have let him anywhere near Laurence.

She put her hand in her jacket pocket needing the reassurance of Bruce's telegram once more: THIEVING CAD STOP BE CAREFUL STOP ALWAYS YOURS STOP BC. *Always yours . . .* How could he always be hers when he was married to someone else? And why did it still matter so much to her? She picked up that morning's *Bulletin*, its front-page splash advertising the upcoming feature about a so far unnamed member of the art establishment. If it didn't take a genius to work out who he was, how easy would it be to connect Leonora with the story? Pickles had promised to play down her part in the exposé, but she had been firmly, if anonymously, positioned as the primary source.

Had she started something she would regret? No, she told herself. She had not. She had done this for Bruce, for the man she had been forced to abandon. Everyone made their own beds, and hers was unbearably empty without him.

To distract herself, she picked up pencil and paper. Without planning what she might draw, she let the lines appear on the page, and as she sketched Villa Clara and its distinctive watchtower, she wondered if he were sitting there right now, glass of wine in hand as he watched the Tuscan sunset. Perhaps he was drawing too, working alongside her as he once used to, but now nearly a thousand miles apart. Better to be grateful for what one had, she told herself, than pine for what one had lost.

As the doorbell rang unexpectedly, she sighed at the interruption. She was in no mood for visitors and had swapped her girdle and day clothes for the shabby silk kimono Bruce bought her many years ago. Hoping whoever it was would go away, she turned up the radio, and it was with some irritation that she put down her sketch pad as the ringing continued. If one of her tenants had forgotten her key again, she'd put the girl's rent up.

'All right, all right,' she muttered as she made her way along the hallway.

She opened the door a crack, then pushed her reading glasses down her nose, in order to be certain she was seeing what she thought she was seeing. 'Good Lord,' she gasped.

'Still wearing that old thing, Nora?' A broad smile burst through his salt-and-pepper-flecked beard.

'What in heaven's name are you doing here?' she said, kicking herself for the inanity of the first words she had spoken to Bruce Cato for twenty-five years.

'You think I'd let you take on that man alone?' He held out a bouquet of dahlias, a bonfire of reds and golds wrapped in a paper cocoon. 'Your favourites.'

'You remembered. I don't know what to say.' She looked down at her state of déshabillé, aware of the grey hair tied back in a scarf, her slippered feet. 'Obviously I wasn't expecting you.'

'I'm glad you weren't. You look beautiful.'

She smiled. 'Now I'm worried about you!'

'Enough to let me in?'

The first twenty minutes or so were a strange dance as they watched one another, seated side by side on the sofa and skirting around the big issues by chatting about the small ones. Eventually Leonora showed him that morning's *Bulletin*, filling him in on everything she had discovered.

'The lying, cheating sneak,' Bruce said. 'He let you think you'd seen a Vermeer disappear off the face of the earth?'

'I know. What sort of person would do that?'

'Nora . . .' As Bruce hesitated, she looked at him closely.

'Bruce, is there something you want to tell me?'

'There is. It's important. But first I just want to look at you.' He took her hand. 'I should never have let you go. Perhaps then you wouldn't have changed your mind about me. Might still have loved me.'

'Changed my mind?' How ridiculous the old lie sounded.

How could she ever have changed her mind about the man she had loved almost all her life? Even now, she was ashamed to tell him why she had pushed him away, ashamed of being the classic idiot knocked up by the boss.

'You wrote to tell me you didn't love me, Nora.'

'I couldn't let you marry me.'

'Because you didn't love me?'

She hesitated. The lie had served its purpose, but what was the point of digging up past hurt? 'Bruce, whatever I felt back then doesn't matter now. You're married . . .'

'Was,' he said quietly.

'Oh.'

'It was a disaster. If she hadn't stormed out after six months, we probably would have killed one another.'

'I'm sorry. I wanted you to be happy.'

He shook his head. 'And you, Nora? Please tell me you were happy. That you found someone you could love more than me.'

She looked at his tanned face, unchanged but for the wrinkles that mapped out the missing years. She owed it to him to be honest at last. 'I could never have loved anyone more than you,' she said quietly.

He frowned. 'Then why leave me?'

'I had no choice.'

'The only choice we had was to love one another,' he said.

'You have no idea how I longed for that, but it couldn't be.'

Bruce snorted. 'You're telling me Leonora Birch couldn't determine her own future?'

'But that's it. It wasn't just my future – it was that of my son.'

His blue eyes widened. 'You have a son?'

'I was already pregnant when we were at Villa Clara, when you asked me to marry you. I didn't know until I returned to London.'

Bruce took a moment before he let out a breath. 'Edwin's.'

'I didn't deserve you, Bruce. I couldn't bring my terrible choices to your doorstep.'

'You didn't think to ask me what I thought? Leonora, I've loved you ever since we were students. You imagine I'd have cared if you brought another man's child with you?'

'But Edwin's?' she said, feeling tears prick her eyes.

'Tell me, what is this son of yours like?'

'Laurence? Kind and clever. He has a prickly exterior, but underneath there's a huge and tender heart.'

Bruce smiled. 'Just like his mother.' He took her hands in his. 'Nora, I came here to help you, but I also came in the stupid hope of being with you again.'

'I don't know . . .' She felt her resistance crumble, the tension in her hands dissolve as he squeezed them and pulled her close.

'Leonora Birch,' he said as he wrapped his arms around her waist, 'would you stop arguing, for once, and just kiss me?'

44

'You know I couldn't have done this without you, Margot?'
Laurence said as they paused on the steps of the *Bulletin* offices,
late-night taxis buzzing past with their cargoes of theatre-goers.

'I just helped with some background.' 'Digging her own
grave' was in fact the expression that had sprung to mind as
she helped plot the demise of her employer.

He glanced towards the imposing façade of the Royal Courts
of Justice, further along Fleet Street. 'I'll bet you anything that
by spring Viner has been tried and found guilty there.'

'Anything?' Margot said, pulling her thin mackintosh
around her. The Indian summer of the previous week had dissolved into early autumn, and she shivered in the early-evening
cool.

He smiled. 'Unless it's another cocktail in Claridge's. Andrei
and the others will disown me. But I do owe you.'

Over the last two weeks she'd realised Laurence's prickliness was just awkwardness, and as he relaxed, she discovered a
dry wit that made her laugh so hard it hurt. No one had made
her laugh like that since . . . well, for ever, and in turn she
found her own demeanour gradually unbuttoning. 'I've enjoyed
it,' she said, shifting to let a couple pass by, hand in hand and
taking up much of the pavement.

'Me too. I mean, I know it's my job—'

'Or, technically, losing me *my* job . . .'

He winced. 'Which makes it even more generous of you.'

'Why wouldn't I? Leonora's been so good to me. Besides, I've got an interview for that new gallery next week. The owner's no fan of Edwin Viner, so I should be a shoo-in after this.'

'I hope so.' He surprised her by taking her hand. 'I'm sorry,' he said. 'I've been an arse to you, and you didn't deserve it.'

'You were an arse, Laurence Birch. But I forgive you.'

He suddenly looked embarrassed. 'Enough to let me kiss you?'

'Maybe.' She smiled, and he pressed his lips lightly on hers, so that she could taste his tobacco, his end-of-the-day chin rough against hers. 'See,' she said as they looked at one another, 'the fabric of society has not come apart because Laurence Birch kissed a Lady.'

His eyes widened as he realised what she was saying. 'What? A Lady lady? You're Lady Margot?'

She shrugged. 'Only to the staff.'

He shook his head. 'Then I shall have to retract that kiss.'

'Don't you dare.'

'I won't if you let me buy you a drink after we've seen tomorrow's paper. They should have the first run out by now.'

'Dinner *and* drinks?'

'It seems a shame just to go home after all this. And,' he added, his hands on her shoulders, 'well, this.'

'Drinks it is. And you get to choose where this time.' She hesitated. 'You do think Joan will be all right, don't you?'

'I think Joan can look after herself pretty well.'

'Still, I don't like to think of her out there with Alf. What if something goes wrong?' She'd been horrified at Joan wanting to be part of what seemed a crazy plan, but if there was one thing she had learned about Joan Carter, it was that she wouldn't be told anything.

'I get the feeling Alf Jackson has had plenty of practice at this. She'll be fine.'

'I hope so,' Margot said, unconvinced. 'Do you think we should have told Leonora?'

'Absolutely not. Now shall we go and see tomorrow's front page? I've heard it's a cracker.'

Margot followed him up the steps to the offices, wishing she shared his confidence.

The anonymous black Wolseley crawled to a standstill on a wooded lane skirting the Charlwood estate, and Alf's driver switched off the headlamps. 'This do, boss?' he growled.

'Good job, Smiler,' Alf said, the leather of the back seat creaking as he turned to Joan. 'You all right, Joanie? Know what you got to do?'

'Yeah. I'll be fine,' she said, listening to the clicks of the cooling engine.

'That's my girl.'

This was it. Joan was Bonny to Alf's Clyde, except it was her job to stay in the car with the driver, looking at a map and pretending to be a couple who had got lost if anyone stopped to ask them. She glanced at the scar reaching up from the corner of the driver's lip, the only source of his nickname, given his permanent scowl. They were an unlikely pairing, but hopefully it wouldn't come to that.

It had taken some persuading for Alf to let her come along, but she wanted to see this through, and besides, it would look much better if she were in the car with Smiler while Alf was gone. It's not like she was dressed in head-to-toe black, like Alf. He'd told her to wear something pretty that would help her sweet-talk her way out of trouble.

'Be careful,' she said.

'Don't worry. This'll be a kids' tea party. Now you keep that seat warm for me, and we'll be back in town dancing at Esmeralda's within two hours,' he said, letting himself out of the car.

Moonlight penetrated the tree canopy above them, dappling the road and casting a blue glow on Alf's face as he muttered instructions to Smiler. He'd be all right, she knew he would, but what if something went wrong? What if Viner had heard about the newspaper article the next day? What if he hadn't gone to the meeting Alf had set up in Mayfair with a fictitious client, and was spending his Saturday night at the country estate? She glanced at the small wooden door set into the perimeter wall, designed for gamekeepers and gardeners, rather than poachers. Alf's contact at Charlwood had promised it would be open. If it wasn't, Viner was at home and the job was off.

Come on, Joanie, she told herself. Stop worrying. Alf knew what he was doing. And besides, it wasn't theft if he was returning something to its rightful owner, was it? One more thing nagged at her as she watched Alf pull a black balaclava from his pocket. She rolled down the window and called out to him. 'What if it's not there?'

'Then I get out quickly, same as I will if it is there.' He leaned into the car and planted a kiss on her lips. 'Don't worry, doll. If that gate's open, I've got a clear run all the way up to the study. A hundred quid made sure of that.'

'Don't do anything stupid,' she said. 'I ain't walking up that aisle on my own.'

He tipped his head on one side. 'Joanie, what sort of amateur d'you take me for?'

She smiled. 'A bloody good-looking one. Now bugger off, or Esmeralda's will be shut by the time we get back to London.'

He slipped the balaclava over his head and waved briefly to her before testing the handle of the gate and delivering a thumbs-up.

They were on.

Margot had half-expected Laurence to be greeted by cheers, but those on the evening shift in the almost deserted newsroom were more interested in typing up their copy. Through the clear glass of the editor's office, a man could be seen pacing up and down, his tie loosened and shirtsleeves rolled up.

Laurence tapped on Pickles' door. 'So, have we got the early print run?' he asked.

'Shut the door,' Pickles barked.

Something was wrong. They should have been celebrating, but Pickles looked as though he'd just been demoted to the post room.

'Why is Smithson here?' Laurence asked.

'Smithson is here because we need our lawyer.'

'But you ran everything past Legal?'

'Of course we did. But some idiot sub-editor did this. Look.' He threw the morning's edition at Laurence, who quickly reshuffled it and riffled through until he found the feature.

'They named her,' he said. 'Pickles, you promised she wouldn't be named.'

'Well, she bloody well has been,' Smithson said.

'Just once,' Pickles said, holding his hands out wide. 'It was a mistake.'

'One that was on sale outside Charing Cross Station for half an hour before we managed to pull it,' the lawyer said, rubbing his stubbled jaw.

'But I checked that copy myself,' Laurence said. 'Leonora Birch was not named – she's my mother. Do you think I'd have let that get through?'

'Well, someone did,' said the lawyer.

'Who was the sub-editor that night?' Laurence asked.

Pickles shrugged. 'New chap. Double-barrelled name. Hennessy something. Oh yes, Hennessy-Stuart.'

'Oh God,' Margot whispered.

'What?' Laurence asked.

'The Hennessy-Stuarts are Viner's wife's family.'

Laurence turned an uncomfortable shade of puce. 'So he's had a mole in here all this time?'

'That's the least of our problems,' Smithson spat.

Pickles leaned back in his chair. 'But we never named Viner.'

Smithson shook his head. 'You fucking idiot, Pickles. This whole story only happened because the editor-in-chief is on holiday and you're not fit to write your own name.'

Laurence glanced anxiously between the two men. 'Viner can't do anything. There is nothing untrue in what we're about to print, and we don't name him.'

'You didn't need to name him,' Smithson went on, his tone irritated. 'With Mrs Birch identified, it's obvious who he is. And now he's got carte blanche to sue the fuck out of us.'

'He can't,' Laurence said.

'You reckon? We've had a D-Notice slapped on us,' Pickles spat.

'A D-notice?' Margot asked, confused.

'Gagging order,' the editor explained tetchily. 'If we publish tomorrow, Viner will have us closed down.'

'And my mother?' Laurence said. 'Is she safe? You promised her anonymity.'

'I can't speak for Mrs Birch, but with even a few hundred copies already sold, the *Bulletin* is in trouble. We're wording a retraction right now. I suggest your mother seeks advice.'

'You can help her, can't you?'

Pickles sighed. 'Sorry, son. We have to distance ourselves.'

'And are you going to find out how her name sneaked in there? Because don't tell me it was just a mistake. It's a bloody set-up.'

'It hardly matters now how it happened. It did, and we need to row back.'

'So you're throwing her to the lions,' Laurence hissed. 'I thought this paper was different but we're just as much in the pockets of Viner and his cronies as the rest of them.'

'Now, let's calm down a minute,' the lawyer said, but Laurence had already put his jacket back on and was making for the door.

'Calm down?' He pointed at Pickles. 'You said this would be all right. You let my mother put herself on the linc. Margot, we're leaving.'

'Laurence, I'm so sorry,' Margot said as they stood on the pavement outside. It seemed impossible that only half an hour ago they had been planning an evening of celebration.

He folded his arms, watching the passing traffic. 'I should have guessed Viner would call on the big guns.'

'You did everything you could. It was a good story, well written. Pickles knows it, and maybe one day when things have settled down, the rest of the world will too.' She tried to place her hand on his arm, but he snatched it away.

'No. It's dead in the water. These people always get their own way. Your people.' He turned to her. 'You know what upsets me most? All the years Mum slogged away to do the best for me, putting herself second . . . I wanted to do something for her, for once.'

'You tried – we all tried, even Alf is trying right now – and that's what counts.'

'It counts for nothing. Can't you see that?'

Suddenly there was no sign of the tender young man who had kissed her only a short while ago. He was worried about his mother, she tried to reassure herself: of course he was irritable.

'Let's talk about it over a drink, work out what we can do next?'

He frowned. 'Drink? We need get to Ludlow Gardens,' he said. 'She's no idea what's about to hit the fan.'

Margot looked along the street, spotting the bus that would take them to Pimlico, a huge advert for Typhoo tea emblazoned on its side. 'We can catch this, but wait . . .' She hesitated, needing to know how he felt about her. 'What happened earlier . . . out here.'

He looked at her. 'Not now, Margot.'

'I just wanted—'

'You? Why does this suddenly have to be about you?'

'It's not.'

'Then why are we still here, listening to you talking about you, when my mother needs me?'

'I know. And I want to help.'

'Why? Who even are you?'

'I'm your friend. You mother's friend.'

'You're not our friend,' he said, shaking her hand from his arm. 'You're one of them. One of the Hennessy-whatnots, or whatever they call themselves, who stitched my mother up. Your whole class is rotten.'

She felt tears burn at her eyes. How could she ever have imagined there was a soft side to Laurence Birch? 'Fine,' she said. 'If you want to behave like an obnoxious oik, then that's up to you. You know, I can't believe I nearly liked you. That I thought you were all right beneath that "poor me" exterior,' she shouted, furious at the tears that gave her away. Yes, he was upset, but so was she.

Laurence hesitated. 'I'm sorry. I'm being a pig.'

Margot tried to hold back her tears as the bus grumbled to a stop, faces peering from its steamy windows. 'You are.'

He sighed. 'Look, we need to get back to Mum. Let's talk about this – about us – when it's all calmed down.' He dared a glance at her. 'If you want to?'

'I don't know.' Had she been mad to imagine that the divide between them could ever be broken down? Even if they did manage to talk this through, she began to wonder whether their differences were just too great and they faced a future of acrimony at every wrong turn.

He turned towards the bus stop. 'We need to catch this. You coming?'

She would rather crawl into a pit of snakes than go with

him right now, but where would that get Leonora? She clutched her handbag tight and set her upper lip to 'stiff' before following him inside the bus just before it pulled away from the kerb.

She could only hope that Joan's evening was going rather better.

Joan looked at her watch. Alf had been gone for too long. In and out, he'd said. Piece of cake. Straight through the trades-men's entrance of Charlwood House and up the back stairs. No one would have stopped him: the family were away, so it was a skeleton staff at the house, and Alf had paid the chauffeur to take the butler and housekeeper into town to see a film.

She clasped the driver's seat in front of her. 'Where do you think he is?' she asked Smiler, his eyes fixed on the rear-view mirror.

He shrugged, but the white knuckles grasping the steering wheel suggested he was worried too. Alf had been clear that if he wasn't back by ten thirty, they should go on without him.

Ten twenty-five.

What were they doing this for, anyway? A stupid painting? It wasn't even very good, if you asked Joan. All wishy-washy, and that daft expression on the woman's face. Except even Alf knew it was a winner.

Alf, into whose business world she had suddenly been thrust. Import–export? Supply–demand, more like. Someone demanded a piece of art, and Alf supplied it. It wasn't like he was selling drugs or guns or anything. Just stuff that posh people kept hidden away, that no one else could enjoy anyway. Alf would never touch museums and the like. He had principles.

The distant chime of a church bell ringing the half-hour

floated across the night air, and Joan began to panic. 'Shall we look for him?' she said to Smiler, but the man's puzzled brow was all the answer she needed. The last thing Alf wanted was two more people piling in and setting off alarms.

Smiler turned the key in the ignition, and the Wolseley's engine coughed into life.

'No, we can't go yet. Give him ten more minutes,' she said, peering out of the back window and willing Alf to appear, a smile on his face and a painting under his arm.

She jumped at the sudden sound of a siren as a police car, blue light flashing, screamed past.

Smiler put the car in gear, but Joan held his arm. 'It might not be about Alf.'

'Boss said to leave.'

He reversed a few feet, then executed a messy three-point turn in the layby. Any hope was quickly extinguished as they cruised slowly past the entrance to Charlwood, where a second black police car had joined the first and was tearing along the drive towards the house.

As Smiler accelerated away, Joan twisted in the seat to see the flashing lights disappear into the distance. Not only was the Vermeer lost, but so was her Alf. It would be a wretched drive back to Ludlow Gardens.

Leonora leaned up on one elbow and looked at the slumbering face on the pillow beside her. If she had known how joyous it was to be with Bruce again, her impatience over the last quarter of a century would have been unbearable. As the distant bells of Big Ben chimed eleven o'clock, she knew she should get up and put the house to bed, but she was loath to break the spell.

There would be explaining to do in the morning, on many fronts, but for now she wanted to savour this moment.

She felt him take a sharp intake of breath, waking himself with the whisper of a snore, his face breaking into a smile as he saw her beside him. He took her hand and kissed it gently. 'I do declare you are worth waiting for, Nora Birch. Will you promise not to make me wait so long next time?'

'I promise.' She frowned. 'Assuming we have another twenty-five years in us.'

'My dear Nora, sixty is the new twenty, I hear. Come back to Italy with me,' he cajoled. 'Let's start again where we left off.'

'I can't just leave,' she said. 'There's Laurence, and the girls . . .'

'The girls?'

'My tenants.'

'You'd turn me down for your lodgers?'

She sat up, pulling the sheet around her. 'They're so much more than that.'

'You always did put other people before your own happiness.'

'You know how much I wanted to go to Rome with you, but—'

He put a finger to her lips. 'I understand. You wouldn't be the woman I love if you'd done anything else. I seem to recall you pulled that "I don't love you" stunt back then too.'

'I did?'

He nodded. 'And then once again after you travelled back to London with Edwin.'

She groaned. 'What a disaster that was. I cannot believe I was so stupid as to believe him about the painting.'

'Why wouldn't you? They were scary times.'

'They took him away at gunpoint, Bruce. They were arresting people left, right and centre. The painting just didn't seem to matter in the moment.'

He stroked her hair. 'I understand. I gave away some thirteenth-century Byzantine icons in exchange for a young boy's life when Villa Clara was raided in forty-one. It was just a painting. It doesn't matter.'

'It was a Vermeer!'

'And at least we now know it's safe.' He frowned. 'Nora, I hate to do this now, but there really is something I need to tell you. Something you must absolutely not tell another soul.'

'Oh.' He looked incredibly serious all of a sudden, and she worried that he was going to tell her about a secret wife, a gaggle of love children, a warrant for his arrest. 'Am I going to like what you tell me?'

'I have no idea.'

'Then I had better brace myself, I suppose.'

She listened quietly as he spoke, nodding as she took in the implications his words held for both her past and her future.

'Thank you for your honesty,' she said as he finished.

'I should have said something years ago.'

'I'm glad you didn't. And it wouldn't have made any difference to what is about to happen.' She held up a finger. 'Wait. Someone's at the door. One of the girls must be back.'

'Haven't they got a key?'

Leonora sighed. 'Probably forgotten it.' Quite how she would explain the man in her bed to Margot or Joan, she wasn't sure, but she slid out from between the sheets and into her kimono.

'Don't be long, Mrs Birch.'

She rolled her eyes as he blew her a lazy kiss, then let herself into the hallway, closing the door behind her. The doorbell rang tinnily once more, this time accompanied by loud banging. 'All right, I'm coming.'

She paused as she reached the front door. Through the stained-glass panels she made out a tall figure that was definitely not one of her girls, and she opened the door just a crack.

'Mrs Leonora Birch?' a man in a cheap suit and trilby growled, stepping so close that she could smell the egg sandwiches he had recently eaten, and was forced to open the door wider.

'What is the meaning of this? You cannot just turn up at someone's home at this hour . . .'

'The law suggests otherwise,' the man said, pulling an envelope from his pocket. 'I'm here to serve you with notice that under Section Two of the Defamation Act 1952, a civil lawsuit will be filed against you first thing on Monday.'

'Defamation? This is ridiculous.'

'If you don't believe me, you might want to read this,' the man continued, pressing the envelope into her hand. 'From the lawyers of Sir Edwin Viner. You will be required to file your response to the court whilst evidence is gathered against you.'

'Evidence? You make this sound like I'm being arrested.'

'I should warn you,' the lawyers' representative said, 'that if you refuse to retract your accusations about Sir Edwin, this will indeed go to trial.'

'What's going on?'

Leonora turned to see Bruce standing behind her in the hallway, dishevelled but fully dressed. 'It's nothing. Just a silly mistake.' Of course it was a mistake: she hadn't been named by the *Bulletin*. 'It seems Edwin has filed a lawsuit against me. For defamation.'

'Defamation?' Bruce said, squaring up to the man. 'That's rich, coming from Viner.'

Leonora felt her blood rise. She was quite capable of dealing with this herself. 'Bruce, that's enough.'

'It's all in the letter,' the man said.

'You may as well go,' Leonora replied, shooing him away. 'I imagine I'll see you in court.'

He tipped the brim of his trilby hat. 'I bid you good evening.'

She was about to close the door when Laurence and Margot appeared, the prickly atmosphere between them tangible and her son's face ashen. 'Laurence, what is happening?' Leonora asked as he pushed inside and into the parlour.

'They named you,' he said, pouring himself a large whisky.

'What are you talking about? Pickles promised they wouldn't.'

'An apprentice sub-editor who just so happens to be related to Viner put your name in.'

'Deliberately?'

'So that Viner had cause to take you to court.'

Leonora pressed a hand to her chest. 'Oh my. This is terrible. But the paper isn't out until tomorrow. It can be stopped?'

Laurence shook his head. 'An early run went out on sale at Charing Cross Station tonight, as it always does. Viner's lawyers are all over it.'

'And all over me, it seems,' Leonora said, holding out the letter.

'Was that man who just left sent by them?' Laurence said.

She nodded.

'And sent packing by Nora,' Bruce added.

Laurence looked him up and down then turned to Leonora. 'Who the hell is this?'

Bruce took a step forward, holding out his hand. 'Bruce Cato. Old friend of your mother.'

Margot's jaw nearly hit the ground. 'Villa Clara Bruce Cato?'

Laurence took in Bruce's misbuttoned shirt, Leonora's dressing gown. 'Oh, no. Please tell me you weren't . . .'

As he turned even paler, the parlour door burst open and Joan stood on the threshold, mascara running down her cheeks. 'Mrs Birch!' she wailed.

Leonora sighed. 'Bruce, this is Joan Carter. And judging by the look on her face, the one piece of good news we might have expected this evening is not forthcoming.'

45

London, 1989

'Let's sit down, and I'll fill you in,' Phoebe said to Tilly as they pushed through the crush of after-work drinkers and found a quiet table in the old-school London pub close to the museum.

'So you found what you were looking for?' Tilly took the slice of lemon from her gin and tonic and chewed it whole.

'Sort of,' Phoebe said, raising her voice a little as the juke-box volume was turned up on the latest Madonna single.

'What does that mean?'

'Well, I trekked up to Colindale this afternoon, as you know . . .' She pulled a face. 'Have you used the Northern Line recently? Grim. Anyway, I looked up the *Bulletin* from the dates Joan gave me.'

Tilly laughed. 'I love how you and Joan Carter are on first-name terms!' She widened her eyes. 'Oh, you should introduce her to your mum.'

Phoebe raised one eyebrow. 'Really?'

'Hmm. Maybe not. So did you find what you were looking for?'

Phoebe pushed aside her white wine spritzer and leaned her arms on the table. 'Well, that's where it all gets a bit strange. The newspaper ran a teaser the day before the article about

Viner was published. Laurence Birch – Leonora's son – interviewed ex-employees who suspected dodgy dealings, women who'd found themselves in compromising situations . . .'

'Wow. He had every angle of creepiness covered.'

'Exactly. The stage was set for outing the man as a cheat and philanderer.'

'I'm sensing a but.'

Phoebe nodded. 'But when I ordered the next day's *Bulletin*, expecting to see Laurence's feature, it wasn't there.'

'The feature wasn't there?'

'The entire paper wasn't there.'

'You definitely got the right date?'

'Yes. Fifteenth September 1963. There was no *Bulletin* published that Sunday. It was pulled.'

'Viner, I'm guessing?'

'Almost certainly.'

Tilly ripped open a packet of crisps and laid it on the table. 'So what happened after that?'

'The following Monday, an apology to the unnamed subject of the teaser was published in the *Bulletin*.'

'Viner got the lawyers in?'

'Looks like it.'

'But what about Leonora?'

'I guess she must have done the same.' Phoebe pulled her notebook from her handbag. 'I found this name in the painting hidden at Joan's place.'

Tilly squinted at Phoebe's surprisingly shocking handwriting. 'Hugo Fairfax, QC,' she read. 'Is that Viner's lawyer?'

'Not unless he sacked the ones who issued the injunction in thirty-nine.'

'Maybe Leonora's, then?'

'That's what I want to find out.' Phoebe took a sip of her spritzer. 'There was something I did find in the papers from that week, though,' she said, unfolding a piece of photocopied paper and passing it across. 'The day after the feature was due out, the *Daily Mail* ran a short piece about a burglary at Charlwood.'

Tilly frowned. 'Viner's place? Where the Vermeer had been seen? Bit of a coincidence.'

'I know. And you'll never guess who was arrested for an attempted heist?'

'Go on.'

'Alf Jackson.'

'Joan's fella? I knew he'd done a stretch in prison . . .'

'He got two years for trying to steal a Gainsborough painting from Viner's study.'

'Not the Vermeer?'

'I suspect Viner found out about the break-in and moved the Vermeer somewhere else, hiding a Gainsborough instead. Alf was arrested before he discovered the switch.'

'Poor Joan.'

'I think she survived.'

'And Leonora?'

'Well, I looked this Hugo Fairfax character up. He's a barrister at Inner Temple. Still practising. He agreed to see me on Tuesday.'

'Need me to run the ship?' Tilly asked.

'Do you mind?'

'Course not. You need the distraction. It's been all funerals and tax bills recently.'

'Oh, Tills, what if I do have to sell the Villa?'

'You can't. I've got a lifetime of free holidays invested in that place.'

'Then perhaps you'd like to pay the bills? Or Angelina's wages? Arrange the olive harvest? Fix the roof?'

'Oh. OK. But you still can't get rid of it.'

'Believe me, I don't want to, but I can't keep the museum *and* the villa going.' She hesitated. 'I rang an estate agent in San Gimignano, asked them to send me a rough estimate of what Villa Clara is worth.'

Tilly looked horrified. 'You did what?'

'I know. I feel awful. But I needed an idea of where I stand, without worrying Stefano.'

'But you wouldn't sell it?'

'How could I? It would mean kicking Angelina and Marco out, apart from anything else.' Phoebe sighed. 'Maybe I'll just let those American wide boys take over the museum.' She saw Tilly's face fall. 'But then we're both out of work. You see why this is hard? It's not just about bricks and mortar.'

'Please don't make decisions based on me. There are other jobs, other museums, other bosses . . .'

'But I don't want to be your boss. I want us to be partners, if the museum survives.'

'I know you do. And I'm really grateful.' Tilly smiled. 'This treasure hunt thing has really helped, hasn't it? Bruce knew what he was doing. You seem much lighter when you talk about it.'

'That's what Stefano said.'

'Then it must be true.' Tilly raised an eyebrow. 'You know Bruce always wanted to get you two together?'

'Don't be silly.'

'Oh, come on. He could see it as clearly as everyone can except you.'

Phoebe felt the beginnings of a blush creep across her face and leapt from her seat in a poor attempt to cover it up. 'Right. Next round is on me,' she said brightly, but Tilly's smirk told her it hadn't gone unnoticed.

46

Laurence sat with his elbows on his knees, face sunk into his hands. 'We never stood a chance.' He turned to Joan, who was still clutching the brandy Bruce had poured for her. 'And now this business with Alf . . . If he talks, we're done for.'

'Not as much as my Alf is,' Joan cried. 'And he won't ever talk. He'd rather do time than get Mrs B into trouble.'

'She's already in bloody trouble!' Laurence shouted.

'And we're all here to help her,' Bruce said. 'Viner will not win this.'

'Thank you, Bruce.' Leonora smiled up at him, then spotted Laurence looking awkwardly away.

'I can't believe you drove all the way here from Italy,' Margot said to Bruce.

'When Leonora Birch calls . . .' He shrugged, his smile deepening the wrinkles sketched across his face.

'Well, I wish you hadn't. You're the one who started all this, with your fakes,' Laurence muttered.

'Laurence, enough!' Leonora said, but Bruce held up a finger.

'Never fakes. Commissioned reproductions and imaginings,' he explained. 'A fine but all-important distinction. Fakery only enters into it if someone wilfully claims them as originals in exchange for money.'

'Like Viner did,' Laurence grumbled.

'Indeed,' Bruce said. 'But our most pressing concern is to get Nora some legal advice.'

Leonora turned to her son. 'Can the newspaper help me?'

Laurence shook his head. 'The *Bulletin* has washed its hands of the whole affair – there's not a chance their lawyers will help. If I even still have a job there.'

'Well, don't look at me,' Joan sniffed. 'Nearest I've come to a lawyer is stopping myself getting pulled on to a High Court judge's lap in the club.'

'Maybe we just go through the *Yellow Pages*?' Leonora suggested.

Margot sat up, looking around the room. 'Maybe I know someone. Give me a minute,' she said, pulling change from her purse and heading out to the hall telephone.

'Mrs Birch?' the young man said, extending a slender hand from within his meticulously tailored charcoal-grey sleeve. 'Hugo Fairfax, QC,' he said. 'Or just Hugo, since we have a mutual friend.'

'A friend she is indeed,' Leonora replied, sitting straight-backed in the leather chair across from his cluttered desk, a pile of pink-ribboned files ready to topple on to their undrunk cups of tea. Margot's former fiancé occupied what one could safely describe as a broom cupboard in the Inner Temple chambers just off Fleet Street. Already the agitation of the weekend seemed a little dulled as she sat, that fresh Monday morning, opposite someone unintimidated by Viner and his lawyers. 'I really can't thank you enough. Especially given . . .' Oh dear. She had already nearly mentioned the thing she'd promised herself she would avoid.

'Not at all,' he smiled. 'I'm only too happy to help.'

She looked closely at him, seeing what a poor match he and Margot would have made. She had known plenty of Hugos at art school, all delightful men but thoroughly unlikely to form a romantic attachment to a woman. This Hugo seemed nice – she was glad they had managed to avoid one of those miserable marriages of convenience. 'And help I most certainly need.'

'As I gather. Fortunately, I am in a position to offer it.'

'Mr Fairfax – Hugo – I appreciate this, I really do, and Margot's efforts, but I should say straight away that I can't possibly afford you.'

He shook his head. 'I have plenty of clients who can. No, Mrs Birch, I would like to act for you pro bono.'

'For no fee? But why would you do that?'

'Because you mean a great deal to Margot, and she means a great deal to me. I wasn't always . . . well, fair in our relationship, and helping you will help me address that. Besides, I'm no fan of Edwin Viner. My own sister was unfortunate enough to have been invited to parties at Charlwood. Let's just say it's about time someone spoke out. I sincerely hope you will agree to my representing you.'

Leonora sank in her seat, overwhelmed by the generosity of this stranger. 'I don't know what to say.'

'Well, that is no use to either of us. I rather need you to say a great deal.'

'In that case, yes, I agree.'

'Splendid. The charge Viner has made against you can only be contested if I have the full story, and if we can persuade others to back up what you tell me.' He hesitated. 'What he will actually want is a full retraction of your allegations—'

'Never.'

'I thought you'd say that. In which case, we may see this all ending up in court.'

'In court?' Leonora said. 'Surely it won't go that far?'

Hugo sighed. 'I'm afraid we have to suppose that it will, without a public apology. And that it will be expensive. Very expensive. You are certain you want to proceed? That we cannot come to an agreement with Viner? There is every chance this will bankrupt you, Mrs Birch, and I would not be doing my job if I didn't warn you.'

She felt a little sick as the reality hit her, but no. She would not give in, even after what Bruce had told her so recently. 'I consider myself warned, in that case.'

'Very well. Then we must brace ourselves. Aside from the fact that the Attorney General is Sir Edwin's godfather, Viner's lawyers are absolute hellhounds. As soon as we file our response to their claim, my bet is that they'll offer you a quiet deal in exchange for an apology. Which is, I suspect, what he is after: his name cleared once and for all, and you effectively silenced.'

'I was silenced once before when that man's lawyers threatened me, Mr Fairfax. I shall not allow it to happen again.'

'I thought as much. Mrs Birch, do you have witnesses to corroborate your accusations?'

'Well, there's Bruce Cato, for a start. It's his work that Viner has been passing off as originals. And Joan, Margot, a baronet

279

in Norfolk who is certain Viner arranged for the disappear-ance of a Franz Hals . . . what's his name . . . ah yes. Roland Blackford.'

'Roly?' Hugo said, smiling. 'Knew him at Cambridge. Decent chap.' He paused. 'Mrs Birch, I cannot pretend this will be easy, but I will do my best for you. Let me make a telephone call and find out exactly what Viner wants.'

It was a tense few moments whilst Leonora listened to one side of a difficult conversation, but eventually he put down the telephone receiver.

'It's good news and bad.' He placed his hands palm down on the desk. 'I was right – there is a deal to be made.'

'What sort of deal?'

'You agree to retract anything you might have said, and promise not to mention Viner's name ever again. Including,' he added, 'in relation to a claim you made against Sir Edwin over twenty years ago?'

'Oh, so he hasn't forgotten he fathered my child,' she snorted.

Hugo's eyes widened. 'Ah. No mention was made of that.'

'I don't imagine it was.'

'In exchange, his lawyers will ensure that costs incurred by you be capped at one thousand pounds.'

Leonora knew she was tired, but was she really hearing correctly? 'And I am meant to be happy about this? That's half the value of my house.'

'Mrs Birch, I cannot pretend that a libel suit is anything less than cripplingly expensive to the losing party. I know we have right on our side, but that is not a guarantee of victory.

I'm afraid that if this goes to the wire and you lose, you will be looking at a sum considerably higher.'

She shook her head. 'He actually thinks he can buy me off?'

'I believe he does.' Hugo smiled. 'But I don't think he realises who he is dealing with. And it proves he is on the back foot. Are we ready to fight, Mrs Birch?'

She thought of her son, her friends, of Alf sitting in an Oxfordshire police cell right now, refusing to talk. No – this time she would not lie down.

'We are,' she replied.

47

London, November 1989

Between the bustle of Fleet Street and the River Thames lay Temple Court, a tiny, densely packed series of courtyards where lawyers crammed into narrow Georgian rabbit warrens. The vast white edifice of the Royal Courts of Justice behind her, Phoebe slipped through a gated alley and into this cobbled Dickensian landscape.

She scanned the huddles of dark-suited barristers chatting on their break from court as clerks rushed back to chambers on the sandwich run. She thought of Stefano, beavering away at the lawyers' office back in Florence as he worked on Bruce's probate, and promised herself she would call that evening. Apart from missing him, she wanted to tell him about the rough valuation she had received from the Italian estate agents, based on comparative sales over the last twelve months. The figure quoted was not a fortune but would save the museum and allow for a deposit on a London flat, if she chose. A simpler, more straightforward life, compared to skippering Villa Clara through debt and restoration, but was it what she really wanted?

Eventually, she spotted a sandy-haired older man standing at the entrance to the Inner Temple Hall, dressed in grey pinstripe trousers and wing collar, and hurried across towards him. 'Mr Fairfax?'

'Ah! You must be Miss Cato,' he said, shaking her hand. 'Unless I have yet again double-booked myself, and you are my Monday lunch a day late.' He chuckled. 'Our clerk will strangle me one of these days.'

There was an endearing scattiness to Hugo Fairfax, despite his fierce reputation in the courtroom. 'Well, I'm grateful he lent you to me for half an hour,' Phoebe said.

'You mentioned Mrs Birch in your letter. Nothing would have stopped me meeting you. Besides,' he said, 'I need lunch, and I imagine you do too. Shall we?' He gestured in the direction of the dining hall, before leading her along carpeted corridors and landings punctuated by portraits of former members. 'Nothing's changed here since I was called to the bar in fifty-six,' he said, 'except the food's rather better and the wine more expensive.'

'You've been here that long?' Phoebe said, as they entered an oak-panelled hall filled with rows of long tables where some conducted on-the-hoof meetings over bone china and others ate one-handed whilst they caught up on case law.

'For my sins . . . or rather other people's. Now, you really ought to try the roast, Miss Cato,' he said as they arrived at a long serving table. 'Guaranteed to induce a good two-hour afternoon nap.' And so it was with a heavy plate that she sat opposite Hugo and began her attempt at the north face of a lunch fit for a family of four.

Hugo glanced up to nod at an older woman passing behind them, dressed in a navy suit that brooked no argument. 'High Court judge,' he whispered. 'We're all petrified of her, except my colleagues who sing with her in the Temple amateur choir. Apparently she has a voice like a hyena. No one dare tell her. Anyway, tell me how you know Mrs Birch?'

'Well, I don't as such. But my uncle did. Bruce Cato?'

'Goodness me.' He leaned back, his long, angular features breaking into a broad smile. 'Dear Bruce. He almost got me barred after a particularly lively night at the Connaught while we were waiting for Mrs Birch's case to come to trial.'

'He had that effect on people. So she did go to court? Did you represent her against Viner?'

He nodded. 'I was persuaded to help by a friend – Margot Stockton. You're in the art business. I'm sure you know of her.'

'Of course.'

'We were . . . well, we very nearly married.'

Phoebe felt her eyes widen. 'Oh. You were . . .'

'The jilted groom.' He nodded. 'To be perfectly honest, Margot did us both a favour, and this was my opportunity to make it up to her. Besides, I became very fond of Leonora. And of your uncle, naturally. They had, by the time I met them, decided to make a go of things. Their timing was unfortunate, however.'

'The *Bulletin* feature?'

'Indeed.' He sighed, taking a break from the huge plate of fish and chips in front of him. 'If the applicant had been anyone other than Edwin Viner, and the respondent anyone other than Leonora Birch, things might have been settled quickly and easily, albeit not cheaply.'

'But his name wasn't even mentioned in the newspaper?'

Hugo tapped his finger on the table. 'No, but Leonora's was in an early edition. It would have been enough to identify

Edwin Viner to anyone in the business. It transpired that a relative of Sir Edwin's family was working as a sub-editor at the newspaper and inserted her name into the copy. Mistake? Design? We will never know.'

'But we can guess?'

'We can indeed. Whatever the truth, Leonora had been thrown into a vat of hot water. Viner filed a libel claim, determined to force a public apology from her.'

'Even though her allegations were true?'

He brushed crumbs from the bib of his starched white shirt. 'I am not at liberty to comment. Anyway, Leonora was given the opportunity to retract her accusations via a statement in open court, but she refused. She believed that if the case went the full distance, she could prove her innocence, and thereby his guilt: "Honest opinion",' he explained. 'A valid legal defence in a defamation trial.'

'And she had witnesses?'

'Indeed. Miss Carter, for one.'

'Joan appeared in court?'

'One could say that. She made rather a splash.'

'And others?'

'Bruce, of course. Oh, and an old pal of mine from Cambridge agreed to testify – Roly Blackford.' He glanced at his watch. 'Oh my goodness. I'm afraid I have to dash. Due in court shortly.' He clearly sensed her disappointment, for he pulled out of his briefcase a thick manila envelope. 'But I do have something for you.'

Phoebe took the packet from him. 'What is it?'

'Extracts from the trial transcript. You are no doubt aware that the trial was held in a closed court – not unusual for defamation cases, since they are about protecting privacy. There was a reporting ban, meaning that newspapers were not permitted to disclose details, and as far as I'm aware, any surviving transcripts are still protected by the thirty-year rule and won't be accessioned to the public for a while yet. This, however, is my personal copy. It will tell you everything you need to know. Well, almost everything.'

'Oh?'

'You may also want to talk to one of Leonora's tenants.'

'You mean Joan? Or Margot?'

He nodded towards the file. 'It's all in there.'

'Are those your instructions or Bruce's?' she asked, smiling.

He winked. 'I think you know the answer to that.'

'Thank you so much for all this,' she said as they retraced their steps.

'It's nothing. I hope you get him this time. Please, let me know if I can do anything.' And as they found themselves outside once more, she watched him stride towards the Strand, his dark jacket tails flapping behind him.

Phoebe made her way out through the maze of narrow streets. Spotting a bus that would save her the short walk to the museum, she broke into a run and jumped on to the back, clutching the afternoon's spoils to her chest. She was getting closer to whatever it was Bruce wanted from her.

Excerpts from *Viner* v. *Birch*

Royal Courts of Justice, Queen's Bench Division

2 March 1964

Judge: The Honourable Mr Justice Thornbridge
Counsel for the applicant: Mr Charles Beresford, QC
Counsel for the respondent: Mr Hugo Fairfax, QC

MR JUSTICE THORNBRIDGE: We are here to ascertain
whether defamatory claims made by Leonora Birch
about Sir Edwin Viner in the *Bulletin* newspaper on
15 September 1963 were intended to cause lasting
reputational damage, or whether they form her own
honest belief. We will hear how Mrs Birch, a former
employee at the applicant's art gallery, claims that Sir
Edwin Viner stole a painting in 1939, and deliberately
sold reproduction drawings as originals through his
gallery.

Sir Edwin in turn will attempt to demonstrate that
Leonora Birch's bitterness over losing her job fuelled a
decades-long vendetta culminating in her defamatory
campaign and a planned burglary from his family home,
one that was intercepted by the police on 14 September
last year.

I would remind the court that this is a civil action,
taken by Sir Edwin against Mrs Birch, and not a criminal
trial against either party. I confirm, also, that all attempts

at alternative dispute resolution have been rejected by Mrs Birch, and that she is aware of the financial and legal consequences of her losing this case.

Mr Fairfax, for one final time, is your client prepared to submit the retraction requested by counsel for the applicant?

MR HUGO FAIRFAX: She is not, My Lord.

MR JUSTICE THORNBRIDGE: In that case, Mr Beresford, please call your first witness.

Examination of Sir Edwin Viner

MR CHARLES BERESFORD: Sir Edwin, can you tell the court why you have taken this action?

EV: I believe Leonora Birch made these claims with the intent of destroying my reputation and career.

CB: Why would she do that?

EV: Leonora Birch was an employee of mine over twenty years ago. She left on such acrimonious terms that I was forced to take out an injunction to protect myself against her.

CB: Why did she leave your employment?

EV: Leonora Birch harboured feelings for me – feelings I obviously did not reciprocate – which made working together impossible. Apart from this, her work was substandard.

MR JUSTICE THORNBRIDGE: Mrs Birch. Please sit down.

CB: Sir Edwin, Mrs Birch claims that you have been selling forgeries by Bruce Cato through your gallery. This is quite some accusation, for someone of your standing in the art community. How do you respond?

EV: Bruce Cato acted as a go-between for me many years ago, sourcing artworks in Italy. I only later became aware of his sideline in forgery. He attempted to sell me some of these forged works in September 1939. They were of an exceptional standard and would easily have slipped through the net for high sums of money, which he suggested we split. I of course refused. I have never, to my knowledge, sold a Bruce Cato copy through my gallery.

CB: Moving on to the allegation of a stolen Vermeer painting hidden at Charlwood, what evidence do you imagine Mrs Birch had for this?

EV: None. She took an incident at Ventimiglia station in 1939, where my luggage was searched and a poor-quality work of art given to me by Bruce Cato was taken, and formed some fantastical story based around it. The woman is deluded.

Cross-examination of Sir Edwin Viner

MR HUGO FAIRFAX: Sir Edwin, did you visit Mr Cato at Villa Clara in August to September 1939, with Leonora Birch?

EV: I did. Cato had some pieces he wanted me to see, but apart from one that appeared to be from the Circle of Veronese, there was little of interest. It was rather a wasted journey.

HF: Despite the Johannes Vermeer painting he showed you?

EV: There was no Vermeer. I believe Mrs Birch either deliberately or mistakenly muddled the Veronese with an imagined Vermeer – the names both begin with V, after all, and she was no expert. It was this I brought back in my suitcase, and this that was stolen at Ventimiglia.

HF: I would now like to draw the court's attention to Exhibit A. [holds up typed piece of paper] Mr Viner, I have here a receipt from Bruce Cato, signed by you and dated 8 September for a Vermeer painting. How do you explain this?

EV: [laughs] Quite simply. Bruce Cato is the finest forger I have ever encountered.

Examination of Miss Diana Viner

MR CHARLES BERESFORD: Miss Viner, what exactly occurred in your father's study at Charlwood House on the evening of 24 August last year?

DV: There was a party at Charlwood that weekend. Everyone was there. Including a nightclub hostess whom a friend – well, no longer a friend – had brought with him.

CB: You refer to Joan Carter?

DV: Yes. A tenant of Mrs Birch, as it happens. I found Joan Carter with my father in his study around nine p.m. She'd lured him there, to seduce him or steal from him, I don't know . . . but she was up to no good. Thank goodness I got there when I did. I've never known Father so grateful to see me.

CB: Was there anything of particular interest in the study?

DV: [glances at EV] He keeps one particular painting of value in there. It's been in my family for generations. She must have caught wind of it. Two weeks later, that woman's boyfriend was caught attempting to steal it. It's clear she was, as they say, 'casing the joint'.

HF: My Lord, if I may interrupt, this is subjective opinion and irrelevant to the facts.

MR JUSTICE THORNBRIDGE: I agree. Please continue, Mr Beresford.

CB: Can you tell us about this painting, Miss Viner? [pause] Who is it by?

DV: The painting is a Gainsborough.

CB: You are certain?

DV: I am.

Cross-examination of Miss Diana Viner

MR HUGO FAIRFAX: Miss Viner, since you work at your father's gallery, you are no stranger to works of art. Is that correct?

DV: Of course.

HF: In which case, you are familiar with the work of Thomas Gainsborough?

DV: Who isn't?

HF: Can you perhaps summarise his work for the court?

DV: Well. [pause] He painted that haycart in a river, didn't he?

HF: No further questions, My Lord.

Examination of Mrs Elsie Risley

MR CHARLES BERESFORD: Mrs Risley, when did you become neighbours with Leonora Birch?

ER: In January 1940, when she bought the house next door to mine. [aside to counsel] Is she allowed to stare at me like that?

CB: Mrs Risley, please focus. What caused you to be concerned about the goings-on at number 31?

HF: My Lord, that is an extremely leading turn of phrase.

MR JUSTICE THORNBRIDGE: Mr Beresford, can you perhaps find another way to express yourself?

CB: Of course. Mrs Risley, why did you telephone the police on 5 June 1963?

ER: Well, aside from the fact that I'd been living next door to an unmarried mother for twenty-three years, I was concerned about the number of Russians coming and going. And then the morning of 5 June, I went to meet a friend at the Regency Café.

CB: Who did you see there?

ER: Mrs Birch. With that Russian who's always visiting her. And another. Younger this time. She was giving him an envelope of cash or something. They were clearly up to no good. What with that son of hers and his communist meetings, I was worried she was involved in some spy ring. So I telephoned the police.

CB: You telephoned the police again on 10 July 1963. Why was that, Mrs Risley?

ER: Because gangsters had started turning up on the doorstep.

CB: Can you elucidate, Mrs Risley? [pause] Explain?

ER: That girl living with Mrs Birch, the nightclub hostess, she was hanging around with some shady characters. The house was crawling with loose women and foreign agents and crooks. I felt intimidated.

HF: My Lord, I fail to see what this has to do with the case.

CB: I am merely trying to ascertain the character of your client.

HF: In which case, my learned friend, may I in turn ascertain the character of your witness?

Cross-examination of Mrs Elsie Risley

MR HUGO FAIRFAX: Mrs Risley, you lodged complaints against Mrs Birch a total of seventeen times between 1940 and last year. I refer My Lord to Exhibit B, a report from the Metropolitan Police, dated December 1963, listing these complaints. I quote here: 'for leaving dirty milk bottles on the doorstep', 'because her lodger came home at ten p.m.', 'for painting her front door a vulgar shade of red', 'for allowing rubbish to collect around the doorstep'. Is it fair to say you had taken a personal dislike to your neighbour, Mrs Risley?

ER: She was bringing down the neighbourhood.

HF: And did the police take your complaints seriously? Did they visit Mrs Birch to investigate further?

ER: No. They did not. This country has gone to the dogs.

HF: That will be all, Mrs Risley.

3 March 1964

Examination of Mrs Leonora Birch

MR JUSTICE THORNBRIDGE: Mr Fairfax, please call forward the respondent. Mrs Birch, be warned that I will not tolerate the behaviour exhibited yesterday. This is the Royal Courts of Justice, not a greyhound track.

HF: Apologies, My Lord. Mrs Birch, you have made two claims against Sir Edwin Viner. I would like to demonstrate to the court that these allegations are based on your honest opinion. Let us begin with the allegation of theft. Going back to 1939, how did the painting come to be in Sir Edwin's possession?

LB: We had travelled to Italy to see a piece Mr Cato had found. With the political situation becoming increasingly volatile, Mr Cato asked Sir Edwin to bring the painting back to London for safety. The Vermeer – for that is what it was, not some second-rate Veronese copy – was hidden in Edwin's suitcase, whilst I took some drawings by Mr Cato in my own. We were taken off the train at Ventimiglia, and Sir Edwin and his suitcase searched by border guards. When he returned, he told me the painting had been stolen by guards. I was not able to check the suitcase myself to verify this.

HF: Might the painting still have been in the suitcase?

MR JUSTICE THORNBRIDGE: Mr Fairfax, that is a leading question.

HF: Apologies. Mrs Birch, this painting you say was

294

brought back from Mr Cato's home at Villa Clara. How would you describe it?

LB: It was of a woman writing a letter, her hair in the Dutch style of the late 1600s. It bore a startling resemblance both in execution and style to the work of Johannes Vermeer. Further research suggested a correlation between this painting and an as yet unidentified missing work.

CB: But My Lord, the witness would say it was a painting of an elephant, simply to contradict my client.

MR JUSTICE THORNBRIDGE: Please, Mr Beresford. The respondent's defence relies upon the nature of this disputed work.

HF: Mrs Birch, when did you become aware that this painting might not have been stolen, as claimed?

LB: When it was seen in Edwin Viner's study by Joan Carter.

HF: And why was Miss Carter in the study at Charlwood?

LB: She was attending a party at Charlwood. When Sir Edwin invited her to his study – not surprising, as she is rather his type—

MR JUSTICE THORNBRIDGE: Mrs Birch. Really.

LB: Very well. While she was there, she saw what she later described to me as the Vermeer I had witnessed packed into Sir Edwin's luggage in 1939.

HF: Let us now move on to the drawings you claim were fraudulently sold. When did you first become aware of these?

LB: In June last year. I spotted something in *Art World*. A trade magazine. There was a photograph of a Breughel sketch, a previously unseen work that had come up for sale at Viner's. Except that I had seen it before.

HF: Where had you seen it, Mrs Birch?

LB: At Villa Clara. In the studio of Bruce Cato. It had been commissioned by Edwin Viner for a client, for personal use only. And then a few weeks later, a Raphael sketch for the head of St Barbara appeared at the same gallery. I brought these two drawings home myself in September 1939. I would know them anywhere. [looks towards applicant] They are not originals, and they were never conceived as such.

Cross-examination of Mrs Leonora Birch

MR CHARLES BERESFORD: Mrs Birch, I wonder if you could tell me whether there is a Mr Birch?

LB: [clears throat] There is not.

CB: But you told your neighbour Mrs Risley in 1940 that you were a war widow, when by your own admission just now you weren't?

LB: I had a right to my privacy.

CB: I'm confused as to why the court should believe a woman who can't even tell the truth about her own circumstances?

HF: My Lord, my client's personal circumstances have no bearing upon this case.

MR JUSTICE THORNBRIDGE: Mr Fairfax, that is for me to decide. Please continue, Mr Beresford.

CB: On the subject of the accusation by Mrs Risley of your consorting with Russians, do you admit that you were seen with two Russians at the Regency Café in June last year?

LB: Of course. Why would I deny it?

CB: You had arranged the meeting in order to make contact with someone inside the Soviet Union. Is that correct?

LB: Well, yes. But it's not how you make it sound.

CB: How do I make it sound, Mrs Birch?

LB: Like some Cambridge spy ring meeting. It was nothing of the sort. My old professor from the Chelsea School of Art has a sister who was very ill in Leningrad. A friend of mine had arranged help to remove her to this country.

CB: A friend?

LB: My tenant Miss Stevenson. She worked for the Foreign Office. She will vouch for this.

HF: Miss Stevenson will be appearing as a witness for the respondent, My Lord. I see no point in pursuing this course until then.

MR JUSTICE THORNBRIDGE: Agreed.

CB: In which case I would like to bring up the injunction served against you by Sir Edwin in 1939. Were you threatening my client at that time?

LB: Sir Edwin was trying to ensure my silence on a certain matter.

CB: A matter that concerned his business practice, as with these more recent accusations?

LB: I prefer not to say.

CB: Come, Mrs Birch. You say Sir Edwin wished to silence you. If he behaved so badly, perhaps you can tell the court what had happened?

LB: I cannot.

CB: Since Mrs Birch is not prepared to tell us what this previous dispute was about, I would like, if I may, to dig a little deeper into her relationship with the man who drafted the drawings she claims Sir Edwin commissioned. You and Mr Cato were old friends, I believe?

LB: [pause] We were art students together in the twenties.

CB: And when you visited Villa Clara with Sir Edwin in 1939, were you still friends?

LB: We had not met for many years.

CB: And when you left Villa Clara? Were you by then lovers?

LB: [glances at applicant and clears throat] We had become engaged. And then later disengaged, so to speak.

CB: Are you still lovers?

LB: Mr Cato and I have recently resumed our relationship.

CB: Is this why you suddenly decided to commence this campaign against Sir Edwin? Was it a plot with your lover Mr Cato to discredit the man who accused him of being a fraud? A man who terminated your employment and against whom you have held a grudge ever since?

HF: My Lord, my learned friend is deliberately leading the witness.

MR JUSTICE THORNBRIDGE: Mr Beresford, could you please consider your use of language?

CB: Of course, My Lord. One more question. Mrs Birch,

if I may. You say this alleged Vermeer was stolen. Did you ever report the theft?

LB: [pause] No.

CB: Because there was no Vermeer?

LB: Because I could not bear its loss. Because it was wartime, and the chances of it being recovered were non-existent. Sir Edwin and I agreed never to speak of it again.

CB: Until it suited you. No further questions, My Lord.

Examination of Miss Joan Carter

MR HUGO FAIRFAX: Miss Carter, where were you on the evening on Saturday 24 August last year?

JC: [smiles at the judge] I was at Charlwood House. At a party.

HF: And who invited you to this party?

JC: [waves at a member of the public in the gallery] Him.

HF: For the benefit of the court, can you name the gentleman in question?

JC: Cosmo. The Honourable Cosmo Stockton-Jones.

HF: Miss Carter, how did you find yourself in Sir Edwin's study?

JC: Well, apart from the fact I knew he had something hidden in there, he thought he was in with a chance, didn't he?

HF: A chance?

JC: You know. Dirty old sod as good as asked me to be his mistress.

CB: My Lord, this is an outrageous and unsubstantiated slur on my client.

MR JUSTICE THORNBRIDGE: I agree. Miss Carter, mind your language. And would someone please fetch Lady Viner a glass of water?

HF: What did you see in the study, Miss Carter?

JC: There was a painting behind a curtain in a cupboard. He said it was valuable. Proper valuable. He'd tried to get it shifted earlier that evening by my Alf. Alf Jackson.

CB: My Lord, Mr Jackson is currently at Wandsworth Prison serving a sentence for attempting to steal the said painting. His statement is hardly reliable.

MR JUSTICE THORNBRIDGE: Miss Carter, please stick to answering the questions.

HF: We have been told by Mrs Birch that the painting stolen – allegedly stolen – at Ventimiglia was of a young woman at a writing desk. Was this the painting you saw?

JC: Yes. She had a long dress and fancy hair. Mrs Birch asked me to mime what the girl in it was doing, and she recognised it straight away.

Cross-examination of Miss Joan Carter

CB: Miss Carter, you are a nightclub hostess?

JC: Not in the way you're suggesting.

CB: And what am I suggesting?

JC: Well, you know. But I'm not that. I'm a waitress.

CB: Have you ever formed personal friendships with any of your . . . clients?

JC: No.

CB: Not even Cosmo Stockton-Jones?

JC: Well, yes. But we're just friends.

CB: The same gentleman with whom you were at the Flamingo nightclub the evening a fight broke out over you between Alfred Jackson and an American GI?

JC: I don't see what that has to do with anything.

CB: Just setting the scene, Miss Carter.

JC: I'm a respectable young woman, I'll have you know. I'm engaged to be married.

CB: To Alfred Jackson, currently serving a two-year sentence for attempted burglary?

JC: He was stitched up. [points to applicant] By him.

MR JUSTICE THORNBRIDGE: Miss Carter, I must remind you to behave in court.

CB: Miss Carter, I am going to show you three photographs of different paintings. I would like you to tell me which is by Vermeer.

HF: My Lord, I fail to see what this has to do with the case. Miss Carter is not here as an art historian.

MR JUSTICE THORNBRIDGE: Then let us find out. Please, Mr Beresford, continue.

[counsel for the applicant shows three photographs to Miss Carter]

CB: Take your time, Miss Carter. And when you are ready, please tell the court which you believe to be closest to the painting you say you saw in the study at Charlwood.

JC: [hesitates] This one.

CB: Miss Carter, could you hold the photograph up for the court to see, please?

[witness holds a photograph up]

CB: Thank you. You have successfully identified a portrait

by Thomas Gainsborough of a woman in a blue gown. The one nearly stolen by Mr Jackson last September.

HF: My Lord, my learned friend has deliberately led the witness. The Vermeer shown to Miss Carter here is a street scene and not a portrait.

MR JUSTICE THORNBRIDGE: Mr Beresford, do you have any further questions?

CB: [smiling] No, My Lord.

MR JUSTICE THORNBRIDGE: In that case, please call forward your next witness, Mr Fairfax.

HF: I call Sir Roland Blackford of Blackford Hall, Norfolk.

[two minutes pass]

MR JUSTICE THORNBRIDGE: Mr Fairfax, is your witness planning on joining us today? [aside, asks court usher to search for witness]

MR JUSTICE THORNBRIDGE: It appears that your witness has decided not to appear, Mr Fairfax. [shuffles through papers] I have a Miss Hillary Stevenson down to testify afterwards. Can anyone tell me whether she is in the building?

[a ten-minute break is called whilst a search takes place]

MR JUSTICE THORNBRIDGE: I'm afraid we have in the last few minutes received official notice that Miss Stevenson will not be appearing. Please strike her name from the record.

48

London, November 1989

Phoebe stepped out of the busy train station, waiting for the traffic lights to pause the heavy lunchtime traffic before making her way to the gardens of the Quaker Friends House opposite. This peaceful oasis, tucked on the fringe of the busy Euston Road, a space where office workers came to read in their lunch hours or passers-by sought a moment of calm, was also conveniently placed for the Security Services' headquarters.

It had been quite some achievement getting through the various levels required to reach the Deputy Director-General of MI5, but Hillary Stevenson's curiosity at meeting the niece of Bruce Cato had eventually broken through the protocols, and she had scheduled fifteen minutes in which Phoebe could ask her questions, if not expect answers.

Following instructions, Phoebe found a bench far enough from others that conversation could not be overheard. As she sat, she wondered who else Hillary had met here, away from the eyes and ears of the office, just a woman on her lunch break, chatting with whoever happened to sit beside her at the agreed signal.

She had seen photographs of Hillary Stevenson, but still it took a moment to recognise the grey-haired woman striding across the park. Wearing flat shoes and a brown dress-and-jacket ensemble that made no nod towards the current shoulder-padded power suits, this was 'woman at M&S', someone you would not look at twice in the post office queue. In Hillary's world, Phoebe supposed, it paid to be invisible.

'I haven't long,' Hillary said in clipped tones as she sat beside Phoebe. 'Cabinet meeting – that wretched woman always assumes we'll just scramble at a moment's notice. As though we've nothing else to do.' She sighed, wiping at the glasses hanging from a chain around her neck. 'Give it a year and there will be someone else pulling the strings, mark my words.'

'Thank you for making the time to talk to me,' Phoebe said, absorbing the rather surreal fact that Hillary's next appointment was with the Prime Minister.

Hillary shrugged. 'You piqued my interest. It's a long time since I thought about Ludlow Gardens.' Phoebe knew that Hillary Stevenson had worked in counter-terrorism in Northern Ireland during the bloodiest days of the Troubles, and was involved in negotiations around Eastern Europe as the Iron Curtain began to fall, country by country. Given rumours that even the Berlin Wall might crumble soon, Phoebe was particularly grateful for her time. 'So what can I do for you?' Hillary asked.

'It's a long story, but my uncle, Bruce Cato, a friend of Leonora Birch, died a few weeks ago.'

'I'm sorry to hear that. I left Ludlow Gardens before the trial so never got to know him, but I heard good things.'

'Anyway, I only recently discovered he'd been friends with Leonora Birch. And then Hugo Fairfax gave me a transcript of the 1964 trial.'

'Oh. I see.' Hillary stopped as a mother and her young toddler walked slowly past. This woman really did take security seriously, Phoebe thought.

'Hugo suggested I speak to a tenant of Leonora's who was called as witness. I wasn't sure who, until I reached the part where Mrs Birch was accused of being a Soviet agent—'

'Utterly ridiculous, of course.'

'Ms Stevenson, I'm sorry to be blunt, but why didn't you turn up to court that day?'

Hillary stared at her. 'You really have to ask?'

'Perhaps not.' She hesitated. 'When I met Andrei Lyov a few weeks ago, he said you had some involvement with his father – Mrs Birch's Russian friend.'

'Goodness me, I've not heard that name for years. I never knew Andrei terribly well – he and Laurence used to try and drag me to the pub. It was never my scene, even though there used to be a bar at our old HQ in Leconfield House. Reasoned that it was better to have your spies drunk at work than blabbing in some Soho drinking den.'

'But you did know Andrei's father?'

'A little. Is he still alive? Probably not. He'd be ridiculously old by now.'

'No, but his sister is.'

One corner of Hillary's thin lips rose in a half-smile. 'I'm glad. Made it all worth it.'

'What do you mean?'

She turned to Phoebe. 'I am only allowed to give you the bare bones, for obvious reasons, but I can explain why poor Mrs Birch had the Russian card thrown at her.'

'So there was something going on?'

'Not in the way that was suggested.'

'So what was the actual story?'

'Valentin Lyov's younger sister was stuck in Leningrad and awfully ill. Back in those days I was a desk officer – nothing terribly glamorous, but I was a Modern Languages graduate and had my uses. Counter-intelligence, weeding out "subversives". There was justified paranoia about the KGB back during the Cold War – Gorbachev and Perestroika were unthinkable back then, and as for the falling of the Iron Curtain we're witnessing this year . . . impossible. Might yet put a few of us out of work if Berlin does open up,' she sighed. 'Anyway, I was working on a unit assessing communist threats, after Burgess and Maclean did their thing. I had a friend who worked with the section managing defected Russians – KGB, diplomats, creatives . . . He knew someone who could move Lyov's sister out. The Lyovs were White Russians, with aristocratic connections, which made them vulnerable.'

'But what did that have to do with Leonora?'

'Lyov was her friend – her old art professor. It was she who asked me for help.'

'Hardly a crime?'

'Perhaps not, but with anti-Russian feelings running high, it was risky. Eventually we got word that the sister could be extricated via Finland, but obviously I couldn't bring Lyov to meet my contact. I'd have been had up for espionage as soon as you could say "Kremlin".' She hesitated. 'Lyov was quite frail then, and so Mrs Birch accompanied him. I'm afraid she was spotted in the Regency Café in Pimlico with two Russians and a wad of cash. It didn't look good.'

'But you were just trying to help an old émigré?'

'That's not how it was painted. And then a file was found planted amongst some "of interest" ones I had worked on.'

'What kind of file?'

'It was the file of Laurence Birch, Leonora's son.'

'You were spying on Laurence?'

'Of course not. I had nothing to do with that file. It was a complete fabrication. Yes, he'd been to Labour party meetings – I knew about those – but the file contained trumped-up reports of his presence at rallies run by the Communist Party of Great Britain. It was Laurence who wrote the newspaper story exposing Viner, and this was the most elegant way to discredit him. Add to that a mother who lunches with Russian dissidents, and Mrs Birch was in deep trouble.'

'Were you able to explain the truth?'

'I was approached by her barrister, Hugo Fairfax, and agreed I would help. The next day at work, however, I found I had been moved to the personnel department – Personal Hell, as we called it – where I would remain for two years. I was taken to an interrogation room and reminded rather forcefully that I had signed the Official Secrets Act. Even if I had agreed to testify that Mrs Birch's Russian connections were innocent, I would never have made it as far as the witness box. And there was the underlying threat of "outing" her son Laurence. She would have hated that.' Hillary's eyes followed a police van, blue lights flashing as it wove through the heavy traffic. 'But still. I will never forgive myself.'

'From what I've learned, Leonora wouldn't have wanted you to sacrifice your career for her. Besides, I expect one more witness would have made little difference.' Phoebe smiled. 'I have an open invitation to dinner with the Lyovs. Perhaps you should come with me. Meet Andrei's aunt, who has had a long and healthy life since you helped her leave the Soviet Union.'

'Perhaps. And now you must excuse me. The Iron Lady waits for no woman.' Hillary readjusted the silk scarf knotted at her throat, then stood, holding out a hand to Phoebe. 'I hope you are able to make good some of the injustices of the past. Viner has it coming, if you ask me.' She winked, so briefly that Phoebe wondered if she had imagined it. 'But of course you never did. Good day, Miss Cato.'

She turned and walked away, blending into the grey London afternoon as though she had never been there at all.

Excerpts from *Viner* v. *Birch* (cont.)

4 March 1964

Examination of Mr Bruce Cato

MR HUGO FAIRFAX: Mr Cato, how would you describe
yourself, in professional terms?

BC: I am an artist, copyist and restorer of works of art.

HF: And where did you learn your craft?

BC: At the Chelsea School of Art, the Royal Academy
and in Rome.

HF: That is an impressive curriculum vitae, from someone
quoted by his former professor as 'one of the most
talented draftsmen' he has encountered.

BC: [shrugs] I have spent many years studying the
techniques of the Old Masters.

HF: What is the purpose of the reproductions you
produce, Mr Cato?

BC: They are commissioned by perhaps film companies,
for use on set, sometimes by collectors – old drawings are
very vulnerable to light, and I provide a copy that can be
displayed whilst the original is safely stored.

HF: How can these copies be distinguished from the
original?

BC: Not to blow my own trumpet, but with difficulty.
I never, however, replicate collectors' stamps or other
identifying features that might cause confusion on the
open market.

HF: Mr Cato, what was the purpose of Edwin Viner's visit to you in August to September of 1939?

BC: Viner had commissioned some drawings for a client – an American collector.

HF: What were these drawings?

BC: A Breughel, a Rembrandt and a Raphael. He didn't want exact copies, but pieces in the style of existing drawings. Viner was very specific about the commissions. I see now that he had deliberately sought out pieces with holes in their provenance.

HF: Let us now move on to the contested painting that left Villa Clara in 1939 with Edwin Viner. What was this work, Mr Cato?

BC: It was, to the best of my knowledge, a missing work by Vermeer.

HF: Where did you acquire this painting?

BC: At a clearance sale in Venice.

HF: [holds up a piece of paper] For which we have the receipt here. And what evidence do you have that it was a Vermeer?

BC: The evidence of my eyes and my experience.

HF: Mr Viner claims that it was not the supposed Vermeer but a piece by the Circle of Veronese that he brought back with him, whilst your witness statement describes you packing the Vermeer into his suitcase yourself. How do you explain this confusion?

BC: [slams fist on witness stand] There is no damned confusion. I sent Viner away with a Vermeer. They were dangerous times. Why the hell would I go to the trouble of packing up some crappy Veronese copy? Viner took that Vermeer, as recorded in my notebook, and Viner pretended it was stolen. Viner also took those drawings – and God knows how many more over the previous years – and falsified their provenance. This should be a criminal trial, not a ridiculous witch hunt.

Cross-examination of Mr Bruce Cato

MR CHARLES BERESFORD: Mr Cato, do you recall entering for a prize at the Chelsea School of Art in 1922?

BC: I entered many prizes.

CB: The Walton Prize, for an original oil painting, came with a substantial cash incentive. Can you confirm that you entered and won this prize?

BC: [shrugs] It's possible, even likely.

CB: And do you remember what you submitted for this prize?

BC: Since I don't recall the prize, probably not.

CB: You submitted a copy of a work presented ten years earlier. Is that correct?

BC: [laughs] Ah yes. I do recall that one.

CB: Do you also recall that you were threatened with expulsion for plagiarism?

BC: It was a joke. The judges paid so little attention to the entries, they could barely remember what they'd seen. I submitted that painting to make a point.

CB: And yet you kept the prize money?

BC: I spent it on a damned fine dinner for everyone who had entered the prize that year.

CB: Moving on to August 1939, Mr Cato, it has been

suggested that instead of Sir Edwin commissioning drawings from you, you attempted to force a selection of forgeries upon him. Is this the case?

BC: Certainly not. He took away pieces he had commissioned, in Leonora Birch's luggage.

CB: Given that you and Mrs Birch are close, and you are known to be an accomplished forger—

HF: My Lord, that is a slanderous claim.

MR JUSTICE THORNBRIDGE: Mr Beresford, please choose your words more carefully.

CB: Very well. Is it not therefore possible, Mr Cato, that you and Mrs Birch identified works sold by the Viner Gallery and retrospectively fitted them to this story of yours, in order to discredit Sir Edwin?

BC: How dare you?

CB: I would like to consider the supposed Vermeer for a moment, and whether such a painting existed.

BC: Of course it bloody well existed.

CB: Then why did you not report it missing?

BC: Are you too young to remember, perhaps, that there was a war on? My friends and neighbours were being dragged to concentration camps or to work in German factories. The art market was essentially frozen. I made enquiries after the war – still have people looking out for it, so be careful, Viner, if you try to sell it—

MR JUSTICE THORNBRIDGE: Mr Cato. This is your final warning.

CB: Mr Cato, do you have proof of purchase for the disputed painting?

BC: I have a receipt.

CB: Which we have all seen, for what it is worth. I would like the court now to consider the following exhibit. [lifts Exhibit 7a] Do you know what this is, Mr Cato?

BC: It looks like an identity card.

CB: Correct. It is an Italian identity card, circa 1930s. Would you now look at Exhibit 7b? For the benefit of the court, I have shown Mr Cato two identity cards. One is genuine, and one is a very convincing forgery given to Edwin Viner in 1939. Do you recognise the second card?

BC: You know damn well I do. I made that card to save his life, if he needed it. Sadly, he didn't.

CB: So you admit that Exhibit 7b is a forgery, made by yourself?

BC: [pause] I do.

CB: Do you therefore see any reason why the court should believe that your original receipt for the supposed Vermeer and the receipt you say Sir Edwin signed for that painting are not also forgeries?

BC: Because one of us is a liar. And it is not me.

Closing speech by counsel for the applicant

MR CHARLES BERESFORD: We are here to decide whether allegations made by Leonora Birch were maliciously libellous, or of her 'honest opinion'. Over the course of the last few days we have seen how a long-held grudge by a former employee was nurtured over two decades. Already the recipient of an injunction for threatening behaviour, Mrs Birch, a woman who consorts with Russians and communists, and keeps gangsters and nightclub hostesses under her roof, attempted deliberately and maliciously to attack Sir Edwin Viner in the national press, the man who spurned her romantic attentions. She would have us believe that Sir Edwin stole from Bruce Cato a priceless painting. She would also have us believe that he knowingly acquired fake drawings from an acknowledged forger and trickster, for sale through his gallery. I put it to you, My Lord, that Mrs Birch and Mr Cato acted together to discredit Sir Edwin, with the intention of pursuing a criminal case and therefore considerable compensation. She claims to have had a witness who would testify against Sir Edwin's business practice, but where was that witness? He thought better of it. She claimed her former tenant would explain the meeting with Russians, but, again, where was that witness? We have here a desperate woman who, beyond all reason, is determined to pursue a course that can only lead to her own demise.

Closing speech by counsel for the respondent

MR HUGO FAIRFAX: It is always difficult in cases of one word against another's, but why else would my client pursue her claims, if she did not wholeheartedly believe them to be true? She has quite literally everything to lose and nothing to gain by refusing to bow to pressure for an apology. Leonora Birch is a woman of exceptional character, a good mother and loyal friend – yes, including to her old professor, a man who, it should be added, escaped the Soviet Union. When she discovered

in June 1963 that Bruce Cato had been cheated out
of the priceless Vermeer, and that his work was being
fraudulently sold, she could keep her silence no longer.
She has demonstrated, through testimony, and through the
exhibits shown here, that the claims she made were indeed
her honest opinion, formed through the evidence of her
own eyes.

49

London, 6 March 1964

'Girls, do stop fussing, would you?' Leonora said, flapping her hand at Linda, attempting to plump the cushions on the velvet sofa once more, and then feeling guilty. Poor Linda had lost yet another job and was only trying to be kind. 'I just want an ordinary evening, not to be made to feel like I've had my last supper.' Given that Leonora had just allowed Linda to cook what was possibly the most revolting lamb stew she had ever eaten, the coming hours would tell whether perhaps she had indeed.

'Well, it'd be no thanks to Pillory if you have,' Joan snorted.

'That's enough. Hillary already risked her job by helping Lyov's sister. Speaking of her work would put her in breach of the Official Secrets Act, and that would be two of us behind bars.'

'Don't say that!' Linda squealed.

Leonora sighed. 'One has to be realistic.'

'But can't you just say sorry, like they want you to?'

Joan laughed. 'Are you mad, Linda? Mrs Birch say sorry?'

'They'll have to throw away the key before I apologise for speaking the truth.' She had one last chance, she knew, to lodge an official apology before the judge announced his verdict the following day, but after the lies that had been said in court about the people she loved, even poor old Lyov, nothing would make her back down. She felt a momentary discomfort recalling the conversation she and Bruce had had the night he reappeared, and the 'something' he had told her, but her accusations of criminal activity stood firm, and she beside them. She would see this through to the bitter end.

'It still doesn't bring back the Vermeer,' Margot sighed. 'Do you actually believe the police searched Charlwood, like they said?'

'I've no doubt they did, in a cursory fashion, but I've also no doubt Edwin was given plenty of notice by his friends. Wherever that painting is now, I doubt it will ever see the light of day,' she said, knowing that this was most certainly true.

'I'm so sorry Alf couldn't get it back for you,' Joan said.

'And I'm even more sorry he's languishing in Wandsworth Prison because of me.' Languishing was not quite the word – Leonora had visited Alf to explain what she knew, and to offer him the opportunity to share the facts, but had found him most comfortable there, and not inclined to cut short his stay. Besides, he had been caught red-handed attempting to steal a Gainsborough. 'Joan, you've been remarkably stoical about it.'

Joan shrugged. 'I get to see him most weeks, and he's already running the place – he had food brought in from the Ritz the other week, if you can believe it. Says his cell is like a little palace, with a telly and everything.'

'Still, two years is a long time,' Linda said. 'What about your wedding?'

'Looks like even you'll beat me to the aisle, Linda.' Joan smiled at Leonora. 'Or you, Mrs Birch!'

'Pah. I'm far too old for that nonsense.' She made light of it, but in truth, marriage was not for her. Companionship, a fresh start, yes, but she no longer wished to play by society's rules.

'But you and Mr Cato . . .?' Linda blushed, still, Leonora noted, shocked at the new domestic arrangements at Ludlow Gardens. Had this generation learned nothing? 'I mean, he's practically your husband, now he's staying here.'

'As a temporary measure whilst this court nonsense is being sorted out. Mr Cato and I will . . . well, let's see what happens. There are already plenty of weddings afoot.' She glanced at Margot, wondering what had gone wrong between her and Laurence. Things had seemed to be progressing nicely, but any spark seemed to have been well and truly snuffed. Poor Laurence. He had felt dreadful about the fiasco with the *Bulletin*, but Leonora was grateful that the story had finally been told, even if it was in court rather than the papers. Laurence had used the enforced six-months' leave to follow up a lead at the BBC newsroom, where he was going great guns. Perhaps things would work out for the best. And at least he and Margot appeared on better terms, even if the romance Leonora had hoped for seemed no longer on the cards: 'We've decided to stick to being friends of sorts,' Margot had told her, explaining that words had been said that couldn't be taken back. Laurence had nothing to say on the matter, but his sheepishness around Margot indicated at least a little regret.

'Anyway,' she said, 'I fear we must admit defeat on the painting. It will probably grace the walls of Edwin's WC until Charlwood passes into his daughter's hands.'

'Given that she doesn't know a Vermeer from a vermouth, that's probably where it will stay,' Margot added. 'I can't believe I was ever friends with that woman, especially after what she said about you in court, Joan.'

Joan shrugged. 'Water off a duck's back. Besides, it's all publicity. I got a letter from an agent this morning, asking to sign me up. I'm handing my notice in at Henry's. The boss is furious – said they put their prices up just because of me.'

'You see?' Leonora said. 'Every cloud.'

'I can't believe you're so relaxed, with the judgement tomorrow,' Margot said.

'How else can I be? We have done everything possible. It is in the judge's hands.'

'Unless you apologise,' Margot said.

'What does Mr Cato think you should do?' Linda asked.

That was a tricky one. Bruce's loathing of Edwin was every bit as visceral as her own, and having had his reputation shredded in court, he would have happily taken Leonora's place the next day. A retraction of her accusation would see Leonora faced merely with a crippling bill, but if she refused to back down and the judge took Edwin's side, she might not be sleeping in her own bed the following night. Either way, she would have to sell Ludlow Gardens.

'Bruce wants me to follow my conscience.' She glanced at the clock on the mantelpiece. Earlier that evening she had sent Bruce out with Laurence and Andrei, under strict instructions to keep him occupied for an hour or two. She needed time with her girls on what might be their final night together at Ludlow Gardens. 'I just hope he's following my advice to behave himself this evening.'

Margot smiled sadly at her. 'He'll be proud of you, whatever you do. We all will be.'

'Thank you, Margot. But we must face facts. I may be away for some time, and this house will not keep itself going.'

'You're throwing us out?' Linda said.

She hesitated, dreading voicing the reality forced on her. 'I'm so sorry, but I have no choice other than to put the house on the market.'

'What? To sell?'

'Yes, Joan dear. That tends to be how it works.'

'But where will we live?'

'It depends upon who buys the place. If it's another land-lord, perhaps you can stay. Linda, you're rather quiet?'

'I didn't like to say, Mrs B, but I was planning on handing my notice in here. Now I've got my new job . . .' She glanced at Margot. 'Thanks for telling me about it.'

'Good job Edwin never took any notice of the staff beneath him. He clearly hasn't made the connection,' Leonora said. 'You're sure you don't mind working there, after everything?' she asked, but Linda shrugged.

'Beggars can't be choosers, and I need a job.' She chewed her lip. 'Mrs Birch, I'm ever so sorry, but I'll be moving out soon. Me and Derek . . .'

As she hesitated, Joan laughed, clapping her hands. 'You're in the family way?'

Linda's cheeks flushed an angry red. 'No! We've just decided to get married in a registry office and spend the wedding money on a deposit for a house.'

'Oh Linda, I'm sorry you won't get your big day,' Leonora said gently.

'It doesn't matter. We've been together since we were fifteen. We don't need a fancy wedding to prove we love each other.'

She glanced at Margot. 'Oh, cripes. Sorry. But you know what I mean . . .'

'Well, at least I shan't have to worry about you, Linda.' Leonora turned to Joan and Margot, squashed on the sofa together. 'What about you two? Will you find yourselves another little attic room?'

Margot turned to Joan. 'It might not come to that. Cosmo and I have found a premises for the new gallery.'

'Oh, I am pleased!' Leonora said. Cosmo Stockton-Jones had so far wasted a perfectly intelligent brain, and she suspected the joint venture with his sister was just the focus he needed. London had long lacked a gallery that would represent solely female artists, and although she was relatively inexperienced, Margot was the woman to do it. 'Where is it to be?'

'Chelsea,' Margot said. 'The King's Road. It's crawling with people desperate to buy art. And there's a two-bedroomed flat above. We were going to let it out, but if you're selling Ludlow Gardens . . . What do you think, Joan?'

Joan stood up. 'I think I should get that bottle of champagne from the fridge. Leaving present from Henry's, and I can't think of better people to drink it with.'

An unusual sensation burned suddenly at Leonora's eyes. Tears, she realised. Something she had not allowed herself to shed ever since the day the doctor had told her she was expecting Laurence. And yet these were not tears of despair at what the next day might bring, but tears of joy for the family she had made here in Ludlow Gardens, the women of whom she was so proud.

She dabbed discreetly at her eyes. 'I think that is a splendid idea.'

Joan pushed the cork from the bottle with her thumbs, and they all ducked as it ricocheted from the mirror, narrowly missing Linda's eye.

'To Linda and Derek,' Leonora said as Joan passed around Leonora's etched champagne coupes.

'To Margot and her gallery,' Joan added.

'To Joan being on the telly!' Linda laughed.

'To justice.'

'Thank you, Margot.' Leonora raised her glass. 'And to the *Girl at a Desk*, wherever she may be,' she smiled.

She woke early, listening to the clink of milk bottles on the doorstep. Beside her, Bruce slumbered, and as she watched him, she wondered whether it would be hours or months before they could be together again.

What miracle could take place, this near to the close of play? Edwin had covered his tracks, manipulated the facts, and nothing she'd thrown at him had stuck. She was no fool: his barrister knew she spoke the truth, the judge knew it – perhaps the reason he had called for the trial to be without jury and without any press presence. Whatever happened, she had forced the world to wonder whether the collective wool had been pulled over the art establishment's eyes. Certainly there were plenty of Viner's clients who would never quite see their purchases in the same light.

Bruce pulled her towards him for a whiskery kiss. 'Good morning,' he said. 'Can I tempt you to a day in court?'

'That depends upon how it ends,' she replied, brushing her fingers across his silver-speckled beard.

He frowned. 'We all know this is a charade, and yet you're still prepared to go through with it?'

'Of course,' she said, sounding more convinced than she felt. 'I will see Viner pay for what he did to both you and the rest of the art world.'

He stroked her long grey hair, released from its pins. 'In which case, I couldn't love you more, Nora Birch.'

'Well, I hope you'll love me in a prison uniform.'

He kissed her fingers then looked up at her. 'If the worst comes to the worst, Viner had better watch out. If I have to come back from the grave and haunt him, I will.'

She prised herself away and pulled open the curtains, gasping at the sight of the press photographers camped on the street outside. One of them saw her, and up went the cry as they trained their lenses on the bedroom window. She closed the curtains so roughly that several of the hooks became loose and one of the velvet drapes hung limply at an angle.

Perhaps she wasn't as ready as she thought.

50

Daily Telegraph, *7 March 1964*

Crowds gathered outside the Royal Courts of Justice yesterday for the culmination of allegedly one of the most acrimonious trials in recent times.

Mrs Leonora Birch, who has laid claims against eminent art dealer Sir Edwin Viner, arrived at court wearing a black suit with Mr Bruce Cato, whose copies of original artworks have come under scrutiny throughout the trial. She was followed by former assistant at Viner's Gallery Margot Stockton, in a navy-blue suit and black sunglasses, and her brother Cosmo, well-known playboy aristocrat and actor. They were accompanied by 'goodtime girl' Joan Carter in a baby-pink ensemble. Valentin Lyov, the rumoured 'Russian' connection, arrived with Mrs Birch's son Laurence, author of the disputed *Bulletin* feature.

Within the limitations of restricted reporting, the *Daily Telegraph* can reveal the Honourable Mr Justice Thornbridge stated in his verdict the belief that Mrs Birch's claims were malicious lies, designed to damage a man against whom she had a long-standing vendetta. These lies were corroborated by her lover Bruce Cato, a man who had over a period of several years attempted to sell forgeries to Viner's Gallery.

Mrs Birch was shown to have had dealings with Russian agents and engaged nightclub hostess Joan Carter not only to search Sir Edwin's home for information to manipulate against him, but to reconnoitre the Charlwood art collection. Miss Carter's fiancé Alf Jackson is currently serving a prison sentence for the attempted theft of artworks from Charlwood House shortly after Miss Carter's visit there.

His Honour closed by stating that despite being given every opportunity to retract her accusations about the man trusted by The Queen as a consultant, Leonora Birch had repeatedly refused, showing no remorse. As well as awarding Sir Edwin the full costs of the trial, the Honourable Mr Justice Thornbridge handed Leonora Birch a six-month custodial sentence, to be served at HM Prison Holloway. Additionally, she and Bruce Cato, along with other witnesses for the respondent, received a lifetime injunction preventing them from publishing in any manner material relating to Sir Edwin Viner.

'My wife and I just want to return to normal,' Sir Edwin told the waiting press outside, as Mrs Viner, looking tired but radiant, stood a little distance away.

Mr Hugo Fairfax, representing Leonora Birch, confirmed that she will not be appealing the judgement.

51

London, November 1989

Phoebe emerged from Notting Hill Gate Tube station and made her way through the icy drizzle towards Portobello Road, Marks & Spencer ready meal in hand. It was time to get her ducks in a row, even if she hadn't quite worked out what to do with said ducks.

Bruce's notebooks clearly laid out the trail of drawings fraudulently sold through Viner's to prestigious art institutions and private collectors who had paid a king's ransom for works bought by Edwin from Bruce at a fraction of their final price. She just needed to know how Viner had done it, and then work out how to prove it.

She also needed to know what to do about the letter that had arrived from the Italian estate agent. She'd missed her weekly chat with Stefano as he was away on business, but they could talk it through as soon as he got back. A major life decision had been pushed a little further towards the horizon for now.

Her arms full, she kicked the front door shut and put down her bags, rummaging through the post that got sorted into flats each day by Moira on the ground floor. Phoebe's only contribution so far to shared house life had been a long-since-dead pot plant for the hallway.

'Phoebe?'

'Hi, Moira.' She paused, halfway up the communal staircase as the door to the ground-floor flat opened and her neighbour peeked out, dressed, as always, as though for a wedding, in a bright fuchsia dress.

'Something came for you,' the older lady said. 'Hold on.'

Phoebe salivated at the smell of Moira's home cooking until eventually her neighbour reappeared with a flat, rectangular package wrapped in brown paper. A typed and franked envelope had been taped to the front, bearing her name and address. She ran up the stairs to her flat and tore it open.

Dear Miss Cato, it read:

> *I realised after our meeting that I have something*
> *intended for you. In my line of business, one receives*
> *gifts for many, often nefarious, reasons. Thus the enclosed*
> *was processed by my secretary when it arrived some*
> *weeks ago, and sent directly to our repository.*
>
> *I hope you will find it useful.*
>
> > *Regards*
> > *Hillary Stevenson*

Even though she knew what she would find inside, she still felt a jolt as she pushed aside the brown paper and bubble wrap to reveal the *Girl at Her Desk*, who had no doubt endured a rigorous examination by the Security Services. The candle in this version, painted on to a piece of board, was burned down to its last inch now, and yet another work hung on the wall. A quick search of Bruce's final notebook identified it as a Dürer sketch of a hand, one Phoebe remembered coming to auction a few years earlier. The only other obvious difference was that the girl was writing with a fountain pen instead of a quill.

Phoebe turned the painting around, finding an envelope taped to the back, addressed this time to Villa Clara, and posted on 4 June 1964. She pulled out a tissue-thin sheet of ruled paper bearing the address of Holloway Women's Prison, London, followed by 'Prisoner number: 70363 Name: Birch L.'

The elegant, sloping lines of the author's writing were clearly from the same hand as the Ventimiglia postcard she had found what seemed ages ago.

Dear Bruce, Leonora had written,

> *I suppose one shouldn't complain at being here. After all, it's the price of telling the truth, despite our evidence about those drawings. Besides, I am finally learning to cook, after a stint in the kitchens. I shall not inflict HM Prisons' version of shepherd's pie upon anyone when I am released, however – I suspect the key ingredient is indeed a shepherd. Other than that, I am managing to stay out of trouble, and time crawls along. I seem to have become a mother figure to some of the younger women in here, whom I'm teaching to read, and have set up a weekly drawing class. Really, it's education and good parenting they need, not punishment.*
>
> *Thank you so much for your visit last week, but you must get back to Villa Clara and your studio. I shall expect it shipshape by the time I arrive in the autumn. Dear Bruce, your idea of driving all the way here in the Alfa is madness. I shall catch the train, as I did twenty-five years ago. At least I shan't have to fend off thieves and Fascists this time.*

I know we talked about what to do next about Edwin, and whilst you are all for going to Bond Street and dealing with Edwin in the way that men will, please don't. I was intrigued by your suggestion, which is a much better idea. We must collect together useful correspondence – even this letter, perhaps! – and trust justice will come around in the end. I always did rather like a cold dish.

I had another visit from Margot and Joan last week. Margot's new gallery seems to be doing well. Apparently there is a market for female artists after all. She has been trying to persuade me to surrender some of my work. Sweet of her, but I think not. Joan, predictably, has benefited from the whole court fiasco and is going to be in a television drama.

Laurence tells me the house sale is going through. I shall miss Ludlow Gardens, but needs must. Bless Hugo for waiving his fee. It is time to move on, and Mrs Parker's Home for Young Ladies has a certain ring to it.

I hear doors being banged along the corridor – letter-writing hour must be over, and there is still so much I want to say. Let us leave all this behind and start the rest of our lives with no regrets. Edwin Viner can wait, for now.

Always yours

Nora

Phoebe felt her heart contract at this gentle intimacy, this window into her uncle's history and the love he shared with a woman Phoebe almost felt she now knew. 'Where are you, Leonora?' she whispered, looking at the letter once more.

She jumped as the doorbell buzzed, dragging herself off

the sofa to pick up the intercom. If it was Jehovah's Witnesses again, she'd scream. 'Yes?' she said wearily.

'Let me in,' a tinny voice said. 'It's freezing out here.'

'What? You're kidding?' Her head still in Leonora's letter, for a moment she doubted what she was hearing.

'Sure, I'm kidding. I came all the way from Italy just to ring your doorbell and pretend to be here,' her visitor said.

She pressed the buzzer and looked around. Shit. The place was a tip. She hurriedly scooped clothes off the radiators and threw washing-up into the sink, running her fingers through her hair and checking for food stains on her slouchy cashmere sweater before opening the door.

'What are you doing here?' she said as Stefano shook the rain off his dark hair and stepped inside the flat. 'You haven't been to London in months.' They had always made time to catch up when he was visiting Jocelyn, with whom Phoebe had established an instant and mutual dislike. She knew Jocelyn's sort: head girl at school, Golf GTi for her eighteenth birthday, mirror-shiny hair, corporate lawyer, all the best-looking boys. The only downside of the relationship ending was that Phoebe saw a little less of Stefano. 'I thought you were away for work?' she said now.

'I am,' he said, pulling away eventually and taking off his damp suit jacket. 'I was in Dublin yesterday, and I've just been asked to see a client in London first thing in the morning. I left a message on your answer machine, to see if I could stay here. You didn't get it?'

She glanced across at the red blinking light. 'Oops. Sorry. Only just got in myself.'

'Oh. OK. I can stay at a hotel?'

'No! You must stay. The spare room's a mess, and I'll need to change the sheets . . .'

'I can do that. I am a housekeeper's son, after all.'

'I haven't eaten yet – want to share a ready meal?'

He pulled a face. 'If I'm saving the company a hotel bill, they can at least stand us dinner.'

She smiled. 'Give me one minute to make myself present-able.'

Stefano shook his head. 'Don't. You look great already.'

'Now I'm worried!'

Phoebe pulled out a new orange belted dress and did as much to her face as she could in the few minutes she dared keep him waiting, before tugging on a denim jacket and knee-high suede boots and dragging him downstairs.

They found a half-decent Indian restaurant around the corner, filling up on lager and chicken bhuna as Phoebe caught Stefano up with Bruce and Leonora's story. It seemed the wrong moment to tell him about the valuation on Villa Clara, and so instead she talked about meeting Hugo Fairfax and Hillary Stevenson, about the court's verdict and the letter Leonora had written from prison, which she had brought with her to show him.

'So what's next?' Stefano asked.

'I'm not sure. I'm going to research all the drawings, to see if I can find a link to Viner.'

'Do you think there's anyone else Bruce wanted you to talk to? All the paintings have led to somebody so far.'

'It's not obvious, but maybe.'

'Here,' he said. 'Let me look at that letter.'

She handed him Leonora's Holloway letter and watched as he read it. 'What do you think?'

'I don't know. Maybe see if this Mrs Parker still lives there? She might be able to point you in the right direction.'

'Perhaps. I must admit, I'd be curious to see Ludlow Gardens. Anyway, that's enough about Leonora. I want to know how things are at Villa Clara.'

He seemed more optimistic about the probate, suggesting that although there wouldn't be much spare, Villa Clara could probably pay its way for the next twelve months. Her stomach hollowed as she recalled the letter from the agency, and watching him animatedly tell a story about his father and a recent goat invasion, she wondered how it had even occurred to her to sell.

His parents missed her, he said, as the waiter cleared away their dishes, but maybe she could go there for Christmas? He reached across the crumb-flecked white tablecloth, his green eyes on hers. 'I miss you too.' He frowned, his expression uncertain. 'I mean I really miss you, Phoebe.'

She smiled. 'I miss you too.'

They looked at one another, and as he stroked his thumb across her hand, she knew she hadn't imagined that moment on the terrace just a few weeks earlier.

'Phoebe, I lied,' he said. 'I have a hotel room booked in town. But I wanted to be with you. Give me the word, and I'll go there tonight. I don't expect anything from you, but please, think about the life we could have together in Italy, if you wanted it.'

332

She held his gaze, her pulse quickening as she understood, as he gave her permission to release feelings she'd perhaps always known were there. 'Bruce knew, didn't he?'

Stefano nodded. 'He knew how I felt about you.'

'"Look after her for me."' She felt tears pricking her eyes.

'You don't need looking after.'

'No,' she said quietly, 'but I need you.'

She woke early the next morning, her body tingling as she stretched naked in the tangled mess of sheets. She reached out a hand, puzzled at the empty space beside her, but she hadn't imagined it: the impression of his head was still in the pillow, the scent of him on her skin. Perhaps he was making coffee, having a shower. They both had work today, after all.

'Stefano?' she called as she pulled on an old T-shirt and padded into the sitting room. There was no sign of him, not even in the kitchen. She felt irritated at her disappointment that he had left without waking her, but remembered he had a meeting first thing. He'd call later, and hopefully they could meet up before his flight home.

She flicked the kettle on and was about to go for a shower when she spotted the pile of post sitting on the table. Phoebe picked up the uppermost letter, open for anyone to see: *Dear Signorina Cato. We enclose here the interim valuation for Villa Clara and grounds and look forward to your further instructions.*

Stefano had dropped his jacket on the table when they got back last night. He must have seen the letter this morning.

'Shit,' she muttered. 'Shit, shit, shit.' There was no way of finding him before his flight home. She would just have to call him when he got back to Italy. Fly out there if she had to. In the meantime, there was nothing to be done but kick herself, wipe her tears and carry on, even though she had potentially broken the one thing Bruce wanted for her more than anything.

52

Phoebe found her way to 20 Portman Square on autopilot, wrung out after another couple of days waiting to hear from Stefano, and as she approached the porticoed entrance, she felt an involuntary panic that she'd forgotten to hand in an essay. The Courtauld Institute, dedicated to the study of the history of art and home to an enviable collection, had changed little since Phoebe's student days, becoming only shabbier as the patina of academic life chipped at its neoclassical framework. And now Portman Square was in its final days as home to 'the Institute' before moving across town to Somerset House. Removals teams were already packing its infrastructure into boxes that filled the marble hallway lit by a glass dome as students streamed to and from the upstairs classrooms and lecture rooms she knew so well.

It had been in no small part down to Bruce that she sailed through her interview, and if she had been intimidated by the priceless works displayed everywhere and by the tweed-suited professors living in its upper reaches, it had not stopped her throwing herself into Institute life. Meeting Tilly when she happened upon a rowdy game of football in the student common room had lightened the experience instantly, as Phoebe found herself welcomed into a clique determined to take its work but not itself seriously.

Where would she be if she hadn't met Tilly? she wondered. Where would the museum be? They had received a letter from the Americans that morning, making a final offer for the lease. If Phoebe did not accept within fourteen days, the rent on Bedford Court would be increased to a level that would make a buoyant business's eyes water, let alone a struggling one. Tilly had stayed calm, suggesting they call a meeting with their landlords in order to thrash things out face-to-face. With Phoebe struggling to focus, and her loyalties torn between Tuscany and London, Tilly had offered to set up the meeting and prepare the paperwork, managing a positivity that eluded Phoebe. In the unlikely event that the museum survived this timebomb and a miracle occurred, there was no doubt Tilly was the one to steer the museum towards calmer waters, whilst Phoebe steered towards their former place of study that afternoon, in order to find some resolution in the story of Bruce and Leonora.

Ironically, given the allegations at Leonora's trial, Phoebe had been in this very building on the day in 1979 when its former director Sir Anthony Blunt had been outed in Parliament as a Russian spy and stripped of his honours. She remembered once attending a lecture from the elderly Blunt on Nicolas Poussin, fascinated by the slightly effete man once entrusted with the Queen's Collection. Had Viner ever consulted Blunt, maybe even brought him pieces from the Villa Clara collection?

She found a space in the library, where overstuffed metal bookcases pressed against the delicate Robert Adam plaster-work. Finding anything here was always a challenge, but within half an hour Phoebe had a stack of volumes piled beside Bruce's notebooks, ready to research the five drawings he had guided her towards.

Following the downward progress of the Vermeer candle, she began with the Leonardo sketch of a horse's flank, marked by Bruce in his notebook of 1928 as 'commissioned by E. Viner for Boston hotel'. Flicking through the definitive catalogue of Leonardo drawings, she found several tantalisingly similar sketches, until suddenly there it was: '*Hindquarters of a horse c.1490.* Metalpoint with pen and ink, on dull blue prepared paper.'

The meticulously recorded provenance of the work took it from the Melzi family who were bequeathed the work by Leonardo himself, through a series of collectors whose stamps appeared on the paper, right up until 1941, when the drawing was believed stolen in Paris by Nazis from a Jewish collector whose entire family perished in a concentration camp. It was acquired by Viner's in 1974 and presented to a London auction house.

On to the Raphael, an early study for the head of St Barbara in the *Sistine Madonna* painting, famous for its two cherubs resting their chins. Whilst she found no photographic evidence for the sketch, a *catalogue raisonné* suggested it was a piece sold at auction by the Prince Regent in 1787, and bought by a French count whose home was destroyed during the French Revolution. The work had been presumed destroyed, until it appeared at Viner's Gallery in 1963.

A drawing by Pieter Breughel the Elder, in which an elderly, short-sighted collector peers over an artist's shoulder, hand on purse, had been a sensation in its day. Bruce's version of this witty comment on the balance between artist and patron was seemingly a study for the finished piece, which had come to light after the liquidation of a Warwickshire country estate. It was one of several stolen from the British Museum in the early nineteenth century by Robert Dighton, a well-known caricaturist and actor. Doubts were raised when it appeared at Viner's, but Sir Edwin was one of several openly convinced of its authenticity, the subsequent sale price reflecting that certainty.

Next Rembrandt's reclining woman, clearly a companion piece to one owned by the British Museum. An intimate portrait of Rembrandt's pregnant mistress Hendrickje Stoffels, this touching work, once owned by William II of Holland, was believed lost in a house fire in 1909. It had, however, come to light in 1961, passing through an Austrian collector before being sold by Viner's to a Dutch national collection two years later.

Phoebe finally identified the drawing of a hand as being by Albrecht Dürer, probably cut out from a sketchbook. Its provenance included a sale through Old Masters specialists Agnew's of Bond Street in 1876, and it was eventually bought by the eccentric collector George Binding in the early part of the twentieth century. The drawing was commonly believed to have succumbed to damp in the basement of his Highgate villa, alongside nearly two hundred other works, which were unwittingly disposed of by the local council after his death. By some miracle, the Dürer survived, having possibly been given away earlier in lieu of debts, and was sold to a private buyer for a six-figure sum by Viner's in 1976.

Five drawings, each listed in Bruce's notebooks as being commissioned by Viner; each with convenient holes in their provenance, and each eventually sold by Viner on behalf of 'a gentleman collector'. Viner had looked for gaps, and Bruce had unwittingly filled them.

'I hope you get him this time,' Hugo Fairfax had said, and now there was a good chance she might, if she knew where to look next.

Later that evening she reread Leonora's letter from prison, wondering if Stefano had been right about there being a clue within it. She had spoken of Margot's gallery, of her own work within the prison, of Joan's career, of gathering correspondence for a trail of clues about Viner. She had also written of Ludlow Gardens, and its new owner.

Phoebe looked once more at the painting sent her by Hillary Stevenson, taking a magnifying glass to every square inch, until there it was, plain as day. The fountain pen held by the girl was inscribed with a tiny logo, almost invisible to the eye: 'Parker'.

'Bingo,' she said, hearing Bruce's chuckle as she cracked the code and half-expecting a sweet to be thrown at her as a reward.

It was time to visit Mrs Parker of 31 Ludlow Gardens.

53

The bus rattled past white stucco villas as gradually the streets became shabbier, interspersed with sprawling post-war housing estates. Pimlico, where already much of the once-working-class terraces had been Farrow and Balled into a tastefully bland palette of creams and greys. She paused on the corner of Ludlow Gardens, trying to imagine how it might have looked in 1963, Morris 100s there instead of Golf GTis, old ladies with shopping trolleys instead of Lycra-wrapped joggers with Walkmans pressed to their ears.

Number 31 had steadfastly clung to its lacy net curtains and sludge-green front door, and as Phoebe pressed the doorbell, she wondered whether she should have called or written first. Did Mrs Parker even live here still? She did not have to wonder for long, however, as the door opened revealing a man of around fifty, his striped V-necked sweater a decade-old C&A classic and thinning hair brushed across his scalp.

'Yes?' he said, against a background murmur of television football commentary.

'I'm sorry to trouble you. I'm looking for someone who used to live here – well, might still.'

'Oh, yes?' he replied in a soft south London accent.

A woman's voice called from within the house. 'Who is it, Derek?'

'Don't know yet, love,' he shouted back. 'Who was it you said you wanted?' he asked Phoebe.

'Mrs Parker,' Phoebe said, peering past him into the hallway that had once belonged to Leonora Birch, and where Bruce had swooped to her aid twenty-five years earlier.

He twitched his nose as his glasses slipped. 'Who's asking?'

'My name's Phoebe Cato.'

'Cato?'

'My uncle was friends with someone who used to live here – Leonora Birch. I think he wanted me to talk to Mrs Parker, who bought the house from her.' It all sounded rather far-fetched now she was standing here. 'I'm sorry. I shouldn't have disturbed you. But if you have a forwarding address, maybe . . .'

'Forwarding address?' he chortled. 'Not unless Mrs Parker's left me in the last two minutes.' He turned back towards the hallway. 'Linda?' he yelled. 'The Cato girl is here.'

54

Margot sat on her bed in the attic room as Joan emptied the wardrobe on to the floor in an attempt at packing, almost exactly eighteen months after the two young women had arrived at Ludlow Gardens. Back then Margot had known only privilege, and now she understood the value of working for one's living, the satisfaction of achievement.

Yes, she was fortunate to have Cosmo's financial backing for the new gallery, but she would have to work harder than ever before, working solo and paying herself the minimum in order to keep the books in the black. There was no better way to run a tight ship than to know every corner of it.

And it was already proving to be some ship. Through representing only female artists, Margot had discovered a gap in the market. She had scoured end-of-year shows at the London art schools that summer, bought lunch for Bridget Riley and Pauline Boty, and searched provincial auction catalogues for any Dame Laura Knight or Barbara Hepworth that had slipped through the net. There was one artist she longed to represent, but even Margot had learned to recognise when she was beaten.

She looked up as Joan called to her. 'Here, what d'you want to do with this?' she said, holding out the wedding gown Margot had arrived in. 'Going to use it again?'

Margot stood, taking the heavy duchess satin between her fingers. The dress belonged to a different Margot from a different world. 'I don't think so.'

'Really?'

'Getting married isn't everything. And besides, things haven't exactly worked out on the romantic front so far.'

Margot and Laurence had never recovered from the almighty row they'd had the night the newspaper was pulled, weeks of relationship-building knocked down in a few angry minutes. They had tried to repair things, but a few months into his job at the BBC, Laurence had been offered a post on the Washington newsdesk, an opportunity he would have been mad to turn down, as Margot had told him. She sensed that if she had asked him, he would have stayed, but how could she be responsible for holding him back? Especially if things didn't work out between them. No, it was the right decision. Definitely. It would just have to be.

'I'll be your bridesmaid instead,' she told Joan now.

'You'll have to wait a couple of years.'

'Maybe Alf will get out earlier if he behaves?'

Joan laughed. 'Doubt it. He's already on a reduced sentence. Besides, I've got my career to keep me busy for now.'

'He must be so proud of you, Joan. We all are.'

She shrugged. 'It's only a bit part in Z Cars, but it's a start.'

Margot looked around. 'I'll miss it here, won't you?'

'It was nice of Linda to let us stay, but it's not the same without Mrs B.'

'It's lovely that they managed to get a mortgage on this place. Do you think they'll get new tenants when they move in?'

'They'd better hurry up. The wedding's in two weeks. Has

Linda shown you that awful brown outfit she bought? I know they're skipping the whole church thing, but she looks like Ena Sharples.'

Margot laughed. 'I don't suppose Derek cares. Here, can you help me get the last of these things in my case? I'm sure it's shrunk since I brought it from Diana's.'

Joan shuddered. 'Don't know how you ever put up with that nasty cow.'

'Probably because I didn't really have any other friends.' Margot smiled. 'And now I've got my Ludlow Gardens family.'

They dragged their suitcases downstairs, lining them up ready for the taxi before saying goodbye to Linda, who was pulling books off shelves and into boxes, her hair tied back in a scarf.

'You all done?' she said, wiping her hands on Leonora's pinny.

'Just about,' Margot said. 'How's it going?'

Linda sighed. 'I'm exhausted. It's all I can do to get my head round the new job.'

'Viner's not giving you bother, is he?' Margot asked.

'No chance. I'm stuck in the accounts office, which suits me. Got my plate full sorting this place before we move in. Leonora said we can keep all the furniture, but I can't be doing with all these knick-knacks. And how many pictures can one person put on the wall?'

'Doesn't she want them?'

'Andrei is taking the pictures. All she says she needs is a suitcase of clothes and a fresh start. Derek wants a bonfire in the yard to get rid of the rest.'

'Stick that awful prison uniform on it,' Joan sniffed. 'You know, I was dying to have a go at her hair when I went last week. She can't go to Italy looking like that.'

There was a tap at the door, and Hillary peered into the parlour, her hair cut shorter and wearing a smart navy suit. 'Front door was open. I just wanted to say goodbye. I heard it was your last day.'

'It's so lovely to see you,' Margot said. She'd missed her gallery partner, and had hoped that once Hillary was off the naughty step at work, they could resume their cultural trips.

'I'm surprised you've got the cheek,' Joan said, folding her arms, 'after you never turned up at court.'

'I wanted to, really. It's just not that easy in my job.'

'And what exactly is this job of yours?' Joan asked. 'Hanging around with Russians, sneaking about. Maybe it's you who's the spy?'

'Joan,' Margot snapped. 'It doesn't matter now. Viner would have won, whatever happened.'

'Is Mrs Birch coming back here tomorrow?' Hillary asked.

It hardly seemed possible that already Leonora was on the final full day of her sentence, which she had borne considerably better than the rest of them. Margot shook her head. 'Bruce has already taken her things back to Italy. She said there's nothing here for her other than memories.'

Linda sighed. 'And the rubbish she's left me to sort through.'

Margot glanced at the notebooks and folders piled on the sofa. 'Can I look?'

'I don't know. She said to chuck them out, but it doesn't seem right somehow.'

Margot took a notebook from the top of the pile. 'It's a sketchbook,' she said, glancing at the pencil and charcoal images dating back to the twenties.

Linda looked worried. 'I'm not sure she'd want us to look at them.'

Margot reluctantly put the book back down. A promise was a promise, she supposed.

'So have you got everything?' Linda said.

'Everything but the dirty sheets. Left those on the bed for you.'

'You wouldn't, Joan Carter!' Linda whined.

A car horn blasted in the street outside, and Margot went to the window. 'That's our taxi.'

Linda brushed her hands on her apron and stood straight. 'Well, I suppose it's goodbye.'

'Suppose so,' Joan said.

'I really hope it works out for you here, Linda,' Hillary said.

'Thanks, Hillary, and do pop back any time.'

Margot glanced around the denuded parlour. 'I wonder if she's glad this all happened. Even going to prison.'

'I know she is,' Joan replied. 'She had her day in court, didn't she?'

'I just wish it were Viner in prison instead of Leonora,' Linda said.

Joan chuckled. 'His day'll come. As sure as that taxi will bugger off if we don't hurry up.'

'Wait,' Margot said as Joan began to pull her away. 'There is one thing I left behind, Linda. It's in the wardrobe. You can have it.'

And as they closed the front door of number 31 behind them for the last time, Margot turned to Joan. 'I couldn't let her get married in that hideous suit, could I?'

55

How strange it felt to be in her own clothes again, rather than the stale dress that never got quite clean in the prison-laundry boil wash. Let some other poor devil wear it now, along with the revolting threadbare cardigan fit only for cleaning floors in the miles of corridors over in the main block. As Leonora's poor knees knew only too well. She was free, or at least would be in a matter of a few minutes, and yet the cabbage-smell and violent shouts of Holloway Prison would haunt her for quite some time.

She stood in front of the mirror in the dingy changing room where prison sentences were sloughed off and an unknown future begun, seeing her reflection properly for the first time in six months. She had lost weight, her once-good suit hanging off her hips, and her silver hair had grown into a shapeless grey curtain that she twisted into a bun, now she was finally allowed hairpins again.

'Hurry up in there, Birch,' the warden shouted from outside the door. The two women would never have been friends in the real world, but a mutual respect had grown between them. 'Let's get you out before they change their minds.'

Leonora took one last look in the mirror, pinching her cheeks and brushing down her tweed skirt. She would have to do.

'Your belongings,' said the warden, passing her a tray as she neared the heavily locked metal door that was her last barrier to freedom. 'Sign here.'

Leonora scribbled her signature on the receipt before putting on her old watch and hooking the slim leather belt into the loops of her skirt. Her pearl earrings had disappeared from the small collection of personal items she'd handed over when she arrived, but she didn't need them in her new life.

She had no regrets. The Vermeer aside, she had stood up for what she knew to be true, and paid the price in this Victorian hellhole that had once housed the Suffragettes who'd fought for the vote she so valued. Even if the details of the trial remained under wraps, the world would always wonder whether Sir Edwin Viner was really what he claimed to be. Never again would he dare pass a Bruce Cato through the doors of his gallery.

'Goodbye, Birch,' the warden said as the heavy door was unlocked and sunshine spilled through on a cloud of North London traffic fumes. 'We'll miss you.'

Leonora turned to the woman squeezed into a woollen uniform two sizes too small for her. 'Thank you. I'm sure you'll understand if I don't return the compliment.'

The warden gestured to the red sports car parked just beyond the high-security fences cut into the tall brick wall. 'Taxi's here, by the looks of it.'

Leonora hesitated, then took the watch from her wrist and held it out to the other woman. 'Here,' she said. 'Have it. My days of watching time are over.'

'You sure?'

Leonora nodded. 'The only thing I shall be counting from now on is my blessings.'

She strode forward, filling her lungs with dirty London air as the gates opened. She was free.

56

London, November 1989

Linda passed a faded Silver Jubilee mug across the vinyl table-cloth to Phoebe. 'I had a letter from your uncle a few months ago, telling me that you'd turn up here eventually.'

'When was this?'

Linda frowned. 'Oh, now let me see. Back in the summer. May? June?'

When Bruce had discovered he was ill, Phoebe calculated. He knew he could do nothing while he was still alive, so he planned this trail for after his death. It was heart-breaking to think of him setting all this in motion, knowing he would be gone by the time Phoebe found her way to Ludlow Gardens and the home of his great love.

'Six months Mr Cato stayed here, while they waited for the trial,' Linda explained.

'Bruce lived at Ludlow Gardens? With Leonora?' How strange it felt, to be at the heart of a life she never knew existed. Strange but comforting, even though she suddenly felt incredibly emotional to be there.

Linda offered Phoebe a biscuit. 'Fig roll?' she said gently. 'Mrs Birch used to say there was nothing a fig roll didn't make better.'

'Thanks,' Phoebe said, taking one.

'I'm relieved you worked it out,' Linda said. 'I told Derek, "What do we do if she doesn't turn up?" And he said, "Linda, stop worrying." I worry too much, you see? Always did. But here you are, so all's well.'

'Yes, I am.' Phoebe smiled, proud she had passed this test.

'He was a card, your uncle. Never told you anything straight, if he could turn it into a riddle.' Linda took a sip of strong, dark tea. 'Speaking of which, wait here a minute.' She headed to the telephone desk in the hall, returning with an airmail envelope addressed to Phoebe.

'This is Bruce's handwriting,' she said.

Linda fetched a pinny off the back of the kitchen door, tying it around her waist to reveal 'Her Indoors' written across the front. 'Now you read that, and I'll get us some tea on, if you're hungry?' She smiled. 'Sausage and homemade chips. Derek insists on it every Saturday.'

'If you're sure?'

As Linda began banging pans, Phoebe carefully tore open the envelope to reveal Bruce's handwriting, as indecipherable as an Old Master's signature, but so familiar.

My dear Phoebe,

If you are reading this, then you are every bit the detective I always knew you to be. I only wish I could dig into that sweetie jar to reward you.

You will have met some of the characters who peopled this story and discovered the deception by another. It was never possible for any of us to bring down Edwin Viner, and I do not ask you to be my avenging angel, but I hope

I have shown you that my role in this tawdry tale was an honourable one. Should you decide to don your wings, however, take everything you've learned, take that brilliant brain of yours and fill in the final pieces of the puzzle.

The light is fading here at Villa Clara, and Angelina is trying to foist my medication upon me. She means well, but we are merely fighting the tide now, and I'd far rather go to bed on a whisky – perhaps the rather fine Macallan Cosmo and I polished off at Ronnie Scott's the night before the trial began. I wish you were here. I wish I could say one last goodbye. I wish you had met Nora. Perhaps you feel you have.

I know things have been difficult for you, and that the museum is struggling (never kid a kidder), but whatever you decide to do with your future, be happy, as you have made me so happy over the years. If all else fails, you have the villa, and people there who love you. One in particular, but I must not meddle, especially from the grave.

Godspeed, my dear girl, if one believes in that sort of thing.

Oh, and don't let Linda feed you. Her cooking is frightful.

All my love
Bruce

'Oh, love,' Linda said, putting an arm around her shoulders. 'Don't you cry now.'

'I'm sorry,' Phoebe said, taking a tissue from her. 'It's just that this feels like the end. Like he's finally saying goodbye.'

'A man like your uncle . . . well, he'll never really leave you.'

'But I miss him so much. This treasure hunt, whatever it is . . . it's kind of kept him alive, like he's looking over my shoulder.'

Linda squeezed Phoebe's hand. 'He'll always be at your shoulder, for as long as you hold him in your heart.'

Phoebe smiled. 'Thank you. I'm glad he sent me here. I'm glad I met you – all of you.'

Linda stood up straight, brushing her hands together, businesslike once again, despite the moistness in her own eyes. 'Don't be daft.'

'I just wish I could find Leonora and tell her what has happened.'

'I wish you could too, love.'

'You don't know where she is either?'

'If I did, I'd invite her here right now to meet you.' She glanced at the letter in Phoebe's hand. 'So,' she said, 'what's in that, then?'

'I think he wants me to go after Viner.' And, she thought with a sinking stomach, to be with Stefano. How happy it would have made Bruce to see them together, if she hadn't messed it up.

'And will you?'

'I don't know . . .'

Linda lowered her voice. 'I don't suppose anyone has mentioned where I work?'

'Not that I recall.'

'Oh, you'd recall, all right.' She folded her arms. 'You're looking at the longest-serving accounts clerk at Viner's Gallery.'

'You work for Viner?' Phoebe could not believe what she was hearing.

'Got my job there not long after Mrs Birch went to Hollo-way. Applied through Derek's address, so no one would cotton on.'

'But why? After everything he'd done?'

Linda shrugged. 'I was about to get a mortgage, and there was a job going. A well-paid one. Besides, it meant there was someone on the inside keeping an eye on things for Mrs Birch. Not that Viner was around much after the trial.'

'And is he still there?'

'From time to time. No nicer now than he was then. So,' she said, 'will you? Go after Viner?'

Phoebe glanced at the letter, thought of the humiliation Bruce had been subjected to in court by Viner, of the Vermeer still hidden away. She had the information and the means to prove those drawings were falsified, a mole on the inside, and motivation by the bucketload. 'You know what? I rather think I might.'

'In that case,' Linda said, wiping her hands on the apron, 'I reckon it's time we got the old gang together.' She grabbed a handful of cutlery and held it out to Phoebe. 'You all right to lay the table?'

She hesitated. How bad could Linda's cooking be?

57

'Well, this is like old times, isn't it?' said Joan, taking a bread-stick from the jar in the middle of the table.

Margot turned to Phoebe. 'We came to Luigi's twenty-five years ago to plot against Viner. If we'd known then it wouldn't work, I wonder whether we'd have bothered.'

'Except they do the best pasta in Stepney,' Joan pointed out as she looked around. 'Even the décor's not changed since then.'

'I rather like it,' Linda said.

It was true that the posters of Sorrento were faded, the fake grapevines dusty and tired, but Luigi's served good food with no pretensions and the sort of family service you only found this far from the West End. Perhaps if Stefano ever came over again – if he ever spoke to her again – she would bring him here.

Across the table, Alf threw a thick, suntanned arm across Joan's shoulders. 'If we hadn't met here back then, I'd have been saved the bother of a two-year stretch, for sure.'

Margot shook her head. 'How can you laugh about it?'

He smiled, revealing a yellow-gold tooth. 'Because it was meant to be four. Besides, I had my Joanie and our wedding to look forward to at the other end of it.'

'Oh, it was lovely,' Joan said. 'Even my old mum made the effort to be nice.'

Alf laughed. 'Only because I'd just made a down payment on a bungalow in Southend for her.'

'Please,' Margot said, 'can we stick to the subject? I'm fresh off a plane, with a raging desire for eight hours' sleep. Cosmo and I have meetings at the gallery all day tomorrow.' She sighed. 'Actually, I couldn't do it without him, although Cosmo can be a bit 1970s with our artists sometimes.'

'Nothing wrong with the seventies,' Alf chuckled, taking a cigar from the pocket of his Hawaiian shirt, then looking around at the assembled disapproving faces. 'I did some of my finest work back then.'

'Anyway,' Margot said tetchily, 'we're here to talk about Viner.'

Joan squeezed Phoebe's arm. 'We'll get him this time. The Ludlow Gardens gang.'

'Minus Hillary,' Phoebe said.

Joan sniffed. 'She wouldn't lower herself.'

Margot sighed. 'You really have to stop blaming Hillary. She had no choice.'

'I always liked her,' Linda said, folding her arms.

Joan's eyebrows shot up. 'No, you didn't. You thought she was snotty.'

'Oh, for goodness' sake, you two.'

Joan looked at Margot. 'You know who you reminded me of just then?' She smiled. 'Mrs Birch, on one of those Sunday afternoons when we'd all sit in her parlour drinking sherry, shouting to be heard over one another.'

'And now here we are, back in Luigi's, without Mrs Birch, still shouting to be heard over one another.' Margot glanced at the mandolin player serenading an embarrassed couple across the restaurant. 'And the music's not improved.'

'Want me to have a word?' Alf said, but Joan and Margot shouted 'No!' as one.

Linda sighed. 'I wish she were here. Why didn't she stay in touch?'

'I don't know,' Margot said, 'but perhaps Bruce is leading Phoebe to her. I wouldn't put it past him.'

Linda smiled. 'Then I hope you find her. And if you do, tell her we all miss her.'

'Hear, hear,' Margot said.

Joan narrowed her eyes. 'Apart from Mrs Birch, there's someone else missing, isn't there, Marge?'

'Who's that?' Phoebe asked.

Joan tapped her cigarette on the ashtray. 'Mrs Birch's son. Laurence. He and Margot were nearly an item back then.'

'Hardly. It never got off the ground.' Margot frowned, but Phoebe sensed a hesitation.

'Because they were just as bloody stubborn as one another,' Joan added, smiling.

Margot tutted. 'Stubborn and totally unsuited.'

Joan laughed. 'See? Still likes him.'

'For goodness' sake, Joan. He went to America, and we've not spoken for nearly thirty years. I've no idea where he lives or what he's doing, nor he I.'

Phoebe, spotting a raw nerve, changed the subject. 'So what happened that night you all came here?'

'Leonora had discovered Viner was hiding the Vermeer,' Margot explained. 'We tried to make a plan to get it back.'

'Except Viner knew I was coming,' Alf said, waving his cigar across the table. 'Little shit I paid to let me know the place was empty was paid more by that old fraud.' He shook his head. 'I broke the golden rule – never trust anyone not in your own firm.'

'So as far as we know, he still has my uncle's painting?' Phoebe asked.

'It's certainly not come up on the open market,' Margot said, fiddling with the oversized Perspex necklace hanging against her plain black tunic dress.

'And I haven't heard it's been shifted,' Alf said. 'Still got my contacts – on both sides.'

'Both sides?'

'Got myself a reduced sentence for agreeing to keep the police informed about certain matters. Mark my words, Viner won't have kept that painting just to decorate his study,' Alf said. 'I never met a man with bigger pound signs in his eyes. He's played a long game, and I reckon now your uncle's passed away – God bless his soul – Viner will think it's safe to move the painting.'

'He can't sell it publicly,' Margot said. 'There's a spoil code attached to it, warning that it's been stolen in the past, and Viner has already denied seeing it. He'll go for a private sale. Linda, have you heard anything at work?'

Linda shook her head. 'I don't even hear if there's a sandwich run going.'

'It's not just the Vermeer, though,' Margot said. 'Bruce specifically wanted Phoebe to know about those drawings. I had my assistant check the collectors' marks against the Lugt catalogue – they're all there.'

'What's a loot thingummy?' Joan asked.

'It was put together by Frits Lugt, a Dutch art historian, in the twenties,' Phoebe explained. 'He catalogued all the stamps from major collectors.'

'Quite,' Margot said. 'We also checked any sales and exhibitions listed in the provenance of the drawings. One or two were added as late entries, on separate typed sheets, but you were right, Phoebe: Viner identified pieces that had fallen through the gaps.'

'So, with Bruce's notebooks, do we have enough to take to the police?' Phoebe leaned back as the waiter came to remove their empty pasta dishes.

'I don't know,' Margot said, brushing breadcrumbs from the red-checked tablecloth.

Alf leaned forward on his elbows. 'You say your uncle didn't add any collectors' marks. Well, I know for a fact that Viner was doing it way back. It was my dad who got hold of the fake stamps for him.'

'That all sounds really complicated. I reckon our best bet is the painting,' Joan said. 'If we can nail him for that, the rest will follow.'

'You ain't going in that study again with him, Joanie,' Alf said.

Phoebe racked her brains. What would Bruce do? He would play Viner at his own game. 'Alf, you say you still have contacts in the business. Any ideas?'

'I might have.' He smiled. 'Miss Cato, how would you like to meet an old friend of mine?'

Three days later, Alf and Phoebe made their way into a Pizza Hut at the rough end of Oxford Street. 'There he is,' Alf said, pointing to a table in the corner, where a middle-aged man in grey shirt and suit was busy challenging the eat-all-you-can salad bar.

'See you've still not started that diet, Harold,' Alf said, sitting himself down on the vinyl-covered bench opposite.

'It's salad,' the man muttered, his accent bearing a trace of his Welsh homeland.

'Pasta and potato salad,' Alf retorted.

'Anyway, it's DS Robbins to you.'

'Whatever you say, Harold.' Alf shivered, pulling his sheepskin coat around him.

'Still not acclimatised?' the detective said, demolishing his last pizza crust.

'London's for mugs,' Alf replied, then turned to Phoebe. 'Miss Cato, meet Scotland Yard Art and Antiques Squad's finest. Even if his choice of restaurants is a disgrace.'

'Why would I waste police expenses on a scumbag like you, Jackson?'

Alf smiled. 'Because you need me.'

'I need to pay my taxes. Doesn't mean I have to like it.' He wiped his mouth with a paper napkin. 'So what brings about this happy reunion?'

'This young lady and I have a proposition for you.'

'And she is?'

'Phoebe Cato. Niece of Bruce Cato. Artist who got stitched up by Edwin Viner in court in sixty-four?'

The detective looked at Phoebe. 'Ah, yes. I remember. And what are you doing hanging around with a lowlife like Jackson?'

Alf spread his hands wide. 'Come on, Harold. Thirty-two lost paintings retrieved, a Ming vase, Stradivarius violin, some nasty Russians banged up for that armed robbery at Welford Hall . . . I'd say that makes us friends.'

Robbins snorted. 'Hmm. So what you got this time?'

Alf turned to Phoebe. 'Want to tell him?'

Robbins listened as Phoebe explained about the Villa Clara collection, the trail that led to the stolen Vermeer.

'Which I nicked you for trying to "return to its rightful owner",' Robbins said. 'Except there wasn't any Vermeer.'

'Cos he'd switched it, like I said,' Alf replied with the air of someone who had explained a million times.

Robbins screwed up his napkin and dropped it on the table. 'Sorry, Jackson, but this is old news.'

'With fresh information.'

Robbins sighed, turning to Phoebe. 'Fine. What have you got?'

'My uncle's notebooks catalogue five of his drawings that were sold through Viner's as originals. He also kept letters from Viner, commissioning the drawings as copies for private use.'

'Wasn't that evidence used back then?'

'Yes, but now I can prove Viner chose each drawing specifically to match pieces with holes in their provenance.'

'My old dad must have supplied him with the stamps to do it,' Alf added.

Robbins rubbed his chin. 'It's still not enough.'

Alf leaned across the table. 'Which is why I've made a few calls, spread the word to see if he's still got that Vermeer. And guess what? He's taken the bait. He wants shot of it.'

'You're sure?'

'One of my old associates made out he had an anonymous buyer with a limitless budget to spend on the black market.

Wanted something really special. Viner came back with what looks like that Vermeer.'

Robbins scribbled in a small notepad then looked up. 'Pains me to say it, but maybe I should have listened to you, Jackson. More than once Viner has lent his connoisseurship to some-thing I'd have bet my gran's pension on being fake. So,' he said to Alf, 'what next?'

Alf grinned, displaying an array of gold teeth. 'Viner is des-perate to get rid of that painting. He's all primed to meet the mystery buyer – a Sicilian, we told him. My contact is ready to hand over to you. If you want the job.'

The detective stared at Alf. 'You thinking what I'm thinking?'

Alf smiled. 'Hilton seventy-nine?'

Robbins tapped his spoon against the table. 'I'm up for retirement in four months. Reckon I'd like to go out with a bang.' He nodded. 'Hilton seventy-nine.'

'What are you talking about?' Phoebe asked.

Alf turned to her. 'A sting operation. Robbins here did a similar job ten years ago in a hotel in Paris. The Hilton. 1979.'

'The thieving bastards never saw it coming, and now there's a very fine Rothko back where it should be, for the whole world to enjoy. Right, Jackson. Do what you need to do. Let's get him.' Robbins stood up from the table. 'Good to meet you, Miss Cato. And now if you'll excuse me, I'd better get going. This young lady has something I want returned to her.'

It was not the only thing Phoebe wanted returned to her, and she arrived home that night to find a message from Stefano on her answer machine: 'I'm sorry I overreacted. If you want to sell the Villa, I can't stop you. It's yours, after all. Let's talk when I'm back from this next trip.'

She tried calling him back straight away, but got his answer machine in response. 'Stefano, I'm sorrier, honestly. I just needed the facts.' She sighed. 'This sounds so lame . . . Anyway, I miss you.'

It wasn't a reconciliation as such, but it was a start.

58

Phoebe sat opposite Robbins in the window of a dingy café, whilst a few hundred yards around the corner, over lunch at the Connaught negotiations were taking place between Sir Edwin Viner and two plainclothes detectives from the London and Rome art squads for the next stage of the Vermeer's life.

Robbins tipped a third packet of sugar into his mug of tea. 'They'd better not mess up,' he said. 'This could be our last chance to get Viner.'

'You definitely can't get him for selling the drawings?'

'Not without evidence that he falsified provenance. But if he tries to sell that painting, I have a warrant ready to search the gallery within a minute of him handing it over.'

'I'd give anything to be a fly on the wall right now,' Phoebe said, glancing up at the flickering TV on the wall and its coverage of the fall of Romania's President Ceausescu, the latest Eastern European communist dictator to topple.

'Me too. Viner would recognise me a mile off, though: I was the officer who dealt with Alf's arrest at Charlwood. No, I have every confidence in DC Wilkins. Top of her year at Hendon and her mum is Italian, so she speaks it like a native, which works for our story of her being Detective Ferraro's interpreter.'

Robbins looked at her. 'Plus she's about the only one who hasn't gone daft since the Italian stallion flew in to the Yard with his floppy hair, natty black suit and stupid sunglasses. Never work with children, dogs or Italians.'

'You think this will work?' Phoebe asked.

'It has to. Viner knows most of my team, apart from Wilkins. And since the painting was technically nicked on Italian soil, those pretty boys in Rome'll kick up a fuss if we don't let them play. As long as Ferraro does the job instead of checking his hair in the mirror every five minutes, we'll be all right.'

'At least he looks the part,' Phoebe said.

Robbins chuckled. 'If he ever wants a change of career, he'd make a convincing Mafia man.'

Things had moved fast ever since Alf's contact confirmed with Edwin Viner that his client, a wealthy Sicilian with a budget in seven figures, was interested in the Vermeer. It was a gamble, but when DC Wilkins, acting as agent and translator for the Sicilian client, received a photograph of the painting from Viner, via the five-star London hotel used as a holding address, a collective sigh of relief had gone around. There was no longer any doubt that *Girl at a Desk* had been brought out of storage. Viner had waited fifty years for Bruce Cato to be out of the way, and he clearly wasn't wasting another moment. If Edwin Viner suspected the Vermeer was being sold to the Mafia, it hadn't stopped him arranging lunch with Detective Ferraro, posing as Giuseppe Lombardo, a representative of the Sicilian 'collector' and with a string of ID as believable as the provenance churned out by Viner himself.

Phoebe looked at her watch. The two detectives had been gone an hour and a half now, which at least meant Viner had showed up. How long did it take to do million-pound deals for a stolen masterpiece? She had no idea, but waiting was unbearable.

'Ey up,' Robbins said suddenly, as the bell rang over the café door and in came DC Wilkins, dressed up to the nines and limping in her high heels, followed by the Italian detective, looking as though he had come direct from cocktails on the Piazza Navona, his pungent aftershave overriding the smell of fried food.

'You keeping those on, sunshine?' Robbins said, indicating the mirrored sunglasses as Ferraro took a seat.

'Think he has to, Sarge. They have them glued on as part of their training over there,' Wilkins said, wincing as she pulled off the heavy costume jewellery dragging at her ears.

'Like the British police have to pass a module in dressing badly,' Ferraro countered, folding his arms.

'All right, you two,' Robbins intervened. 'Keep the squabbles out of school, please. So, I hope you made the bastard pay for lunch?'

Wilkins nodded. 'Too right we did. Bloody good it was, too.'

Ferraro shrugged. 'The steak was overdone and the wine poor.'

'So, restaurant reviews aside,' Robbins said, 'will this young lady get her painting back? Have we got him?'

Ferraro straightened his black tie. 'The Carabinieri always get their man.'

Wilkins rolled her eyes. 'I think, Sarge, what our friend here is trying to say is that we need a large sack of cash and a room at the Davenport Hotel in two days. Miss Cato, we'll get that painting if it kills us.' She tipped her head towards Ferraro. 'Or, with any luck, him.'

Finally, Phoebe allowed herself to feel optimistic that Bruce's Vermeer might be returned. Things were looking promising. And even better, Stefano had left a message to say he was passing through London in a couple of days on a string of client meetings. Did she want to meet for a quick drink at his hotel to talk things through?

It was hard to gauge whether his intentions were reconciliation or just business, but Phoebe scribbled the name of the hotel near Buckingham Palace in her diary. Drinks, not dinner, was definitely a relegation, but it was a start.

With the trap set, two days later Phoebe spent the morning chatting with the occasional visitor and cataloguing pieces kept in storage at the museum, keeping busy while she waited for news that Viner had been arrested. She was also wondering what the hell would happen to over a thousand pieces if the Cato did have to close. In the office, meanwhile, Tilly prepared ammunition for the meeting that would decide the museum's future, fighting inevitability with indomitable hope. Phoebe felt awful: she had done almost nothing, other than suggest a tour for the Americans. More and more, she realised that Tilly was far better than she at managing the place, whilst Phoebe had the flair for curation. What a team they could make, given the chance.

Shortly before lunch Tilly came to tell her a call had come in, and Phoebe picked up the telephone receiver, heart thumping at the sound of DS Robbins' voice. 'It's off, isn't it?' she said.

'Not quite.' He hesitated. 'We've hit a slight hitch. DC Wilkins has got herself a vomiting bug. She wants to come in anyway, but as far as I know there's never been a sting in which one of the police officers can't keep her breakfast down.'

'Can Ferraro do it on his own?'

'Not a chance. We told Viner that his Sicilian contact doesn't speak English, so we could get Wilkins in as his interpreter.'

So it was over. The Italian detective would have zero credibility if he suddenly turned up having learned English in forty-eight hours. 'I guess that's it, then.' She tried to keep the disappointment from her voice – Robbins had wanted Viner caught almost as much as she had.

'Well, not quite, if we can find an Italian speaker who knows this case as well as I do.'

'Is there someone else at Scotland Yard who could do it?' she asked.

Robbins sighed. 'I wish. Now, Miss Cato, this is most irregular, and I wouldn't even suggest it if we weren't in danger of pulling the plug, but what are you doing right now?'

Phoebe checked her appearance in the mirror above the sitting-room fireplace in the hotel suite where Edwin Viner would shortly hand over a Vermeer in exchange for a hold-all he imagined was stuffed with cash, but which in fact held DS Robbins' son's football kit. As crime scenes went, it was a sumptuous one, antique furniture placed discreetly around the thick white carpet and the large picture window framed by floor-length silk curtains. To avoid arriving at the Davenport looking like she'd been dragged off the street, Phoebe had called the only person she knew who owned the kind of wardrobe that would cut the mustard. Now sporting heavy jewellery, a figure-hugging black dress and stiletto shoes, she could tell from Ferraro's approving gaze that she looked the part. She worried whether Viner would recognise her, but their paths had not crossed since she was around eleven years old. With her blonde bob slicked back, and wearing enough make-up for a bit part in *Dynasty*, even her closest friends wouldn't have known her. Joan, waiting in the basement bar with Margot, had done a good job, even if Phoebe did need to change into her own clothes before heading off to meet Stefano in a couple of hours.

'How you doing?' Robbins asked, popping a nicotine gum into his mouth.

'I'm fine.'

Robbins nodded. 'This should be over pretty quickly. They usually grab the money and run. Or try to.' He smiled. 'Once Viner's in here, I'll be on the landing, just outside. As soon as the handover takes place, Ferraro will make the signal. Within ten seconds there'll be enough coppers through that door to film an episode of *The Bill*.'

'I'm reassured . . . I think,' she said as she watched Ferraro clip a microphone to the inside of his jacket.

Robbins grabbed his walkie-talkie as it crackled into life, replying with a 'Roger and out'. He slapped Phoebe on the shoulder. 'This is it. He's just been seen walking into reception with a briefcase. I'd better scarper.'

And then she was alone with Ferraro, ice cool and every part the Sicilian gangster in his shiny grey suit and black shirt, a heavy gold chain around his neck. As she perched on the sofa beside him, listening to his final instructions, it seemed like hours not minutes before there was a gentle tap at the door.

Ferraro smiled. '*Andiamo*. Let's get the bastard.'

As arranged, Phoebe went to the door, finding herself face-to-face with a polished elderly gentleman, his grey pinstripe suit and silk handkerchief a perfect disguise for the crook beneath the surface. Edwin Viner, who had forced a place at her parents' dinner table, maligned and continued to cheat her uncle, even in his eighties – and who clearly still thought it acceptable to give young women the once-over.

'Good afternoon, Sir Edwin,' she said. 'Please come in. Signor Lombardo is waiting for you.'

'I don't know you,' he said, his vowels dripping with privilege. 'Where's the other woman?'

'She had to attend to an emergency. I work with Signor Lombardo's boss frequently – you can trust me to be discreet.'

Viner followed her inside, clutching a slim leather briefcase in one hand, his eyes searching the room. 'And your colleague has the . . .?'

She nodded towards Robbins' holdall sitting on a silk-upholstered armchair beside the window. 'He does.'

Ferraro stood, his sunglasses hooked into his jacket pocket. '*Benvenuto*,' he said, shaking Viner's hand and gesturing him towards the opposite sofa. '*Potete parlare con la mia collega.*'

Edwin sat, the briefcase at his side, looking uncertainly between Ferraro and Phoebe, seated across the marble-topped coffee table.

'Signor Lombardo welcomes you on behalf of his employer,' Phoebe said, 'and invites you to speak through me.'

Ferraro whispered in Italian into Phoebe's ear: 'Get him to open the briefcase. Make sure it's there.'

'What did he say?' Viner asked briskly.

'Signor Lombardo looks forward to seeing what you have brought. Would you please show him?'

Viner looked uncertain, but turned to his side, undoing the combination lock on the briefcase and flipping the lid open slightly. Phoebe tried to see inside, but the painting remained tantalisingly out of sight. 'Before I do,' Viner said, 'I need assurance that his employer has agreed to the sum we discussed?'

Phoebe spoke quietly to Ferraro, who nodded. 'He has,' she said. 'The full amount is waiting for you over there.'

'And this transaction will remain between us? I remind Signor Lombardo that the painting has a complicated history.'

Again she spoke to Ferraro, who whispered, 'Just get the arsehole to hand me the painting. Once it's in my hands, this is over.'

'Signor Lombardo understands the need for discretion. The painting is for the sole use of his employer.'

Did she detect a reluctance about Viner as he donned a pair of white gloves and removed the soft cloth wrapped around the unframed painting, a hint of regret that it would become little more than Mafia currency, swallowed up in a shady world of drugs, guns and honour killings? She did not. She saw only pound signs and the satisfaction of completing a job that had waited fifty years.

As Viner hesitated, Phoebe struggled to appear emotionless as she set eyes at last on the work that had been stolen from her uncle all those years ago, the work she already longed to share with the world. The thirty-sixth Vermeer.

'This is the right one?' Ferraro asked her quietly, and she nodded.

The seconds dragged as they waited for Viner to move, but eventually he leaned across the coffee table to offer the painting to Ferraro for examination.

Ferraro took the painting, glancing at it briefly before muttering something into his hidden microphone.

Viner frowned. 'What did he say just now?' He glanced towards the door, through which low voices could be heard on the landing outside.

Phoebe sat up straight, staring into Viner's grey eyes. 'On behalf of my uncle Bruce Cato,' she said, 'I want you to know that Detective Ferraro of the Rome Carabinieri just ordered your arrest.'

Before Viner even had time to register the name of his old nemesis, DS Robbins burst through the door, flanked by two uniformed officers.

'Afternoon, Viner,' he said, popping the gum from his mouth and pressing it into an ashtray on the coffee table. 'Think we're long overdue a bit of a chat, don't you?'

'Now, look here—' Viner began, but Robbins pointed at him.

'No, sunshine,' he whispered, 'you look here.' He turned to Ferraro. 'Nice work, Al Pacino. Mind if my boys deal with this from here?'

Ferraro shrugged. 'Feel free. He and I will talk later.'

Robbins nodded towards his police officers. 'Right, lads. Cuff him while I authorise that search of the gallery.'

'How dare you?' Viner called back as he was led out of the suite. 'I know people, you know?'

'Yeah, yeah . . .' Robbins muttered, then turned to Phoebe. 'How you feeling?'

'Like I wish my uncle could see this.'

'If it's any consolation, you just got yourself a genuine Vermeer. I'd say that's justice, wouldn't you?'

She smiled. 'It'll do.'

'Right,' Robbins shouted, 'get me that kit bag before it crawls away. If my Darren doesn't have his football boots in time for practice tonight, I'm a goner.'

59

A slightly stunned Phoebe found herself half an hour later nursing a brandy in the hotel basement bar, back in her own clothes, face scrubbed free of make-up.

'We finally got him,' Margot said.

'Twenty-five years late, but we did.' Joan pointed at Phoebe. '*You* did! I'd like to see the look on the face of that daughter of his. If she had two brain cells, I'd think she'd been in on it.'

'Definitely not Diana's style. She has a rather more passive attitude to acquiring money.' Margot sighed. 'What I wouldn't give to have seen that painting just now.'

'So when do you get it back?' Joan said.

'Not for a while. It's evidence, and DS Robbins needs to get it checked over, to prove it's genuine.'

'Well, we all know it is,' Margot said. 'Frustrating, though.'

Phoebe shrugged. 'Six months ago I didn't even know it existed. I'm just pleased we found it – for Bruce.'

'Cheers to that,' Joan said.

Margot looked around. 'You know, this is the hotel where I got ready for the wedding-that-never-was. Diana Viner was my bridesmaid. It seems a lifetime ago.'

'Any regrets?' Phoebe asked.

Margot thought for a moment. 'No. Look at me now, the archetypal career woman. If I'd married Hugo, I'd have been miserable.'

'So you married your work instead?'

Margot rolled her eyes. 'We can't all find our Alf, Joan. No, if I've any regrets, it's that I never had a chance to see Leonora's work, apart from a few sketches.'

'Did she start painting again in Italy?' Phoebe asked.

Margot shrugged. 'I have no idea. As I've said, we lost touch.'

'That's so sad, after everything you all went through.'

'Maybe she went to join Laurence in America,' Joan suggested.

'Wherever she went, Bruce had been – is still – making regular payments to her,' Phoebe said. 'So she must be somewhere.'

Margot smiled. 'Then let's hope she is well.'

'Amen.' Joan finished her drink. 'But right now, we need to celebrate. How about dinner? I've practically got my own table at Langan's.'

'I'm sorry, but I can't,' Phoebe said.

Joan took a gold-cased lipstick from her handbag and smeared it on her lips. 'You'd miss a night on the town with Joan Carter?' she said, fluffing up her helmet of blonde hair.

Phoebe looked at her watch. It was still only five, but she didn't want to risk being late for Stefano. 'I'm meeting someone.'

'Ah, that sort of someone.' Joan winked. 'Why don't you bring him along?'

'You just can't help yourself, Joan, can you?' Margot stood. 'I'm taking this woman away before she embarrasses herself further.' She leaned over and planted two light, Chanel No. 5-scented kisses on Phoebe's cheeks. 'Off you go. And if it's who I think it is, I hope you have fun.'

Phoebe smiled as she watched the two women walk away, the best and yet most unlikely of friends, and suddenly she missed her own best friend more than ever. It was time to sort out this rift with Stefano once and for all.

Early Christmas decorations lit Phoebe's way as she walked the short distance to Buckingham Palace Road. In just a few weeks the year would end, a year that had seen the death of Bruce, worry over the museum, the discovery of a Vermeer and uncovering of a fraudster. If nothing else, she had learned she could never let Villa Clara go. What had she been holding on to here, after all? A city that suffocated her, a mouldy flat she couldn't afford and a business on its last legs. Well, at least there was an outside chance of the museum surviving. She worried about Tilly, but if the Vermeer was genuine, her friend had a job for life.

The Vermeer. It had still not hit her that she might by a circuitous route have inherited something of such worth. No wonder Bruce had sent her after Viner. The painting had the potential to change everything, and yet she realised she wanted nothing more than to repair things with Stefano.

As she arrived at the hotel, an upmarket tourist stopover, she realised she was early by a good half an hour, the bar not yet open. She was directed by a concierge to a huddle of sofas across the foyer, and picked up one of the newspapers lying there. She looked unseeingly at photographs of Thatcher, Bush and Gorbachev celebrating the official end of the Cold War, Bob Geldof touting an upcoming Band Aid Christmas single, and realised she was nervous. What if Stefano really hadn't forgiven her?

She glanced up at a familiar laugh, spotting Stefano as he walked into the lobby from the hotel dining room, looking film-star smart in a navy suit and open-necked white shirt. Her heart thumped in recognition, and she was about to jump up and head towards him when she realised he was not alone. A couple of paces behind was a face she recognised.

Jocelyn, in full battle dress of tight shoulder-padded suit and stilettoes.

Phoebe lifted the newspaper higher, hiding her face as she watched them embrace and execute a series of continental cheek kisses. Jocelyn took Stefano's hands and they smiled at one another before she pulled away and allowed the doorman to let her out into the street.

You idiot, Phoebe chastised herself. She'd messed up, handing Stefano to his old flame. There would be no reconciliation, only a hard conversation in which the apology she had prepared now threatened to stick in her throat.

Phoebe watched as Stefano went to talk to the receptionist, and as soon as his back was turned, she slipped out of the hotel.

He tried to call her several times that evening, leaving messages wondering where she was, but Phoebe remained glued to the sofa in her pyjamas, the triumph over Viner tempered by yet another heartbreak.

The prospect of a future at Villa Clara suddenly looked somewhat different.

60

'Thanks for coming in, Miss Cato.' A week later DS Robbins led Phoebe along a corridor of closed doors, deep inside the nerve centre of Scotland Yard, until they reached the Art Squad office, where he shifted a pile of fast-food wrappers from a chair. 'Here, take a seat.'

'Thanks,' she said, taking in the paintings stacked against overstuffed filing cabinets, the pinboards covered with photographs of artworks, maps and mugshots, Robbins' desk littered with card indexes and trade magazines. 'And, well, thanks for everything.'

'All in the line of duty, as they say. And we couldn't have done it without you. That was quite some act you put on there.'

She smiled. 'Maybe I missed my vocation.'

'Not from what I've heard about that museum of yours. I must visit sometime with the wife.'

'You'll get the VIP tour, in that case.' Tilly's inspired presentation having fallen on deaf ears during their meeting the previous day, Phoebe had stalled the Americans with news that a work of priceless value was on its way to the Cato. She had watched their accountant assess either closing the museum or maximising the PR attached to supporting a Vermeer on its premises. A discreet nod had led the lawyers to agree an extension of their deadline until verification of the painting had been confirmed. If Bruce's plan had been for her to have her cake and eat it, it had worked. The Vermeer would keep the museum more than buoyant, and possibly even help fund the maintenance of Villa Clara.

'So what happened at Viner's Gallery?' she asked Robbins. 'Did you find the Villa Clara collection?'

'We did. Nice woman called Linda was very helpful and showed my colleagues where the cupboard was. Not much left in there, but we did find a set of stamps hidden in a drawer in Viner's office.' He glanced at the Lugt catalogue balanced on one of the packed bookcases. 'They match up with genuine collectors' stamps, made to order. Our friend had probably falsified countless works. We'll never know for sure.'

'Is he still saying my uncle deliberately misled him with the drawings?'

'He can say what he likes, especially with Viner's correspondence you gave us from your uncle's notebook. Plus,' he added, 'we pulled together some of the provenance attached to Villa Clara drawings sold over the years – receipts typed on old paper, exhibition flyers and what not. All typed with the same typewriter. And guess what?'

'The typewriter belongs to Viner?'

'We found it locked in a cupboard in his office. Cheeky sod had even been to the V&A library and planted a fake auction addendum about another Villa Clara drawing in a Sotheby's catalogue from 1951, in case anyone checked it out.' DS Robbins tapped a manila folder on his desk. 'It's all here in Mr Cato's notebooks. Details of each commission and its intended destination. Your uncle might have been naïve, but he was no criminal.'

Phoebe smiled. 'You obviously never played him at cards.'

He sighed. 'I see a lot of forgeries, but to my mind Eric Hebborn was the only one who produced drawings of the craftsmanship of Bruce Cato.' He winked. 'Except, unlike your uncle, Hebborn made a game of defrauding the art market. Not that that will be much comfort to the owners of these drawings.'

'Ouch.'

'Ouch indeed. Some even found their way into national collections. Viner may find himself facing a string of civil lawsuits – it'll cost him more than his reputation.'

'And you're not worried about him being out on bail?' she asked.

Robbins took a packet of Polo mints from his pocket, offering it to Phoebe before taking one himself. 'He can't move for cameras,' he said, crunching the mint. 'Besides, how fast can an eighty-six-year-old man run?' He slapped his palms on the cluttered desk, sending a pile of paper dockets flying. 'So, enough about Viner. There's something else I'm guessing you want to know?'

She glanced at an easel squashed in the corner of the room, hidden beneath a cloth. 'Is that it?'

'Just back. It's a beauty, all right . . .'

'I sense a but?' Phoebe said.

He paused. 'But it's not a Vermeer.'

'You're sure?' she said, trying to cover her disappointment. 'Bruce was almost certain it was genuine.'

'Sadly, not certain enough,' he said. 'For a start, there's no signature, which doesn't discount it being genuine, but although the pigments used are common to Vermeer's own studio, X-rays show it's been painted on top of a rather poor nineteenth-century landscape, two hundred years too late. I'm sorry, Miss Cato. We can get him for the drawings, but in terms of handling stolen goods, this is a non-starter.'

'My uncle had paperwork, though – the provenance wasn't solid, but it was pretty convincing.'

'Well, if there's one thing we've learned from this, it's not to trust the paperwork.'

Phoebe couldn't help feeling that she had let Bruce down, and not just by messing things up with Stefano. All she'd done was demonstrate her uncle wasn't quite the expert she had always believed him to be, and without the Vermeer to dangle under the Americans' noses, the museum was still in trouble. 'Do you mind if I look?' she said, curious anyway to see the subject of so much drama over the last fifty years.

'Be my guest – in fact, take it home with you. It's no longer any use as evidence.' He turned towards his desk as the phone rang. 'Mind if I grab that?'

'Of course not.' The painting was so familiar, and yet as she looked closer, she saw it was not quite identical to the one in the museum. The candle in her version had burned down to a stub, the wet, pooled wax suggesting it had just been extinguished. And yet here, there was still the tiniest flicker of a flame.

'Look carefully,' she imagined Bruce whispering, and she examined closely every detail, from the woman's gown, the letter on the desk and the crumpled paper on the floor, the light breaking through the latticed window, the blonde curls escaping their pins, and finally the artwork on the wall.

This time, however, it was no drawing. It was a tiny painting, a landscape populated with cypress trees and a sixteenth-century villa, a heavy stone watchtower just visible close by.

Phoebe recognised it instantly.

61

'What's up with you?' Tilly asked as Phoebe crashed through the front door of the museum and flew up the stairs.

'I need to check something,' she shouted as she let herself into the Vermeer room.

Tilly ran up to join her. 'What did the detective say?'

'That the painting Viner stole is a fake.'

'What? So Bruce didn't find a Vermeer?' Tilly sighed. 'All that drama, for nothing. What do we tell the Americans?'

'Nothing yet.'

'Why?'

Phoebe stood beside the painting created for her eighteenth birthday by Bruce. 'I might be completely off here, but do you see the map on the wall of our version?'

Tilly peered closely. 'Yeah . . .'

'The version Viner took didn't have a map. It had a painting of Villa Clara.'

'But why would Bruce give it to Viner, in that case? Why all that fuss over a fake? It doesn't make sense.'

'Doesn't it? What if my uncle sent Viner back to London with a copy . . .'

Tilly's eyes widened. 'Because he didn't trust him?'

'Exactly. In which case, what did he do with the original?'

The two women looked at Phoebe's painting once more, and then back at one another.

'Tilly, can you grab my magnifying glass and that Vermeer catalogue from my office?'

Whilst she waited, Phoebe looked once again at the lace foaming at the cuffs of the woman's gown, the translucency of the brushwork and the play of light on her plaited hair and the hand poised above the table; the dazzling blue and yellow pigments concentrated in a small area of the canvas; the paint that seemed to float and shimmer beneath the surface glaze; the map she was almost certain she'd seen somewhere else. Was *this* the painting Bruce had discovered in a Venetian palazzo fifty years ago?

'Here you go,' Tilly said, returning.

Phoebe took the magnifying glass and examined the monochrome map, exclaiming as she discovered what she had hoped would be there. 'See these tiny spots dotted across it?'

'Barely. What are they?'

'Where were you when we studied the camera obscura?' she asked.

'Probably hungover.'

'These spots are *pointillés*,' Phoebe explained. 'Small dots of lighter-coloured paint that Vermeer used to mark up the projection from the camera obscura. Find *Woman in Blue Reading a Letter* in that catalogue, would you?'

'Here,' Tilly said, handing it across.

Phoebe looked at the map in the background of the exquisite portrait of a woman in a gathered blue gown, reading a letter as she stands beside a window. 'It's a map of Holland and

Friesland, identical to the one in our painting, even down to the folds and the way it has crumpled slightly. And you see how the land looks blue on ours? That usually means he intended it to be green, but the yellow pigment has faded, leaving only the blue. It's something that's happened in a few of Vermeer's paintings. And look, there's even a *pentimento*.' She pointed to the light pencil workings beneath the surface, a sign that the artist had changed his mind.

'What's that in the top-right corner?' Tilly said.

Phoebe held the magnifying glass to a tiny signature tucked in the corner of the map.

'J . . . VM,' Tilly whispered.

'There's one more thing I want to check.' Phoebe pulled on a pair of gloves, gently flipping the painting over then placing it on a soft blanket on the table and carefully removing the tacks securing it to the frame. If there was any resistance, she would have to stop, but the frame came away easily, revealing something tucked just out of sight. Phoebe used a pair of long tweezers to remove a piece of folded, yellowed paper. 'Oh my God,' she said as she opened it.

'What?' Tilly said.

'It's a handwritten receipt. From 1696.'

'The year of . . .'

Phoebe nodded. 'The Dissius sale of Vermeers. "Lot 19. A young lady writing a letter, by the same, very beautiful. Sold for 200 guilders to Baron Charles de Roussillon."'

'Holy smokes,' Tilly said. 'Are you thinking what I am?'

'If it's that Bruce switched the paintings and created an elaborate way to give the original to his niece, via exposing Edwin Viner for fraud, then yes, I am.'

386

'Jeez, Pheebs. What are you going to do?'

Phoebe looked at her watch. 'What time is it in LA?'

'LA? What, are you planning a trip to Disneyland?'

'No. But I am planning a phone call to the Getty Institute.'

It was a frustrating few days whilst Phoebe waited for news. Having had one Vermeer discredited, the stakes felt high, and with Christmas only a fortnight away, there was a danger things would be held up. She had given as much information as possible to the Provenance Index Department, set up by the Getty Institute to create a database of known works. If a work had appeared on the open market at any time, it was recorded here alongside details of sales and previous owners. Of course what she was saying sounded ridiculous – genuine Vermeers did not just appear from nowhere, but who was to say that one of the lost works from the 1696 sale had not found its way to the basement of Count Minotto's Venetian palazzo? Bruce had believed it.

She was desperate to call Stefano and talk to him about it, but still smarting from seeing him with Jocelyn, she resisted, and he seemed to have given up his attempts to make her pick up the phone. Despite all this, she'd made the decision to spend some time at Villa Clara in the New Year, work out what needed doing and start the task of sorting out Bruce's belongings. There would be plenty of opportunity to talk to Stefano then.

And then, finally, the day before the museum closed for Christmas, Phoebe was in her office when a fax came through. 'Tilly!' she shouted. 'This is it.'

The painting matched records for something sold at the Dissius sale to a French baron, Charles de Roussillon, who had paid 200 guilders for the painting of a girl at a writing desk. The work then disappeared until it was exhibited at the Paris Salon in the Académie des Beaux-Arts in 1754, and was auctioned as lot 265C ten years later on behalf of a Mr Henry Walker, on 13 December 1764 at Christie's of London. The buyer was Count Niccolò da Minotto, whose estate and palazzo on the Grand Canal was eventually sold off by the remaining family members in early 1939. No mention of the painting appeared in an inventory, although it was believed several works had perished through water damage in the basement of the palazzo.

Phoebe dug around in her desk, eventually pulling out the receipt Bruce had given her with the painting years ago – 'Just to prove I actually bought it!' he'd joked. 'Here,' she said to Tilly. 'Receipt from the Minotto sale in Venice for a "water-damaged painting of a girl at a desk in the Dutch style", 10 April 1939. Now we just need to match all this up with our painting.'

'The receipt's not enough?'

'It's a very strong start.'

'OK. Anything we missed on the back of the picture?' Tilly asked.

'There's that exhibition label.' Phoebe ran upstairs to check. Amongst various dusty chalk marks, she found a yellowed piece of paper glued to the frame, bearing the words 'Exhibit 389, Paris Salon 1764. HW'. Henry Walker, surely? She searched for further markings, and then, suddenly, there it was. Fading into the patina of the painting's wooden frame but still visible: a distinctive Christie's auction house stencilled lot number: 265C.

Bruce had finally beaten Edwin at his own game.

62

Further scientific tests were required, as well as some explaining to the experts who had recently dismissed the Viner Vermeer, but with the provenance watertight, the general consensus was that sensational news would hit the art world in the New Year. Exciting times for the Cato Museum lay ahead, with the Americans already talking about expanding the premises.

'You are coming back to work in the New Year, right?' Tilly said as Phoebe tidied her desk on the last afternoon before the holidays.

'Of course. But I need a break, and Villa Clara needs me for a little while. Besides, you're Joint Director now, and so much better than me at running this place.'

'I just do the spreadsheets.'

'. . . and the school visits, and engage the visitors, and fill out the funding applications. Seriously, Tilly, you can manage without me. And Villa Clara can't.'

'So why aren't you spending Christmas there?'

'Angelina keeps asking, but I don't know . . .' Stefano would be there, and she didn't want to get in the way of their family Christmas, even if they did manage to sort things out. 'I thought about going to see Mum in Cornwall—'

'—but you'd have mucked up her plans with this new chap?'

'Exactly.' Given that Phoebe's mother had stopped tele-phoning once she realised her brother-in-law hadn't left her so much as a paperback book, Christmas was a tall order. Just as well she didn't know about the Vermeer yet.

'Still time to take up the offer of coming to my folks',' Tilly said. 'Northampton at Christmas isn't the most glamorous, but there's always sherry and a good fight.'

'You know what? I'm just going to stay at the flat. Eat chocolate and drink Baileys and wear pyjamas. Margot said I could join her and Cosmo for their annual non-Christmas Christmas Day dinner party, but I'm not sure I can be bothered.'

'That's the spirit.'

'I'll get my act together and go out to Villa Clara after New Year.'

'And Stefano . . . ?'

Phoebe hesitated. 'I'll see him when I get there, I guess.'

'With the lovely Jocelyn?' Tilly muttered.

'I don't know.'

'You have spoken to him about what you saw?'

'No. Not yet.'

'Phoebe . . .'

'Stop bullying me. Anyway, what are you still doing here? Haven't you got to catch the Christmas Express?'

Tilly groaned. 'I can't stay with you, can I?'

'No! Now go.'

Phoebe locked up the museum and joined the throngs released from work for the Christmas break. She knew she should be elated about the Vermeer, but the proliferation of Santa hats and bulging shopping bags, the cheeks pink from lunchtime drinks, served only to dampen her mood as she squashed on the Tube back to Notting Hill.

If she was going to forgo company, she was not going

to forgo luxury, however, she decided, grabbing a trolley in the eye-wateringly expensive deli supermarket around the corner from home. She threw in finest Alpine cheese and hand-carved Parma ham, marrons glacés and Swiss chocolate – everything she was always too broke to buy. Urged on by the nonstop loop of jingling Christmas music, she paused at the single-malt whiskies, deciding instead that it was champagne she wanted. Champagne she bloody deserved, in fact.

She wasn't the only one to have had that idea, however, and had just reached to the back of the shelf to grab the last bottle when someone else beat her to it. 'Come on. Really?' she said, stepping back, ready to get into an argument.

He smiled. 'Share it?'

'Stefano?' She wasn't sure whether to laugh or hide. 'What are you doing here?'

'Buying champagne with which to persuade you to come back to Villa Clara for Christmas. Mamma will kill me if I don't.' He held up the bottle. 'So?'

'I don't know . . .'

'You're still angry about the estate-agent thing? Phoebe, I'm sorry. I overreacted. Of course you'd want a valuation done, after I gave you the scare story about the finances. I wanted to say sorry in person, but you stood me up.'

'I didn't stand you up . . .'

He frowned. 'I waited in that bar for an hour and a half, then called you God knows how many times. Why didn't you come? I wanted to make it right – get us back to where we were that evening before I left.'

'How could we go back to that?'

'What? After just a silly misunderstanding?'

She sighed. 'No. After I saw you with someone else.'

Stefano shook his head. 'I don't understand. What are you talking about?'

'About the fact that you and Jocelyn seem to have got back together.'

'Me and Jocelyn? I'm sorry, you've lost me . . .'

'At the hotel, that evening, I arrived early. I saw you.'

'And you assumed . . . ?' He laughed. 'Phoebe, we'd just had a meeting with a client she introduced to my firm. A meeting at the hotel.'

'You were hugging her. In the lobby.'

'Yes, because she'd just told me she'd got engaged. I was congratulating her.'

'Oh.' She looked up at him. 'I'm an idiot.'

'We're both idiots. We should stick together.'

'Even though I just accused you of seeing someone else?'

'And I threw my toys out of the pram because you got your own house valued?'

He put the bottle back on the shelf and took her hands. 'So, can we go back to the bit before we were idiots?'

'You mean the bit where we spent the night together?'

'Yes. But this time, instead of my running off the next morning, you come to Villa Clara with me for Christmas.'

She smiled. 'I like that part.'

Phoebe jumped as another customer squeezed between them, reaching for the champagne bottle. She snatched it back, wrapping her arm around Stefano's waist. 'Sorry,' she said. 'This one's spoken for.'

63

As Christmas turned to New Year, Phoebe gradually settled into a new rhythm at Villa Clara. Firewood was now stacked beside the huge drawing-room fireplace, sheets airing on the washing line and rugs beaten to within an inch of their lives. She and Stefano had found an old gramophone and danced through the empty house to Bruce's jazz records, toasting him with the last of his wine cellar.

Only once did they go into the studio, to check the recent heavy rains hadn't caused damage. It was impossible to check the roof without getting into the first-floor space, but despite looking everywhere, there was no sign of a key to the padlocked hatch door, and Stefano hadn't yet organised anyone to open it up. Besides, Bruce's stories of rats had stuck with her. The watchtower had lasted six hundred years – it would be fine for now, and he promised to get someone over as soon as he returned from a short business trip to Naples.

In the absence of news about the Vermeer over the holidays, things seemed to be ticking along as the museum reopened for the new year. With Phoebe's original painting now in Amsterdam for assessment by experts at the Rijksmuseum, the Viner copy was on display. In the aftermath of his arrest, and with rumours flying about the potential Vermeer, visitor numbers had gone through the roof and the museum books were already looking healthy.

And then one day Tilly telephoned.

Girl at a Desk had officially been declared an original Vermeer.

Amongst the reasons cited, experts had uncovered an underdrawing of an early working of Vermeer's well-known *Lacemaker*, and had discovered the presence of tin in the yellow paint of the girl's jacket, a substance not used after 1700. Her plaited hair and its red ribbons were of a style popular for only around two years, and dated the painting to approximately 1670, placing it amongst Vermeer's late works.

The painting would remain safely in Amsterdam until plans were in place for its secure return to the Cato Museum, when Phoebe and Tilly would form a strategy for its future.

Meanwhile Phoebe had the gargantuan task of making an inventory of the contents of Villa Clara. She gradually worked her way through the house, listing everything from the art on the walls to the crockery in the vast kitchen dresser. Bruce's bedroom was a particularly tough challenge, and here she carefully catalogued the antique bedspread and carved oak furniture, tried to hold it together as she bagged up his clothing. Alongside Bruce's signature shapeless linen suits she found various items of women's clothing, their dated style suggesting the fashion of the fifties or sixties. A battered, wide-brimmed straw hat hung on the back of the bedroom door, matching one worn by Leonora in the framed black and white photograph of her and Bruce that sat on the dressing table, arm-in-arm in the Villa Clara gardens, sometime in the late sixties.

So where was she now, and why had Bruce been sending her money for nearly twenty years?

And then, suddenly, the payments bounced.

'What do you think is going on?' Phoebe asked Stefano in Angelina's kitchen the night he returned to Villa Clara, a noisy game show playing out on the small television while his mother stirred a pot of pasta sauce.

Stefano shook his head. 'I don't know. Our accounts department just told me that the payments for the last few months haven't gone in. Maybe she heard he died, and cancelled them.'

'But if she knew, why wasn't she at the funeral?' Phoebe turned to Angelina. 'Do you really remember nothing about her?'

Stefano's mother shrugged. 'We came here in 1971, just before you began visiting. There was no woman living here. I'd have remembered.'

Stefano smiled. 'Nothing gets past Mamma.'

Angelina frowned. 'Including you sleeping over in the big house.'

'Mamma, I'm thirty-one next birthday . . .'

Angelina cuffed her son's head playfully. 'Anyway,' she said to Phoebe, 'maybe you need to ask in the village? Someone might remember her.'

'A few do, but they also remember she suddenly went away. Bruce would never say where.'

'You could talk to my predecessor?'

'You know who she is?' Phoebe asked.

'Marianna Casini.' Angelina tutted. 'How could I forget that old battleaxe? She did not want to retire, and she did not want any other woman looking after Villa Clara.'

'Is she still alive?'

Angelina shook her head. 'I don't know. She'd be very old by now.'

'Where is she?'

'She moved to Poggibonsi to live with her son.'

'That's only about fifteen kilometres away.' Phoebe looked at Stefano. 'Reckon we can find her?'

'You, I'm afraid. I have to go away for a couple of days. Unless you can wait until I get back?'

She smiled. 'Seriously?'

Marianna Casini was very tired – she was ninety-one, didn't you know? – but would give Phoebe a few minutes of her time, since Signor Bruce had been so good to her. As Phoebe sat in Marianna's gloomy parlour, she realised she had seen the old lady before, distinctive with the jet-black-dyed bouffant hair that was surely a wig, and her lavishly applied red lipstick.

'You were at the funeral, weren't you?' she said.

The old woman nodded. 'My son brought me over. We both owed him a great deal. I only stayed for the service. Couldn't bear to go back to the villa. I knew that new housekeeper would never keep it as well as I did.'

'Signora Casini, I wanted to ask you about your time at Villa Clara.'

Her eyes moistened. 'I loved that place like it was my own. You know Signor Bruce saved my son's life there, back in the war? He got him away to safety.' She looked around at the swirled carpets and pearly patterned wallpaper, the photographs and Capodimonte ornaments. 'I wouldn't be living here with my boy if it hadn't been for your uncle.'

'He was a very special man.'

Marianna smiled. 'I remember the day he found out you'd been born. What a celebration we had.'

'I just wish my parents had let me know him better, sooner. They never wanted to visit, and his trips to London when I was very young were so infrequent.'

'At least you knew him. You are one of the lucky ones.'

'I wanted to ask you about someone else he knew, Signora Casini. Someone he knew very well, in fact. A woman.'

Marianna Casini straightened in her armchair, its vinyl cover creaking. 'Not the floozy from Rome?'

'His first wife?'

Marianna folded her arms over her floral housecoat. 'They were married for five months. Five months too long.'

'And after her? Do you remember Mrs Birch?'

'Leonora,' Marianna said, her face softening into a smile. 'If only she and Signor Bruce had got together years earlier. She was there the night my boy was beaten by blackshirts. She was a kind woman.'

'She came back to Villa Clara in the sixties, I believe?'

'Yes, to live with Signor Bruce.'

'But where did she go? She seems to have disappeared twenty years ago. No one knows where. And if she was this great love of his, why did Bruce keep her secret from me?'

'To protect her, perhaps. Or himself.'

'What do you mean?'

Marianna sighed. 'It was a terrible shame, what happened. After they'd waited so long. Life can be cruel.'

'She died?' Phoebe asked. It explained her disappearance,

but if that were the case, why was Bruce sending her money, right up until the end?

Marianna shook her head. 'It might have been better if she had.'

'Please, Signora Casini, tell me what happened.'

She let out a slow breath. 'It was gradual, so gradual that we didn't notice for some time. But she began forgetting things – losing her sketchbook, asking Signor Bruce the same questions over and over.'

'Was she unwell?'

The older woman nodded. 'And then things got worse. She would get lost in the grounds. He even found her wandering on the road towards San Gimignano, with no recollection of why or how she was there. She was frightened, confused. He brought her home, and for a few weeks everything seemed fine. She even began painting again, in that studio of hers.'

'Studio?'

'On the first floor of the watchtower. You had to climb a little ladder to get to it.'

'Bruce always told me it was storage space.'

'Storage? No. It was Leonora's. He had to ask permission to go up there.' Marianna laughed. 'He couldn't help himself interfering when she was working, and so she had a bell put in. If he wanted to come up, he would ring, and she decided whether to let him up.' She leaned closer to Phoebe, smiling. 'A good plan for all husbands, I'd say. Have you looked in there yet?'

'I didn't know there was anything to look at. And besides, it's locked,' Phoebe said.

'Even after all these years?' Marianna sighed. 'That tower was their special place. They would spend hours over there, working away. I'd bring them lunch, sometimes even supper. They were happy times.'

'Until her health deteriorated?'

'Of course. It wasn't long before the mood swings started. She would throw things at him, scream that she didn't know him. She wanted Bruce, she'd say, not this old man.'

'Do you think she had Alzheimer's?'

'Possibly. We didn't know what it was called back in 1969.'

'She was young still, surely?'

Marianna nodded. 'Too young. Bruce had hoped they would have twenty years together, but in the end, they had just five before she became ill.'

'That's heart-breaking.'

'It certainly was. That last summer, she declined rapidly. We tried to care for her at home, but it was distressing for everyone, especially her. She didn't know Bruce, kept asking when she could go back to London.'

'So what did Bruce do?'

'There were decisions to be made. Leonora's son came over from America. He was a journalist there, I think. He and Bruce talked endlessly. They both wanted the best for her, but it was hard to know what that was. She would become violent when any of us tried to wash or dress her, even feed her. She needed professional care, and so they found the best place they could. A converted palace on the outskirts of San Gimignano, with round-the-clock medical care, the finest chefs, art and music therapy. She was as happy and safe there as it was possible to be.'

'Poor Bruce. He must have hated taking her from Villa Clara.'

'I packed the poor woman's bag for her. It was a terrible day. They drove off together in that little red car of his, and you could have imagined it was the old days.' She shook her head. 'Poor Leonora never came back.'

'How long did she survive?'

'Years. I don't know how Signor Bruce kept paying for it, but he did.'

'He was paying for her care?'

'That was the plan. He set up a trust with her son – in case something happened to him before Leonora died – and paid into it every month.'

L. Birch . . . of course. Bruce hadn't been sending money to Leonora, but to her son Laurence.

'Signora Casini, you don't happen to know the name of the care home, do you?' Phoebe asked.

The old lady thought for a moment, then wrote a name down on a piece of paper. 'Here. But you're too late.'

'What do you mean?'

'Leonora Birch died six months ago, in July.'

Phoebe looked up. 'But Bruce only died six months ago.' 20 July 1989, the day imprinted on her memory. 'Signora Casini, may I borrow your telephone, please?'

20 July 1989

Bruce put the telephone down and made his way over to the watchtower. He climbed the steps to Nora's studio and stood in front of the easel bearing her last work, a still life of dahlias from the Villa Clara garden, now long-dead in a vase nearby. Only then did he allow himself to weep. They'd had twenty-five more years together, and yet those few when she was well would never be enough. His darling Nora was nearing the end, and his life might as well be over.

He spotted a note beside her easel and opened it. She must have written it whilst she was still well enough to understand what was happening to her, for in it she gave him permission to share her work with Margot Stockton, after her death.

You will always be the love of my life, Bruce Cato, Leonora wrote at the end, *even when I am dust and our story is a long-forgotten song sung only by the stars.*

He scrubbed at his eyes. What was he doing, wasting time? Nora needed him, and he must go.

He bolted and padlocked the trapdoor, then locked the studio behind him and grabbed the keys for the Alfa, making the winding, dusty journey to San Gimignano for one final time.

She had rallied a little, the nurse told him as he arrived, but the chest infection that had gripped her for weeks had developed into pneumonia. Her weakened lungs had deteriorated further, and Leonora had only hours left. He made his way through still, cool corridors to the elegant room he had chosen himself for her, its tall windows giving on to the kitchen garden, from where he had hoped birdsong would wind its way into Nora's troubled consciousness.

Something had changed since his visit the previous day. There was a new stillness in the air, like a held breath, a peace reflected on her pale, shrunken features as she lay in a white nightdress within crisp white sheets, thin muslin curtains swaying in the morning breeze.

'My darling Nora,' he said, sitting on the bed beside her.

He took her frail hand in his, smoothing her grey hair from her forehead while she slept. She already felt like a memory of his beloved Nora, and yet still he talked, on and on, even though it was years since she had responded to him. He talked of their student days, of the first time he told her he loved her, of seeing her on the terrace of Villa Clara years later, and how she had captured his heart all over again.

'And yet I do believe, in this moment, you are more beautiful than ever,' he said, leaning over her.

Her breathing was shallow as her body clung to life, but as his tears fell on her cheek, there was a sudden catch, a disruption to the inexorable march towards death. Her eyelids flickered a little, slowly prising open, as though her pale, thin eyelashes were made of lead.

'Bruce?' she whispered through dry lips, and he was shocked to hear his name after so long. She had come back to him, just as it was time to leave.

'Nora, talk to me, my darling, please.' But all she could manage was a smile, one that made the world unbearably bright for the few seconds it lasted before the clouds blocked the light once more and her breathing became harsher and more infrequent.

'Nora, take me with you,' he sobbed as her free hand began plucking at the sheet. 'Don't leave me behind, please,' he begged. 'Please don't make me live without you.'

And then suddenly, with one last exhalation, she was free of pain, her spirit dancing briefly in the sunbeams that burst through the window before she was gone.

Three hours later, Bruce Cato's car was found crashed just off a narrow road leading from San Gimignano to Villa Clara.

He had survived his beloved Leonora by less than an hour.

It was dusk as Phoebe arrived back at Villa Clara, the cypress trees casting long needles of shadow across the drive. She was tired, hungry and in need of a restorative bath, but instead she headed across the courtyard, longing to be in the space where she felt her uncle's presence more than anywhere else.

The setting sun was level with the old tower, rosy-gold light bouncing from the medieval stone. For once the door was unlocked, the cool space inside the studio exhaling as she entered. Everything was the same, if a little dustier since she had last been here, tightropes of spiders' webs criss-crossing the beams and glancing off abandoned easels.

'Hi,' a voice said.

'Stefano. What are you doing here?'

'I got back early from my trip,' he said, getting up from Bruce's armchair and coming across to kiss her.

She pushed his hair back from his eyes. 'It's good to see you. But why are you in here?'

'I heard you'd been to see Signora Cassini. I thought you might find your way here.'

'Oh, Stefano, it was so sad. She told me where Leonora had been.'

'I know where,' he said. 'I know what happened to her.'

'What? You've known all along? Why didn't you tell me?'

'I only found out today. I've had a small package from Bruce sitting in my desk. I wasn't allowed to open it until

403

Signora Cassini's son let me know you'd visited. Which he did this afternoon. I went straight to the office from my meetings and opened it.'

'Bruce was playing you too?'

'Of course.'

'And what was in the package?'

'A note explaining what you were about to find out. And,' he added, 'something he's kept from us both for years.' He looked down, pulling over his head a piece of string tied around his neck. 'It's for you.'

She took the string from him, finding a small rusty key hanging there. 'What's this?'

He glanced up towards the trapdoor in the ceiling, the rickety wooden ladder, the bell she had always imagined was to call the housekeeper. 'Want to take a look?'

'Are you coming too?'

He shook his head. 'This one is for you.'

The ladder was heavy, but they managed to drag it across, resting it against the lip of the hatch door, Stefano steadying it beneath her. She climbed steadily, then gripped the top rung, sliding the key into the heavy padlock and releasing the bolt, which came free, dropping to the stone floor with a clatter. Phoebe pressed her hands against the hatch door, and with a shower of dust and grit it finally loosened.

As she climbed through the gap, all she could see at first was a framed view of the jagged skyline through the window. She probed in the dark, looking for a light switch and crying out as a bat scooted close by on whispering wings. Eventually, for the first time in twenty years, the overhead strip light buzzed into life, illuminating the ordered, peaceful space that had been Leonora Birch's sanctuary.

In contrast to Bruce's studio, the workbench was neatly arranged, brushes washed and stored in jars according to size and type, bottles of linseed and turpentine labelled and lined up on a shelf, whilst unfinished tubes of paint had been stored, lids tightly closed, in colour order in small, open wooden boxes. A bookcase held a series of what looked like sketchbooks, and Phoebe pulled one out, admiring the rough pastel sketches of Villa Clara's gardens and the familiar views from the olive grove.

A folded note addressed to Bruce in Leonora's handwriting gave him permission to share her work, if he chose, after her death – 'when I shan't give a fig what the world thinks of it,' she had added playfully. 'Margot will know what to do.'

It was the paintings resting against the walls that beguiled Phoebe most: small, dazzling still lifes of flowers in earthen-ware jugs, a blue and white vase that appeared over and over, a coffee pot, glass bottle, striped china beaker. The brushwork was swift and sure, a burst of papery yellow narcissi singing against the soft mauve glaze of a jug, and a tiny posy of violets resting on the studio windowsill against an impressionistic wash of green and pink depicting the hills beyond. Colours danced and shimmered, defying convention as they created new rules.

Bruce might have been the craftsman, but Leonora was the visionary.

An easel was placed in the middle of the room, beside it a well-used palette, reds, yellows, oranges frozen in the process of being scrubbed together. A desiccated bouquet sat in a tall glass vase whose water had long since evaporated, the indigo-blue linen cloth on which it stood now dusty and faded. The flowers had shed into an autumnal drift at its base, threads of gold still discernible in the tissue-dry petals. Phoebe stood back to admire the ghost of these long-dead blooms, dahlias from the gardens of Villa Clara, resurrected on the canvas into a fire show that crackled with movement and life and light.

The last painting of Leonora Birch.

64

London, September 1990

'So, Phoebe, how on earth did you get those two talking again?' Linda asked, peering across the top of her champagne glass.

Joan chuckled. 'More than talking, if you ask me – and about time.'

Phoebe glanced across the gallery, to where Margot and Laurence Birch were deep in conversation in front of a pastel landscape. From the smile on Margot's face, it was hard to tell whether she was more pleased finally to be exhibiting Leonora's work or to be speaking to Leonora's son again.

It had been quite a journey to this September evening graced by an Indian summer, the overflow of guests from the private view spilling out on to the sun-drenched pavement, exhibition catalogues tucked under their arms. Around the Chelsea gallery Phoebe recognised a few names from the world of art journalism, including a reviewer from the *Guardian*, taking copious notes as she examined each of the paintings and sketches Margot had curated for the Leonora Birch retrospective.

An added frisson of interest had been injected with the recent conclusion of the trial of Sir Edwin Viner. Evidence against the eighty-six-year-old Bond Street art dealer had been incontrovertible. He was now one month into a seven-year sentence at an open prison, and in all probability would end his days there. Had he even once admitted his guilt or apologised for the damage he had caused, the Honourable Lady Justice Fellows had said in her summing-up, his sentence might have been shorter, but rarely had she come across someone so utterly unrepentant.

Phoebe would almost have felt sorry for Viner if he hadn't still insisted on defaming Bruce from the defendant's stand. And besides, he would enjoy considerably more comfortable conditions than those endured by Leonora at Holloway. It wasn't as though he had a home to go to, in any case: Charl-wood House had been put on the market and the gallery sold to cover some of the astronomical compensation claims building up against him. It was said Diana Viner had been forced to leave her King's Road flat and was now living in a shabby Bayswater bedsit.

This night was not about Viner, however, nor about the Vermeer, which had recently returned to London. It was about the woman who had stood up to Edwin Viner, and who, fifty years later, was finally having her moment, if the price tags listed in the exhibition catalogue were anything to go by. It was said that both the Tate and the Dulwich Picture Gallery had already approached Margot Stockton, representing the artistic estate of Mrs Birch.

Across town at the Cato Museum, a further room had been styled to recreate Leonora's studio space at Villa Clara, and now accommodated half a dozen paintings donated to the museum by Laurence, whilst in the room next door, *Girl at a Desk* was on display for twelve months before embarking on a world tour to include the Metropolitan Museum of Art in

New York, the Kunsthistorisches in Vienna, the Paris Louvre and Prado in Madrid before being exhibited in Delft, Vermeer's hometown.

Phoebe had not known what to expect when she was visited at Villa Clara by Leonora's son Laurence, having been warned about his prickliness, but was pleasantly surprised by the softly spoken political correspondent with a Washington DC tinge to his voice. He had visited his mother several times a year in the care home, he'd explained as they stood together in Leonora's watchtower studio. They were difficult visits, in which she didn't know who he was, and it had been awful to see her gradual decline. Laurence was eternally grateful for the care Bruce gave her, still visiting her several times a week even though she no longer knew him. This at least made sense of the frequent absences Phoebe remembered, and which Bruce never explained. It didn't explain, however, why Bruce had kept Leonora a secret from her.

'The woman Bruce loved – we all loved – had essentially gone,' Laurence told her, 'but he could at least protect the woman she had become, and allow her dignity, rather than pity. He was so angry at the unfairness. It broke his heart to talk of her, and so he kept her to himself.'

And then had begun the conversation about what to do with her work, the studio's worth of paintings and sketches. It seemed obvious for Phoebe to suggest talking to Margot Stockton, and Laurence's subtle probing did little to fool Phoebe that his interest was in more than gallery space. A meeting had been arranged for a fortnight's time, and Phoebe had welcomed Laurence and Margot to Villa Clara for a long weekend in which it was agreed that Margot would represent

Leonora's work. Whilst everything in the studio was catalogued by Margot and Laurence, Phoebe sensed she was surplus to requirements in the long conversations taking place in the watchtower each evening.

During that weekend Margot asked Phoebe what she planned to do with the villa, now it had cleared probate. Phoebe had discussed several options with Stefano, including using the space as an artists' retreat, and so Margot's suggestion of opening a Tuscany branch of her gallery seemed an obvious development. Things had progressed quickly, and with renovations to the watchtower underway, the first exhibition would take place in Leonora's old studio the following spring. Proceeds of any sales would help fund renovations to the villa and enable Phoebe to ensure the museum was financially secure for the next few years, with Tilly as its joint director. Meanwhile, in the main house, January would see the first intake of students on the Villa Clara residential art restoration course, under an Italian tutor who had learned from Bruce back in the fifties, and who considered the late Signor Cato the best in the business.

With Villa Clara now firmly her home, Phoebe suddenly felt like a visitor to London, and she took one last tour of the gallery, knowing she had to be up early for her return flight to Florence. She smiled as she passed Andrei Lyov and his aunt chatting in Russian with Hillary Stevenson, clearly uncomfortable as Irina poured effusive blessings on the woman who had helped her escape the Soviet Union. 'Do you think Hillary would be able to send her back?' Andrei had whispered in Phoebe's ear earlier as he attempted to navigate his aunt's need to stand up, sit down, drink something, drink nothing, stay at the party, be taken home.

Further along, Cosmo, dressed in his signature velvet jacket, shirt unbuttoned just a fraction too low, was regaling a group of wide-eyed young women with stories of Chelsea in the sixties, a glass of sparkling water in his hand. Her saw her and waved, throwing her his best blue-eyed smile. If she were thirty years older . . . if she didn't love Stefano quite so much . . .

Further along, Sir Hugo Fairfax, QC, and his partner, a well-known journalist with a taste for natty ties, were deep in conversation with the elderly lady who had bought three Leonora Birch still lifes before the exhibition even opened, and who had recently found herself thrust into the public eye. Upright despite her years, and immaculately turned out in a black suit and steel-grey beehive, Ursula Knight had been an essential element in the prosecution of Sir Edwin Viner, guiding the investigation towards further sales that she now believed to be part of a larger scheme to defraud the market.

Phoebe smiled as she watched DS Robbins, uncomfortable in the tie and collar his wife kept fiddling with, attempt to avoid Alf, who having announced his retirement saw no reason the two men couldn't now be friends.

'You need to rescue Robbins from your husband,' Phoebe said as she reached Joan and Linda once more.

'You'd think Alf would have had enough of coppers by now,' Joan said, straightening her tight, electric-blue satin dress. 'He's got this idea of them writing a book together. Like Alf's ever read anything other than the *A to Z*. Right, I'm going in. Hold my champagne, Linda.'

'Oh, but I was about to leave . . .'

Phoebe smiled. 'I'll take it.'

'Would you?' Linda said, handing her the glass and slipping

on her beige mac. 'Got to get back. My Derek'll be wanting his tea.'

'Say hello to Ludlow Gardens for me,' Phoebe called out as Linda headed for the door.

She felt a hand on her waist and turned, smiling, to see Stefano behind her. 'Am I allowed to take you home yet?' he said.

'To the hotel? Home's tomorrow.'

He kissed her lightly. 'Home's wherever you are. Ready to go?'

She looked around at the packed room, the smiling faces, bursts of colour beaming from frames on every wall, the subtle clasp of Margot's little finger around Laurence's. Leonora would be so happy. Bruce would be so proud.

She took Stefano's hand, threading her fingers through his and answering the warm smile in his green eyes. 'I'm ready.'

Epilogue

Leonora shielded her eyes against the sun as she leaned over the rail to watch the Newhaven coastline disappear over the horizon, the six months in a women's prison already a distant memory.

'We made it, Mrs Birch,' Bruce said, turning her towards him. 'You are worth the wait, even if you need a damn good haircut.'

She laughed. 'You're one to talk.'

'Good job only the seagulls can see us.'

She rested her head against his shoulder, closing her eyes as her hair blew about her face. 'It was all worth it, wasn't it?' she said.

'Even doing time for a stolen fake?'

'Especially that.'

'You went to court, even though you knew Viner didn't have the original.' He whistled. 'You are some woman, Leonora Birch.'

'Maybe he didn't have the Vermeer, but he certainly conned the market with those drawings of yours.' She shrugged. 'The principle was the same. I wanted to make a point. Besides, I love the idea of Edwin coveting a Bruce Cato for all these years.'

Bruce chuckled. 'And if he ever does try to sell it – unlikely, as it'll have more red flags than an eighteen-hole golf course – he'll find himself in hot water. Besides, anyone prepared to pay the sort of money he'd want for a black-market Vermeer would do their homework and spot the deliberate howler.'

'I still can't believe you painted Villa Clara into it,' Leonora said. 'How did you know he wouldn't notice?'

'I made sure the copy was as tarnished as the original. It's almost impossible to see what's in the painting on the wall. Anyway, Edwin sees only pound signs.'

She paused as the ship's horn blew, deafeningly loud on the deck. 'And I can't believe you didn't tell me you'd switched it, back in thirty-nine.'

'You had to be completely innocent, Nora. If anything happened and you were stopped, you couldn't know what I'd done.'

Leonora waited until a young mother had scurried past, clutching the hand of her green-faced child, a casualty of the ship's gentle lurch. 'And what of the original?' she said eventually. 'Will you sell it?'

Bruce shook his head. 'I thought a good deal while you were on your little sabbatical at Holloway. Even if I were to offer the Vermeer to a public gallery now, no one would take me seriously. My brother and his wife have a young daughter. Perhaps it would make a good gift for her one day. And perhaps she will be the one to expose Viner. What did you think of my plan, by the way?'

'It's complicated, but then you always were complicated!'

He sighed. 'I'd love to see the Vermeer out in the world, for everyone to enjoy, but it will have to bide its time, perhaps until I've had my time.'

She turned to him, placing her hands on his arms. 'Don't say that.'

'But it's the reality of love in old age.' He raised a finger. 'Old*er* age. We're not there yet.' As he kissed her, the years of separation, of hurt and anger, slipped away.

'We will never get old, Bruce Cato.'

'Maybe not,' he said, 'but in the meantime, Mrs Birch, we can get dinner.'

She took his arm, and as they strolled along the deck of the boat, the sun on the horizon offered a final, hot-dahlia burst of golden light before sinking beneath the blue-grey surface of the sea.

Author's Note

Anyone who has read any of my previous books will know that I am an inveterate researcher, and writing my new novel opened up some fascinating avenues, particularly for someone with my love of art.

There is usually a seed that plants itself as early inspiration for any novelist's work, but in the case of this book, there were two.

In a nod to my debut novel *The Missing Pieces of Nancy Moon*, I was keen to write a second book set in the sixties, and through an old friend came across an exhibition about Christine Keeler, one of the young women caught up in the Profumo sex scandal of 1963. Christine's story had it all: showgirls, philandering aristocrats, elegant fashion, Russian spies, the gradual overturning of the class system and a sense that the Establishment closed ranks to protect itself. I tried to imagine what it must have been like for the women at the heart of the chaotic press frenzy that killed Stephen Ward, led to a sparkling career for Mandy Rice-Davies and destroyed Keeler, whilst playing its part in bringing down a government. I hope the story of Leonora Birch and her 'girls' at least communicates some of the atmosphere of that time.

The hook from which to hang my story is one close to my heart, and it was a joy to give myself permission to delve deep into the world of Old Masters, and those who sell, buy, curate and even copy them. The memoir of roguish forger Eric Hebborn was a huge help in researching this last aspect. Hebborn was an exceptional student at the Royal Academy, but after moving to Italy, he made a career of trying to pull the wool over the art world's eyes with his faultless forgeries, many of which he claimed reside in national collections. Hebborn's mysterious murder in a Rome backstreet in 1996 was very likely a result of pushing his luck just a little too far.

Choosing an artist whose imagined work could become central to my story was a simple and pleasurable task, and a trip to Holland enabled me to look closely at Vermeer's paintings and work out how I might dare to invent a new one. Waking up in Delft and listening to the very church bells that would have greeted the artist himself each day was hugely inspirational, and archival evidence of the 1696 Dissius auction of Vermeer paintings, at least two of which have never been found, provided the impetus to take liberties with the catalogue of known works.

Talking to experts is one of the perks of the job, and as well as plaguing the library staff at the Courtauld Institute, I was lucky enough to have a private tour of the British Museum drawings collection by Dr Olenka Horbatsch, Curator of their Dutch and Flemish Collection. Olenka not only brought out some treasures from the collection to show me, but explained about provenance and the process of authenticating works via means such as auction and exhibition records and the Lugt catalogue of collectors' marks.

I am also incredibly grateful to staff at the Getty Research Institute in Los Angeles: Sally McKay, Head of Research Services, and Anna Cera Sones, Provenance Index advisor, were able to tell me in detail how their database of artworks might have been accessed and utilised in the late eighties. Anyone who has watched a few episodes of *Fake or Fortune* will be aware of the importance of the Getty Provenance index, and so it was wonderful to be able to talk to the real people behind it!

The life story of any work of art is usually a complex one, and Patrick Toynbee of Bonhams was very generous with his time and expertise, explaining to me how a piece is brought to auction, and how experts might conduct their own research in order to verify an artwork. This glimpse behind the scenes was invaluable in creating the setting of Viner's Gallery, although I must stress that Sir Edwin's practices are born entirely of my imagination!

Thanks also to Lisa Kenny of the British Library News Reference Team, who explained how the newspaper archive in North London would have been accessed back in 1989. There really is no substitute for talking to someone who was on the spot.

I have no background in Law whatsoever, and therefore I owe much to Rebecca Glenn, KC, a Lincoln's Inn criminal defence barrister who took time out from her busy schedule to describe to me the process, etiquette and language of a High Court trial. I'm very grateful to her for proofreading my attempt at a transcript written within the strict parameters imposed on those leading the arguments within the court setting. A visit to the Royal Courts of Justice allowed me to sit in on trials and witness this first-hand, something I would recommend to anyone interested in how our justice system operates.

One particular research highlight was interviewing two police officers from the Metropolitan Police Art and Antiques Squad in London, who reassured me that my plot is 'totally plausible' (their words). Nothing in the world of art theft and forgery is too ridiculous, it seems, and they even provided me with some golden nuggets with which to enhance the story (I wonder if you can spot them . . . ?). I wish I could name these fantastic individuals, but they know who they are, and coffee is on me any time!

Thank you to Sarah Bance for her excellent work in copy-editing the manuscript, and, as ever, to my agent Gaia Banks for her wisdom and patience (I wouldn't want to work with authors!). Massive thanks also to Bea Grabowska, my editor at Headline, with whom I have been happily reunited after working together on *The Lost Song of Paris*. She really is the best.

Discover Sarah Steele's heartrending and deeply moving story of hope in the face of war.

The SCHOOL TEACHER *of* SAINT-MICHEL

'My darling girl, I need you to find someone for me . . .'

France, 1942. At the end of the day, the schoolteacher releases her pupils. She checks they have their identity passes, and warns them not to stop until the German guards have let them through the barrier that separates occupied France from Free France. As the little ones fly across the border and into their mothers' arms, she breathes a sigh of relief. No one is safe now. Not even the children.

Berkshire, present day. A letter left to her by her beloved late grandmother Gigi takes Hannah Stone on a journey deep into the heart of the Dordogne landscape. As she begins to unravel a forgotten history of wartime bravery and sacrifice, she discovers the heartrending secret that binds her grandmother to a village schoolteacher, the remarkable Lucie Laval . . .

Available to order

REVIEW

Uncover an unforgettable story of lost love, danger and espionage
and one remarkable woman's bravery in World War Two.

The LOST SONG of PARIS

1941. Darkness descends over London as the sirens begin to
howl and the bombs rain down. Devastation seeps from every
crack of the city. In the midst of all the chaos is a woman gripping a window ledge on the first floor of a Baker Street hotel.
She is perched, ready to jump. And as flames rise around her,
she is forced to take her chances.

1997. Amy Novak has lost the two great loves in her life: her
husband, Michael, and her first love, music. With the first anni-
versary of Michael's death approaching, Amy buries herself in
her job as an archivist. And when a newly declassified file lands
on her desk, she is astonished to uncover proof that 'Agent
Colette' existed – a name spoken only in whispers; an identity
so secret that it has never been verified.

Her discovery leads her to MI6 'godmother' Verity Cooper –
a woman with secrets of her own – and on to the streets of
Paris where she will uncover a story of unimaginable choices,
extraordinary courage and a love that will defy even the darkest
days of war . . .

Available to order

REVIEW

Inspired by the incredible stories of the heroines of
the Italian Resistance, discover Sarah Steele's powerful and
heart-wrenching exploration of how far we will go
to protect our families.

The
TRAITOR'S
WIFE

Naples, 1943. Luisa Giordano has faced many losses: her mother to a deadly illness, the man she loved to the Nazis when war came to Italy, and her unborn child at the hands of her own husband. All Luisa has left is her voice, and when she learns her husband is colluding with the enemy, she knows she must use it to fuel the women of Naples with fire.

Los Angeles, 1962. Hollywood starlet Lola Hart has come a long way from the backstreets of Naples, the glamorous parties a way to dull the pain of the past. When she is offered the role of a lifetime portraying a heroine of the Italian resistance, she knows returning home means confronting old ghosts. But as she seeks out the story behind the film, she realises there are many in Naples with secrets, and that the woman she is to play held the greatest one of all . . .

Available to order

REVIEW